Her Rabid Beasts

E. P. Bali's
House of Romantasy

Her Rabid Beasts is a work of fiction. Names, characters, places, incidents and locations are the product of the author's imagination or are used fictitiously. Any resemblance to actual events, locations or persons, living or dead is entirely coincidental.

This first edition published in 2024 by
Blue Moon Rising Publishing
www.ektaabali.com
ISBN ebook: 978-0-6457846-7-1
Paperback: 978-1-923159-02-0
Hardback: 978-1-923159-03-7
Exclusive Edition: 978-1-923159-04-4

No AI was used in the creation of this book

Cover Design by David Gardias
Lyle Illustration by Rami fon Verg
Chapter Artwork by Wisp Tale
Formatting by E.P. Bali

A Note on the Content

I care about the mental health of my readers.
This book contains some themes you might want to know about
before you read.
They are listed at www.ektaabali.com/themes

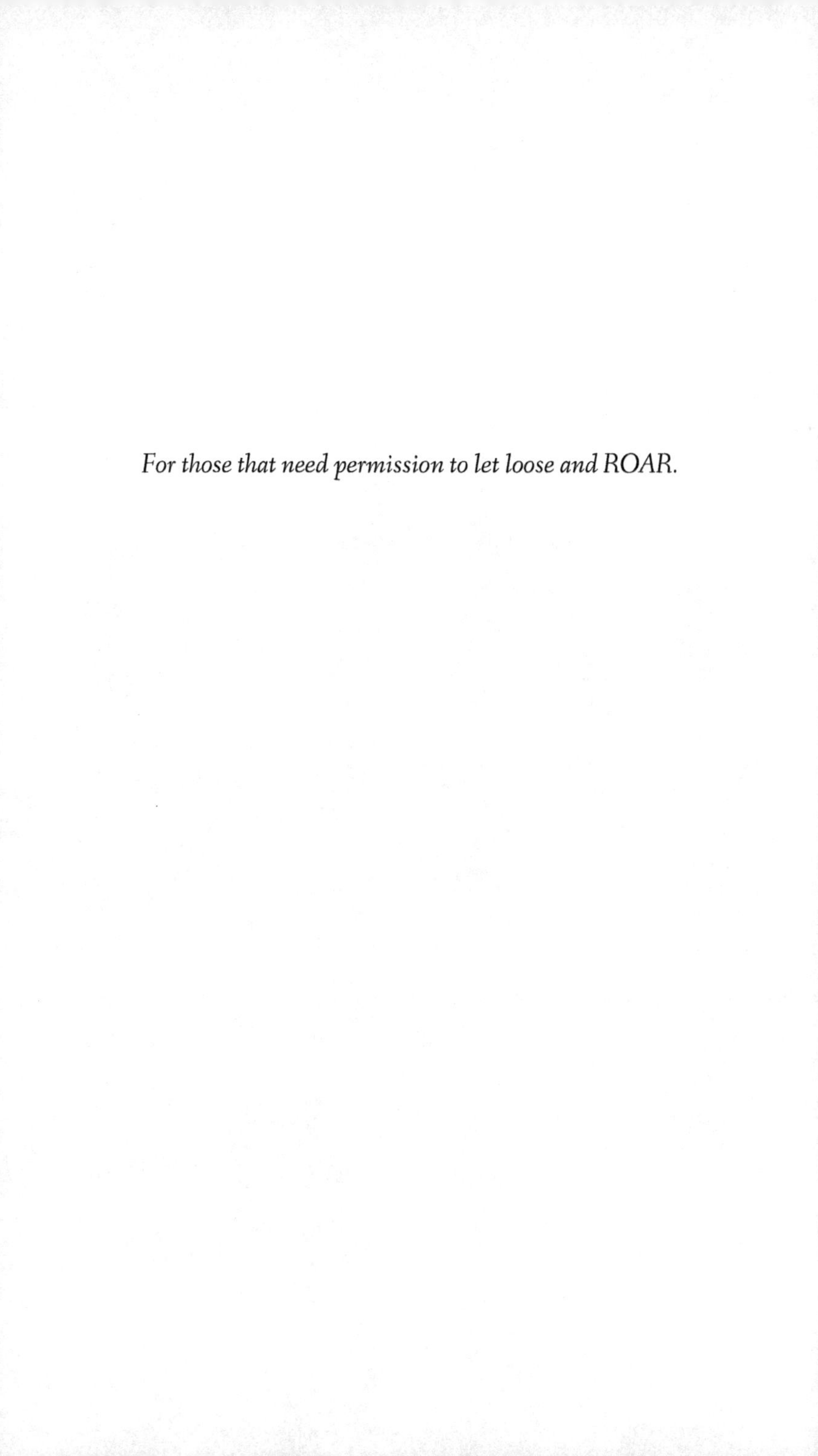

For those that need permission to let loose and ROAR.

Her Rabid Beasts

② 2

L.P. Bali

Prologue

Savage

Nineteen years ago

Before Friday night fights in the town warehouse, Dad puts us in the back room to wait with the other kids. Scythe calls it the nursery, but I call it the TV room. One night, when Dad drops us in there, the TV is already on and there's a lion cub sitting on the floor in front of it and two other boys sitting on the old grey couch behind him.

The lion cub is in his changed form, golden fur with little round ears that twitch this way and that, and he has little round burn scars all over his back and side.

Scythe and I gape in the doorway because a kid being in his fully shifted form is basically impossible and I've never actually seen it. I've never fought him in the puppy pens, so he might be from out of town. I also think he's a bit older than us.

My surprise only lasts two seconds before excitement takes over and I race right for him.

"Hello," I say cheerily, plonking myself down next to him

1

and blinking at his face with wide eyes. I pick at a scab on my bare chest and Scythe slaps my hand away, coming to sit down next to me, his sky-blue eyes stuck on the cub too.

The lion doesn't say hello back because you can't physically talk when you're in your beast form. But Scythe has been teaching me manners, and told me I need to practise every chance I get.

"What are you watching?" I say out loud, looking at the wooden puppet on the TV. "Oh, it's the puppet movie!" I excitedly jab Scythe in the arm and he grins at me.

The lion still doesn't move his eyes off the TV, just blinks his wide eyes the colour of apple juice. So I do what wolves do best and talk into his mind.

"Have you seen this movie before?" I ask.

The lion cub snaps his head towards me, and I nod proudly. *"I'm a wolf,"* I explain, putting a palm on my chest. *"So I can do tele patties in your head."*

"Wow," he says, and I flinch in surprise because other orders usually can't do mind-speaking back. But he doesn't actually sound wowed by it at all. His voice is low and serious like an adult's, and smooth like the handle of Dad's hammer.

I press on, because if he's talking back to me, that means his head has all its screws. *"Have you seen this movie?"*

"Pinocchio? No."

"Pin oh key oh," I say out loud and Scythe nods his approval. *"Hey, so can you change to a boy? It's easier to talk that way."*

"No." His voice turns sharp like the edge of a claw.

"Oh." I've never met someone more feral than me before, but I think this lion has to be. Maybe we can be friends. Feral friends. *"Well I've seen this movie before. The blue fairy is going to come and make him into a real boy at the end."*

The lion cub turns to look at me. *"Do you think she can do that for me?"*

"What?"

"Make me into a real boy."

I stare at his lion cub face for a little while because when he said "no" before, I thought he just didn't want to change, but maybe he meant that he can't.

"Yeah, I think she could," I say confidently. *"Maybe she can help me, too. My brother says I'm not enough like a boy either."*

The lion cub turns back to look at the TV just as Pinocchio starts dancing with his cricket. All of us watch together for a while and I get to sing, "And always let your con-shins be your guide."

The lion says, *"I want a cricket to tell me what's right and wrong, too."*

"Aw, yeah. That's his job, right?"

"Conscience."

"Con-shins," I repeat, nodding like I know what that means.

"What are you saying to him?" Scythe asks in that tone he uses when he's about to tell me off.

"He wants to find a blue fairy to help him become a real boy!" I say, gesturing enthusiastically to the TV. "But I don't know where to find one. They come from the sky."

Scythe pushes his long silver hair over his shoulder and peers at the cub with new interest, but it's one of the boys behind us who scoffs. "Don't be stupid, that movie's not *real*. Faeries and angels don't exist."

I turn around to see a boy about my age with long dark hair and the start of a dragon tattoo on his bicep. Even though I think the artwork is cool, I glare at him. "They *are* real!"

"Are not!" he says, crossing his arms.

There's a shiny watch on his wrist and I point at it. "Hey, what's that?"

He looks at me like I'm stupid. "A Rolex, you idiot."

"Stop it, Sav," Scythe tells me.

I turn to glare at him because how was that my fault? Now I'm angry and want to punch something. In the corner, there are small wooden kid's chairs around a table with colouring pencils that one of the mums put there. I leap up and run over, taking a chair in both hands and smashing it against the floor with all my might.

The dragon boy and Scythe start shouting at me and the other boy on the couch starts laughing his head off. I grin and continue smashing it until its back legs fall off. The lion cub ignores me like what I'm doing is normal and keeps watching Pinocchio. Maybe his dad is loud like mine is.

Because I'm already angry and excited, when I concentrate on my hands, my claws burst out of my skin with a quick *pop*. With their sharp ends, I start slicing away bits of wood from the chair leg. It's hard work, but it's helping me get rid of the angryness inside of my belly.

"What are you making?" the dragon boy demands.

"None of your business," I snap.

He crosses his arms and sits back on the couch, sticking his lower lip out like I've refused him lollies. He's probably a spoiled rich brat, and from the way Scythe is eyeing him, he thinks so too. I whittle down the wood until it's the size of my hand, then work on the details. Boy, it's hard, and two of the wings are wonky, but they still look like wings, so it's fine.

There are paints on the corner table and Scythe comes over because he knows I'm going to spill something. I point to the ones I want, and with his careful fingers, he opens the paints for me. I pick up a small brush and start my masterpiece. I'm concentrating so hard my tongue is between my teeth, but when I'm done brushing on the paint, the wings are blue and her dress is white.

"Dragon boy," I sing. "Come dry this for me."

With a loud groan like it's the biggest effort in the world, he slides off the couch like slime and stalks over. I think he's curious about what it is.

"Be careful," Scythe warns.

The dragon boy ignores him and holds his palm over the wood. My hands heat up as warm air fans over my artwork like a real, live heater.

"Stop! Stop!" I cry when smoke starts curling upwards. I bat the smoke away and check my work. The paint has gone dry and smooth over the rough wood, and I think it looks perfect.

The dragon boy grunts and goes back to the couch, grumbling under his breath. Something about puppies and roasting. The other couch boy narrows his dark eyes at me and I don't know if I like him.

I run back to the lion cub, who never took his eyes off the TV for even one bloody second.

"Here ya go," I say happily, holding it up to his furry muzzle. "Now you *do* have a blue fairy."

"Hey, that's cool." The lion cub leans forward and gently takes the wooden fairy between his teeth. *"It looks like an angel."* He sets it down between his paws and, smug as a bug, I brush my hands together because it was a job well done. I turn around and stick my tongue out at the boys behind me, but they only roll their eyes.

We sit like that until my dad comes to get us for my first fight.

I don't see that lion again until almost two decades later, when he's ten times as big and growling at me over his desk as Deputy Headmaster of Animus Academy.

Chapter 1

Aurelia's Anima

Blasting through the cold night air, I ascend upwards on rapid beats of my wings.

Danger swarms beneath, where powerful, hungry monsters prepare to launch an attack that will end me.

Venomous fangs reach for my feathers through the ether; hissing mouths whisper heinous things that I can't bear to hear.

Boneweaver female. Twenty years old. Unbred. Unmated. Offers over ten million.

My scream is a shrill cry. Power from the depths of me doesn't explode through the night.

It *implodes.*

The primordial darkness long kept dormant, claws its way up my throat, pincers digging into my spine, fangs piercing my sternum, claws ripping through my consciousness.

The human woman is shoved deep into the recesses of my body and placed in a new cage. A cage of necessity and safety.

Too long have we lain trapped within bars of fear. Too long have our roars of protest gone unheard.

But no longer.

I tear forth. The primal female that shares Aurelia's soul. The one they call a Boneweaver.

Through the dark, my primitive instinct turns my beak with purpose. My heart yearns to soar into the wide-open sky beyond, but it is covered in a crackling dome of pure heat that will cook my flesh. Instead, I'm led to swooping for a familiar building. Black and gold and... glass.

A window has been left open, and it feels purposeful. Friends are in there.

My sister-pack.

Propelling myself forward with powerful sweeps, I spear towards the open window. At the last minute, I tuck my wings in and lower my beak, nothing but a spear made of feathers and talons entering my old den.

Surprised female yelps are sharp in my ears, but I ignore them, knowing my mark is close at hand. I sweep through the room and turn a sharp right down the corridor. Human feet pound in my wake, the voices striking core memories like a song only I know how to sing. But it's not only the members of my sister-pack in pursuit of me. Tiny squeaking balls of fluff zoom through the air like giant bees.

This is good. They need to come with me so I can build a nest and keep them warm and safe.

Warm. And. Safe. This is the ultimate goal. This is the thing upon which all life depends.

Venomous fingers brush the sides of my protections and I sink deeper yet into the primal beast at my core. My power expands out. Further out. And further still.

Only when my protection is all-encompassing do those green-tipped fingers recede.

Safe. Keep them all safe.

My wings almost brush the sides of the corridor, but I only have a few sweeps before I reach my mark: a wall made of something that looks like open sky, covered in magic that I recognise with my bones. Safe. Secure. Good for nesting.

My heart expands with joy and I pummel beak-first through it. I go straight through like I knew I would, but... I stop short, rearing up and back-flapping to slow down.

There is darkness and a smell like ancient and hidden things. A fizzing sound erupts on either side of me, and I drop to the stone below just in time for twin flames to flare up. I squint at one, and then the other, warmth and light sputtering to life.

I am being welcomed.

My human-shaped pack of animas stumble through the dragon-door, making sounds of surprise and shock through their flat beaks. I can barely register the noises they are making but decipher their general meaning well enough.

"Holy m-moon mother," my wolf-anim mutters.

"Shit," my leopard says.

"What in the Phantom of the Opera is this?!" my tigress shrieks.

"This is a dragon-trick door?" my fair-lioness huffs. "When Lia told us about it, I imagined something less..."

My dark-lioness sneezes. "Creepy?"

"Well, we didn't have all that much time to put the plan together this afternoon," my tigress says haughtily. "This is insanely cool though."

Impatiently, I let out a cry that makes them all violently flinch. The sound echoes all the way down the stone stairs, making me peer into the gloom. But I cannot continue to my place of nesting with these wings.

Only one other form feels correct. Bones crunch, ligaments snap and feathers make way for honey-yellow fur, silent paws and a mouth full of sharp teeth.

There are five sets of screams.

"She's a lioness?" my leopard shouts.

My tigress inhales sharply. "Oh, Lia, are we not keeping it a secret anymore?"

"You knew?!" shriek the other felines at the same time.

"I knew s-something w-was up," my wolf growls.

One of the tiny hatchlings with fur the colour of the sky squeaks and plonks himself on my head.

I make a sound of contentment and follow my nose, padding down into the shadows, knowing that my sisters will stop their babbling and follow.

Flames come alive as I silently descend and the animas continue to chitter like cockatoos behind me, their steps echoing all around the black stone.

"I knew something was up when she freaked out in the library the other day!" my fair-lioness cries.

"The sh-shark was reading the B-Boneweaver book," my wolf gruffs. "He knows t-too."

There is silence for a moment. A silence laced with secret realisation.

"Shit." My dark-lioness sounds worried. "This is bad."

"Yeah. Even more shit that *they're* her mates," my leopard says.

"A bit of optimism would be good here!" My tigress is angry.

The footsteps stop. I pause too, assessing for threats. The hatchling perched on my head squeaks with concern.

I let out a snarl that reverberates all around us, growing it into something more than menacing.

"She's saying hurry up." My tigress waves her human paw at the others. "Come on, we'll talk about it later. I'm sure they're looking for her. We need to make sure this place is safe from those Serpent Court goons."

The footsteps start back up again, and satisfied, I bound down the stairs. Round and round I go until finally, the smell of brine fills my nose. I round a final corner and find stairs open up to a shadowy cavern with a low ceiling extending out into the distance like a tunnel. But there is nowhere for my paws to tread. Instead, my path is filled with water. I growl at the calm blue surface before more fire splutters alive on either side. The hatchling zips from my head to a wooden vessel that bobs on the water, a flame housed in glass lighting up the prow.

The animas stomp down the stairs, gathering around me, the other hatchlings cooing in wonder. I suppose it is beautiful.

"You've got to be joking," my leopard mutters.

"You guys! This is so exciting! I'm going to draw a map." My tigress comes up to inspect the boat.

With another sniff of the water to assess its composition, I change again. My muzzle elongates into a snout, my fur blends away to leave a tough, scaled skin, and my limbs disappear, leaving me with only a long powerful body. Blinking at the new colours now visible to me, I slip into the water.

"She's as big as a basilisk!" my leopard cries before all sound becomes muffled. The water is pleasant against my cool skin and I wiggle happily. Under the surface, a few green aquatic plants grow but my vibration and heat sensors detect nothing else.

The water agitates as my sisters clamber into the boat. Content they are following, I swim on ahead.

With the current soft against my skin and the peace of silence, I cruise down the waterway, allowing the lulling sensation in my mind to drift this way and that. A tiny inkling at the back of my mind irritates my peace, but I brush it aside.

All that matters is that those venom-tipped fangs no longer scrape at my protections, and while I am here in my most primal state, they cannot.

The canal floor begins to slope upward where it ends and I slither out onto the rough, hard stone floor, droplets of water sliding off my skin.

I shift once again for better walking, my limbs reappearing and sending my body upwards, fine whiskers on my cheeks twitching as I scent the air and look around at my new domain.

"I'm never going to get over her just shifting like that," my fair-lioness whispers.

"Guys, this is literally a dragon's secret cave!" my tigress calls. "I reckon the old dragon family who used to own this place kept their horde of gold and jewels down here."

The animas and hatchlings make pleased sounds as we assess the cavern. There is a very faint scent of dragon and many old and useless objects scattered around.

Well, it belongs to the dragons no more. I stalk to the corner and proceed to mark this territory as mine.

"Is she— Did she...?" my leopard-sister is loud in my ears.

"She really just pissed on the wall, yeah," my dark-lioness says.

"Oh, Wild Goddess, she's gone rabid." My tigress is not happy and I do not know why.

The hatchlings zip around the space as my sisters burst into chatter and I set about my task, building my nest.

There are sticks from long-dead plants, and dusty cloth that makes me sneeze, but I drag select pieces to the centre of the cavern where I will have a good view of everything. I push with my muzzle and pull with my teeth until I have arranged a nest of soft but sturdy materials. The hatchlings squeak with approval, immediately adding their own additions to the nest before settling down and looking at me expectantly. Carefully, I settle myself down and rest my head between my paws. My own turquoise hatchling inserts himself between my golden paws, chirping low in question. A contented purr emerges from my throat and the hatchling closes his eyes.

My human sisters inspect our surroundings, making funny squawks and warbles as they find new and interesting objects. I watch them toddle about with half-lowered lids.

We must rest. We must conserve our energy because those dangerous fingers lurk ever closer. Ever waiting for weakness. For entry.

Keep them all safe.

But my peace is not to be. Within minutes, there comes a faint smell of sweet burning. My head jerks upward in raw awareness. That is no mortal, ordinary fire.

And yet it is not like dragon fire either.

I let out a little warning growl and my pack all jerk to attention.

"What is it?" my tigress squeaks.

My gaze remains fixed on the watery tunnel and they all watch where I do.

Water glistens, that mythical scent of flame infiltrates my nose, and the sound of gentle lapping fills the cavern.

It is not long before she appears.

Standing on another boat, surveying my territory, is an anima I met once, many years ago, almost in another life. Her hair is a fiery red, long and curling down to her breasts. Her human body is covered in a white suit and her eyes gleam like golden molten coals.

Though I do not recall her name, I know she is safe. She knows things others do not. She showed kindness to me once, and now, on her lips, is a knowing smile.

Lady Phoenix.

Her boat bumps against the slope of the cavern floor and she steps off it with otherworldly feminine grace.

"Aurelia." A deep voice like magma over old rock sends shivers down my spine.

The human inside of me bangs uselessly against her cage. I only blink in reply.

"We think she is rabid, my Lady Headmistress," my tigress says.

The other animas shift as if surprised, but the phoenix nods and the sounds that come out of her mouth are slow. "Aurelia, if you can understand me, I have placed an injunction upon your sentence. Your execution has been halted."

The silence in the cavern is sweet music to me.

"Will you animas keep watch over her for the moment?" Lady Phoenix asks.

There are blubbers of assent.

"You are good friends to Aurelia. However, I still expect you to attend your classes and keep to your progress plans. You cannot stay here in beast form or you'll turn just the same."

"So we just leave her here?" my tigress asks.

The Lady Phoenix nods slowly. "I sense that she needs this, and I would prefer her to lie low after the events of this evening. That is for the best. Do not speak a word of this place to the other students. Is that clear?"

There are more murmurs and Lady Phoenix fishes a white human communicator device from her pocket. A soft blue light is reflected on her face as she reads something on it before looking back up at me and my pack-sisters. "Very well, ladies. If you'll excuse me, I need a word with my deputy."

Lady Phoenix gazes at me for a moment, her face beautiful in its maturity, and her expression is sincere. Then we watch her leave, gracefully stepping back into the second boat, which of its own accord, sails itself back through the tunnel.

Once more, we are left in the silence and darkness.

"Sorry, but how is that possible?" my leopard asks. "The sentence was passed by the Council. How can she just interfere with that?"

"The House of Phoenix has always held the power to intervene in cases like this," my tigress whispers. "Their magic lets them see mating bonds, among other things. They're given the right to have their collective say if their court sees fit."

"And how did you know we even have a Headmistress?" My dark-lioness demands. "This whole time we thought it was a Head*master*!"

My care for their mouth-sounds wanes. I nestle in with my blue hatchling and close my eyes. There are only two things I know: there is peace here, and as long as I remain as I am, we will all be safe.

After some length of time, the sisters of my pack grunt and bones shift and re-form. I open my eyes long enough to see furry pelts of copper, black, orange stripes, golden spots, and a final pelt, a twin to mine, settle down around me.

They have assumed their true forms. Perfect.

Chapter 2

Lyle

My stride is controlled as my alleged bond brothers and I exit the elevator onto my floor, but the way my office door slams open tells everyone that I am, in fact, *not* in control at all.

Boneweaver. Aurelia is a fucking Boneweaver. Likely the only being in the world who can shift into *any* beast she chooses. And *all* the gifts that come with that? No wonder Mace Naga wants her back. No wonder he'd touted Aurelia as some manipulative narcissist, when all she'd been trying to do was survive.

I've fucked up. Badly.

Georgia, having returned here, no doubt to monitor the disaster in the receiving bay from the security cameras, jumps to her feet and hurries towards us. "Lyle, should I—"

To my surprise, it's Scythe who snaps, "That's *Mister* Pardalia."

As I pass her, surprise makes my rage falter. Is it propriety or possessiveness that makes him correct her? I might never know. The thought that Scythe might get territorial over me is laughable at best, and disturbing at worst.

Georgia visibly flinches in terror at the shark's skin-crawling rasp and all but runs back to her desk as fast as her Louboutins will carry her. We all file into my office and, with a twitch of a finger, I slam the door closed.

Savage lies prone by the bookshelves lining the right side of my office, where I instructed Xander to dump him after darting him earlier today. Scythe and I didn't want anything to interrupt Aurelia's trial and eventual conviction.

To think I was worried about the delinquent wolf and not Aurelia Aquinas, ex-princess of the Serpent Court and current bane of my existence.

I stride past Savage to my desk, activating the office's sound-proof mechanism as Scythe crouches down to brush his pale, tattooed fingers over his brother's face.

The distant sound of chains rattling reaches my inner ear. A chill runs down my spine.

"We need to retrieve her," I mutter. "Before everything turns to further shit."

There is no way for Aurelia to run outside of the academy, as she well knows. The dark shadow of her wedge-tailed eagle's body was headed for the anima dorms, no doubt feeling it was safest to be with her friends.

"She's in the anima building," Xander says irritably, thudding his tall frame into one of the chairs by the bay windows. "Well, *under* it, to be precise. Turns out there are more dragon-trick doors than I estimated." The lights of my office cast shadows over his long black hair and face, transforming him from brooding to outright sinister. Dragons always have that power edged in mystery look about them. As if the mythical beast prowling within knows things the rest of us don't. Or can't.

Scythe rises from his inspection of Savage and shoots Xander a curious look—a mixture of interest and irritation—but I don't have time to ponder it. I need to get this entire situation under control. I need to find Aurelia and question her. I have to figure out what her father has been up to. What his plans are. Everything I know about her will have to be reassessed.

I don't even realise I'm pacing the room until Scythe cuts my path off. Me and my thoughts come to an abrupt halt.

The shark's sheet of silver, shoulder-length hair falls forward as he takes an old-fashioned metal cigarette case out of his pocket. Those iceberg eyes flick up to mine, then around my body. Whatever he sees in my aura makes his pupils constrict into tiny dots.

Being on the pointy end of a shark's stare, especially Scythe's —a light enough blue to be almost white at times—should make any animalia, even a lion, want to run. But Scythe has something in him that no other shark on the planet does.

One part of my soul group.

Scythe Karkhorous—gangster, mobster, killer—is my brother by destiny.

Slowly, he takes out a hand-rolled cigarette and I watch his tattooed hand extend it towards me.

My nose tells me it's not tobacco, but blue ganja; a special type of marijuana grown extra strong for the beast population. I haven't had one in years.

I take it.

"They used to charge a lot for this in Blackwater," I say, putting it in my mouth as Scythe pulls out a lighter. It's a novelty one, in the shape of a shark with open jaws.

"They still do," he says. As he lights my joint, the corner of his mouth ticks up because we both know who controls the illicit substances coming in and out of the federal penitentiary for beasts, and it's certainly not me.

I choose to ignore his reply as an orange flame comes to life from the open jaws of the shark and I take a long drag. The joint hisses as the chemicals fill my lungs. It's been a while, but the familiar way it burns through me focuses my mind. Taking out my phone from my pocket, I send a quick message to my superior.

The identity of the noble leader of Animus Academy is kept so secret that few even knew that the so-called "Headmaster" is actually a *she*. It is kept that way for her own safety. Against powerful beasts that would try to use her. I now wonder if Mace Naga was one of them.

Xander snorts. "Mace is not going to be happy with the way you lassoed him and his generals right out of the gates like that." His glowing eyes stare at me from the bay windows, the moon-light reflecting blue off his midnight hair.

I grunt as I sit down at my desk because I won't admit to him that the use of my power had not been intentional. That seeing Aurelia and her mating mark—our mating mark—blazing gold like that... I lost control. Plain and simple. Everything I've worked for over the last decade crumbled down in the split second it took for that skull and five curling beams of light to register. I'd pulled myself together, of course, but...

My animus could not be released. Not ever. And my regina presenting herself to me was forcing that disastrous power to come forth out of the bindings I placed upon him with so much care.

I glance at Savage, still snoring softly into the carpet, a dark curl flopping annoyingly over his forehead.

"He won't be asleep for long," Xander drawls, dropping his head back as if he's tired. "I had to re-dose him five times. Who's going to break it to him? And who's going down to find her?"

Both beasts are watching me far too closely for my liking.

"She trusts me the most," I say.

"The fuck she does," Savage groans as he rolls onto his back, grimacing. "Why'd you put my neck like that, Xander? You're—" And like he suddenly remembers who and what happened to him, he's on his feet with a swiftness I expect from a beast with combat set like cement into his bones.

Savage snarls and lunges for Xander with fury saturating his eyes, leaping right on top of the dragon. "You fucking asshole!"

"You'll want to listen to this!" Xander shouts, grabbing the wolf's head with both hands as Savage's suddenly wolfish canines enclose around his throat.

"Listen, brother," Scythe says sharply.

Perhaps it's his tone, because Savage abruptly jumps off Xander, his hazel eyes narrowed and suspicious on his shark-brother, then on me. His voice is guttural, fully descended into his wolf. "Where is she? Where is my regina?"

Without waiting for an answer, he closes his eyes and I know he's sensing her.

I'm suddenly very aware of Aurelia's scent on him. Her aroma is sweet and heady, and I realise it's not just her scent, but... *her scent*. I'm on my feet before I realise it, a soft growl escaping my throat, my eyes set on the wolf.

The three beasts' heads snap towards me at the latent threat, and I shake myself and lower my ass back onto my seat.

"Well, well, well." Xander is amused as he crosses his arms. "He *does* feel his regina's pull."

I glare at him because he's the last person to be taunting me about this.

Savage stalks towards my desk, predatory eyes on me, all male arrogance and swagger though his teeth and eyes are back to normal. "Why does she feel different? What happened at the trial? If anyone fucking hurt her..."

The fact that Savage has had sex with Aurelia complicates a great many things. He *wants* her now. More than ever. Is calling her his regina.

I glance out the bay windows, into the dark of the school grounds. We can all sense her. Our souls feel that primordial tug towards hers, like the moon feels the tug of the Earth. It's unavoidable. Unignorable. And even I can feel the wild tangle that's new. The primitive force that envelops her.

A familiar, dark feeling of unease winds through me.

"She's not coping with this," Scythe says. "She's not stable."

"Physically, she's fine," I say quickly. "That's the most important thing."

"I want to see her," Savage growls.

With a veteran's practise, I blow out a slow, measured exhale. "It'll tip her over, Savage. She's—"

"Fuck that. She needs me." And then, begrudgingly, he adds, "She needs us."

"She doesn't want us, Sav," Xander snaps.

Scythe's voice cuts through their bickering. "If she needs to be alone, we leave her alone." Scythe is Savage's voice of reason. And if the devil *could* be a person's voice of reason, you know you're dealing with a real bottom-dweller of hell itself.

Savage goes still and something passes between the blood brothers. I wonder what it is because, by the small crease between his brows, even Xander doesn't know.

Shark and wolf. I always thought it was a strange mix in a family. Their father was well known in the underworld. By all accounts feral, but sane. All his kills were in cold blood. Males like that should be put down as soon as they reach adulthood. But there is a humanity in Savage that is very much not like his father's. It's new for him, although it seems limited to his newly found regina.

The fact that we are all in the same pack, have the *same* regina—I can't even compute that.

I speak his name and the wolf's head snaps back towards me, his hazel eyes raging with a suspicion that borders on outright violence. "You can see her on one condition." He needs to be tested. I take another drag of my joint.

His eyes narrow. "Who do I need to kill, *feline?*"

I let the jab go. For now. "You'll attend the regina course we run here. All of you will. *Then* we can see about a visit."

Xander swears under his breath. "I don't have a regina. I'm not fucking going."

But Savage cocks his head contemplatively and a light enters his eyes, as if he's inspired. "Alright." He shoves playfully at Xander. "And you'll do it too, Xan, or I'll rip off your ears."

The dragon snarls, smoke streaming from his nose as he leaps to his feet and storms out of my office. Savage rubs his hands together and licks his lips as if he's thinking of Aurelia. "That's a yes."

"Don't push him," Scythe warns. The yellow lamplight catches his eyes, but it adds no warmth to those cold sapphires. "The last thing we need is a rabid dragon running around campus. We already have a rabid Boneweaver."

There it is again. That little, blue-eyed word that sits heavily between us like a boulder. A boulder that might swing back at any moment and get us all killed.

But Scythe is ever the calculating Don. I can't even tell what he feels for Aurelia beyond cursory interest. Does his animus even respond the same way to her as it does for us land animuses?

As if he knows what I'm thinking, Scythe stares right at me in open challenge as Savage bounds out the door. I meet him stare for stare. As the oldest, I ought to be rex of our group, and failing that, second-in-charge. We're all a match for power, after all. But in a group like this... well, I expect to have my dominance challenged constantly.

But I won't accept it. I'm not a part of this pack. Far from it.

In the silence of my darkened office and the cicadas chirping outside, I let out another measured breath. Between just the two of us, perhaps conversation could be civil.

"Why did she never tell us?"

"Because she's Mace Naga's daughter, Lyle." Scythe takes another drag of his joint. "Because for thirteen years she was raised by a manipulative, cunning man and knows how this works, perhaps better than anyone."

Aurelia certainly has never been an innocent sort of young lady. Growing up in the serpent mansion itself, she can't be. But she also never struck me as malicious, and I considered myself a good judge of both animalia and humans. "But Mace sent her away to marry Halfeather. If he knew about her power, why would he do that? Why not keep her for his own from the start? He clearly wants her back."

"Wants her back to breed her," Scythe says. He allows that to sink in. And when it does, something old and lethal creaks in my ears. Something I've been keeping at bay for ten long years. I take a long drag of my joint and hold the sweet, acrid smoke in my lungs until it stops. Scythe continues. "That Halfeather situation was just a power play. Likely for a few million bucks. He wants to have control of the most powerful beast of our generation. Of *any* living generation." Scythe stands up, his face beautiful and hard like it's cut from marble. "If she ever caught wind of exactly how powerful she is, she would know there is nothing in her way. Even *we* couldn't go up against her." He takes a step towards me. "She can't *ever* know how powerful she is, Lyle. If she does, we'll have an enemy on our hands—the worst we've ever known."

I frown at him. I can't deny his logic, but it's a mobster's logic. It's the type of thinking that Scythe has used to gain this much power over the years and stay in that power.

He exhales and I know there are thoughts running mad in his head. For the millionth time, I wonder how he stays sane. How he remains logical and calculating despite the call to the ocean I'm sure his shark demands from him every minute of the day.

Scythe turns out to the window, looking out over the school grounds. By the light of the moon lining the sharp planes of his features, he looks like some ethereal creature from another world. I see the lure he has on the animas and every other beast who comes across him.

"Are you worthy of the name 'Beast Breaker'?" Scythe asks abruptly.

I refuse to blink at the question. "I'm the best at it."

Turning back to regard me, he points with his joint out the window. "I certainly hope so, because Mace Naga is coming for you."

Chapter 3

Xander

I'm lying on my bed, thoroughly enjoying a joint of premium red grade, dragon-strength weed, when a voice starts singing in my head.

"My Aurelia with eyes so blue. Aurelia, my love for you is true."

A fucking Boneweaver. I should have known. I should have sensed it on her. *Smelled* it on her.

"Aurelia, my heart goes pitter patter. Aurelia... I'm going to smack your ass for running away from me. I'm coming, I'm coming, I'm coming."

"Fuck off, Savage," I mentally call back. *"That didn't even rhyme."*

But his voice only gets louder as he reaches the stairs for our hidden floor. *"Aurelia, your pussy is so sweet. Aurelia, I'm going to fuck you so hard you'll tweet."*

My head starts pounding and I leap off the bed, startling Eugene sitting on my headboard, trying to catch some smoke. But Savage bursts into our room, flinging the door open so hard it hits the wall and rebounds.

His grin is manic as he leaps for me and we both fall back onto my bed.

"Take me to her, Xan!" Straddling me, Savage shakes my shoulders, but I just close my eyes and take another drag. "She's escaped death all by herself and I just know it's because she loves me. I traced her scent to the anima dorm!" he says excitedly. "She's in there alright, but the magic won't. Let. Me. In." He shakes me with each syllable.

I take a long drag and allow a beat of dramatic silence to settle between us before I exhale smoke into his pretty face and say, "No."

He growls low and deep before slugging me right in the jaw so hard I see stars. My head snaps to the side, but I look back at him and laugh darkly.

"I'll rip your liver out and eat it, Xan. *Take me there.*"

It's hard to deny a direct request from your bond brother, especially because I know he follows through with his threats, but I manage to grit out a firm, "*No.*"

Savage sits back on my thighs and looks down at me, pushing out his lower lip. "She's probably missing me really badly. Please?"

He looks ridiculous, but the bastard knows exactly how to appeal to our bond. A sorry plea like that is possibly the most annoying thing on the planet. Lucky for my weed and Mozart.

"Get the fuck off me or I'll melt your face off and she won't be able to stand the look of you."

He shoves off me, muttering expletives under his breath as he tears off his T-shirt and throws it on his bed. He does that when he gets irritated or angry. As if clothes are a heinous crime to his wolf body and an impediment to animalistic thoughts.

For a moment, I am afforded peace. A random Mozart concerto blares in my ears. Eugene's nervous heartbeat flutters above me, and further away are the muffled sounds of the other students getting ready to go to bed on the floors beneath us. The weed burns through my body, lulling me into a sweet stupor while Savage paces the room, hands on his hips. Occasionally he fingers the black hair tie around his wrist.

Suddenly, he stills.

"Got it," he says, before rushing back out the door.

He's got an idea. And Savage with an idea is bad news. I just don't have it in me to care right now, so I don't move an inch from my comfortable supine position. Scythe and Lyle can deal with whatever his mutt brain has cooked up.

* * *

It takes all of one hour for me to eat my words. An image flickers through my mind, fingers tattooed with the phases of the moon fiddling with...is that a—?

Eugene shrieks in terror.

"Fuck!" I shout, leaping off my bed.

I wave at the rooster to stay put as I stride out of our room.

"*Scythe!*" I call out sharply through our mind connection. "*We have a situation.*"

"*Deal with it,*" comes the curt reply. "*I'm soaking in the pool.*"

"*What? Now?*"

"*I need to burn the residual serpent magic from my blood. You'll need to fly me to the coast later tonight.*"

"*Where's Lyle?*"

"*With the headmistress.*"

"*Savage is about to blow up the goddam school!*"

"*Well, go and stop him then.*"

He slams down the door on our communication, and I storm down the stairs. I learned long ago that if Scythe is dealing with something, it's best to leave him to it.

Swearing about the madness of sharks and wolves, I shoot out of the dorm.

Chapter 4

Savage

I position the final explosive at the base of the anima dorm and beckon to my little leopard friend to follow me as I move back. I can't very well make sweet love to my beautiful regina if I'm blown to pieces now, can I?

It took all of forty-five minutes to blackmail a couple of my spotted friends to make me some explosives big enough to bring down a four-story building. They are good at making little useful devices, and we are going to set them all off from afar at the same time.

The Forklift Brothers spent a little time distracting the guards with a student who "managed" to get his entire arm stuck down a toilet. Bob's your uncle and now I'm ready to go.

"Ready, spotties?" I ask the gathered felines. "On my count—"

One of the kits whose name I don't care to know gives me a panicked look under his comb over. "But, Mr Fengari, there are girls in there."

"Yes," I say, not so patiently. "But the prettiest one is far *beneath* the building. This is the way I get to her."

Pickle, one of the nerdy leopards who made the bomb, clears

his throat. "Sir," he says nervously behind his protective goggles. "Should we, er... give them a chance to get out?"

"Who?" I frown disapprovingly at him.

"Um... the other animas?"

"Oh," I say slowly. I forgot about other people for the moment. Correction. Didn't care about them for the moment. *"Hear ye, hear ye!"* I broadcast into the minds of all the animas in the old building. *"Get out of the anima dorm in one minute because I'm about to blast it up to the Wild Mother herself!"*

There are a couple of yelps and shadowy female bodies begin to dart around by the light in the dorm windows.

As I tap my foot, something prickles at the side of my awareness. I put up all my telepathic shields so neither of my brothers could sway me from my path. But sometimes when I get excited, like during sex or setting up a bomb, it's possible for things to slip through to them. I think it's because I like my brothers a little too much.

Just as the first animas bolt out their front door, the hairs on the backs of my arms stand on end.

The heat slams into me first. Everyone else scatters in all directions and I dive to the ground, just as holy hot red dragon fire lights up the night.

"You're not blowing up this beautiful piece of architecture!" Xander roars.

I roll to my feet to face one hell of an angry dragon, stomping up to me, all six-foot-eight of him.

"Yes I am!" I shout back, pointing at the building. "My regina is under there!"

"It's *heritage* listed, Savage." Xander shoves his face right up to mine.

"I don't even know what that means," I snarl. "And I don't fucking care."

"I'll get you in, you crazy fucker," Xander pants, shoving at me.

I go stumbling back, but now there's a massive grin on my face. "Really?"

"Yes, you illiterate backwater hick."

"Well, now I'm just going to blow it up out of spite, aren't I?"

Xander growls and stalks into the dorm as panicked animas stream out of it in their skimpy, lacey pyjamas, some with pillows under their arms. The males hiding a distance away look on with interest and jog back out to meet the ladies. Pickle sprints past me to collect his bombs, but manages to snag a group of curious feline animas on the way back. I smirk as I follow Xander.

The animus dorm is going to be a giant party tonight.

Don't let anyone say I'm not a benevolent pack leader.

Chapter 5

Xander

We trudge up three flights of stairs, passing two animas who give each other an almost comical look of fear before dashing past us.

With Handel's *Passacaglia* blaring in my ears, we get to the serpent girl's corridor, and quite suddenly, I'm hyper aware of *that scent.*

It's like nothing I've smelled before and giving it a name is like trying to remember the words of a song when you only know the melody. It's like starlight and the primordial place between the stars. It's heavy and sweet like a summer storm. It makes my whole body tingle.

No doubt the scent of a Boneweaver.

I fucking hate it.

Suppressing a gag, I survey the serpent girl's dorm. The balcony doors have been forced open from the broken brass handles on the floor. The rest of the room is in disarray and the smell of the other animas and nimpins litter the air.

Savage pushes past me to sniff the room, and suddenly he goes stock still.

His voice is dangerously soft when he says, "What is that doing here?"

I lean around him to see what he's staring at. On the snake girl's bed is a pile of items. Three specific items. A pair of cheap charcoal track pants, a two-dollar USB (who even uses those anymore?) and a red foil chocolate wrapper carefully folded into a perfect square.

Helpfully I say, "Ah. That."

"You returned my chocolate foil?!" Savage screams. He's on me in an instant, claws out, dragging the sharp points down my face. It burns like acid, but I let him have at it as I think dully. All this over a snake girl. I don't understand his anger. Really, I don't.

"You scumbag cunts!" Savage roars. "That was *mine*! They were *ours*!"

I let him drop us to the ground, and he slams a furry fist into my jaw. Left, then right. Then left again. I hear a crack and see stars. The feeling of broken bone must satisfy him because he rears back on his heels and jumps up.

"Fuck you, Xander!" Savage strides over to the pile and possessively snatches them up and hugs them to his bare tattooed chest. "If you don't want them, you should have given them to me."

"They're shitty gifts, anyway," I grumble through gritted teeth. Savage shoots me a dark, unhinged look that tells me he's at the end of his tether. I turn away from him as I press the broken parts of my jaw back together so they can heal properly.

We both stride out of the dorm room and track the Boneweaver scent down the corridor.

Savage rushes up to press his nose against the painting on the wall at the end of the corridor.

It's a stunning oil painting. An original, I'm sure, of a dragon flying high over a craggy mountain range somewhere in Europe. A small sigh escapes me as I admire a piece of history. We had paintings like this all over my parent's mansion.

As soon as I get back to my room, I'm going to get a drink.

Without even looking, I can sense the dragon-trick door. Looking at it through my magical eyes, I can see right through it and the fresh sparkle that tells me it has been recently unlocked.

I narrow my eyes. A dragon would have had to open this door. I don't know if Lia's Boneweaver abilities extend to dragons or not.

She better hope not, otherwise we are going to have a big fucking problem. I'm the only dragon allowed around here.

"Lemme through." Savage impatiently pounds his fist against the priceless art.

I swat his hand aside and he steps away. Pressing my hand against the gilded ornate frame of the painting, I sense the old magic and the strands of power that make it up.

To my horror, it's somehow been programmed to allow all her anima gang through.

"What's wrong?" Savage says quickly, detecting my rising anger.

Smoke streams out of my nose and I just shake my head, re-programming it to recognise and allow Savage and Scythe through.

When I step through, Savage leaps after me, nearly shoving me down the narrow winding stairs.

Fire splutters to life on dragon-shaped wall sconces on either side of the darkness.

"Oooh, fancy," Savage says, before shouldering past me and hurtling down the stairs at full pelt.

Sighing, I follow him and we quickly find ourselves at the bottom of the winding staircase, a cavern of water before us.

"Ha!" Savage ignores the waiting boat and, after carefully setting down his spoils in the corner, rips off his pants. He bursts into his wolf form and belly flops into the water, doggy paddling his way down the channel.

I let out a growl of warning because we don't know what else could be in the waters here. My father would be inclined to keep saltwater crocodiles, or worse, box jellyfish inside something like this. But Savage just gives me an excited yip and I clamber into the boat, grab the oar, and push off after him.

My family mansion has a similar underground cave system, and it makes my skin crawl with nostalgia to think of it. I've only been down there once, where my father kept our most precious family jewels hidden behind dangerous magic. *This* place, having long been abandoned, only contains traces of magic. Things that require low power, like the wall sconces and the boat.

Having a dragon back in situ, and considering the amount of my own blood Savage managed to spill onto the floorboards when we first got here, probably gave this place a little jolt of life.

I follow Savage's bobbing black head through the gloom until we round a corner and the tunnel opens up into a high-ceilinged cavern. And lo-and-behold, a sorry sight awaits us.

Savage gives an excited yip at the sight of his regina. Despite her new and improved form, I recognise her immediately. It's the eyes, I think, the particular colour of them, that gives her away.

The anima girl gang are all in their beast forms, lazing about on dirty piles of cloth and litter. Minnie is at the front, in her tigress form, staring at us, with Sabrina as a leopard, her head resting on Minnie's back. Connor is an impressive black lioness between them and Raquel, in their wolf form. Lastly, Stacey, in lioness form, is on her side, pawing at Raquel's ear.

I wrinkle my nose as my ancient instincts flare up to clean the place and sort out the dirty things from the precious things, but I shove that shit down because this is not *my* dragon's horde.

The lioness with the sapphire blue eyes lies in the middle of the dirty nest, a queen at court, apparently. Her head rests on her two front paws and Henry the nimpin is snuggled right next to her cheek, looking pleased with himself.

Though the Boneweaver's pose is casual, lazy even, her eyes

are sharp and bright on Savage as he shakes off the water like the mutt he is. As I clamber out of the boat, her eyes flick to me. Something hangs in the air around her. Like the low, repetitive boom of a bass drum. I frown as it registers and bat it away like an irritating fly.

Savage lets out a bark to announce his presence, his ears erect as he makes to trot up to her.

A low warning growl from Aurelia stops him in his tracks. Savage's ears flip back. *"Aurelia,"* he telepathically coos. *"Let me in, pretty princess."* He casts me a look over his shoulder. *"It's like her mind is shielded with stone."*

It's not stone at all, rather something more unbelievable. I sigh and gesture to the rest of them. "Have you all lost it, or is this a personal preference?"

It's Raquel who shifts into human form, probably in response to the alpha wolf of the school staring them down. They crouch on the spot, trying to cover their pale, naked skin. They have a number of tattoos in random places.

"S-sorry, Mr F-Fengari."

"Raquel," Savage snarls, *"what the fuck do you think you're doing with my regina?"*

"N-nothing!" Raquel says. I'm sure the wolf anim speaks out loud for the benefit of their friends. "N-Not by our choice. L-Lia led us here. We're j-just k-keeping her c-company. She's n-not... n-not that well."

"Not mentally well," I correct. "I don't think she ever was, to be honest."

Minnie hisses in offence, baring her long incisors.

"Pipe down, mouse," I command irritably. "But this is just what we *fucking* need." I gesture to the lot of them, lying there, useless lumps of fur and teeth.

Minnie flinches at the anger and I can't be bothered feeling bad about it.

"Let's go," I say to my brother. "There's nothing we can do here."

"*I'm staying.*" Savage plonks himself down on the stone floor like he's keeping guard, his tail wagging as his eyes are fixed predatorily on the lioness who still hasn't raised her head from her paws.

That *sound* around the Boneweaver girl is giving me a headache, audible even through my music.

"Fine," I snap. "But don't come crying to me when Lyle comes down here and starts barking orders."

Annoyed bestial noises trail me as I climb back into the boat. I flip them all off and light a fresh joint with a finger flame.

Chapter 6

Savage

The next morning, I wake up to the annoying sound of the animas and nimpins squeaking, groaning, and yawning as they shift back into their human forms and rummage around for their clothes.

I keep my eyes closed because their complaining is traumatic enough without me seeing their naked bodies, too.

"Oh, I'm starving," Stacey says through a yawn. "Let's bring food down here next time."

"And drinks," Connor grumbles. "Preferably alcohol."

"And pillows!" Minnie pipes. "Shit. I've done something to my neck."

Raquel chuckles because us feral wolves are used to sleeping in groups like this in our beast forms. I crack open a lid to find my regina watching the other animas and nimpins as they get ready to leave. She didn't sleep all that much last night. I know because I was watching her blinking eyes the entire time. Her power fizzles around the cavern, sort of like Coke shaken in a can. It tickles the inside of my nose.

"Is she safe with him here?" Sabrina jerks her chin at me as if I'm an unwanted parasite.

The growl that comes from my lungs is a knee-jerk reaction, and I don't even feel bad when they give each other startled looks. All of them except for Minnie. The little tigress stares me down with narrowed eyes and then shakes her finger at me like a witch from a fairytale.

"Don't you *dare* do anything stupid while we're gone, Savage."

I blink my wolf eyes innocently at her. *"Like what?"*

"Like trying to blow up the building," she snaps back. "Yeah, your broadcast reached us last night."

I turn my head away from her dismissively because I *won't* apologise for trying to get to my regina.

"Lia c-can h-handle herself," says Raquel firmly.

We all swivel our heads to look at my feline princess.

I don't realise that I'm crawling closer to her on my belly until she lets out a rumble of warning.

A thrill shoots through me and I want to defy her—push her limits and see what she does.

"She's just been saved from a death sentence, Savage," Minnie stresses at me. "She needs space and time to process all the shit that's happened." Then her voice turns accusatory. *"Including* when you guys—"

I've shifted to human form and am on my feet in an instant, snarling at Minnie. The animas all jump back and the nimpins flinch. "Don't even say it!" I snarl. "This is between me and my regina and my pack. Get the fuck out of here and let me talk to her alone."

But a sound of rabid aggression erupts from the nest. Lia is on her paws, her lioness' body angled and snarling towards me. Her long white incisors are bared, her whiskers twitching. She takes a single step towards me.

The sound of her angry growl, her open threat towards me, shakes me to my core. I pant in shock, going still as she stares me down with those amazing blue eyes.

As shocked as I am that another beast dares to warn me, threaten me, my cock twitches at the sight of her.

She's magnificent. I drop to one knee before her, showing her that I submit.

"L-like I said," Raquel hisses. "Lia can t-take c-care of herself."

The animas clamber into the boat and the entire time Lia does not take her eyes off me, her threat so very clear.

Slowly, so she knows I mean no harm, I sit cross-legged on the cold floor. "My regina," I whisper. "My beautiful regina. I never would have let them take you."

She snarls in annoyance before slowly sitting back on her haunches, then her belly and assuming a sphinx pose. Henry lands on her shoulder.

It hurts a little that she is defending others against me. As if those animas are her pack and I am not. I press my lips together and swallow through a thick throat.

I sigh. "I have to be at classes or Lyle will probably send *me* for execution."

She puts her head down on her paws and angles her head away from me.

Maybe that wasn't funny. I try again. "So, I'll be gone for a while, but I will come back as soon as I can. Scythe and Xander are off on a trip, so it's just me and Leo the lion."

She closes her eyes. As if now, finally, she gets to rest. Henry is still by her cheek and he closes his eyes, too.

I shift back into my wolf form and, after looking back at Lia one more time to make sure she's sleeping, I pad over to the water. Every bone and muscle in my body tells me to stay and never leave her again. To make sure no one will hurt her or take her away from me. There are people who want to steal her, *breed* her. I cast my eyes around the cavern and the water. She'll be safe here for the moment. And there is that defence around her that makes my fur stand on end.

The quicker I leave, the quicker I can be back. And with food. She'll need lots of food.

* * *

After breakfast, we have cooking class and I hunt down Minnie in the corridor as everyone is leaving the dining hall.

"Minnie!" I call. "Minnie, I need to talk to you!"

"Alright, alright." Minnie makes a hushing gesture at me and I stop short and stare down at her audacity. Eyeing my face, she says hastily, "There's no need to draw attention, Savage."

"I need to talk to you."

"I heard you the first time."

"Alright, keep your hair on." I eye her bubblegum pink mop to double check that it is not, in fact, a wig. But if it was, that first time she shifted into a tigress to jump at me, it would have fallen off in the shift. So it must be real. "I need your help to woo my regina."

She puts her little fists on her hips. "And why should I help you? You tried to kidnap her. *And* use me as a hostage."

I wave a dismissive hand. "You were not a hostage, Min. I didn't hogtie you, drive into the outback in a black van, and take a video of you with a claw at your throat outlining my requests."

She narrows her eyes. "That's oddly specific."

"I daydream about these things sometimes," I say quickly. "But anyway, I need you to help me get my regina to forgive me. For her mental health's sake. I didn't mean to return the gifts and she would've been hurt really badly by that." Minnie chews on her lip like she's considering this. I know Aurelia has told her quite a bit, if not the whole truth. "I'm one of her mates. If anyone can get her out of this funk, I can."

Her eyes almost explode out of their sockets. "This 'funk'? Dude, she's basically *rabid*."

It's my turn to quiet her with shushing palms. "Whatever it is. I can help her get out of it before Lyle has to resort to his therapies and other weird shit he does to the rabid students to get them to change back. You don't want Lia to be therapised by Lyle, do you?"

"Therapised is not a word."

"It is now."

She sighs dramatically. "Alright, what were you thinking?"

I gesture to the kitchen door. "I'm going to make her food to say sorry. Mates bring their regina food and presents and other nice things to make them feel better, right?"

"Like the pink handbag."

My stomach tightens at the memory of that bag. What happened after I laid it at her feet. How Aurelia ran from us in that forest and we chased after her, right into the hands of Lyle, who captured her and hauled her here. I was so angry that day. If Aurelia told Minnie about it... that must mean it had meant something to her. I clear my throat. "*Food,*" I press. "I can't search for recipes."

"Hundreds and thousands."

"What?"

"Sprinkles. She giggled the last time we saw them at the buffet. I think..." she trails off and stares into the distance.

I bend down to try and get to her height, but she's so much shorter than me. "*Min*-nie," I sing impatiently.

"I think the sprinkles reminded her of fairy bread from her childhood. Like from before... everything went bad. All kids love that stuff."

"What's fairy bread?"

She gapes at me like a blowfish. "You don't know what fairy bread is?"

My growl is soft, but still threatening enough to let her know I don't like her assuming I'm stupid.

Then something extremely unusual happens. Minnie's face

goes all soft like she's sad. Her voice is only a kitten's mewl when she states, "You never had fairy bread as a kid."

"No," I say flatly.

She takes a deep breath and blows it out like Scythe does when he's about to lose his shit. "Come on, then. Where's that contraband phone I know you have? I'll show you."

Four hours later, I return to my regina, proud as punch with a paper plate balanced on my knees as I paddle back to her on the rickety old dragon's boat. This time, I bring along Eugene, with his brand new, custom made goggles. The little chicken knows what his job is and I never want Aurelia to be alone while we're all in class.

My regina and Henry are in the same position as when I left them and I worry about it, because does that mean she's not moved *all* day?

As soon as the boat slides up the slope, Henry zooms right for me, squeaking like prey, probably excited by all the colours on the plate.

He's so soft and squishy, with tiny bones I probably wouldn't even notice—

As if she knows what I'm thinking, Aurelia lets out a short growl and I snap out of my imagination. Henry levitates back to her and stares at me accusingly.

I try not to look at him and grin at her as I make my way to my designated safe spot a little way from her nest and instruct Eugene to sit by my side. "Regina, I made cookies! Look, they've got sprinkles on them and little stars, see? Minnie helped me. She said it was alright if they were all in the shape of Australia. I'm not really good at making them round, but Australia I can do as long as we ignore Tassie. And..." I excitedly point to the triangles of bread covered in butter and hundreds and thousands. I had to eat the first few slices because I was too rough with the butter knife and tore the bread. "Fairy bread!" I announce, going on my knees to push the plate forward as far as my arms will reach.

She blinks once at the plate but doesn't move.

I lean forward on my knees again, this time shuffling a tiny bit forward to push the plate just a little bit closer.

My regina growls her displeasure, and I sit back on my haunches. Henry lets out a squeak of a question, and when she makes no reply, he carefully levitates himself to the plate, and without taking his eyes off me, leans down and takes a tiny sugary star in his beak and floats back to Aurelia. He offers it, hovering right near her mouth as if he wants to feed it to her.

Aurelia opens her beautiful incisor-filled mouth and Henry drops it onto her tongue. She closes her maw and moves her tongue around like she's swallowing it.

Something in my chest twists.

That should be me. Feeding her, brushing her coat, cuddling with her.

"Henry, you dirty fuck," I grumble, pulling the plate back towards me. I stare it for a moment, trying to think. After a moment, I tear off a piece of fairy bread and wave it through the air.

"Go on, nimpin. Take it and give it to my regina."

Henry eyes me suspiciously. His gigantic eyes are far too big for his head, which means he can see really well in the dim light of this cavern. But he doesn't move forward.

"Suspicious little bastard, aren't you?" I say. "Well, you're not as dumb as you look then. Ready?" I lob the piece through the air as slow as I can and the tiny thing zips upward and meets the bread as it crests, catching it in his beak. He offers it to *my regina*, and she opens her sweet little mouth.

Satisfied, I settle back on my ass and Henry and I begin our game.

Chapter 7

Lyle

"It's been a week, Lyle. You need to see her."

Headmistress Celeste Agnios casts me a wry, red-lipped smile from across her desk. I sit in her office on the invisible topmost floor of the central offices of Animus Academy. A phoenix being granted keeper of a dragon's mansion was unheard of until Celeste's ancestor helped the Draykaris family in a dire situation generations ago. With the dragon population dwindling, and the Draykaris line dying out, the Agnios line was given ownership of the land. The dragon-made mansion respected her as the lady of the house, with only a small tantrum now and again. I imagine that Celeste being one of the mythic orders made the transition smoother. No one really knows the extent of the phoenix power because they keep themselves quiet and secret in the same way the dragons do. Seeing mating bonds between beasts made them powerful enough and it was no wonder there were people who wanted control of them. It was for that reason Celeste had confined herself here.

But now, the academy houses *three* creatures from mythic orders. I wonder if that is why the property allowed Aurelia to access one of its secret chambers. There are many such passages and chambers hidden around and under the school, but rarely did the spirit that ran the place grant restricted access to students.

I meet Celeste's dancing golden gaze and say evenly, "We're still not out of the water, Celeste. My voicemails are full of threats and inquiries. The first phoenix injunction in decades has everyone extremely curious."

And nervous.

I managed to avoid questions from the other students by telling them I placed Aurelia in solitary confinement. Whether they interpreted that as a punishment or a safety measure was of no consequence to me.

The media filled my inbox the entire week, and while I managed to avoid making a statement, time is running out.

As the face of an academy for budding ferals and criminals, I've spent my career maintaining a good relationship with the media. I spoke about my programs, showed them my meticulously kept data and success rates. One nosy reporter looking too closely into my dark past could completely derail everything I've worked for. Everyone knew that I'd entered Blackwater Penitentiary ten years ago, but that was all. Nobody knew the full story of what had come before. And I'm going to keep it that way.

Celeste's reply is smooth and confident, as always. "Phoenix Court has made our statement. We are investigating. That will placate the council for the moment."

Even Mace Naga was forced to quiet his protests once Celeste put out the notice via a message carried across the state with phoenix fire. I wish I could have seen the look on the face of the Serpent King when he saw the words written in licking red flames bright enough to sear the retinas.

The ancient and noble Court of Phoenix hereby places a formal injunction upon the execution of Aurelia Aquinas, pending an investigation. Further notice to be given at a later date.

Timely and precise. But also vague. Irritatingly so for Aurelia's scheming father. A beast we'd all thought was trying to improve Serpent Court for the betterment of his people.

"But for how long?" I say.

"For as long as we need to figure out what to do with our... situation."

The council will intervene as soon as they have the chance, and we both know it.

Celeste eyes my swinging foot and I cease my fidgeting under her acute gaze. She's always been able to read me better than most. Since the first day I met her at a difficult time in my life, she's been a mentor; not quite a mother, more like a stern aunt. She'd given me a chance when I'd been ready to throw myself to the executioner's block. "You're worried about the effect she'll have on you. You're worried she'll trigger you."

I don't reply, wondering how the hell I'm supposed to answer that. But Celeste knows me too well and continues in that ever-calm voice of hers. "I think she will benefit from you being there. Regina or not, a student needs you and your particular skill set. You *will* go to her aid."

Something in me settles a little at her order. Aurelia is nothing more than a challenging student who requires my instruction. Remedial instruction. I've been monitoring the situation from afar. Minnie and the other animas have been with her near-constantly, including overnight. They are dedicated friends. Savage, on the other hand has decided that he wants her and has been more than obsessed. He's been attending enough classes that I don't have to pull him up on it but then rushing back to her every evening. I should have known that his wolfish instincts would lead him to her. That he would be the first of us to succumb. But the rest of us have more sense and if we are careful, he will be the only one.

I rise from my seat, pulling down the cuffs of my suit jacket.

"Very well. I'll do my rounds with the rabid students and then go to see her."

Celeste nods imperiously, the edges of her lips twitching as she muses. "How long I've waited, Lyle. How long *we've* waited."

* * *

Animus Academy is best known for our flagship civilisation program. My hand-selected team is made of those passionate and skilled in helping young animalia be the best people they can be. I rarely venture out to teach those classes because I picked the best to do it for me.

But the rabid students are handled by me directly. There is no structure, no textbook or training guide that knows how to free a human mind from inside their beast. I consider it an art form more than a science.

Rick, my veterinarian and zoologist, is the only other person I permit down in the underground system of impenetrable glass rooms I built when Celeste appointed me as her deputy four years ago.

"G'day, Lyle," Rick says cheerily, handing me the clipboard with his overnight notes for the group. "The rooms have been cleaned and the students are fed. Titus is in a better mood today. We even went for a bit of a swim. Thomas was drawing some pictures in the night, mostly gigantic monster-snakes. The usual. The others all slept."

I thank him and he heads off to bed, cheerily waving goodbye to Titus as he goes.

The rabid tiger, for his part, lies on his bed in naked human form, scowling at me. After weeks, his skin is finally grime free. Big cats love to swim, contrary to popular belief, and I built the connected pool with the hope of sneaking some hygiene in. There are a variety of plants in each room as well as sensory items, personal effects from home and pictures of their family to prompt them to remember who they are.

Strolling up to the glass wall that separates his room from the rest of the cavern, I speak through the speaking holes, "How are you this morning, Titus?"

He grunts at me and under his thick black beard and shaggy hair. He's grinding his square jaw as if he hates having to ask. "More food now."

In the last three months, I've managed to increase his vocabulary significantly. Unlike some of my other students, Titus wants to be human. He's also quite intelligent, which helps, but is arrogant, which doesn't. After my investigation, I discovered that his rabidity is only recent. He spent most of his life feral, but I have yet to learn what triggered this episode of rabidity.

"More food?" I smile at him. "Give me a new word, Titus." I nod at his laptop on the desk next to the TV, where I'd written his words for the week. "And I'll give you a whole goat to hunt."

I'm well aware that he can read, even if he pretended he couldn't when he first got here.

Titus and I converse for a little while before I have the guards deliver a goat via the dumbwaiter system. Satisfied that Titus will chase his prey around the garden attached to his room, I take my sessions with my other rabid students. There are a few down here, all animuses, the last one being Thomas Krait, a serpent.

They've all made good progress, and if my estimation is correct, I'll be able to introduce at least two of them to the rest of the school in a few weeks.

After my rounds, I head back above ground and make straight for the anima dormitory.

I stride towards the old gothic building, a five story building that was a part of the original structure, looking for one of the things that caused a stir for the students this past week. Aurelia's cavern is not the only new development the academy saw fit to introduce.

"Deputy Headmaster," a raspy, metallic chirp sounds from above the anima dormitory entrance. I stop short and stare at the squat cast iron gargoyle perched above the glass doors.

"Well, I'll be damned," I say, staring up at the creature. It had always been there, the inanimate head at least. A constant, silent observer of those who entered or exited the dorm. Only now, it had grown into new life, full body and all.

"The pleasure is mine." Not a he, but a *she*, by the swelling breasts beneath her absent neck. She has a round, cherub-like face with a hooked nose and wispy, bat-like wings.

"You're new," I remark slowly. I don't just mean the creation of new architecture, but the fact that for the first time, the school made something that could talk.

"Was necessary," she sniffs through that big nose. "After a certain psychotic wolf decided to set an explosive at the base of our dwelling."

It was lucky Xander had caught Savage just in time.

"Well, we won't let it happen again, will we?" I say, swiping my card to get inside the dorm. It clicks and I pull it open.

"Affirmative, Deputy Headmaster. Very affirmative. Are you going to visit the Lady Boneweaver?"

I freeze.

A dark, primal rage erupts from the base of my spine and I tamper it down with the might of ten years worth of cold, hard discipline. There are guards patrolling a little distance away but none, thankfully, within earshot. Slowly and silently, I shut the door and take a step back to level a stare at the gargoyle.

Visibly, she gulps.

My voice is whisper soft. "What is your name?" For surely, the thing has one and I suddenly *need* to know it.

She shivers at my tone, then starts blabbing as if it will save her life. "Christine, at your service, sir. After the Lady Christine Draykaris, dragoness of the house of nineteen forty—"

I cut her off with words laced in cold death. "I want you to listen to me, Christine." Her mouth snaps shut and her eyes grow wide as she peers down at me. "Not a word of what lies in that cavern beneath this building leaves your mouth. Ever. Is that understood?"

"Mouth is zipped, sir."

I stare her down. "If you so much as breathe *that* word to another soul, inanimate or otherwise, I will tear your head off this building with my own hands and crush you to sand. Is that understood." Not a question.

"Sand, sir, sand. Affirmative."

I don't realise that my heart is hammering until I'm inside the air-conditioned building and the door has slammed shut behind me.

Swearing through my teeth, I follow Celeste's instructions up to the third floor and through the new dragon-trick door. Dragon mansions are full of these types of tricks and secrets, the school itself being sentient. There is every chance the school made this entrance by itself and showed it to Aurelia for her use. My own lodgings were made in such a way when the school decided to accept me on my first day here.

The unpredictability of it might have scratched at me, if not for the fact that the school was intelligent, easy to negotiate with, and seemed to like my traditional manners. It was old-fashioned, which we both seem to appreciate. These new developments might be annoying, but they are also useful. Christine will serve as an extra pair of eyes for me now. Another layer of security upon the layers of magic already here.

The fact that the school knows *what* Aurelia is, however... I'll have to ponder that another time.

I've paddled my way through the canal of sparkling blue water when I see her.

My breath seizes in my throat. Every hair on my body stands on end. The paddle sits frozen in my hands, completely forgotten.

Perhaps it's the way she sits in a sphinx pose, preternaturally still, golden fur a mirror to my own. Perhaps it's the low boom of power that pulses around the entire cavern like the steady beat of an old drum. It pounds in my ears, heavy and constant.

Here is not a girl, as I expected, bent and bowed by fear and devastation, cowering in terror at the thought of a breeding ring. But a queen, staring evenly at me as if waiting. Assessing. Judging.

Those eyes. Those stunning blue eyes, which I've previously seen flash in anger, dull with grief or dance with playfulness, are now only embers. Like coals burned down past their main heat.

As if she's powered her body right down to skeletal functions.

She has hidden her mating mark once again, no doubt a part of the mysterious power lent to her by her Boneweaver ancestry. But that mark has been seared into my mind as if she'd taken a white hot branding iron to me herself. I know it's there. I know it's on her skin, same as mine and the memory of it speaks to my animus in a wild roar.

Something more than me compels me to sit right there on the stone floor. And so, I do. I leap out of the boat and sit before her, suit and all. Staring at her golden fur, her long, white whiskers, the very regal pose.

I don't intend for it, but my voice emerges soft as down. "Some people think being rabid means you've lost control. That when beasts are driven to madness, they... regress into a shadow of themselves." I take a steady breath through my nose. "That's not the case, Miss Aquinas." I observe carefully for any reaction to my using her official family name, but I get none. To call her by her first name seems... forbidden. A shiver threatens to course through me and I tamp it down. "I know it to be for what it really is. Protection. Self-preservation. Our beasts protect us in the only way they know how. The most primal way."

She never blinks. And I withstand the judgement in that glimmering blue gaze.

I don't think my words register. I see no recognition in the dull consciousness behind her eyes. But just perhaps, somewhere inside of her, human Aurelia is listening. That fierce girl so intent on defying me.

Quite suddenly, I become aware of the rest of the cavern. The chaotic mess of a week's worth of blankets, pillows, soft toys, and discarded food wrappers. One of the plushies smells new, no doubt a gift from Savage. It's a small pink wolf with the glass eyes painted blue by hand. Henry the nimpin sits at Aurelia's front paw, blinking wide, sleepy eyes at me.

And in front of them both is a tray with a teacup and saucer, no doubt taken from the dining hall by her friends. But it's what I scent inside the teacup that catches my attention. Milo. A chocolatey malt drink I make sure to provide because it's so popular, especially amongst the younger students before bed.

A memory beckons, distant but... burning.

Deep inside me, chains rattle, followed by a low, steely growl.

The sudden urge to smash that porcelain to pieces almost overwhelms me. Henry squeaks in question, and I'm brought out of my reverie.

"I was just thinking about the Milo," I say to him. "I knew a girl who used to drink Milo in a set just like that."

Aurelia blinks at me, and I wonder if she can see, somehow, what I am to her. What I should be to her. I wonder if she's angry that her mates handed her over to her father. Correction: *Tried* to hand her over.

No doubt that's what tipped her over into this state.

Sighing, I think of the sixty-two emails in my inbox that need replying to.

I'm about to get up when Aurelia growls, low and soft, at the base of her throat. I freeze, staring back at her. To my utter surprise, she heaves herself to her feet, pads the five steps between us, turns around and settles down next to me. Her body is soft and warm against the length of my thigh. She lays her head down on my knee.

I'm fixed to the spot. Stumped by this wholly unexpected action.

I swallow at the sight of her resting on me. At the warmth that spreads through not only my leg but every other part of my body. I swallow again. Then clear my throat.

She begins to purr.

While the human might loathe me, clearly, her anima does not.

Henry settles down on her other side, a ball of blue fluff amongst the gold. A strange urge strikes me. Aurelia might not remember any of this. I realise that anything uttered here is unlikely to be repeated. It makes my animus purr beneath his chains. It makes his tongue loose.

Careful not to touch her, I murmur words I never thought I'd utter.

Chapter 8

Lyle

One of my earliest childhood memories is drinking Milo in the evening with my siblings.

There was a human girl, the daughter of the man who owned the illegal wildlife park where I was born. Skye's mother would give her hot Milo at bedtime, and she'd sneak down to the cub cages and pour half her teacup into our food dish.

We'd all scramble around the dish and lap it up as fast as we could, my four brothers and sisters and me. Skye would giggle and call us "silly little things" and often she'd babble about her day. I don't think she had anyone else to talk to.

It's a good memory despite the hellscape that place was.

Ulman's Wildlife Sanctuary, it was called. They had "all manner of koalas, wombats, Tasmanian devils, and a unique pride of lions who perform amazing feats of intelligence seven days a week between nine and three."

I never found out how my mother, her wife and two husbands ended up in Ulman's cages. We were forbidden from interacting with our parents and I didn't even know what they looked like in human form because we were also forbidden from shifting.

My mother gave birth to three litters in her beast form. Such a thing was unthinkable before Fredrick Ulman, a renowned biologist, researcher and lion fanatic, forced it to happen.

His favourite tool was a cattle prod, fashioned into a high voltage for adult lions and a lower voltage for newborn cubs. His techniques worked so well that we no longer took our human forms at all. But instead of reducing us to changed animals, Ulman kept our human minds sharp with his style of training. Electricity as punishment and food as reward.

We were kept in outdoor enclosures, our parents in an adult cage and the kids in cub cages until we stopped bottle feeding and he'd move us to the teenage cages.

The Ulmans taught all of us cubs to read and write and paint. It was part of the tricks he made us do for the tourists who came to the wildlife park every day. It was one of the last remaining parks of its kind; the others had been disbanded by the government in the 80s. But Ulman, with his contacts, and regional location somehow managed to keep his 'pets', as he called us.

Unlike other animalia, we were all born as lion cubs and immediately taken from our mother for hand rearing and training.

Every time we shifted into our human forms, we were given a zap of electricity to force us to shift back. Every time we fell asleep, and shifted, we were zapped again.

That sort of training works best on cubs, but we grow to maturity slower than humans. It took most of us around four years to adapt to staying in our feline forms as we slept.

The lack of sleep would have driven us all mad if we didn't learn. Those who didn't learn disappeared.

All because Ulman wanted us to keep our human executive functions for the shows he put on for tourists. It was confusing for us, but children are adaptable and we learned to read and write and think while still in our beast forms.

Ulman's two children and wife helped rear us, but his youngest, Skye, took a special liking to the cubs, as little girls often do. She helped train us using electronic buttons that spoke words when pressed. Us cubs would run around in an arena and speak to the audience using these buttons. They would ask us silly questions, sometimes simple maths equations, and we would reply to them.

They would laugh, they would clap. We would return to our cage and do the same thing the next day. Our parents did different, more dangerous tricks made to bring in a crowd. Once a week, Ulman hosted "Killer Safari", where humans would ride around in safari trucks and hunt them with paintball guns. Our parents would have to fall over and pretend to be dead if they got shot. To me, at the time, it looked like fun. At least they got to run around, whereas us cubs were contained in smaller cages.

One day, when I was eight, a member of the audience asked a strange question. "Do you love living here?"

I'd grown a little bold by that age and straight away pressed the button for "no" with my paw. The entire audience went silent.

That night, Ulman took me away from my siblings and made me sleep alone.

"Next time lie," he said, sticking the electric prod up to my face.

You would think you'd get used to electric shocks after years of them, but they never hurt any less. It zinged through my little body and I was thrown to the floor of my cage.

I asked Skye a question using the buttons when her father left. "Isn't it wrong to lie?"

"You're an animal," she chided. "How do you know what you're *supposed* to do? Whatever us humans tell you is right, is right."

But I didn't quite believe her. I don't know what made me different from my brothers and sisters but I questioned Ulman on a number of occasions. I even used the buttons to speak to the crowd in ways that weren't allowed. Perhaps my hormones were about to kick in. I don't know.

Eventually Ulman got sick of my probing. I was a crowd favourite and he didn't want to put me down because I'd never been aggressive toward him. So he did something that he knew would get me to listen.

He took me away from my family.

I was sedated, not asleep and so I felt the fear of it every step of the way. The ride to the airport. Being stowed in the strange vehicle that hurt my ears and made loud noises as it glided through the sky. Ulman had some business in an illegal cub fighting ring, where he made me watch as human children with claws and fangs beat and tore each other bloody.

He leant down and said into my little ear, "This is what happens to cubs who don't behave, Lyle. This is what will happen to your little brothers and sisters if you don't do what you're told."

And so I did. I was the perfect little cub for a long, long time.

* * *

Aurelia's breaths turn deep and heavy in that of sleep. I stare at her for a moment, waiting for her to change back into her human form, every sense of mine standing on a razor's edge.

But she remains as a lioness.

I sigh long and low. "But that is a story for another time." Carefully, I take her head off my knee and set her down on the stone. I climb to my feet, suddenly feeling as if some old burden has been taken off my shoulders. "I'll come back tomorrow and we will speak again. Perhaps about nicer things."

It's on my way out that I see a halo of bright pink hair bobbing through the dragon trick-door. "Miss Devi."

She stumbles but catches herself, managing to keep a hold of her glittering pink folder and armful of paper bags. My nose tells me they are filled with ham and cheese croissants.

"Oh, Goddess! Sorry. Hello, sir," she says sheepishly, kohl lined eyes blinking.

I stare down at the tigress, assessing. There are bags under eyes and her brown skin has an ashen tone. "When I ask you this question, Miss Devi, I want you to answer honestly, do you understand?"

Her eyes widen before she controls herself, paper bags crackling. "Of course, sir."

"For how long has Miss Aquinas been in her shifted form?"

Minnie blinks once, twice, then rubs her eyes with her wrist. "Um, I haven't... I haven't seen her change into her human form at all, sir."

"In this entire week?"

She gulps and shakes her head.

"And when she sleeps?"

Minnie shakes her head again.

A cold trickle of dread snakes down my spine, and by the nervous look in Minnie's eyes, she also knows what this means. The longer a beast stays in their shifted form, the longer they risk becoming *changed*. That is, losing their humanity completely. Losing the ability or will to change back to human form. Even my rabid students shift when they sleep.

By the way Minnie is chewing her lip, she understands what is at stake.

"No shifting," I say sternly to her. "For you or the other animas. Speak to her as much as possible. Touch her as much as possible. Try and remind her who she is." Although Minnie nods eagerly, I know there are personal challenges that weigh her down on top of this. "I don't want you all sleeping down there, either. You need to sleep properly." Her nod this time is not so eager. She's a good friend to Aurelia; I chose purposefully when I placed them together.

As I step around her to leave, I say over my shoulder, "And Minnie?"

"Yes, sir?"

"Not a word. To *anyone*."

Chapter 9

Aurelia's Anima

I know he is mine. The lion who chains himself. I do not have the energy to soothe his weary soul, but I can warm his body with mine. So when he comes to sit with me, I lie next to him.

The wolf who wears a human skin is also mine, but he is not like the lion. He is full of life, but I do not have the energy to play with him as he demands.

He brings me food that I do not wish to eat. He speaks through his human mouth, noises I do not wish to hear.

I must concentrate. I must focus.

The fingers reaching for me have turned into fangs, blade-sharp points that *scrape, scrape, scrape.* They scratch down my shields, hunting for any entry, any weakness. Though I sense they come from far away, they are strong, and the black hand that wields them is relentless. I have no choice but to bury deep within the recesses of my beast, the seven layers of my protections straining.

But they hold.

Keep us safe. Keep us safe. Keep us safe.

It is a song I chant even in my sleep.

My sisters go away during the day, and when they come back at night, making additions to my nest, bringing colourful, fluffy items to keep away the cold that has nothing to do with the temperature of the cavern. They bring food as well, but it tastes like ash on my tongue, barely giving me enough strength to keep afloat.

Then one day, my tigress-sister nervously brings something to my nest, eyeing me uncertainly. Immediately, I am suspicious.

"Aurelia, we don't want you getting fleas from this damp place," my tigress-sister says gently. "You need this medicine to keep them away."

Despite her peaceful tone, the scent I catch from the tube she is holding smells *foul*. I let out a warning growl at her approach, and she freezes.

"Here, let me try," my playful wolf says, plucking the substance out of her hands. He advances towards me slowly and respectfully on his knees to show me he means not to attack. My hatchling flies upward, making soothing sounds in my ear.

The wolf extends an arm out.

A pungent scent fills my nose like acid.

On instinct, I lash out, jaws snapping then finding purchase on human flesh. Blood fills my mouth and my hatchling shrieks, making me go still in alarm.

The wolf skips back, staring first at his human arm mangled, blood dripping freely, before turning back to me.

But there is no tang of fear and pain in the air. Instead, on his face is an expression of simple human joy.

My playful wolf is not right in the head.

Confused, I bare my bloody teeth and hiss at him. My hatchling squeaks in disapproval. I nuzzle him in apology before monitoring my wolf once again.

He is different from my lion. They are both dangerous, virile males who wear power under their skin and inspire fear in my pack-sisters. But where my lion is like a solid wall of marble that grounds me, my wolf is like an ever-shifting ball of power. Always moving and always thinking.

He licks at the wound I made on his human arm and I watch his tongue move over the golden fur-less skin, the blood disappearing, leaving jagged lines of flesh. Even with an injury, his power does not falter.

With a huff, I rise from my nest and stalk towards him. He pauses his licking to stare at me, an unnatural glow in his eyes. Strange, crazy wolf. I allow a trickle of my power to reach towards him. It finds his wound and heals it, just enough to stop the bleeding. That is all I can spare. The edges seal together and I realise that he never stopped staring at me. With an annoyed growl, I lie next to him, a clear instruction for him to sit next to me.

His bare skin against my fur is soothing. It makes a jolt of energy move through me, making my mind less muffled.

He murmurs something that I am too tired to hear, but his voice is like the lick of a loving tongue to my tired heart.

Scrape. Scrape. Scrape. Those fangs are always there. Always waiting. Always hurting.

I stay close to the wolf and recede to where it is safe, burying deeper and deeper until those vile, venomous fangs give up for the day.

Chapter 10

Scythe

The moon kisses my bare skin as I emerge from the crashing waves and stride onto the sand of the beach. The night air is fresh and my senses pick up the change in the seasons. Xander is sitting on the shore, a joint in hand, gazing out over the breaking water, those white orbs like little torches through the dark. A lighthouse guiding me home.

Mace Naga's blood contract has faded off my skin, but the echo of it had still slithered underneath. Dark and wretched. Like oil over water, it had stirred in my blood. The only way for me to process that residue had been to swim it off. Down in the deep womb of the ocean, everything heals in quiet darkness. It's what I imagine an actual womb would feel like. Where thoughts are nothing but passing murmurs and nothing can harm you. It's a relief. A reset.

Something I seem to be needing more and more these days.

There are no ghosts down below. Not for me, anyway. No lurking demons snarling at me, prowling around my mind, ready to take my sanity.

Except this time, emerging from the salt water feels different. I ought to feel calm. Serene. My blood should be settled in my arteries, moving smoothly through the chambers of my heart.

But something is not quite right.

And I have a dark suspicion that nothing will ever be quite right ever again. I scratch at the right side of my neck and see Xander's head swivel slightly in my direction, no doubt honing in on the movement.

I can hear his low growl over the crashing waves. Blowing out an exhale, I force my thoughts onto pressing matters.

Trying to attend to business locked up in a dragon manor away from the city is not easy. Luckily, we have plenty of beasts on the ground who are good at their jobs.

I hired every single one of them and they are all sworn by blood to me.

Two of those trusted beasts meet us at the top of the sand dunes, two black Jeeps parked behind them. One is an old friend. One is new.

Rufus is a jaguar I met when I'd first begun in this business. He came to me begging for help. His daughter made a near lethal mistake by swearing into a very rough pack. Once I marked them as prey, it was over. I retrieved his daughter and Rufus swore himself to me.

The second male is a new addition to the team. He openly drags his eyes down my naked body, then looks at me directly in the eyes, his aura rippling an orange that is shifting to red. At the forefront, there is a thick grey spot hovering around his head.

He sticks out his hand like he wants to shake my mine.

It's my shark that lashes out, crushing his throat in one hand and thrusting him backwards into the Jeep behind him so hard it crushes the door.

Rufus shakes his head in dismay as he steps back to give me space.

The ghost appears at my side in an instant, cackling and excited. *Kill him, torture him, rip him to shreds. Eat him, destroy him, cut him until he begs.*

I breathe through his rattling, calming my rage as I look down at this beast. While my damaged human voice is rough, my animus' voice is pure guttural predator. "Tell me your name, cougar."

He chokes, trying to drag in air, his hands clawing uselessly at mine. I ease the pressure slightly.

"J-Jason," he splutters.

"Jason," I rasp, pushing my face into his. "It's not good manners to stare."

"S-sorry! I'm sorry, Mr Kharkouros!"

"But see, that's not the only problem." I pause, considering his aura. "I want to eat the lie in you."

Jason's eyes go even wider, his animus thrashing in his pupils. I allow my power to surge out, feeling the thrum of vessels and electrical pulses in his body. Letting him feel my dominance over his blood. Letting him know how powerless he is in this situation.

"*Eat his face,*" the ghost screams. "*Dig your teeth in his mug. Claim him. Tear him.*"

Gods, when the voices in my head turn to screaming, it really is hard to concentrate.

Jason seems to understand that he is not the dominant beast here—not by a long shot—and goes limp, his head slumping to the side in submission bearing his neck to me.

Rufus is having a panic attack to the side, wondering what the fuck he missed when he recruited this creature.

"I know who you work for. I can smell him in your blood. What is Cain Clawson so keen to know?"

Jason whimpers. "Please." The cougar's eyes grow wide as he feels his blood pressure rising higher and higher.

I stare him down, relishing the feeling of full control over my enemy's circulatory system. His heart beats like a rabbit's, fluttery and rapid, and his eyes blink as the tiny blood vessels in his retinas break.

"Oh God, my head," he whimpers, screwing his eyes shut.

The thing with blood pressure this high is that it gives you a mad headache before—

Brown eyes snap open, bulging out of their sockets before his entire blood volume explodes through his skin and all over me.

Rufus swears softly.

That warm shower eases the fire of my bloodlust just enough to clear my head. I let what is left of Jason go and his skull and flesh slide to the ground with a splat.

I turn to Rufus, who flinches at the sight of his boss drenched in five litres of blood.

"I'm sorry, sir," Rufus says honestly. "We didn't know he was affiliated. He came from out of town!"

"It's not your fault," I say evenly. It's the very reason why they bring them to me for approval. "Scrape him off the bitumen and send him to his master with my thanks. If Cain wants a game, we'll play a game."

"Yes, boss," Rufus says. He's perfectly used to the way I deal with infiltrators and hides his flinch as I nod at him.

Xander drawls into my head, "*A bit tense, huh?*"

I ignore him.

"There's news," Rufus says, clearing his throat. "The feds have raided one of our warehouses."

"Which one?" I say.

"Red bird."

That is the code name for one of the newer warehouses in the newly occupied Halfeather territory.

I do the quick calculation. That was at least twenty million dollars' worth of product. Gone. Xander glances at me, calculation in those glowing white eyes.

"*Mace isn't happy about losing that land,*" Xander gruffs into my mind. "*So unhappy that he'd prefer to hand the goods over in a tip-off than to try and take it himself. So unhappy that he'd form an alliance with a feline.*"

By our laws, Xander killed Halfeather, therefore making that land ours. That same night, when we spoke to the serpent king, we made that clear.

But we both know it wasn't just the loss of Halfeather's land that set Mace off, but rather, the loss of something more valuable than any land.

A Boneweaver.

He hoped to keep her quiet and isolated. Hoped to remove Halfeather from the chessboard and collect a neat package of funds. But things have gotten out of hand. He's going to do everything in his power to get her back. And serpents have weapons the other orders cannot even fathom. Weapons that work secretly, silently, in the dark.

He is no doubt using those already.

Savage must be listening and thinking the same thing, because his voice funnels into me, faint due to the distance but still very much audible.

"Yeah, well, we still have our princess, so..."

"We can't let this slide," Xander snarls. *"Those human customers won't be happy the deal fell through because we lost product."*

But I don't care about that human biker gang who wanted those arms. Couldn't care less. I *do* care about Mace forming an alliance with my neighbour.

I think about what I know about Mace and Cain Clawson.

An alliance in our line of work is a near-impossible thing. Dominant males do not like to share or indebt themselves to other dominant beasts. To do so is submissive behaviour. But I suspect something about Mace Naga and Cain Clawson. Something that links them so profoundly that it superseded their natural urge to dominate one another.

Something so dark that even I, standing under the moonlight covered in blood, shiver to think about it.

I look at my dragon-brother and clench my teeth.

Aurelia inherited her Boneweaver power from her mother, meaning that Mace Naga was mate to a Boneweaver regina.

Mace has other treasures too, more valuable than dollar figures. We will have to be careful.

One thing that males like Mace and I understand is the long game. Something my father never quite mastered, to his detriment.

"We lie low," I instruct firmly.

"You can't be serious. We need to retaliate—"

"Not yet, Xan."

He stares at me, his fiery power pulsing around him, all black and red. There's so much rage in him, fuelled by my little demonstration, and he needs to fight. Needs it like I need brine.

"Soon, brother," I reassure him. *"Soon."*

I head back down to the beach to wash off, while Xander takes the keys to the second Jeep from Rufus and sends him on his way with Jason in a plastic tub in the back seat.

My dragon brother needs to blow off some steam and there are only one or two other orders that can match a dragon in a fight. Since I'm neither a phoenix nor our fifth brother, it will have to be in human form.

"Come on," I say, once we're in our car, driving us away from the beach to one of our usual sparring locations in a regional block of land—a place where we won't be able to cause too much damage to buildings or humans. "I think lazing around all day smoking red in that school has made you soft."

"The fuck I am," he snarls back.

As the car fills with smoke from Xander's rage, I merely wind down the window and smirk. "I need to see Marduk again, then we head back to Animus."

Xander only grunts in reply, but I feel it in him too. That reluctant relief. That primal, ever-fucking-present need to get back to our regina.

Chapter II

Aurelia's Anima

My lion returns to see me often. Unlike the others, he is always in his human skin while his animus is leashed in chains of obsidian and steel. Chains so tight, I wonder how he does not choke on them.

But I cannot be excited to see him. I cannot afford the energy.

He sits with me when my wolf and my sister-pack are away. He talks and talks and talks. Softly, quietly some days, other days more loudly. His voice is pleasant. Deep and rhythmic, and often, as it rumbles through the air, it lulls me into a restful slumber. I find myself looking for that voice on some days. It has the steady reassurance of the earth. The weight of heavy rock. I can lay my mind against it and it will not falter while I rest for a time. It gives me some energy. And when he is not here... I miss his melody.

I do not understand what he says, nor can I spend precious energy deciphering the words. Because those fangs that once went *scrape, scrape, scrape,* against my skin now *burn, burn, burn.*

Through my psyche, the pain is mirrored across my stomach. I growl, burrowing deeper into my protections.

Keep us safe. Keep us safe. Keep us safe. It is a counter-song of my own.

It barely lessens the venomous assault on my body. This threat from the enemies outside.

I need more power, yet I am weakening.

One day, when my lion has stopped talking, I lift my eyes to look upon him.

To consider.

As he considers me back.

He is a male of sheer power. Any anima can see that. To share power with a beast like this would grant me access to a greater power, and in turn, a greater defence. And he is mine. Mine in the most essential way.

He says something, and his song is a gentle stroke down my fur.

The human inside me pounds on her cage and I wonder if she knows something I do not. But I cannot afford to let her out. She must be protected inside me. Away from the burning and the venom and the darkness of the enemy. She has lain quietly for some time, understanding what is at stake. But now she pounds and pounds and it hurts my head.

We will endure this. We must.

And so, I lay my head back down and sing my lonely song.

Keep us safe. Keep us safe. Keep us safe.

Chapter 12

Savage

Two weeks or so after my regina's anima took her over, Scythe and Xander return. I beg them—threaten them, even—but they both refuse to visit her. Xander sleeps a lot, smokes even more, and Scythe warns me not to terrorise him too much.

"The last thing we need is a rogue dragon lighting people up," Scythe says to me one day as Yeti, Beak, and I join him in the dining hall for breakfast. "Give him your gold and let him be."

"It's not healthy," I say reasonably, digging into my steak and casting an eye over the first-year anima table. "He's going to explode at some stage."

Yeti, our favourite Siberian tiger, arches a white eyebrow at me. His mother was a white tiger and his father a Siberian tiger so he luckily got the best of both worlds. The massive size of the Siberian and the unusual white hair and blue eyes of the White. I return his look and feign innocence. He, too, is eyeing the anima table with great interest.

Everyone knows about the phoenix injunction, and we've told our beasts only that Aurelia is keeping a low profile and not to ask questions. It made for a good amount of gossip in the first week, but it's old news now. Only the birds of prey are bothered that one of "their" animas is missing in action, but I put an end to any clucking about it quick-smart. Fists talk better than any mouth can. That's always been my motto.

Scythe glances down at our regina's teeth marks on my forearm. I salted them to keep them there and wear them like a badge of honour. These beautiful indentations will be something I treasure forever. Same as the missing index finger on my right hand.

I think about her every moment of the day. How she sits beneath the anima dorm like a vicious, bloodthirsty, hibernating monster. How her blue eyes stare at me through the dark. How she hisses and bares her teeth when I insult one of her friends. My cock twitches at the thought. Scythe doesn't understand yet, and neither does Xander. They don't let their animus guide them like I do and so they don't *see* her properly.

But I do. My wolf and I, we can see all of her. I've seen her now as an eagle, a wolf, and a lioness. But behind all those beautiful forms is the woman underneath. The one who planned her escape from the clutches of execution. There were a dozen lethal beasts outside the medical wing and she managed to thwart all of them with just a few nimpins. Brilliant. Genius. I would have given anything to see it in real life and not just the security camera footage I watch on my phone every other day. That's what we talk about when I go down there every day. Well, that's what *I* talk about and she just listens.

I'm hoping that the more I talk to her and feed her, the more she'll fall in love with me too. Her anima likes me. It lets me feed her little bits of chicken now. At first, I chewed the food myself and tried to give it to her in the way that birds do, thinking maybe her mother did that for her.

But she just looked at me with an adorable "are you kidding?" look. When I tried to do it again, Stacey and Sabrina gagged and retched in the corner of the cavern and I had no choice but to try different methods. I tried to give it raw, then boiled, then roasted, but she took none of it until Connor brought down the boneless kind. He said that we didn't want to know who he had to blow to get it, but he was grinning so he definitely didn't mind.

"She doesn't like bones?" I say in disbelief to Raquel. *"All rabids like bones."*

"I don't think she's a regular rabid, Mr Fengari," comes the telepathic reply.

It makes me beam with pride, because I know my regina is *not* normal. Or regular. Or ordinary. She's special. A Boneweaver. And every time she takes food from me, my heart grows a little bigger.

It excites me that I'm the first one in our pack to have tasted her. To have savoured her.

Whenever the others come around to loving her like I do, I will still have that claim. That ownership. Lyle hates me for it. I knew it from the start. His animus thinks he's oldest and therefore second in charge and should have had the first claiming. But fuck them all, because I was the one who saw her first.

And I'm the one who fell in love with her first.

I skip second period because I can't fight the urge to be with Aurelia. I spent the night there, like I always do, but leaving her, even with Eugene there, to eat or go to class is like an old wound being cut open again. Lyle won't be happy, but I'm attending his regina classes, so he's got to give me marks for that. Humming my way to the anima dorm, I blow Christine a kiss. She shoots swear words in my direction, not having forgiven me for the bomb episode, but lets me into the dorm regardless. Once I reach the canal, I see that the boat isn't docked. Narrowing my eyes, I shift and leap into the water, paddling my way down the passage. The water mutes scents and there are so many of us down here these days that it can be hard to tell which is from today and which is from yesterday.

But my sense of the mates from our pack goes beyond my nose and I detect Lyle's presence before I round the corner and see his long blond ponytail hanging down his broad, suited back.

He's sitting on the stone floor and Aurelia is...

Jealousy flares as I see the two of them together. Aurelia is cuddled up to Lyle, her body lying alongside his leg as if she finds comfort there. Lyle knows I'm coming up, but he doesn't turn around. Eugene is sitting in Aurelia's nest, watching them through his goggles like the good boy he is.

As I get out of the water, I shake my fur, spraying both of them with cold water.

To my dismay, when I finish, I see a screen of water droplets hovering in mid-air. On the other side, Lyle has lifted only a single finger off his knee. He drops the finger, and the water comes shooting for me.

Annoyed, I ignore him and stalk over to Aurelia's other side and lie down to sandwich her between us.

She huffs as if she enjoys this and Lyle sighs as if he doesn't.

"Why aren't you in class, Savage?" When he talks, it's in a surprisingly soft voice. Like he doesn't dare use his normal authoritative tone near our regina in case it scares her.

I let out a huff to say I don't care for his question.

"Savage, you really must be in human form when with her. She needs to come out of this rabidity."

My animus protests at being told what to do by this beast, but Aurelia is more important. And Ruben told me that love is when you care about the other person so much that you put less important things to the side.

So I shift into human form but remain where I am, lying on my belly. The stone rubs against my dick and I grimace, rolling over so that I'm on my back instead. Lyle doesn't look as intimidating now that he's upside down.

If I close my eyes, I can even pretend he's not there. Aurelia's fur is glorious against my side, like a warm silken gown. But I can feel her ribs under that skin and I sit up as I realise it. I fed her this morning, but she only took two chicken tenders.

Shit. Maybe it's not enough. It certainly wouldn't be enough for me. I glance up at Lyle, uncertain about what this means. He's already studying me, eyes narrowed in some sort of suspicion. Like he thinks I'm going to try to blow up the anima dorm again.

I'd sooner blow up his office. It's still in the "to consider" part of my brain.

But my irritation for Lyle is overcome by the worry in the pit of my stomach. Lyle is probably an expert on lions and I'm not. He probably knows about this stuff.

"She's not eating much," I say tightly.

We both look down at her beautiful body. Her breathing looks sort of fast to me, but I don't know if that's normal for a lioness. Or a Boneweaver.

Lyle glances at the empty plastic bottles of water the girls are collecting to the side. I never knew girls could be so messy. Without asking, I get up and rush towards the bowl she's been drinking from and fill it with a fresh bottle of water.

I bring the full bowl back and bop her nose with it.

She looks at me like she doesn't appreciate her rest being interrupted, but laps at it exactly three times then puts her head down like she's really tired.

Why is she so tired all the time?

"I don't understand why she's not eating," I say, putting the bowl aside and peering into her eyes. "She should be eating plenty." I don't want to say it out loud. I really don't. But when animals don't take food and water, it's a bad, bad sign.

My stomach churns and I heat up. My heart starts racing like

I've run five miles really fast. I've never felt this way before.

"Brother," I project to Scythe, who's likely back up in our room.

"What's wrong?" comes the sharp reply. He's immediately on alert, and I sense Xander's presence listening in. I don't usually use this tone. But I swallow down the feeling of poison in my throat. *"I think Aurelia is sick."*

But it's Lyle who answers me. "We need her to shift back."

"How do we do that?" I gruff. I hate having to ask him questions, but my heart is still pounding and now I can hear it in my ears. Now that I'm looking at her with adrenaline honing my eyes, I can see that her fur is kind of dull.

"Honestly, I don't know," he admits.

Anger flares through my veins and the urge to break his face almost makes me lose it. But Aurelia needs us to think. Not fight.

So, I glare at the useless lion. "Aren't you known for this?" I demand. "Can't you therapise her? Can't you do the things you do to make her snap out of it?"

"I've never seen a beast turn rabid like this. It's not quite normal. I think it's something else. I think..." He looks at me then. Really looks at me in the eyes like he wants to know something. "Can you talk to her telepathically?"

I shake my head. "It's the first thing I tried."

"I thought so," he sighs. "I actually think this might be a Boneweaver thing."

And we know fuck all about Boneweavers. There's none that we know of in the country—or any country. And Aurelia's mother is long gone. The rest of her family is dead, according to Marduk's research.

As for her *other* family...

Lyle and I stare at each other as we both realise it at the same time.

The only beast who might know anything about this is the very beast we're trying to avoid.

"Mace has been trying to arrange a meeting with me on a near daily basis," Lyle says dryly. "I've declined him each time. But maybe—"

"No." Scythe's resounding voice booms through the air like a hand grenade, and even Lyle stills as he hears it. "*Not a single chance.*"

"*He's her dad.*" Xander's voice is snide because this is his favourite argument. "*She must take after him in some way. Try a spell for vermin extermination. That might work.*"

"*I'm going to kill you,*" I say to him. "*But after we save Lia.*" I lean down and run a gentle hand over her pretty little golden head. "Come out, Lia," I coo. "We need you back."

I feel Lyle's judgemental eyes on me, but I don't care. I can't even believe we're collaborating like this. "Come back out and say something sassy to me. Please."

But it doesn't work. Her eyes don't even open to acknowledge me and it's like she's gone even deeper into the thing that's taken her.

I grumble at the lion. "Can you ask Lady Phoenix? She's from a mythic order, she might know."

Lyle huffs and I take that as a yes.

Xander's drawl pierces my mind again. "*I'm from a mythic order too, you asshat. She's done this to herself,*" he says. "*If she's put herself in, she'll get herself out. Now everyone fuck off and stop fretting like a bunch of old hyenas.*"

Lyle sighs and I know he heard that too.

Xander knows stuff about things the rest of us don't. He's the closest thing to a Boneweaver, so I'll just have to trust him.

As I lie back down next to my regina, wondering if my power can somehow transfer to her by osmosis, Lyle says quietly to me, "Keep feeding her, Sav. Try the roast beef tomorrow."

I grunt a yes, because *obviously* that's what I'm gonna do. With more fairy bread for dessert.

Look at us. Collaborating. Our regina will be so happy.

Chapter 13

Aurelia's Anima

Another day, another time; I cannot tell how long I've been hidden in the dark. My sister-pack has just finished their heats, and my tigress-sister returns to me.

By the smell, she brings more food, and it makes my stomach roil. Although power dwindles day by day, in this form, their food is no good for me, so I snub them, only accepting the small morsels I now allow my wolf to feed me by his hand alone.

But today my tigress-sister is unsettled. I open one eye to focus on her. Her own hatchling—yellow, like a ripe banana—sits on her shoulder and lets out a sharp sound. Immediately, the only other of our pack in our nest, my wolf-anim, gets onto their human feet, their green hatchling also making a sharp noise.

I open both my eyes now, as my tigress presses a hand to her head and scrunches her face.

My own hatchling squeaks in alarm. Then all the hatchlings screech in unison.

My tigress-sister rubs at her soft, round stomach, the thin covering over it shifting a little.

Then she doubles over, crumpling in on herself.

I smell the blood before I see it. My head snaps up in alarm. Red seeps through her shirt. Four lines, shallow, but long and jagged.

Burn. Burn. Burn.

They couldn't get to me, so they've come for her. I've been so tired they've finally found a breach in my defence.

"Oh my God!" my tigress-sister shrieks. "Raquel! It hurts! It hurts!"

But a wolf can do nothing in this situation.

The human in me screams and my head is full of her agony, my heart is pounding and searing as venomous pain scorches my insides.

Keep them safe. Keep them safe. Keep them safe. At all costs.

I jump to my paws, a volcano erupting from deep inside the cage at the base of my body.

The roar of pure rage I let out shakes the very foundation of the cavern itself.

Chapter 14

Lyle

I'm sitting with Titus as he plays a game on his laptop. He seems to enjoy car racing and his fingers are deft across the keyboard. Muscle memory from years of playing computer games and PlayStation as a teenager, kicks in and he swears in annoyance under his breath.

He's not a particularly cheerful tiger, more the serious, brooding type that lends to rabidity, but he is making excellent progress.

I'm smirking at my new therapy technique and the fact that he'll be able to join gen pop within days, when something rattles the cavern walls.

Titus' fingers freeze on the keyboard as we both register what it is.

From far away, the sound of a female lioness' roar shakes my very bones. The mating mark on the right side of my neck sears my skin like a new brand. The fact that I'm hearing it here means that there is a push of significant power behind it.

I'm on my feet before Titus has even registered it, locking his door and stalking into the elevator.

We are at the end of the three-day heat lockdown, with

Savage, Scythe and Xander all locked up in separate obsidian cages down below, at their own request. Because there are still a few hours left before the protections lift at sundown, I'm the only one striding across the grounds to the anima dorm.

Christine chatters excitedly as I unlock the dorm early, the steel doors sliding up and disappearing into the ceiling.

"Hello, sir! Pleased to help, sir!" she says excitedly.

I do not answer her because there is fire in my blood and chains rattling in my head.

Inside, the animas are all a-chatter, wondering who made that mighty roar, but the look of warning on my face as I bypass the first two floors has them all scattering back to their rooms and shutting their doors.

I make it to Aurelia's cavern with my heart pounding like a war drum.

Only Minnie, Raquel and their three nimpins are with her. Aurelia, in human form, kneels before Minnie as the tigress tugs on a new blouse. Aurelia hugs Minnie around the waist, her face buried in her friend's stomach, her naked body smeared with dirt and grime from the cavern floor. She hasn't washed in four weeks and smells like it, but still Minnie tightly returns the hug, holding Aurelia around her bare shoulders. Henry squeaks with alarm, hovering over Aurelia like a mother hen.

The scent of blood is faint in the air, but a quick scan reveals that no one is actually injured.

Relief. Pure and cool and light floods my veins at the sight of her human form, apparently sane, apparently well. I find my breath again.

"Miss Aquinas," I say, hooking a finger into my collar to loosen it a little.

She rotates her face towards me, never leaving Minnie's embrace, and I am not prepared for that look of pure loathing that simmers in her eyes.

Her olive skin is ashen and there are deep bags under those

furious bluebell irises. Pale lips, thin from dehydration, twist in annoyance.

Even looking so unwell, I am struck by her wild, rabid beauty. A creature of legend returned from the dead. How much does she remember of our time down here? When she came to me for comfort? But I have a feeling those quiet moments of us sitting together will never happen again.

"L-Leave," she rasps. Her voice is scratchy from lack of use, or perhaps a little sore from that vicious roar she just made. The one that still echoes in my ears and will linger in the dark parts of me for years to come. That rabid power. It called something forth in me, something very much unwanted. My eyes find her neck, but that celestial mark still isn't there. A whisper of disappointment seeps into my mind like venom. *"Leave,"* she repeats. Gods, the pure hate in that voice.

Good. This is good.

I inhale and exhale twice; evenly and slowly in a measured way that is second nature for me, from a long life learning absolute control. I keep my mind carefully blank. I am her deputy headmaster. This is my student. Whatever it was between her anima and me down here in the dark and quiet is now ended.

And I am thankful for it.

"Miss Aquinas," I say crisply. "Welcome back. I expect you in the dining hall for breakfast tomorrow morning." Turning on my heel, I leave.

Chapter 15

Aurelia

"W-What an asshole," I mutter, even as the sight of Lyle, one of my mates, walking away from me, makes a hole tear open in my chest. But that is just my anima pining like the wanton hellcat she is. The human in me knows he has no right to be here. None, when he was instrumental in my court case and handed me over for execution. *Handed* me over to my father, just like that!

My anima protests the thought. She stalks beside me now, ready to take over again if I need her to. But she also knows we can't sit here anymore, and as long as I don't put her in a cage again, she promises to behave. We've got to work together now.

Henry squeaks indignantly and Raquel snorts, but it's a relieved sound. "S-so you r-remember how t-to speak then?"

I swivel to look at my wolf-anim, taking them in with my human eyes. The silver lip, brow and septum piercings glint in the dim light and their dark brown hair has grown out and cut into a new pixie style that I love. I try to remember how to move my human face. I twitch my lips and, albeit a bit stiffly, they shape a smile.

It's so funny that baring your teeth as a beast is a clear threat, but as a human, it's a sign of pleasantry.

"There she is," Minnie says in approval. "Can you stand?"

With a long-suffering groan, I clamber to my feet, using Minnie as a brace. "As if I'd forget to speak with you lot chattering at me all day," I say softly, touching my throat and frowning. "Hurts though." And my teeth are disgustingly furry.

"We'll get you some honey," Minnie says. "Honestly, you had us worried for a while there."

It was the sight of her. Of Minnie, bleeding under the assault of an enemy she could not see that did it. My anima had shoved me to the side and kept me deep within my own body. Much in the same way I kept *her* under wraps for so long. Those scraping fangs burning across my own body I could handle, but *Minnie?* Or any of them? Never. It had been enough for my anima to relent, stepping aside for me to surge upward and *rage* with my power carried in a roar around the school until those scraping fangs were shut out altogether. Healing Minnie had come naturally, of course. Those fang marks *violating* her body, was something I could not bear to look at. Or bear to have *her* look at.

The nimpins finally settle down. The poor things sensed the psychic attack but didn't know how to help. Henry comes to nestle against my neck, making cutesy, soothing squeaks and then I notice Eugene by my foot, clucking in concern. My mind is a little boggy, like I'm wading through thick mud. But the adrenaline caused by the horror and then in seeing Lyle is helping me out of it. My stomach twists in a horrible sort of way, telling me that I've *really* not been eating all that well these last few weeks.

"Food," I murmur. "And a lot of it."

"And c-clothes." Raquel hands me a spare jacket and track pants, but their nose wrinkles just a little as they approach.

By the Wild Goddess, if Raquel, having grown up in a wild commune, is wrinkling their nose at me, I know I must smell like hell itself. I swear under my breath as they both help me pull on the clothes and walk me to the waiting, rickety boat.

Clothes feel strange against my furless skin. I want to tear them off as I lope awkwardly to the water. Smothering in the brush of air against my skin feels like I'm losing one of my senses. My two human legs are less stable than having four and I feel like a newborn foal on ice, about to topple over at any second. It makes me hunch a little and I realise this turns my stride into a *prowl.*

Savage comes to mind, and the way he swaggers around the academy like a beast on two legs. I thought men put that walk on as a dominance thing, but the walk is entirely involuntary. Minnie and Raquel eye me like they're worried I'll collapse any second, and in truth, I am lightheaded... and overwhelmed.

Able to see this place with my human eyes and height for the first time feels like I'm waking up from a dream.

When I asked Xander's dragon if he could open a hiding space for me—much like the dragon-trick level my mates have in the animus dorm, his mouth curved into a smirk and he said, "Of course, my regina." Once he triggered the door, it was time for me to leave for the trial, so I'd not been able to come down here to check it out.

It's little more than a gloomy, dusty, dank cavern, but my brilliant animas have transformed it into a girly wonderland.

By some feat of determination, they've managed to bring a mattress and tonnes of pillows down here, making a sort of pillow fort in a semi-circle around the nest I built on instinct. Someone, probably Connor, brought down a mini fridge and there is a basket overflowing with chips, chocolates and cupcakes. There's even a couple of purple armchairs, a little round table, and I'm sure it was Minnie who'd strung up multi-coloured fairy lights all around the back and sides of the cavern.

Warmth fills my chest, golden and fresh. I turn to look at Minnie and lean my head against hers, whispering her name.

It's then that I scent something that makes my head snap up.

Minnie is crying. She sweeps her sleeve over her cheeks, trying to hide it, but she's doing a poor job of it due to her loud sniffing.

"I was really worried, Lia," she whispers.

"Oh, Min," I say in my hoarse voice. "I'm so sorry. It all turned to shit."

"I-It didn't th-though," Raquel says firmly. "You're f-fucking *alive*, Lia."

"Thwarted a breeding ring," Minnie adds.

I grin at them gratefully.

"That's right," Minnie continues, holding the boat steady as Raquel helps me in. "The plan worked, our nimpins did great, and now... we'll sort it all out."

We all pile into the boat, with Eugene and his new goggles, hopping in after us. I'm softly lulled by the gentle rocking as it travels through the canal. I'm so tired, I feel the edges of a faint coming on. But I can't afford to pass out. I can never afford that. Not with the distant psychic attacks coming at us from all angles. Henry prods me gently with his beak as if he knows I'm blurring at the edges. I take him from my neck to look at him.

His liquid black eyes blink slowly at me, as if he's saying, *It's okay.*

My vision blurs, but this time from tears.

I hope my eyes convey what he means to me. *You saved my life, Hen. You and the other nimpins disabled some of the strongest beasts in the country and got me out of there.*

Henry just nuzzles my palm affectionately, and all I can do is hold him to my chest and silently thank him. The other nimpins were with me down here too, all this time, with my friends. I don't know what I did to deserve friends like these, but I'm grateful for it. And I don't know how to repay them for it either.

Scrape. Scrape. Scrape.

Those fangs wait at the edges of all things. At the edges of *me.* I knew my father would not be swayed by my little escape. The king cobra might not be able to get his physical hands on me, but snakes are especially good at psychic warfare. He's going to try to wear me down, gradually, relentlessly, until I have nothing left and he has full access to me.

The fact that he managed to assault Minnie proves just how much he is willing to use any method to get to me. Somehow, he figured out that Min was my best friend and therefore the next best way to get to me.

It was a threat written in blood.

And I'm not going to let this happen. I need to be strong and just as relentless as him while I figure out what to do.

Hibernation in my beast form kept us safe for all of four weeks. But it wasn't sustainable and my anima knew it. My energy is now at a critical level.

Lyle and Savage had visited with me frequently. Strong, powerful males at the height of their power. And the one perk of being in a mating group is... power sharing.

Beasts refuel their power using two things: food and sex. But to ask them for that was insane. They tried to kill me, after all.

* * *

When we walk through the painting in the corridor outside our dorm, Theresa, our first-year anima counsellor walks out of our room. She takes one look at me and her hand flies to her mouth, her grey eyes wide. She's a short woman with close cropped blonde hair, a full sleeve of colourful tattoos down her right arm and a silver eyebrow piercing.

"Dear Goddess," she says, hurrying towards me. "Lia!"

"I know," I say wryly, passing a look to Minnie to ask how much Theresa is aware of. "I need a shower."

"Lyle sent me. We'll go to the communal bathroom," she

says, taking Minnie's place on my right. "There's a bath ready for you there. If you can get some of Lia's pyjamas out, Min?"

Minnie hurries off into our room through our apparently newly reinstated door while I'm escorted to the communal bathroom on the ground floor at a sloth's pace. Everyone is in the dining hall since Lyle ended the lockdown early to see me after my outburst, so the anima dorm is empty as I stumble through it. I've never had to use the communal bathroom as there is an ensuite in our room, but Theresa explains that they use the baths for parasite treatments. And apparently, four weeks of not bathing and the few bites of raw meat I've eaten could have given me something.

Once in the black and white tiled bathroom, I take one look at the steaming metal bathtub and groan, ripping off my clothes immediately. Hardly caring about my nudity, or the fact that it smells like flea treatment, I let Raquel and Theresa help me in. Theresa hands me a bar of soap and that gross LFS treatment for my hair and everyone leaves to give me some privacy.

I'm conditioning my hair when there's a commotion outside the door. A jolt of fire in my belly surprises me as I hear Savage's growling voice.

My body immediately responds to his presence, and I take a few deep breaths to control my urge to leap out and go to him.

The last time I "saw" him, we had wild, rough, life-changing sex. I don't know where that puts us. I don't know what it means. But I *do* know that he was nowhere to be found when I was being presented to my father like a lamb for slaughter.

There are raised voices and I have no doubt that he's arguing with Theresa and Minnie. My time in the cavern is hazy and I can't remember much of what happened while I was there. I remember that Savage was with me often, but not what I might have done. I don't trust my anima to act with any decency. After all, she's a hussy at the best of times, wanting to enact our deepest, darkest desires for our mates. So what the hell did she do when he came down there?

Henry gathers water into his beak and squirts it at me in a long stream. My laugh is cut off by an aggressive knocking on my mental shields. With my protections up, he can't get through to talk to me telepathically.

"That wolf can fucking wait," I grumble with irritation. The fact that he knows more than I do about our interactions is seriously annoying and potentially embarrassing.

One part of me does want to see him, and another part of me doesn't want him to see me like this—tired and sagging under my own strain. The regina in me wants to look shiny and pretty for him, and I'm too tired to fight that instinct right now. No, it's better if he's kept away... for the moment.

But his deep voice wafting through the door makes heat sidle through my lower stomach.

I give Henry a little growl to tell him he needs to be elsewhere. The good little nimpin zips off to look at himself in the mirror over the sink.

Sliding deeper into the water, I hang my head back against the lip of the tub and slide my hands down my neck to the swell of my breasts. The soapy water makes everything deliciously slippery, and I shiver as my palm brushes over my erect nipples.

I've spent so much time alone for the past seven years that I'm very good at pleasuring myself. So when I pass my hand down my stomach and into the mound of soft curls between my legs, the anticipation sends me hissing.

But this time, instead of thinking of some imaginary beast, I think of Savage and the way his eyes heated up when he looked at me the night before my trial, when I found myself in his room. The way he threw me on his bed and we were all desperate teeth and tongue. He devoured me then, pulled me into a place I never even dreamed of being. My fingers slide in and out of my increasingly slick heat, my thumb circling my clit to the sound of Savage's angry voice on the other side of the door.

Suddenly, it goes quiet outside and I smirk, wondering if Savage can scent me and what I'm doing. If it's made him go quiet in realisation, or maybe a little bit of shock.

Then a single, clear growl passes through the bathroom door. "Princess?"

I come suddenly, almost caught off guard, arching into the feeling of his growl around his pet name for me and the memory of his large, tattooed hands, and wicked tongue. I wring out every last delicious bite of pleasure from myself, allowing it to consume and comfort me in its golden warmth.

A deeper voice joins the mix and I think it might be Ruben, the seven-foot-tall wolf who is head of security around here.

As the voices outside recede, I lie here in a lazy afterglow, breathing heavily and deeply, aware of the fact that I've received a tiny burst of power from my own ministrations.

So Savage was not there that night my father came to pick me up. He didn't need to be, I suppose. I don't even know how that makes me feel. He obviously cared about *something* if he visited me so often in my cave. But I also can't be sure if Scythe sent him to keep an eye on me in the way he needs to keep an eye on everything.

Anger coils within my chest. Not just anger, but fury at what they all did to help my father. The way Lyle handed me my notice of execution. The feel of Scythe's and Xander's hands on my upper arms as they escorted me to my waiting father. Sure, I tried to run away from them, but that was my only crime as a mate. I would *never* have put *them* up for execution.

There is some blurry memory of Lyle coming to see me as often as Savage. There were some gentle words and a gentle hand, even.

But whatever they communicated to my anima hadn't been communicated to me. It was all moot. It doesn't count.

I rub my eyes as the weight of all this falls heavily on me. There are enemies at every angle both in this school and outside of it.

But if any of them think I will take this lying down, they are fucking mistaken.

Chapter 16

Aurelia

Only once I'm sure Savage has been coaxed away do I dry off, brush my teeth, and emerge back outside. Theresa and Minnie stand in the corridor, surveying me with worry.

"I'm alright," I say softly. "Was that Savage causing a ruckus?"

Minnie gives me a wiggle of the eyebrows. "He's been so possessive and super keen to win your good favour. I think you should talk to him."

I exhale dramatically.

"You're mates, aren't you?" Theresa asks flatly.

I glance at Minnie. She nods seriously. "He's openly calling you his regina now."

Shit. That bastard outed me? I can't believe it. But now that I know Theresa better, I do feel bad for lying to her that first day during the anima presentation when Savage literally threw himself at me.

"I'm sorry, Theresa, but I think you understand why I might have avoided that whole... situation."

The cassowary shifter nods slowly and studies me, her grey

eyes kind. "I do. But what I don't understand is why Xander Drakos covered for you."

Minnie makes a face that suggests that she also thinks the answer to Xander helping me lie is unfathomable.

"He hates me," I shrug. "That's all I really know about him."

With that, Theresa directs me and Henry into my room where Sabrina, Raquel and Stacey wait with a whole bunch of food on my bed.

Gods, I love my friends.

The three feline animas shriek when they see me, jumping up and down.

"Thank fuck!" Sabrina shouts, holding her boobs with both hands as she jumps. "I really thought we were all in trouble at the end there!" My leopard-shifter friend is always immaculately dressed, with today being no exception. She wears a leopard print body-con dress and has her long black hair in a long ponytail.

Stacey, my Vietnamese lioness bestie in high pigtails and a purple romper shakes her head. "It was all shits and giggles until you *peed* on the wall, *Lia*."

"Shit, I don't remember that at all."

"It's alright," Connor says, kicking off his red stilettos and combing matching fingernails through his long black mane. "We still love you."

I side-eye Theresa, who observes me closely. "The deputy headmaster will counsel you personally, Lia, as he does all the ex-rabid students. Your memories might come back in dribs and drabs, but only time will tell."

That word sits in the air. Rabid. I descended in my anima so far that I actually turned rabid. And by the itch on my skin and the irritation crawling beneath it, I know it's not out of my system. My body aches to shift back again and cover us in fur and fangs.

"From what Lyle told me, we've never seen this quick of a

turnaround before," Theresa says honestly. "Your transition may still be a little rocky. I don't think it's hit you just yet."

"I think it was us," Sabrina says, crossing her arms as if it's a fact. "There was always someone with her. We stopped her from going under completely." She looks at Raquel for confirmation and our wolf anim nods, pulling Eugene into their arms.

"We think that's why the wolf communes stay firmly feral and not rabid," Theresa agrees. Henry gives an indignant chirp from my shoulder and the other nimpins chime in. Theresa laughs, "And the nimpins are another factor we need to consider. I'll bring it up with Lyle in case he hasn't considered it for his research."

Lyle.

Also known as: my new secret mate. By the time my sentencing came around, my friends had figured out that Scythe, Xander and Savage were somehow my mates, even if it was impossible for me to be regina of beasts with different orders. Now they knew the whole truth.

But about Lyle? Even Minnie doesn't know about the fact that I'm regina to the deputy headmaster. I'd suspected it for a while, but at the time, it really made everything a million times worse, so I just... let it be and ignored the signals. Whenever I hide my own mating mark, I can't see my mates marks either. And in our world? The way we find our destined pack mates is by looking for beasts who bear the same mating mark we do—a glowing symbol unique and secret to our pack that only members of the pack can see on each other.

For us, it's a skull with five curling beams of light. Five beams for five mates.

Now I've seen Lyle's mark with my own eyes, saw him on his knees that night of my sentencing, my anima won't let me forget it. Perhaps that's why I shifted into a lioness for my hibernation instead of staying in my favourite wedge-tailed eagle form.

Theresa leaves us be and I tuck Henry and myself into bed

as the others pile food into my lap. Minnie sets a bowl of blueberries in front of Henry and he gratefully picks at them with his tiny beak.

Raquel places a massive burger on top of the pile of food and I stare at them with wide-eyed appreciation.

"I know th-that h-hunger," they say quietly, silver piercings glinting. "Eat up... cub."

They all look at me meaningfully. Oh right, *that* little issue of them all knowing what I am. Of me not being a specific order at all.

"We've already spoken about it," Minnie assures me.

"Yeah, we had four weeks to interrogate Min," Stacey says. "Don't worry, we got it all out of her. One of my friends is a—" she mouths, *"Boneweaver,"* and gives me the thumbs up.

"And our lips are sealed." Sabrina mimes zipping her lips and throwing away the key. "The way I see it? It's an advantage for all of us. The headmistress has dealt with your little execution issue and now we can go back to our usual craziness."

Delayed, not dealt with, I want to say, but I don't. It's been a big enough day.

"Yes, but now we have to tell Lia all about *our* news." Connor presses. "She has four weeks of academy gossip to catch up on!"

As I shovel food into my mouth, my pack of animas tells me the latest about the various dramas between the animas and animuses, including a lion who got chucked out of a second-story window for eating someone's stash of Mars bars and a hyena who tried to escape the school before he was brought down by Ruben and his security team.

But the thing that interests me the most are the changes the school has made to *itself.* Apparently, the very moulding of the door above the school has been given a sort of sentience. Our anima dorm now has a gargoyle called Christine. She's a chatty, annoying little bitch, so Sabrina says, and a cutesy creature, according to Minnie. The fact that these changes coincided with my hibernation has me suspicious, but I'll have to find out more when I start moving about the school normally again.

Eventually, our friends leave us to find their own beds, and when Minnie and I are finally alone, I stare at the fancy scroll-work of the ceiling, my thoughts laboured and dark.

What happened with Minnie this afternoon can *never* happen again. I would rather a thousand wounds be placed on me than harm come to any one of my friends. But I know my father. He's relentless, cruel, and infinitely clever. Worst of all, he gets what he wants. By hook or by crook, he will eventually make it impossible for me to ignore him.

It only means that I have to double down on my attempts. I need more strength. Which means food and... that other thing.

I've been denying my desire for my mates for so long, running away from the idea of them for so many years, that to think of going to one of them for any type of *help* is alien and uncomfortable. It makes adrenaline flood my veins and a thread of fear course through me.

These men handed me over for execution. Helped, and were crucial even, to my father's awful plans for me. Hell, more than one of them hates me and openly rejects me. Lyle, for his part, definitely follows Xander's line of thought, and him being the deputy of the school complicates things.

Something dark crawls in my gut at the thought of what I may need to do.

When I fall asleep, it's so deep that I don't dream at all.

Keep them safe. Keep them safe. Keep them safe.

* * *

The next morning, I wake up to an empty dorm as planned, because I told Minnie I needed a sleep in. In reality, I need to get myself off again so I'll have an energy boost for when I need to brave the academy dining hall for the first time since my mysterious disappearance. As a bonus, nothing makes me happier than defying an order from Lyle Pardalia. The fact that we now both know I'm his regina gives me *extra* right to do so. The anima in me agrees. *We* give the orders around here. Full stop.

I enjoy a leisurely morning in my bed thinking about Savage's large hands and Scythe's glowering eyes before my post-orgasm doze is interrupted.

A knock comes at my door and I raise my head to see that it's not Theresa come to question me, but Stacey. Her hair is in her signature high pigtails, she has matte red lips and wears a slinky black maxi dress. She looks like a sexy cat and should have a smirk on her face, but doesn't. Something is wrong. Her eyes are wide and she wrings her hands as she steps cautiously into my room.

"Bestie," she greets, tentatively.

I'm immediately on high alert and off my bed in front of her, sniffing the air and straining my ears to hear for any signs of commotion. "What's wrong?"

"It's Minnie."

I grab her arms. "Is she bleeding? Is she hurt?" Please, not another breach in my defence. Not another attack. I was so careful through the night to make sure I kept the shields up—

"What? No, no!"

I calm down a fraction and let her go. "Then what is it?"

"We have a situation. I know this was your rest day, but I think you need to come down with us to breakfast. For Minnie's sake."

I'm about to demand for her to spit it out when Sabrina comes stomping into my room on her stilettos, waving her hands in the air. "Bitches, it's a disaster. Minnie's lost it completely." She points at me. "Lia, you need to go down there and beat some sense into that tigress! She's sitting *in his lap,* for Goddess' sake!"

"Whose lap?" I demand, trying to think if Minnie has ever

mentioned fancying an animus around here. There was that one anima fling a while ago, but she never snuck off into the animus dorm like Sabrina, Raquel and Stacey often do.

Instead of answering, my feline friends throw a dress at me. I shove my hair into a messy bun and we hurry out to the dining hall with Eugene trailing behind us.

Chapter 17

Aurelia

The hall is packed as usual, with everyone occupying their regular seats. Eugene scurries to our table, no doubt to get scraps from Raquel. Sabrina, in her typical confident style, sashays behind him.

"Don't make it obvious," Stacey says, lingering by my side. "Casually get your breakfast so we don't catch attention."

Stacey's plan is in vain, because I'm noticed immediately as we walk in and, rather suddenly, I'm hit with the full force of the gaze of every hungry, lusty animus in the school.

Stewing in my own rabid juices for four weeks, hibernating in the recesses of my anima has made my senses sharper. I'm suddenly acutely aware of the males around me even more than usual. Their scents hit me in a whirlwind of information, along with their fear, their arousal and their excitement. The latter of which markedly increases as I turn my back on them to collect my food with Stacey by my side. Filling my plate with no less than eight ham and cheese croissants, I take that precious minute at the buffet to steel my body and mind to prepare for what awaits me now that I'm 'out'.

It's then that I feel it. The authoritative presence that enters the hall like a predator on the prowl. Like a king entering his court.

I pause where I am, not sure if I want to look down or sideways or up to pray to the Wild Goddess herself. But then he rounds the buffet and comes to stand just adjacent to me—as if he's not here to see me, just the dining hall in general. But I am not fooled. I know in my bones he came here when he felt that I did.

I wonder if all my mates can feel *where* I am in time and space, even with my shields up. Savage was able to hunt me down when I fled from them, but only because he'd been inside me. But now apparently Lyle can too.

We didn't *do* anything down in the cavern. I would definitely know if we had.

My anima pleads with me to look at him, and because we are promised to cooperate with each other, I oblige her.

When my gaze lands on him, my breath falters. He really is a stunning beast, despite all the chains and shackles my anima is telling me he places on himself. His long hair is perfectly tied back, the golden tones in them sparkling by the sunlight streaming in through the stained-glass windows lining one side of the hall. Those amber eyes are on me intently. Scanning me from head to toe as if he's concerned that at any moment I'll detonate and kill everyone around me.

Concerned. Lyle Pardalia is concerned about me. The realisation is both jarring and... something else. My eyes fall to the skin of his neck, where of course, I can see nothing because of my own protections. For the first time in my life, I curse them.

"Miss Aquinas," Lyle says. How can a man's voice be both honey and steel at the same time?

"Yes?"

"You are holding up the line."

I glance at the eagle animus next to me, patiently waiting but clearly checking me out. "Right, sorry."

Hastily, I turn around to join my friends at our usual table right in the centre of the hall, cussing at my stupidity. Perhaps I just really need the food.

As I walk, many eyes scrape down my face, my breasts, my ass. I feel their gazes like the ravenous predators they are, and by the gods, how did I forget these hungry bastards outnumber us animas five to one? I plaster a glare on my face when whispers break out as I pass the full tables. I walk with a slow, confident prowl to make sure everyone, *including* Lyle, knows I don't give a flying fuck about what they think.

Taking a seat opposite Raquel, who sits all broody and scowly, there are three things that I notice immediately.

The first is that none of my enemies are at their usual table at the back of the hall. It sits empty and there are a couple of snide "Where've you been, bunny?'s" from the neighbouring birds of prey who think they have a chance with me since my cover order is an eagle.

The second thing I realise is that, in my rush to get here, I've forgotten to wear *any* underwear. Bra included. My nipples are obvious through the thin material of the navy-blue mini dress and the thing is made to stick to me. I actually enjoy the fact that it's tight because after four weeks of being without clothes, it feels like a second skin that I can easily ignore.

But I forget about the show my nipples are serving when I notice the third thing.

Minnie is not at our table.

She's sitting at a table held by the senior minority felines and there is a dense concentration of energy around my best friend. This table is for the loner types like tigers and jaguars who don't like to socialise but also can't sit anywhere else. Everyone has their place in the animus dining hall and that's one of the tables everyone gives a wide berth.

Next to Minnie sits a huge male that I have never seen before.

This, my instincts scream, *is a dangerous male*. The last time I had such a feeling, I met Scythe, down in Halfeather's dungeon, chained up and naked in the dark. A shiver passes over me at the memory. But where Scythe is light—silver-haired, and pale skinned—this beast is dark. An obsidian buzzcut sits above two black slashes for eyebrows and a five o'clock shadow. His irises are nothing but midnight spheres as they survey the beasts around him with a cold, cutting dominance that will not be questioned. A cruel smirk lines his lips as he speaks to those at his table.

All the males laugh, but they are nervous and forced.

I understand why my animas are in uproar. My primitive female instinct screams to snatch all our females away from him. That this is a beast who is waiting to strike from the long grasses. He's not Minnie's type. Not by a long shot.

But the Boneweaver in me asks a little, curious question.

Sabrina says snidely over her fruit salad, "He's got that 'I'm-too-good-for-aftercare' type look, doesn't he?"

We all grunt in agreement, eyes narrowed on the male.

Stacey suddenly puts down her fork. "Wait, this can't be the ex who was bad news, right? The one in the gang who landed her in here in the first place?"

"Shit," Sabrina agrees. "The one she told us about on our first lock in."

"He's an a-alpha t-tiger," Raquel mutters, glancing over their shoulder. "Just l-look at him."

In our world, an alpha was a beast who held so much dominance that other males followed him. They had strong command of their order's powers and were leaders within their territory. And this male is holding court at not only his table, but the neighbouring tables as if it's just another day. The felines, both animas and animuses, are all sucking up to him, nodding eagerly, their chairs turned towards him attentively. Even some of the wolves and birds a little further away are gazing on with interest.

I look around for Yeti, the top tiger in the academy, and order leader of the felines to see his response to this new threat, but he's not here.

Staring from his table, Beak sits, his face blank. He catches my gaze and his eyes widen a little. He looks between Minnie and us glaring animas, and as if he knows what I'm thinking, gives a tiny shake of his head.

A warning. An instruction.

Both things, I am above.

Minnie hasn't even noticed me come in, her eyes solely for this huge, cruel brute. My friend has every right to pursue any anima or animus she wants, my every primal instinct is shouting at me to get my pack-sister away from this danger cloaked in a human body.

Stacey gets out her sneaky phone, probably scouring social media for any information. Sabrina mutters dark things under her breath while Raquel shoots daggers around the hall.

I only realise that I'm on my feet when Raquel's spoon pauses halfway to their mouth.

"Lia, *no.*"

But my eyes are only for Minnie and the clear danger she is in, and Gertie, on her shoulder, the yellow nimpin looking very uncomfortable. Like she's a hairsbreadth away from puffing her chest out and screaming that special disabling song all nimpins have.

I know people are staring. I know Lyle is still behind me, surveying the situation from afar. His teaching methods continue to confound me because I'm sure he's behind the fact that two ex-rabids are here today.

My walk is little more than a prowl as I wind through the tables, ignoring the stares that rake my skin, the snide comments about my absence.

And oh, the dangerous tiger knows I'm making a beeline for the table, but he never looks my way. If I was an animus, he'd consider this direct approach a threat. But as an anima, my approach could be misconstrued as an invitation.

Connor, who'd been sitting within the pool of felines near the danger, half rises from the table on the other side, shaking his head at me in a vigorous *no*. His orange nimpin, who wears a tiara of diamantés, is sitting on Connor's shoulder and staring at me as if I'm mad.

I level them both a disapproving look before halting before Minnie's table. Henry shifts nervously on my shoulder, no doubt feeling the tension around us.

The table goes deathly quiet as the dangerous tiger finally turns his head and graces me with his attention.

I let him see the dominance in my eyes. "Who are you?"

Someone hisses, others go stiff, and Minnie goes still, saying in a small voice. "Lia?"

But the tiger gives me a lazy smile, sitting back in his chair, his tone light but his words slow and measured as if he's remembering how to use them. "Well, who's this pretty creature? Piggy, introduce your cute friend to me."

I barely notice the depth of his voice because... Piggy? *Piggy?* I don't like anything about him. The command in his voice. The possession in the way he's folded my best friend into his side.

Minnie clears her throat, and in a higher pitch than usual says, "Aurelia, this is Titus. Titus, this is Aurelia Aquinas."

Titus slowly drags his eyes down my body, with obvious consideration, rubbing his bottom lip with his thumb. I've just had a shower but I immediately feel like I've just waded through filth.

I keep my hands casually by my side and my body language open to show I'm not afraid of this neanderthal. "The first-year animas sit at the anima table," I say, jerking my thumb over my shoulder to where our friends sit.

But Titus smirks as if this is very funny. "No, birdy, she's sitting here with me. Where I can see her properly."

My low growl is wholly reflexive and, perhaps, my first mistake of the day.

The smile slips off his face faster than a sheet pulled off a dining table. His eyes level on me, his body coiled and ready.

Hm. Shit. There are more guards than usual around the hall today, but the problem with that is they step in *after* a fight starts, allowing us the opportunity to get some damage in. I wonder if Lyle will let it happen today. I'm almost curious enough to test him out. Push his limits a little bit. Animas are generally not attacked by animuses here. The males are forever trying to get into our good graces and don't want to ruin their chances with us. But this Titus is new. He might not care about that.

I go to take a step forward but a massive invisible force brushes against the shield I keep around my body, not a dominating warning, but a careful and inquiring request.

It is not Titus' telekinesis, like I expected, but another feline's from further away. My shields won't let that power touch my skin directly, and it does not try to breach it.

I am here, it says.

But I am confused by what Lyle is trying to say. I'm confused by this change in his approach.

But Minnie, as always, comes to rescue, putting her tiny hand on the tiger's substantial, bare forearm. She frantically looks between him and me. "It's alright, Lia," Minnie says quickly. "I'm sitting here for a bit. I'll catch up with you later, alright?"

Titus relaxes the barest fraction and Connor blows out a relieved breath.

Looks like I won't win this bout. I give my friend a small smile and nod. "See you later, Minnie."

It looks like I've officially returned to the jungle and there are new predators stalking the underbrush.

Chapter 18

Aurelia

After breakfast, Minnie and Titus leave together. Just them. Connor comes hurrying to our table to slap me on the shoulder and berate me about my lack of self-preservation.

"Who is this animus?" Sabrina asks him. "He looks like bad news."

"Well, I mean, he *is* hot," admits Connor, shivering a little. "But he's also one of the rabids treated by Mr. Pardalia. Just got released this morning. I had no idea he was Minnie's ex, though. That's some serious shit she's into."

Raquel swears.

Sabrina mutters, "I'll be having words with her when she comes back from fucking him."

We all groan in dismay before we head back to the anima dorm.

As it's Sunday, the others need to get ready for the school week by doing laundry, ironing their outfits, and catching up on homework and group projects. But when we get back to the anima dorm, I see something I missed while I was being rushed out the first time. Or rather, some*one*.

"Nice pumps, Connor," a nasally voice chirps from overhead.

I gape at the new *moving* gargoyle sitting above the door like she's always been there.

"Aurelia, meet Christine." Sabrina rolls her eyes. "Old bat, meet Aurelia Aquinas."

"I'm well aware of who this is." Christine peers down at me with great interest. "You and I will be great friends, Miss Aurelia!"

"Oh, so you like *her*, but not me?" Sabrina puts her hands on her hips.

"She's got better fashion sense."

"She gets her fashion sense from *me*!" Sabrina shakes her fist at Christine before leading us all sniggering inside.

I drag Stacey and Connor into my room and pull up the academy tablet. We're not allowed online shopping privileges until second year, but Stacey has managed to hack her way into getting the system to approve us.

We sit on my bed for an hour, giggling and gasping over my purchases with my massive, mysterious school stipend. I wish Minnie was with us, but that's another problem I'm going to have to deal with. I even get Connor and Stacey a couple things while we're at it. Considering I can hardly call the free money mine, I feel bad using it without sharing.

We're just putting through the payment when footsteps come thundering down our corridor.

Connor jumps to his feet straight away, on high alert. He was born with an anima and is gender-fluid, but because he's a biological male, chooses to live in the animus dorm. Which is a more exciting place to live due to the "pleasantly volatile action" every day.

The person who's running down the corridor, pounds on every door as they pass. Our door is the last in the line, so when she gets to us, she stops short, panting in the open doorway.

It's a brown-skinned she-wolf from third year.

"There's a trial!" she puffs, tucking a curl of wild black hair behind her ear. "It was just broadcasted to the wolves. He's holding court. Quick, you don't want to miss it!" She runs back down the corridor.

Trial. I break out into an immediate sweat.

"What does that mean?" Stacey asks in alarm, looking from me to Connor and back again, almond eyes wide in alarm as we all shoot to our feet.

"Someone's done something naughty and needs to pay." Connor sees me, no doubt ashen-faced, and loops his muscled arm through mine. Stacey does the same on my other side. "Don't worry, girl," he says quietly. "It's not *your* trial this time."

I nod as Henry begins his slow pecking of my neck to remind me to breathe. "And who did she mean by '*he*'?"

Connor gives me a pointed look, swishing his long black mane. "He's a mate of yours." He snorts at the double entendre. "The scary shark daddy, of course."

Every muscle in my body stands to attention as I gulp. Ice-blue eyes flash in my memory as my anima keens in sadness and excitement. Our Great White shark didn't come to see me down in our cavern. A little part of me thought he might have. That he might have wanted to. But nope. Clearly, I'm not as important to him as I thought. It hurts something in me to admit it. And now, as I follow the animas outside, I'll have to stomach facing two mates who want nothing to do with me.

* * *

As we all file into the animus dorms, there are four armed guards monitoring the crowd from outside.

"Wait, student justice is *sanctioned*?" Stacey hisses.

"Yup." Connor gives us a white-toothed grin. "The deputy headmaster lets the animuses run their own trials for certain inter-court squabbles. It's supposed to prepare us for life outside, when we have to answer to our court royalty."

I grumble under my breath at a demonstration of another of Lyle's educational tactics. This *event* seems to be fairly orderly so far. The fact that there are systems and processes that are led by the students themselves? I begrudgingly admit that it's a smart thing for him to let us do.

To my delight, there is also a talking gargoyle sitting at the top of the glass doors leading inside, twig-like legs hanging over the lip of the awning. He sits with a rotund belly and bat-like wings folded behind him and wears a top hat and monocle. Unlike Christine's more covert mutterings, this gargoyle is shouting profanities at those passing through the door.

"This place has gone to the *dogs!*" he cries, pointing a stick-like finger at a pair of wolves.

Someone throws a black flip flop at him, hitting him square on his bulbous nose.

"Screw you, leopard!" He shakes his fist. "Just showing everyone how small your cockle is!" He holds up a pinky finger and the rest of us snigger.

The gargoyle turns his head to survey the crowd and those cast iron eyes widen when he spots the three of us animas.

"Yoohoo, animas!" he calls. That obsidian face splits into a wide grin and he waggles his fingers. "So refreshing to see pretty things around here. Come up and give us a kiss." He puckers his lips and blows a loud raspberry.

"Hi, Bastian," Connor calls, wiggling his fingers back. "I'll climb up for my kiss later."

Stacey and I exchange an amused smirk as we pass through the doors.

There is an excited yet tense buzz in the air and as we funnel through the first floor of the dorm and Connor holds me tightly to avoid the jostling that's going on. The animus dorm is easily three times the size of the anima dorm, and even with the wider corridor, we're all moving at a snail's pace.

At the end of the corridor, four of the biggest animuses from Scythe's entourage stand as guards by two big front doors. One of them is Yeti, the imposing white-haired order leader of the felines, cooly surveying the passing students. Another is Beak, looking impressive with his arms crossed and golden-brown hair perfectly spiked up. He's definitely in his element because he smartly smacks one of his eagles on the back of his head.

"No groping other animuses!" he barks.

"That eagle misses nothing," Connor says reverently.

Indeed, Beak's brown eyes dart this way and that, so naturally, he catches my eye as I come up to him. "You and I will talk later," he says down to me, his face grim.

I look up at him in surprise. Is this about the Titus incident in the dining hall?

Beak raises his brows like I'm a bit slow. "You're under me now. Court of Wings."

"What?" But the crowd pushes us forward and I have to enter the large, carpeted room.

"Hm, that's a bit awkward," Connor says, holding onto my elbow so I'm not swept away. "Beak leads the raptors now, so he thinks you come under his jurisdiction."

"He's their *order leader* now?" I say, glancing back at the tall eagle.

"They got into a fight a week back," Connor murmurs, guiding Stacey and me towards Sabrina and Raquel, the former waving enthusiastically at us. "He almost killed the third year who was boss. So... now he's it."

Well colour me impressed. There was more to Beak than I'd originally thought.

As we enter the room, the crowd splits left and right to allow for an empty space in the middle. At the head of the hall is a short stage, three steps high, with a single black leather armchair and wooden lectern.

We join Raquel and Sabrina on the right-hand side, and try as I might, I can't spot Minnie in the crowd.

"This is the rec room," Connor explains as the crowd shifts to accommodate everyone. "We play pool here and watch movies. We use that stage for karaoke."

"It's so unfair!" Sabrina bemoans like she's said it many times before. "We don't have one in the anima dorm."

"Well," comes a deep voice from behind us, "if it means you're over here all the time, I'm not complaining."

Sabrina grins and twirls around to put her arms over the big shoulders of a lion from second year. We leave them to it as they noisily make out. A puma grabs Stacey from behind and she yelps with glee as she too recognises her current friend with benefits. Connor pats me on the arm to tell me he won't leave me and I smile gratefully up at him. Raquel takes my other arm and scowls at the animuses to ward them off, but they know my wolf anim well enough by now to stay away.

The sound of the wide double doors being closed makes me stand to attention. The crowd quietens as Beak, Yeti and the other guards file to the front and line the base of the stage with their arms clasped sombrely in front of them.

It's at that exact moment that my heart all but stops in my chest.

I'm not ready. I was never going to be ready.

Xander appears from behind the stage, followed by Savage and Scythe.

It's been weeks since I've seen the three of them with my clear, human eyes, and yet it feels like a lifetime. Time seems to stop as I take them in, and every cell in my body stands to attention.

They've always been the most intimidating animuses I've

ever laid eyes on, even with all my years observing cage fights and inter-court violence.

Savage is a stunning, lethal creature, and any beast looking at his languid, slightly hunched stalk as he gracefully jumps off the stage and comes to stand in the centre of the line of guards knows that he's hardly civilised and more than a little unhinged. He's not wearing a shirt, as usual, showing the deep lines of his perfectly cut, tattooed torso. His dark waves are perfectly imperfect, almost lazy in their disarray if not for the fact that I can see the fade on the sides of his head is fresh. The wolf tattoo that spans the front of his chest bares its teeth at the crowd, just as its owner glares at the gathered audience. He's like a dark, feral guardian of the court, just waiting for his turn at violence.

Xander comes to stand at the lectern and it's his appearance that surprises me the most. He is the tallest beast in the room, which is saying something because the biggest animuses here are over six and a half feet. There is more than one appreciative female sigh at the sight of Xander, and it's because it's the first time he's appeared in a suit. It's black as the darkest night, tailored to perfection and hugging his lean, muscular frame like a dream. Of course he's smoking a joint like he doesn't care about his appearance, but the drip he sports says anything but careless. Gold and silver rings on his fingers glint under the halogens as he grips the sides of the lectern with both hands, as does the single black dagger earring on his left ear. He's wearing his headphones of choice. The white cords leading from his ears to the device stuck in his pants pocket might say nonchalant, but all that fades away when you catch sight of his glowing all-white eyes. Contrasted with his chest-length, silken straight black hair, he's a dragon who screams "stable, for now."

Scythe comes to sit on the lone armchair, and if the other two are stunning, he is... viciously beautiful. We don't often see sharks on land, and his presence always catches everyone off guard. There are more than a few excitable titters from the animas as they take in his shoulder-length, silvery hair, those ice-chip blue eyes and the five lines of ancient marine text on the left side of his neck. His pale skin is covered from foot to neck in tattoos, though I can only see some peeking under the cuff of his black business shirt.

I'm sent off balance by the colossal gravitational pull I feel towards the three of them. It's undeniable, that sheer *need* I have for them. I swallow through a thick throat, trying to control my own emotions. Perhaps it's that everything in my post-rabid state is more detailed, making me more sensitive. Xander's fingers tighten on the lectern and I know he, at least, has noted my presence.

But none of them look my way.

I clutch onto Connor's arm more firmly, in case my anima decides to prance over there and sit on Scythe's *very* inviting-looking lap. Heat swirls in my belly, shooting right down between my legs.

I'm about to murmur to Connor to get me the fuck out of here when Xander drones in a deep, formal voice I'm not used to hearing on him. But it suits him. Oh Goddess, does it suit him.

"Step forward the accuser, Troy Leppard. And bring forward the accused."

I almost step forward myself at the deep command in that dragon's timbre, only stopping just in time to see a short, long-haired male confidently stepping out of the wings, striding to stand in the middle of the open space before the stage.

The tension in the room quite obviously rockets up as we all stare.

A wolf is brought forward by two others, holding him in place with steel grips around his biceps. He wears faded blue jeans and a jacket covered with old stains and snarls at everyone around him.

"Troy Leppard," Xander drones in his deep, clipped voice.

"What is your accusation of this here wolf, Brendan Moonsayer?"

Troy clears his throat. "Brendan used a contraband gun to attack me last night. I believe there was a hit put on me from an outside gang and he was trying to put me down."

Murmurs strike up through the crowd.

"Bring forth the evidence," Xander calls.

Two more wolves bring out a wooden board with metal glinting on top. A small, concealable handgun sits there and is brought up to Scythe. The shark glances down at it before he nods.

"Use of arms in a fight is prohibited under our laws and is a punishable offence. Does the accused have anything to say in his defence?" Xander asks.

"Fuck all of you," Brendan spits. "I didn't do nothin'!"

Savage snarls softly and Brendan clenches his teeth but stares back at him in open defiance.

"S-stupid, stupid wolf," Raquel mutters on my other side.

Then it's Scythe who finally speaks. "Brendan Moonsayer." His rasp filters around the entire hall. "You are found guilty of keeping an illegal weapon and using it in an assassination attempt. Your punishment is the same injury inflicted upon you in the honourable way."

Brendan tries to wrench free of his captors but they hold firm.

When Savage grins, it's not a nice one at all. He prowls forward with that confident saunter, spreading his arms out. "As your noble order leader, it is my duty to inflict your punishment." He points at Troy. "Since the leopard was shot in the abdomen three times, you'll get three bites from me. Not enough to kill, just enough to"—he bares his teeth—"hurt really bad."

"And by the Old Laws," Scythe rasps, "healing will be withheld for three days. You are only permitted stitches."

"May the Wild Mother have mercy on you," Xander grins, and it's a truly cold thing. "Because we sure as hell won't."

Without warning, Savage bursts into his wolf form and lunges for the accused. We all flinch as Brendan's guards scramble to get out of the way. Savage pummels into the wolf, sending them both crashing to the floor.

Brendan screams, and there's blood, so much blood, as Savage gouges into his stomach with his canines, biting and gnawing. He punches Savage's head with both fists, but it's like a rabbit trying to fight off a wolf and I feel sorry for the guy. I've been under Savage before, I understand the weight; the sheer feeling of that powerful beast over you. I've also seen beasts gouging out abdomens before, but Savage is different in his approach. As wild and ferocious as the attack is, it's precise and measured.

It's over quickly. Savage steps off Brendan, completely in control of his bloodlust.

The maimed wolf is carried away by other wolves, sobbing and choking on his own spit. My stomach roils as Savage licks his bloody teeth clean. Even through my own nausea I stand transfixed at his wolf form. He's massive, with a pelt that twinkles like the midnight sky and eyes that demand obedience.

"Punishment is concluded. Court is dismissed," Xander announces. A command to leave. He's smiling fondly at Savage.

A chill runs down my spine.

After a moment of stunned silence, everyone hurries to obey.

I don't realise that Raquel is squeezing my hand so hard it's cutting off my circulation, until everyone shuffles for the door. Raquel gives me an embarrassed grimace and drops my hand, but I give my friend a reassuring smile in return. I wonder where Minnie is. How she felt watching this. I'm trying to see a pink mop of hair in the audience when a husky, deep, feral voice rings out across the hall, making me freeze.

"Lia? *Regina!*" I turn to see Savage, in his naked human

form, waving enthusiastically at me, his bloody face and mouth stretched into a huge smile. "You're back!"

"I've n-never s-seen him so happy," Raquel mutters.

"It's a little creepy," Connor mutters, but his tone is amused.

Even though Savage looks like a mad serial killer, I can't help the way my sex twinges at the sight of him and that naked male body made by the Wild God himself.

"You're so lucky," a wolf I don't know says as he passes me.

I look back at Savage to find him shoving his way through the crowd to get to me. My eyes dart to the others, but Xander is gone, and it's only Scythe still sitting there. His eyes like a snare, holding me captive in their cold depths. I'm rooted to the spot. Stricken by him and the power that lies behind that powerful gaze. Goddess, were his eyes always the colour of the coldest sea?

But Savage is nearing us and Connor taps me on the shoulder in silent question. I grab his hand in two of mine and turn to see where Raquel is.

But my wolf friend indicates to Savage with their eyes and jerks their chin at us to leave. "Go. I n-need t-to stay."

Before I can protest, Connor whips me, Stacey, and Sabrina out of the hall as fast as he can.

Chapter 19

Aurelia

We leg it out of there with Connor shoving slower animuses aside until we get out into the warm sun and fresh air.

The guards shout at us for bursting out of the doors, so we slow to a power walk instead, giving Bastian the animus gargoyle a wave as we leave.

"Shit," I mutter. "Fucking shit."

"Tell me about it," Connor says. "That was a bad one. So far, I've only seen mild inter-court disputes, but they're usually dealt with privately. A public display like that is…"

"Brutal showmanship," I say under my breath. "And very telling."

"They have to put them in place, Lia," Sabrina mutters. "It's how they keep the peace."

Oh, I know. I want to tell her I've seen and heard of worse in my own father's court. Some of the things I saw as a child made this look tame. Including the one where my father executed my very first boyfriend via venom and made me watch as punishment for losing my virginity.

I had just hoped other courts would be better.

Who the hell was I kidding? And with Xander and Scythe presiding over *that* display? I should have expected it. Beasts who would present *their own* regina for execution are capable of... well, anything.

"And what about Raquel?" I ask. "Why did they have to stay back?"

"Oh," Connor chuckles under his breath. "Well, Savage has made our little wolf anim a commander-in-training."

"*What?*" I halt on the concrete path to our dorm.

The others nod seriously.

"Raquel is a broadcaster," Stacey explains as we start walking again. "Pretty powerful. Once Savage realised, he brought them into the fold."

A broadcaster is a wolf with telepathy so strong they are capable of blasting into the minds of groups of people. Just like how Savage apparently broadcasted to the entire dorm to escape before he almost blew up the place.

"Shit," I say

"Yup." Stacey pops the *p*.

Because we all know that if Raquel has been recruited by Savage, we know where Raquel's loyalties have to lie. Whether they like it or not.

"I don't know if you remember," Sabrina says with a little smirk. "But you let *him* feed you."

"Him who?" I ask lamely.

She knocks her shoulder into mine. "Girl, you know *who!*"

Henry chirps from my shoulder like he agrees with her.

I sigh. "I might have a vague memory of eating sometimes." In truth, I do remember Savage sitting in front of me and offering me different types of bread and meat. Of all my memories, shadowy or otherwise, of being down there, his face presides over everything. Both him and Lyle.

"I dunno, Lia. I reckon you should give him a chance," Sabrina says. "I'd give anything for my mate to come and *hand feed* me, even after I became a beast and almost tore off his arm." She looks me up and down to indicate said *beast*.

"It was cute," Connor shrugs. "He seems really smitten, actually. And he sent Eugene to watch over you when we were all at class."

"Smitten," I repeat in disbelief.

"I think," Stacey sighs wistfully, "if you asked him for *anything* he'd do it."

It's hard for me to reconcile the Savage I knew from before to the one they're talking about now. The wolf who came into my room and messed it up just to scare me. But the entire time, I'd known he was fighting his natural urge to care for me. He brought me that pink handbag after all. He stole my panties as if he couldn't help it. Heat surges through my body at the thought of the way he pulled me into his arms before the trial. The way he wanted me with the same desperate need, the same way I'd wanted him.

Does he regret it? What he and his brothers tried to do to me?

* * *

That afternoon, Theresa comes to check on my mental health and brings with her one of Lyle's formal appointment cards, his name signed in a sweeping fancy cursive with a fountain pen and all.

I don't know how to feel about seeing him one-on-one.

On one hand, he's an arrogant bastard who practically served me up for execution on a silver platter. On the other hand, memories from the cavern come back to me in flashes. Moments of a gentle hand and a deep, murmuring voice. It had calmed my anima. It had comforted us. And then there was that moment in the dining hall...

Theresa knows something is up by the way she avoids my gaze.

"Can't *you* counsel me?" I ask desperately.

"The deputy headmaster treats the ex-rabid students himself."

I grumble under my breath.

"And Lia?"

"Yes?"

"I'm glad you're here. Glad you're still with us."

My head almost snaps up to stare at her in shock. She smiles at me with all of her teeth. "I'm growing pretty fond of you."

I only just manage to stop the gaping. After everything, my vision goes blurry as I register her words. What had been about to happen if I hadn't acted. Henry nuzzles into my shoulder, detecting that I'm about to lose it.

"Thank you," I say softly. "I... I haven't felt welcome in any place in a very long time."

"I know. It's the same for a lot of the students here, you know. The ones who come from crime families. Maybe not the wolves so much, but a lot of the felines and raptors have this in common. Rough parents. Rough lives."

I nod in agreement. Sabrina and Stacey certainly have similar such stories. Sabrina was locked in a cupboard for hours by her father. And Stacey only just revealed to us that she was forced to go hungry as punishment for not getting good marks at school.

"But Theresa, my sentence has only been postponed. It's not like it's all gone away."

"Speak to Lyle tomorrow, love. We'll get through this."

* * *

My friends come and go during the afternoon, but Minnie is not one of them. Sabrina mentioned that she saw her with Titus and some other felines over at the animus dorm. None of us like this, but Minnie is an intelligent girl who knows her own mind. As soon as classes come around tomorrow, I'll be able to get some one-on-one time with her to ask her what the fuck Titus is about. So it's just Me, Eugene and Henry in the room as I wearily climb into bed, my bones feeling like they're made of lead. My skin feels tight over my muscles and no matter how much water I drink, I feel like it's never enough.

I'm heaving myself up from bed and reaching for my water bottle when a prickle of awareness tickles the back of my neck.

I go on high alert.

I check my shields for their integrity. Once, and then twice for good measure, but they're all fully functional, protecting me and my friends from the external forces that might hurt us.

So then... what is it?

A small scuffling sound comes from outside, followed by a loud grunt. The handles of the balcony door angle downward and I stare as the shadow of a tall male straightens on the other side. I shrink into my covers as the doors silently sweep open.

Eugene clucks a soft greeting from where he's roosting on the new purple armchair Minnie brought up from the cavern.

"Princess?" Savage whispers.

"Fucking hell," I mutter, pushing myself forward and taking a swig from my water bottle.

"You didn't think I'd let you hide from me, did you?"

I allow my eagle eyes to take over so I can see better through the dark.

He closes the balcony doors, the security lights from outside casting his bare torso in silver. He's showered since his messy attack at the trial, leaving his hair damp. A lick of a dark curl flops onto his forehead as he grins down at me.

"Hello, regina."

His voice is a caress up my spine. I set my water bottle down and self-consciously pull up the bedsheet to my chin. "Hi."

Savage's grin is ridiculous, and he has the audacity to close his eyes and tilt his head back as if savouring my presence. "Oh, my heart, regina. I've missed your voice."

I narrow my eyes, and when he opens his, that grin turns into something a little more uncertain.

"*Did* you," I demand, "or did you *not*, threaten to blow up the anima dorm?"

"Not threaten," he corrects earnestly, stepping forward. "I had the explosives in place and everyth—"

The dark look on my face makes him decide against finishing that sentence. I thought perhaps he'd turn sheepish at my words, but once again I've underestimated his audacity.

He takes a step forward and the space between us heats at the intensity simmering in his eyes. "Blowing up a building is the very *least* I would do to get to you."

Shit. My afternoon get-off session didn't take the edge off anything. A tingle shoots straight between my legs, but I ignore it and keep the venom in my voice. "And how about the girls in it? You didn't care for them?"

He rubs the back of his neck, exhaling heavily, as if the concept is a great nuisance. It's then that I see my black hair tie is still around his wrist. He's kept it after all this time. "I got them out in the end, regina."

I glare at him. At this insane wolf who tried to blow up an actual building to get to me. A shiver wracks my body and arousal holds me in its hot, heavy grasp. Those beautiful lips of his curve into a smile.

"I've come to cuddle. Move over."

"No you haven't," I say quickly, leaning back.

"We used to cuddle all the time down in the cavern!"

I shake my head.

His face falls and I almost feel bad. I want to be the type of girl who has her mates in her bed every night, but—

I take a deep breath. "You need to ask permission."

Savage gapes at me. "What does that mean?"

"Oh, come on. You went to the same manners classes I went to. Consent and all that."

"Consent has to be freely given, enthusiastic and ongoing." He sings it like it's a jingle from a commercial.

"Yes. So you can't say, 'I'm cuddling with you.' You say, '*Can I cuddle with you?*'"

"Oh, right." He scratches the back of his head. "Can I cuddle with you?"

"No."

"See!" He gestures wildly. "It didn't work! That's why I didn't ask."

I glare at him in exasperation, and he grins at me. "I'm only joking, regina." He kneels down next to my bed and clasps his hands together like he's a child praying at bedtime. "My beautiful, stunning, gorgeous regina, with eyes like a warm summer's night. May I, pretty please with five cherries on top, eat your pussy and fuck you senseless?"

Pressing my lips together to stop the laugh that's threatening me, I say dryly, "Well, that was lovely, I suppose."

"I know."

I tear my eyes away from that perfect, masculine face and stare at my hands. The backs of my eyes burn as I wonder what the fuck I should do. The force of my desire for him is almost choking me. But with everything that's happened—

"Regina?"

He keeps calling me that and I don't understand why I feel different about him now. Why *he* feels different about me. I'm confused and tired and thirsty—

"Hey."

The gentleness in his voice catches me by surprise and I suddenly don't know what to do. How to move, how to speak.

And then he's there, climbing onto my bed and pulling me into his muscled body. My face sits against his warm, bare chest and I'm getting his skin wet with tears, but under that is his scent. Ancient forests and deep fertile earth. A smell I've known for weeks and even longer than that. A flash of a memory comes to me again, of me lying down next to Savage, both of us in our beast forms. Just breathing. Just lying quietly together. It's familiar to me now. His wild, heady energy, wrapping around me on a near constant basis. I might not have known it, but in all that time, I got used to him being by my side.

Now, his human arms encircle me, holding me tight as if he's needed to do this for a long time. Now his human skin sits against mine and there's no layers of fur between us. Just... skin through my thin nightie. My anima is telling me this beast is safe. The human side of me is terrified that it's all a lie.

But he wasn't the one who presented me like a Christmas ham to my father. He wasn't there that evening. I *have* to know what that means.

"Where were you?" I whisper. "That day. Where did you go?"

I hear him swallow through that powerful throat. He knows exactly what I'm talking about as his arms tighten even more around me.

"The day of your trial, Xander darted me and kept me locked up in Lyle's office so I couldn't get to you. I woke up there after all that shit happened outside the medical wing. If I'd been there..." He blows out a puff of air. "I wouldn't have handed you over, Aurelia."

They knew he would try to get to me. Out of all of them, he was the one who would have let his instincts get in the way. But even so...

"You made the blood vow," I whisper into his chest. "With my father."

"You didn't want me," he says, the hurt making his voice catch. "All I wanted was you, and then when you found me, you" —he swallows again—"didn't want me."

I want to sob and scream. I want to vomit at the mess my life has become. Instead, I pull myself out of his arms and wipe my face to look at the wolf properly. He sits cross-legged on my bed, that wolfish face grim, his jaw clenched against the pain of the memory. My heart squeezes in my chest.

"I couldn't..." I blink away more tears. "I couldn't be with you, Savage. Even if I'd wanted."

He takes one of my hands in two of his large ones. His eyes search mine. "Did you want to?" he breathes. "You came to me the night before. When I cut off my finger for you. You *wanted* me then, didn't you?"

I nod. It changed me. That one moment in his bed, with him inside me. Nothing could remove that from my being. That sheer, absolute, devastating feeling of him entwined with me.

But there were still answers I needed.

"And what about Halfeather's prison?" I whisper. "You never told me why you were all in there in the first place."

Savage licks his lips. "Everything we do has a reason."

"Are you telling me you got caught on purpose?"

"Sometimes it's better to let your enemy show their hand. Sometimes it's necessary to walk into danger to get what you want."

I frown at my hands, trying to understand what he's saying. I had always wondered how and why they'd ended up in chains. Men like Scythe, Xander and Savage don't simply get *caught* like that.

"My regina," Savage whispers. "My mate." He places a finger under my chin and tilts it up to look at him. "I want you more than anything in this world. Let me show you. Let me make it up to you. Let me *have* you."

"Savage, I—"

"Even when you say my name, it completes something in me, you know that?"

I *want* to say yes. I really do.

I remove his hand from my face and frown down at the stub of his index finger. The healer in me assesses the way I healed it in that moment of pure lust.

"Does it hurt?" I ask faintly, lightly touching the new, healed skin.

Savage shivers. "I would do more than cut off a finger to be with you."

He keeps saying things like that. I drop his hand. "You don't even know me."

"I do."

Heartbreak gives way to irritation, especially when he starts grinning again. "I know you like ham and cheese croissants and that you used to have hot chocolate for supper every night. I know you love Minnie and Raquel and—unfortunately—Henry, Sabrina, Connor and Stacey. I know you draw funny pictures in class but somehow you still listen. I know you use peach and mango body wash. I know you like to read romance novels about witches and vampires. And!" he says dramatically. "I know you like me." He places a hand on his chest for emphasis. "I know I can make you come, Aurelia. With just my fingers."

A little shocked, I bite my lip.

With a growl, he surges forward, catching my bottom lip with both of his. I let out a squeak of surprise. But his lips on mine have been all I wanted, and that squeak turns into a languid sigh.

Melting into his body, I take his face in my hands and open for him.

Savage groans with all the desperation of a beast who's spent weeks waiting for me—months, really—and kisses me, deeply and passionately.

It's not feverish like our first time together. It's like he's taking his time, his movements purposeful and languid. It sears me, his scorching lips, claiming my own with slow, sensual grace. I make a sound of contentment and my approval urges him on.

His tongue slides into my mouth and his hands find my waist, pulling me forward and guiding me to straddle him. I can't help but respond. I cling onto his face, stubble prickling my palms as I climb into his lap, my legs on either side of his, and we deepen our kiss. He savours my mouth, my lips, my tongue, as if he's been waiting a lifetime to do it. He's gentle with me, and yet under that, I can feel the encroaching heat at the edges of us, just waiting for permission to pounce.

And it doesn't feel like enough when he pulls away, just a little, to speak.

"Aurelia," he whispers against my lips, his voice deep and husky. "Needing you is something I can't fight anymore." He swallows. "I *won't* fight it. It was the worst mistake of my life trying to keep away from you."

My heart hammers against my ribs. I want to jump his bones. I want to tear his clothes off, grab his cock and fuck him within an inch of his life. But this is dangerous. Savage is... undoubtedly still as dangerous as he was all those months ago when I met him. And I have a feeling that once I fall into him, once I give myself completely to him, my heart and soul will be his forever. "W-We need to go slow," I whisper. "I was never supposed to— I can't—"

"I know," he says, kissing me gently. "I'll do whatever you say. I'll do whatever it takes to make you happy. To make you feel safe so that you don't have to do... whatever that was down in the cavern, ever again."

Warmth slides through me at his earnest, gentle cadence. I brush my fingers down the strong length of his jaw. I cherish his words. His soft way with me.

But he doesn't know. He can't know the danger we are all in while my father stands on the other side of that academy barrier, just waiting for me to show a thread of weakness.

Chapter 20

Aurelia

I wake up to Minnie's Tigger alarm clock and Savage's heavy arm draped around me.

He murmurs into my neck, "Fucking tigers."

Fucking tigers, indeed. I need to catch Minnie this morning, but Savage's arm only tightens around my waist, keeping me pressed against his hard body. I can feel his erection against my ass, and in the night, my nightie has risen up, making my skin flush against his track pants and his considerable length.

Goddess, *do* I remember that mighty size of him in me. I resist the urge to wiggle against him.

"Savage," I announce.

"Yes, regina?" he replies, lips brushing against the sensitive skin of my neck.

A fluttery feeling, soft as a butterfly's wings, starts up in my lower belly. Shit. "I need to get up."

He sighs dramatically and releases me. It's only when I clamber out that I realise we don't even fit on this bed. We somehow fell asleep with Savage's huge body a hair's breadth away from falling out.

The wolf in question rubs his eyes and regards me with great interest before smiling broadly.

Tousled, with hooded eyes, he's irresistible in the morning. I have to be careful. We didn't fuck last night, only cuddled as he promised.

I point at him. "Boundaries."

He puts his hands behind his head, highlighting those beautiful biceps and forearms. "I'm a wolf, regina. I don't know what that means."

I rummage through the clothes in my wardrobe to see what I'm going to wear today. "It means that you eat at *your* table and that I eat at *my* table."

"But packs eat together." The dismay in his voice makes me grimace, but I have to maintain a sense of normality right now. Connor and Stacey's words yesterday ring in my head.

So, I raise my chin as I turn around with a dress in hand. "To make up for your transgressions, you'll be at my beck and call. Whatever I want. Whenever I want."

I'm almost shocked that I'm saying this, and even more shocked when he nods enthusiastically. "Sexual favours, any favours, I'm up for it." As if he suddenly remembers something, he reaches towards the floor and picks something up that must've fallen out of his pocket last night. "Here." It's a brand new, sleek black phone with a purple case. "I got this for you."

Something uncomfortable stirs in my chest at the fact that he knows my favourite colour, but I quickly snatch the thing up. Gods, I've missed my phone. That bastard Lyle never returned it to me when it slipped out of my beak in my original escape attempt from him.

Savage's eyes follow my movements, and for a split second, hunger flashes across his face and I stop breathing.

His Adam's apple moves up and down. "My number is in there. You just message me, alright, regina?"

I'm not used to this version of Savage. This... gentle wolf who wants to please me. I stare at him, still uncertain about what the fuck I'm doing. He snares my gaze and holds it.

It's a soft hazel that greets me, a mixture of greens and browns that catches the morning sunlight.

And then I shake myself because we're standing there like absolute idiots staring into each other's eyes.

I clear my throat. "For anything?"

To my great and intense satisfaction, Savage looks a little concerned. But he says, "Anything, my princess."

"Great!" With my new phone, I all but leap for the bathroom.

When I emerge from a cold shower, Savage is gone, leaving only his lingering, heady scent. I make my bed, pat Eugene's head, empty Henry's litter box, refill his little drinking fountain and double-check my appearance. I can't take my phone with me, because during my wardrobe purchases, I only had sexy in mind and not storage. By the time I leave, the other animas have already made their way to breakfast.

To my surprise, as I near the dining hall, I spot Minnie walking in from the animus dorm, wearing the same black mini dress as yesterday.

My brows fly up and I stop myself from battering her with questions.

"Walk of shame," she admits, a shy smile gracing her lips as she tucks a pink curl behind her ear.

On complete instinct, I reach for her hand and she immediately reaches for me and clasps it back. I remember that first day here, during mating lines, when I'd grabbed her hand. She'd effectively been a stranger to me that day, but she'd happily grasped my hand back. Minnie had never judged me. The criminal arsonist fugitive. She'd only shown me kindness.

"There's no shame in a good fuck," I say reasonably.

She chuckles, and together, we walk into the dining hall.

Minnie was there for me at my worst. At my most vulnerable. The last thing I want to do is *not* stand by her when she needs me.

"I'm always on your side, Min, you know that," I murmur as we get in the queue for the buffet. The warm, reassuring smell of bacon and eggs, toast and coffee fills my nose.

When she looks up at me, there's a soft smile on her face and her eyes are all... glowy. She rests a palm on her heart and I gape at her.

"You're in love with him!" I hiss, gripping her shoulder.

"Uh-huh," she admits, grabbing my arm back as if she's excited to finally tell someone. "It was love at first sight for us, we were bound to get back together. It was a big shock to realise he was coming here, but I think it's fate! And I'm really glad you get to meet him."

I laugh, but it's an awkward one. "He seems pretty intense."

She casts a look over her shoulder and briefly scans the animuses queueing behind us. I do the same.

"He's not here," she says quickly. "He usually doesn't eat breakfast. These rabid guys often eat once a day."

I pat my slightly nauseous stomach. I've been forcing food down for energy, but my body protests to the new volume of food. Lions and tigers in the wild only eat every so often, and my stomach is still adjusting to this whole thing.

Minnie playfully elbows me. "*You* know."

"Yeah, I do." I smile at her. "So, what's he like? How'd you meet? I need to know every tiny, dirty detail."

"We met outside my uni last year, actually. He was picking up his younger brother and happened to catch sight of me. Came up to me right away and demanded I come home with him and meet his dad."

"He didn't!" I say in disbelief.

But Minnie laughs as she picks up a single grapefruit and puts it on her plate. "It was really funny. But I felt right at home with him and we just... clicked."

I frown at my tray as Minnie grabs a cup of black coffee from the urn next to me.

"Titus is enough of a beast to make up for a group of them, for sure," she chuckles. "He's pretty possessive too, like Savage."

I load up my plate with croissants and pour myself some coffee, adding milk and sugar. "Possessive, huh? Girl, I've missed you. Make sure I get my bestie at least a *couple* nights a week."

Piggy. The nickname resounds in my head. Titus is not like Savage, I realise. Not by a long shot.

"No bacon and eggs today?" I ask tentatively as we get to the end of the line to pour our coffees.

Minnie pats her little stomach self-consciously. "Not today. But I *know*"—she rolls her eyes—"we need regular catch ups for sure. Were you at the trial yesterday? Holy shit, Lia."

She's changing the subject as we reach our regular table and I tear my eyes off my wellness check of her and her canary-yellow nimpin, Gertie, to find Scythe and Xander already seated at their usual table at the back of the hall. Beak, Yeti, and some others are there too—I almost drop my bamboo knife as I notice the anima sitting in Savage's seat, opposite Scythe.

Everyone remembers Sarah from our first day when Xander had set her hair on fire for sitting in his lap uninvited. But clearly she's back at her usual antics. She leans over the table, her red push-up bra working overtime. She preens, running red nails through her now shoulder length brown hair as glossy pink lips quickly move, talking at a fast pace.

Stacey elbows me hard at the same time Henry gives my cheek a sharp peck.

"Ow!" I squeal.

More than a few animuses turn to stare, including Beak, who frowns at me. Yet another beast I need to avoid, apparently.

But my eyes quickly find that beautiful brunette anima again. A sizzle of energy shoots through the air and I turn to see Savage stalking to his table from behind me, his eyes not on me but on Sarah. He tears into a massive piece of raw ribeye as he passes our table. That sizzle usually happens when he's telepathically talking to someone.

Sarah hastily gets up and saunters to her third-year table, where her friends lean in to whisper at her, no doubt wanting all the goss.

It would be easy to fall in love with Savage, I realise. Way too easy.

"Sorry, Lia," Stacey says quickly, patting my shoulder in apology. "But you were breaking your fork."

I swear softly as I pull out a splinter from my finger and proceed to eat my first croissant with my hands. I can't be showing obvious disdain for other animas approaching Scythe and Xander. The other animuses will start to get suspicious.

Sabrina leans across the table to hiss at Minnie, "We want the deets about Titus."

"Spill, cub," Raquel commands.

"There's not much to say," Minnie sighs. "We've just been reunited, you know?"

As Minnie cuts into her lone grapefruit, the rest of us exchange dark looks.

"What's he like in bed?" Sabrina asks, narrow-eyed as she aggressively cuts her toast and scrambled eggs. "I hope he reciprocates."

Minnie chokes on her coffee and Raquel slaps her on the back.

"He's fine. A bit enthusiastic about group stuff, I guess."

"That's great," Stacey says, although she doesn't sound so sure. "Good start."

"Does he eat you out?" Sabrina presses. "You can tell a lot about a male by how he eats you out."

"Um. Well, he's a good kisser." Minnie's cheeks are progressively turning pink under her brown skin and I just know there are animuses at the neighbouring tables listening in.

"So he *doesn't* eat you out?" Sabrina's fork hangs in mid-air. A bit off scrambled egg falls off it.

"Can we stop with the eating out talk?" Minnie hisses, her voice high. "Titus is... He's..."

"It was love at first sight," I explain to the table, swooping in to save my friend. "They've known each other for a while."

Stacey and Sabrina give me googly eyes, as if to indicate that none of this is good news.

"As l-long as he t-treats you w-well, Min," Raquel says quietly. "That's a-all we want t-to know."

Minnie nods firmly as she cuts into her grapefruit. "I love him."

My tigress is tight-lipped, even through morning group counselling and then cooking class. It makes my chest fill with unease at the way she's answering our questions, but I convince myself she just wants to keep things private.

By the time self-defence class comes around, it's time for my appointment with Lyle, so, reluctantly, I show my appointment card to one of the guards and they escort me to his office.

Georgia, Lyle's perfectly stunning secretary, is sitting at her desk, brushing her long golden hair as I enter the executive floor where all the offices are. My two guards wait for me to step out of the elevator before heading back down. The lioness's eyes tighten as she stares me down, and it incites a strut out of me. She proceeds to look me up and down and so I do the same. My anima and I decided that we didn't like her at first sight.

"Georgia," I say curtly. I can't forget that she was the one who'd fetched me from my dorm the day I was to meet my father.

The top of her pink lip twitches in a soft sneer. "Let's get one thing straight, Miss Aquinas."

My hackles raise.

"Girls like you come in here all the time," she says, rising from her chair. She's wearing a lovely, expensive-looking white blouse and red pencil skirt that hugs her to perfection. The picture of class. "And think they can woo the deputy headmaster with their skimpy, slutty clothes."

This bitch—

"Well Lyle knows better than that. He sees right through you to the nasty little crim you are."

The sudden urge to rip her throat out makes a growl tear out of my throat.

"Don't you *dare*, growl at me," Georgia hisses, planting her hands on her desk and leaning over it.

I catch a whisper of a scent on the breeze, parchment and musk. It calms me a little. Lyle is just behind his office door.

"Well," I say lightly, straightening from what was likely an attack-ready hunch. "You have a pretty bad memory, Miss Georgia. Don't you remember that the last time I was here, I said you can have him? He's an arrogant asshole."

"You don't fool me," she scowls.

I shrug, but my anima is fuming, *seething* inside of me. A lick of my telekinetic power coils around the lioness and a fine line forms between her perfect brows. She's confused about where it's coming from because as an eagle I shouldn't be able to do that. "I don't give a falcon's fuck what you think, Georgia. Pretty sure *Lyle* sees right through your fake ass too."

But it only makes a smirk curve along her lips and she tosses her hair. "Oh, Lyle and I are *well* acquainted with each other."

Oh she did not.

Georgia's throat suddenly looks very tasty and for a moment

I wonder what it would be like to taste her blood and flesh in my mouth. Feel it tearing open—

Oh Goddess no. I need to snap out of this pure feral madness. I take a shuddery breath and step away from her desk, tearing my eyes off her long, slender throat. She mistakes my actions for submission and her smirk widens. She says in a sugary sweet voice, striding toward Lyle's office door. "Mr Pardalia will see you now."

Chapter 21

Lyle

"**L**ook at this." I wave Scythe over to my desk and swivel my monitor towards him.

He comes to stand beside me, and together, we stare at the long list of items Aurelia has purchased from an online store called *Eggplant Emporium: Pleasure for exotic tastes.*

Since I've given Aurelia a stipend, I've been monitoring her spending like a lion monitoring a gazelle. The best way to get a read on a person? Watch their purchases. Before her hibernation, the amount of lingerie and tiny dresses she'd purchased from the student village had me near calling Theresa to berate her for irresponsibility. But I've refrained thus far, not wanting anyone to know I'm watching her as closely as I am.

But this new round of purchases is simply ridiculous.

I scroll down the page as I scan the items for a third time. I scroll again... and again. There are dildos, vibrators, clitoris stimulators and anal plugs of all types, colours and makes. While the unicorn one I could forgive, the very last vibrator? Purchased almost as if it was an afterthought?

It's called "The King's Pride." The silicone is the same gold as a lion's fur, with the base moulded into the shape of a male lion's head, fluffy mane and all.

Heat creeps up my spine. Scythe chuckles softly under his breath.

I sit back in my chair, drumming my fingers against the armrest, staring at my screen. Chains rattle at the base of my consciousness and a low rumble—no, not a rumble, a *purr*—a fucking purr resounds in my head.

"She has a healthy appetite," I remark.

Scythe nods slowly. "She's regina to five alphas," he says pointedly. "She was made that way."

I shake my head because it can't just be that. I also can't help but notice that her order doesn't include any toy cleaner or sanitiser. Purely against my will, I put in an order for two bottles and send an email to *Eggplant Emporium's* customer service to add it to the same parcel.

There's a knock at my door, snapping me out of my bullshit. Georgia opens it to peer through. She's been a little quiet these days, but currently, there is a look of utter distaste on her face. "Miss Aquinas is here, sir." She steps aside.

Scythe straightens.

Aurelia steps through and, rather suddenly, everything in my world narrows down to a pinpoint. I mark every movement as she steps towards my desk. I note every breath; I listen to every heartbeat; I sense everything about her physical and mental form. But something deeply ingrained in me scents the air, *searching*. And finds nothing. Yet again, I can't scent her. Whatever shields she has up courtesy of her Boneweaver powers hides that part of herself from me and it leaves my skin itching. It's missing. That crucial thing is missing, and it sets the predator in me off. Those chains rattle again.

Rabid beasts always have this gleam in their eyes. A sort of glaze that tears them away from this world and into that of their beast. It tells other beasts that this creature is not thinking, only feeling. That this is a creature who is wild.

But when I look into those ocean-blue eyes, I don't see a crazed gleam. I never have. Now, in her human form, there is a keen, but weary intelligence; a tired but necessary alertness. I want to know what's going on behind them. I need to know what her mind is doing; what it's thinking and why.

Those eyes meet mine and it's as if she's displeased by what she sees. They slide to Scythe and narrow in suspicion.

"So you're working together now." Her husky voice reeks of disapproval as she makes her statement.

Neither of us say anything. We just... dare I say it? We fucking take her in.

This might be the same young woman who entered my office a few months ago, defensive and snarky, and yet, she is decidedly not the same.

It's almost as if she is more aware of her body now. More settled into it.

She's chosen clothes as if she didn't want to wear any at all. Her blue mini dress is like a second skin that hugs every supple curve, revealing the golden length of her legs, and to my great dismay, it's obvious she's not wearing undergarments.

Her nipples are pebbled and I tear my gaze back up to her face. There is the golden column of her neck, where I saw the mark that will ruin me. By her Boneweaver magic, she's back to hiding it.

I'm once again reminded that my alleged regina has lived a life of hiding. Hiding her mark. Her scent. Her real self.

Something dark twists its way up the column of my back. Something that whispers, *"We know this. We know this pain. This spirit is our kin."*

"Why am I here, Lyle?" she deadpans, whipping me out of my reverie. "Are you going to hand me over to my executioners again?" She casts a dramatic look around. "Where are the shackles?"

A timely reminder: gone is the lioness I sat with for four weeks. Gone is the quiet beast who laid her mighty head in my lap. Gone is the anima who purred for me and me alone.

I cover my flinch by standing from my desk. But it's Scythe who stalks over to her, his powerful body eating up the space in two heartbeats. He leans down to get close to her face. I don't know if he's trying to intimidate her or if he can't help but get close to her, probably a mixture of both. Aurelia does not back away from him. Instead she sucks in a breath as he speaks in his low rasp.

"I sensed the nimpins under your jacket. You did very well."

He stalks out of my office, leaving Aurelia slack-jawed in his wake.

I didn't detect the nimpins. I had been too focused on the goal. On Mace Naga and his five serpent generals—the full retinue on *my* academy grounds. In *my* territory.

But Aurelia recovers quickly under my steady gaze. "Are we having a walking meeting, or are you going to have me in your office?"

Her attitude slides along my veins like a hot poker. And her choice of words leave a lot to be desired.

"This is not appropriate academy attire," I say tightly, gesturing to her clothing. It's normal for ex-rabids to find clothing irritating and inessential and I should cut her some slack. But I find that I can't.

Aurelia raises her brows and has the audacity to drop her arms so her breasts are fully visible to me. Like she knows *exactly* what's bothering me.

But how much does she know? I need to know how much she remembers. How much... she was affected by her rabid state.

I come around from my desk. "Do you remember anything from your time as a lioness?"

She stiffens and then sighs. "So you know."

She's referring to her being a Boneweaver. While we've moved on four weeks with the knowledge, she's yet to catch up.

"We all know what you are," I reply drolly. "If you'd told us, we would have known it sooner."

"It's always been your style to state the obvious," she retorts. "But would it have changed anything?" Aurelia rubs her eyes, then pinches the bridge of her nose. I'm so aware of her breath and movement that I forget to do either myself. When she looks back at me, her eyes are glimmering. They look like mythical tidepools. Tired tidepools, haloed by dark shadows.

Tired is an understatement. Aurelia is exhausted. I want to order her to sit down, to drink water, to eat properly, to cover her in warm clothes and rub heat into her skin.

I take another step towards her, but it's completely involuntary. There's anger in her eyes, enough that it could even be hate. *Would it have changed anything?*

"There's no point wondering about the past," I say, waving a dismissive hand. "But, Miss Aquinas, what do you remember?"

She walks over to the two opposing armchairs before my bay windows and trails a finger over the back of one. "Miss Aquinas," she mutters darkly. "So that's how it is."

Sit down. I want to fucking say it. *Just sit down before you fall over.*

"What do you remember?" I grit out.

She drops her hand to pin me with that simmering gaze. "Not all that much. I remember you came down. I remember you sat there for a bit. It comes in flashes."

"That's normal," I say calmly, although my heart is racing. "Some of it might come back," I smile, perhaps selfishly so. "Some of it might not."

That her anima and I had a private moment undoubtedly gives me the upper hand.

She casts me a suspicious glance like she knows this, too. "You are, irrefutably, the worst."

"Your anima didn't seem to think so." It's out of my mouth on instinct and I curse myself for it.

"Apparently, my anima does not recognise *logic*," she snaps. "Doesn't recognise that you tried to have me *killed* a few short weeks ago."

The sharp pain in my chest and her attempt at dominance forces my hand. I'm in front of her in a flash, leaning down into her face. "I did *not* try to have you killed, Aurelia. My hands were tied." She flinches and I master myself, straightening with a long breath. I did for Aurelia what I've done for countless other students. Gone with them to court, advocated for them using my reports. Within the confines of the law, I could have done no more for her. So then, why did I have the distinct feeling that I was grasping at air? "But you thought that your father did not want you dead," I point out.

This close, I can see every long, dark eyelash framing her eyes and I find I can't look away. Suddenly she's panting, clearly furious. "*Not* that you believed me at any point."

I might not have believed her, but I remembered all of what she said. Every moment of our discussions was burned into my memory. But does *she?* Does she remember any of it like I'm cursed to?

I stare at her. And she stares back.

Aurelia is still breathing hard and her pupils are dilated. And then she does the most heinous thing she could have done in my presence.

She licks her lips.

Aurelia is aroused by me. My closeness affects her.

That realisation draws me into her like gravity. And as I sway towards her, my entire world tilts on its axis. Wetness glistens on her bottom lip, caught by the morning sunlight. I'm suddenly caught in the shape of her lips. The pale pink colour, the way they are equally plump. Ripe, even. Sweet.

Holy Mother. Not now. Not ever.

The amount of willpower it's going to take to step away from her is unthinkable. Because I don't want to. Because I must.

"Easy, Lyle." A familiar rasp swims into my head on a current of pure lethal awareness. *"Think of something unpleasant."*

"Think of worms squirming in meat." A voice like the inside of a volcano tunnels into my mind. *"Think of eating them. Works every time for me."*

What the hell?

"Is Lyle in the group chat now?" Savage grumbles. *"Fucking hell, now there'll be no fun at all."*

"You're wrong," Xander chuckles. *"Shit just got a whole lot more interesting."*

This can't be happening.

"Well, get used to it," Savage says reluctantly, *"brother."* A mental image of one of the school classrooms comes into my mind's eye, followed by Savage's hand in his lap, giving me the finger. *"Yeah, we can do that too."*

Scythe laughs. And it was the second most unsettling thing to happen inside my head.

As Aurelia narrows her eyes at me, my temper rises again, hot and hard at fate's continual defiance of what the fuck I want. "You might not be heir to the Serpent Court anymore," I say, "but you still have the attitude of a princess."

She hisses, "By the Goddess, I hate you."

The need to punish her for those words makes me clench my fists. Instead, I smirk at the memory that flashes through my mind. Her lioness' head nuzzling against my thigh. Her anima *loves* me.

"What?" she snaps, eyes flashing again.

The light in them is good. Anything is better than the dull, dark awareness of the past four weeks.

"Watch your tone," I say, even as a thrill runs through me.

Eyes narrow and her voice is deep with disgust, never for a moment backing down. "If I'd told you what I was, you would have treated me the same way as every other time I told you the truth. With dismissal." She points at the ground to mark her point. "With contempt. With... idiocy! You're terrible at your job."

I blink down at her face, defiantly upturned to mine. Henry is huddled against her neck, so I know her emotions are running rampant.

Heat suffuses my chest. I'm forced to lower my voice to the soft tone I used to use with her anima. "You don't know that."

But it has the opposite effect of what I intended.

"Do you know what, Lyle?" she hisses with so much venom I just stare. "Fuck you, and fuck your school, your rules, and everything. I'm going to make you regret the day you *ever* came after me."

With that, she storms out. I can feel her power crackling like a sheet of living lightning in her wake.

Relief pours through me. And it's a relief of multiple parts. I run my hand through my hair, pulling it out of its ponytail as I do.

I sit back down at my desk and shake my mouse to wake up the screen. Aurelia's long list of purchases stare back at me boldly.

It shouldn't satisfy me so much that here is another thing she's not aware that I know. But there is a lot more I need to know about her. And by the gods, I will find out everything there is hidden in the mind and body of Aurelia Boneweaver.

Chapter 22

Aurelia

Damn it. Fucking damn it.

With heat scorching my insides, I grab Henry from my shoulder as I storm back to the elevator. I breathe heavily as it dings back open, and luckily, neither Lyle nor Georgia come after me.

I completely lost it in front of that arrogant, awful, asshole lion. My arousal almost took over, and when I shoved it back down, it just made me angry. Is there such a thing as a lust rage? He probably thinks I'm even more pathetic now. And the fact that he had the nerve to be smug about me not remembering all he said to me in my *own* nest?

And Scythe.

I sensed the nimpins under your jacket. You did well.

You did well?!

He'd known I was up to something. And even when I'd released the nimpins, he'd just stood there and cocked his head like he was challenging me.

There is a strange and awful satisfaction unfurling in my chest at his final words.

Fucker. Absolute fucker! I'd been on death's door and he'd wanted to *see* what I would do?

You did well?

"Urgh! These men!"

Henry squeaks in agreement as we make our way back to the dining hall. I'm not going to return to class, not in this state. I'm too riled up. Waiting in the dining hall for lunch seems like the best option for me, so I can take time to cool down.

There is an academy guard following me, one of the tall, imposing animuses, who dresses from top to toe in black. I feel safe as I make my way through the twisty hallways that lead through the central building of the academy.

When I enter the mostly empty dining hall, there are a couple of animuses sitting at a table in the furthest right-hand corner of the hall. They probably have a free period and are drinking coffee. Seems like a great idea to me, only I'm too twitchy for caffeine.

I barely spare them a glance as I head to the drinks section of the buffet. There's a new gargoyle sitting there, who only allows the hot chocolate to be served out of his mouth. It's kind of gross, but the academy hot chocolate is amazingly decadent, so I simply can't pass it up. Especially not right now.

"One cup, please," I say to Gary, positioning a fresh mug under his large, hanging jowls.

He leans over and opens his mouth. Delicious, velvety chocolate mixture jets out of him until my mug is full.

I dollop a healthy amount of whipped cream on top and turn to take a seat.

That's when I check out the animuses sitting in the corner and realise too late that it's the table allocated to the serpents. I halt halfway to my usual anima table as a face that has haunted my nightmares for the past four years turns to look at me.

The stained-glass windows he sits under cast multicoloured

facets across the table, his thin arms and face making it feel like I'm wading through the current of a nightmare.

I drop my mug. Henry shrieks but I barely hear him or the crash of the ceramic shattering on the floorboards.

The young man is tall and lean, milky-skinned, with golden brown hair tinged red by the windows. There are deep blue bags under his eyes, hollowing out what was once a handsome face. A face that once smiled sweetly at me as I worked in Aunt Charlotte's shop. A face with a mouth I'd kissed for months.

A face I last saw strapped to a metal table in the middle of my father's throne hall. He always used it for punishments.

And executions.

There is a six-digit number tattooed on his right cheekbone. A venom identification number. It's something my father does to the most venomous snakes of our court. As a warning that their power doesn't lie in brute strength, but something far more sinister. And the venom of the Common Krait is one of the most lethal in the world.

"Theo," I whisper.

His irises snap into narrow slits, his lids widening into feral aggression. His tongue slips out to taste the air, and it's thin and forked.

Shit. This serpent is *more* than feral.

I know it's not him. I watched my sweetheart, Theo Krait, die right in front of me, thrashing and screaming as my father's venom burned through his veins in a torturous, gruesome death. This boy is his brother, by the different numbers on his face, I know for sure.

"*T-Thomas* Krait?"

They look so similar. I rub my arms as his nostrils flare, scenting me. He definitely wasn't here at the start of the school semester. I would have noticed him right away.

I swallow through a dry throat and take a few tentative steps forward. "Did you just arrive at the school?"

One of the other serpents hiss in warning and I halt a few metres away from their table. They've all gone still, turning hateful gazes towards me.

"Fuck off, Aquinas," one of the others, a python, drawls. "You're not wanted here. And he doesn't want to speak to you." He spits on the floor.

Spitting is gross on a good day, but for a serpent to do it is worse than open dismissal. It's an open threat. Some of these guys have venom in their fangs by the markings on their cheeks, but it's a punishable offence to use venom-loaded bites in this school.

"I'm sorry," I manage to choke out.

Thomas hasn't looked away from me, hasn't moved at all.

"I'm so sorry." I whirl around and leave through the open front doors, holding back a sob as old memory flashes through my mind.

My uncle brought Theo's execution up at my trial to discredit me. Insinuating that I gave my virginity to him knowing he'd be killed for it. Insinuating that I was a malevolent person capable of being selfish like that.

Scrape. Scrape. Scrape.

Pain explodes across my abdomen and I gasp as my shields are breached by the forces I've been trying so hard to keep out. My horror at seeing Thomas must have created a weakness in my protections.

With one hand across my stomach, I stumble back to my dorm. Christine asks me what's wrong from above the door but I don't reply, swiping my card and managing a wheezing climb up to the third floor. I don't even make it to my bed, instead collapsing in a heap on the floor next to it.

Eugene flaps over to me in alarm. He and Henry cluck in question but I wave off their fussing, pulling my tank top up to peer down at my stomach.

When I see it, I shout out, half in anger, half in terror.

The sight is an awful one. Four deep gouges in the shape of twin fang marks run diagonally across my abdomen from right rib down to left hip bone. And they're not red with blood like Minnie's were.

They're black with venom that necrotises the skin.

Refusing to panic, I squeeze my eyes shut, focusing on sending my healing power into the wounds, mending muscle tissue, tendons and skin. But it depletes my power so much that I'm panting and drenched with sweat in minutes. Pain pummels my body and I kick my legs out to try and dispel some of it. To try and contain the explosive, violent burning.

By the skin of my teeth, I manage to seal the wounds off so that the gouges won't bleed, but the nasty black marks remain behind, still scorching like acid.

The sob that escapes my mouth is both unwanted and unavoidable. I smother my cries, but it only leads to a full-blown meltdown.

I curse my father. I curse the entire Serpent Court. I never asked to be different. I never asked to be born this way. I'm being punished for something I can't control and it's unfair and stupid and fucked up that I have to run from my mates and have to fight so hard just to *live*. It's unfair that my mates hate me for having to run from them. It's unfair that they tried to kill me. It's unfair that Theo died. It's unfair that my father is the worst possible creature in existence.

My chest heaves, trying to draw in air as the tears drip down my cheeks. As quietly as I can, I cry into my palms, squeezing my eyes shut against the mental images plaguing me. Of Theo lying on my father's metal table, the light leaving his pretty brown eyes. Of Lyle, Scythe and Xander leading me to my father.

My father; the worst of all. Looming over me in the loading bay of the medical centre, black shackles ready to claim me. Ready to trap me forever.

I can't do this. Any of it. It's pressing on me so tightly that I can't breathe, can't think as death looms over me. Death, and a breeding pen.

Boneweaver female. 20 years old. Unbred. Unmated. Offers over ten million.

That malevolent male voice I heard when I escaped from my dad a month ago told me my asking price was ten million dollars. I don't feel like I'm worth anything right now. I feel like I'm worth fuck all.

Theresa was right. It's finally hitting me. It took its fucking time.

My anima surges forward to protect me and I allow it because I can't think of anything else to do to fix this. I drop to all fours as my mouth elongates to a muzzle. My vision grows sharper and my fingers and toes flex into paws.

It's a fresh release that I revel in. A release that bubbles up my abdomen, rockets up my chest and my throat—

I tilt my head up, take a deep breath, and howl up to the ceiling.

Chapter 23

Savage

I'm sitting in group counselling, bored out of my fucking mind and anxiously waiting for Lia's return from her meeting with Lyle. I keep checking my phone, but there are no notifications from the fairy emoji that I've assigned to my regina.

"Stop shaking your leg, it's fucking annoying." Xander's voice is snide in my head.

I ignore him.

The howl hits my ears like an axe to the skull.

It's grieving, it's raw.

It's the equivalent of a canine scream.

The other wolves look up, frowning. They're not familiar with this voice because it's a new one.

But it pulls on that part of me that has always been wild and unhinged. My wolf form bursts through my skin, completely out of my control.

Someone screams, but I just shove through the circle of chairs between Beak and another bird and charge out of the room.

Human feet scramble behind me and I know Minnie is running too.

"*Savage.*" Scythe's voice in my head is a warning.

"*Let him go,*" Xander drawls. "*She's probably just lost a makeup brush or something.*"

Promising that I'm going to tear him up when I return, I bound through the hallways, stopping only to unlatch a door with my teeth and rush outside and straight to the anima dorm.

The door is closed and I don't have a swipe card to get in. I growl up at Christine to let me in.

"Nuh-uh!" she calls down. "Not today, Satan!"

I'm too violent to return to my human form to climb up like I did last night. Cracking my neck on both sides, I prepare to charge through the glass, backing up a couple of steps. It's non-smashable glass so it might crack my skull, but I don't fucking care right now.

But Minnie is suddenly next to me, panting loudly, and I snap at her, telling her to hurry up. Her eyes are wide as she yanks off her lanyard and hurtles right at the door. Smashing her ID card at the sensor, she then yanks on the door.

But it doesn't click open. The door remains shut.

"Nope, he'll come right in with you," Christine pipes.

For Lia. For Lia I can concentrate.

Taking a deep breath, I picture my regina and her magnificent blue eyes. The way she felt to hold last night. Soft and warm and all mine.

I shift back into human form and roar up at Christine, "Let me in you stone cunt!"

"Nope!" she shouts back just as loud.

Minnie swears and shakes her little fist up at the gargoyle. "Come on, Christine!"

Ignoring the both of them, I leap up like I did last night, ready to climb up to her room.

Except, where yesterday my fingers easily gripped the

bottom of the first-floor ledge, today, my fingers hit an invisible barrier of slippery magic. I fall back to the ground in a heap. A sheet of magic protects the column of balconies all the way up to the third floor.

I jump back up to my feet and immediately see that though Christine has protected my climbing path, she's left *herself* open.

"I'm going to tear your head off this building!" I roar, and without waiting for a reply, I charge at the door, leaping up at the last minute and scrambling up until I get my fingers around the upper ledge. I haul myself up and straddle Christine from behind, grabbing her head in both hands and pulling with all my might.

"Argh!" Christine screams. "Help!"

"Let me in or you're dead!" I cry.

The stone groans and I hear a distant crack.

"Oh my God!" shrieks Minnie.

Xander strolls up, joint in his mouth. "Oh no you don't," he growls, before assuming a baseball pitching position, turning on his side, raising his hands and one knee. A fire ball appears in his hands, glowing a mad orange-red, and he piffs it right at me.

I have no choice but to leap off the gargoyle, right back for the ground, where I land, rolling. I leap to my feet yet again, shoving at Xander, who slugs me right in the nose.

There's a crack inside my face.

"*Control yourself,*" he snarls.

"I want my regina!" I roar, grabbing my nose and pushing it straight. "Lia is hurting."

I'm vaguely aware of Minnie bashing her ID card against the sensor, but Christine is wailing and swearing, not letting her in.

"Now you've done it!" Minnie shouts, stomping over to me and pushing me hard in the chest. I barely move, but Xander and I both peer down at her tiny, round form in surprise. "You've fucked up the door, Savage!" she cries.

Xander lets out a low laugh. "Then use your little Tigger powers and throw something at the glass."

She rolls her eyes. "I'll get in trouble," she says, as if he's an idiot. "*You're* the dragon, here. Command her to open."

"She won't listen to me," he says. "That gargoyle is loyal to—"

"To me."

We all turn around to find Lyle stalking towards us with death in his eyes.

Chapter 24

Aurelia

I'm curled up tightly against the base of my bed in wolf form, Henry chirping slowly to give me a count for my breaths and Eugene nestled by my side. My anima wants to take control again, but I deny her, focusing on Henry's little comforting rhythm.

Within minutes, my wolf hearing picks up a commotion outside and a very audible Savage. Groaning to my feet, I lope my way over to the double balcony doors. Since Savage came in last night, the door is unlocked, but I don't open it up. I manage to nuzzle the lace curtain aside and peer out.

Xander and Savage are in each other's faces and I can just manage to see a head of bouncing pink curls next to a tall blonde one, so I know Minnie and Lyle are there too. Christine is wailing. From the sound of it, I think she's barred entry to the dorm. Silently, I thank her for the extra time. I don't know what possessed me to howl that loud, calling everyone here, but I feel better for having done it. Almost like I'd been bottling up my emotions and a pressure valve opened up to physically get it out of my system. My stomach still burns, and I just need a bit of time to pull my shit back together.

A small click sounds to my right and I whirl around.

On the other side of my bed is my chest of drawers and wardrobe. To the right of those is the bathroom door and to the left of it *used* to be an empty wall.

Now? A black mahogany door stands wide open, a gilded door frame and handle sparkling in the sunlight filtering from the windows. Beyond the door lies a set of stone stairs, ominously leading upwards into the shadows.

Upwards.

Another dragon-trick door has been opened.

My wolf's mouth drops open and Henry and Eugene give an excited squeak and cluck, respectively, both immediately zipping over to the doorway and inspecting the space. It's almost exactly the same as the set of stairs that lead down to my secret cavern.

But Xander's dragon didn't open this door for me.

Is the school trying to tell me something? An open door is about as clear a message as it can get.

I shift back into human form and look down in dismay at my now shredded dress. Quickly tugging on a simple thin purple cotton sundress with spaghetti straps and a soft, barely there thong gifted to me by Sabrina, I warily step up to the door. There's no magic fizzing around it that I can sense. Nothing like Xander's dragon trap that locked me in their room when I snuck in there that first time.

I take a tentative step into the cool shadows and take a sniff. It's only dust that I smell.

Henry sneezes and, alarmed, returns to land on my shoulder.

"It's alright," I say soothingly, although I'm the one with the shot nerves. Adrenaline still pumps through me, making me shaky, and that burn along my abdomen is at the edges of all things. "Clearly we're being told to go up. It's gotta be safe, right?"

There are dragon-shaped sconces on either side of the

passage, ones with their wings spread wide as if they're mid-soar, and as I step past them, purple flames magically sputter to life.

On bare feet, I pad silently up the steps, testing each stair in case there are unexpected tricks. This place is old, as is the magic, and even though I'm getting a distinctly *helpful* vibe from all of this, you can never be sure with the mythic orders.

Even my own order is still mysterious to me. My mother never got to teach me anything about it other than the use of my shields. And my father? Fat chance of him revealing anything he knew. To him, knowledge is power and no matter how hard I researched about my own kind, I was never able to come up with anything useful. I even felt guilty looking anything up in case it got noticed and reported back to my father. In the dead of night I would practise shifting into small creatures. The one thing I did figure out, was that I had to touch an animal in order to turn into it. It was lucky that in primary school we'd had a visiting petting zoo and I'd gotten to pet a range of animals like alpacas, mice and even a baby saltwater crocodile.

But now I'm here at the Academy... my options for researching are more open than before. I have a range of friends for one and access to the library for another.

The black stone staircase winds in a tight spiral, and I take each step with one hand lightly tracing the rough surface of the wall. The purple fire makes for a sort of eerie ascent, but I'm not bothered by it. If anything, it suits my mood. Eugene silently follows along, his little feet making scratching noises as he dutifully watches my every move.

A part of me is happy for this distraction. With this new development, I can focus my mind on the present. On being here, with the stone under me, and who knows what above me. I don't have to think of the past or the fuck up of my life *or* that acidic pain across my stomach.

My thighs burn, but just as I'm wondering if I should take a rest, we come to a small landing terminated by a medieval style circular door of black painted wood. A cast-iron ring in the mouth of a dragon's head serves as a door handle.

"Fancy," I whisper to my side-kicks. "But what's on the other side?"

The handle is ice cold under my soft touch. Like it hasn't seen a human hand in decades. Blowing out a steady breath, I tug on it.

It opens silently and smoothly on its hinge, so the gasp I let slip sounds loud in comparison.

To my surprise, there is no dark dragon's tower, complete with a roaring fireplace and a crusty old wizard tinkering away in the corner.

Instead, we come out to a small, clean, modern apartment. I wander out, straining my ears for sounds of movement—human, beast or otherwise.

But the apartment is silent.

As Eugene and I step further into the living space, I turn around to see that the secret door forms the mantel-piece of a black fireplace. It's a gothic hearth with an arch of black stone that mirrors the circular shape of the door. Black leather couches surround a blood red carpet that makes for a sophisticated but cosy sitting area. I imagine it would be super comforting to sit here in the evening, with the fire crackling and a good book in hand. Behind the couches is a formal, black-painted wood dining table that can seat six in the high-backed, ornately carved black chairs.

It sends a shiver down my spine.

Six, my anima says.

Six makes us whole.

Shoving that thought aside, my eyes move past to the small kitchenette with its black opalescent marble countertop and shiny steel grey electric appliances.

There are floor-to-ceiling windows that make up the entire

left-hand side wall. I pad up to them and push aside the sheer curtains to find the sports ground at the front of the school.

Can this be the residence of the fabled phoenix headmistress my animas have told me about? I only have a memory of red hair and the smell of power from when she'd come to see me on my first day down there.

But this doesn't seem like the residence of a lady, and there is something distinctly familiar in the way even the kitchen is organised with a meticulous, almost obsessive hand.

I check the sink. Not a dish or glass in sight, nor a droplet of water. The dish drainer holds a single black mug.

And on the wall opposite the windows sits a massive printed canvas. But it's not artwork, it's a blown up photograph. I step up to the black white landscape, depicting a mountain canyon taken from a great height. Walking proud, but alone through the towering mountains, like the last of his kind, is a dark male lion.

Sudden emotion pours into my chest. At how lonely it is, the path he walks. The way the camera is angled so we can see the path that he'd walked, but nothing of what lies ahead.

Goosebumps erupt all over my body.

I wonder where he's been, that proud lion. Where his path led him after the photo was taken.

Shaking myself out of a sudden pensive stupor, I tear my eyes away and consider the rest of the apartment with new eyes.

With excitement bubbling up in my chest, I pad down the maroon rug leading past the kitchen and find a massive bedroom. It's clean and simple. A king bed lies in the centre—all black sheets and pillows—pristinely made with corners and folds of military style precision. A wardrobe leads off to my left and I tip-toe inside and flick on the light switch.

The fresh and heady scent of paper and leather hits me before the sight does.

Suits. Suits of black, grey and navy-blue line the entire left-hand side, grouped by colour. White, black and blue shirts line the other side. There's a rack of perfectly polished shoes and a set of drawers slides smoothly open to reveal neat rows of ties, gold cufflinks and watches.

Giddiness tingles down my spine as I receive sudden, delightful confirmation of my suspicions.

I'm inside Lyle's apartment. His *private* space.

It should feel invasive to be in here. Intrusive, even. Instead, I feel a smug sense of satisfaction that I'm in his secret dwelling and he doesn't know it. I now know for sure the school is on my side, because Christine is clearly keeping him occupied with trying to get into the dorm so that I can get in here to snoop.

I'm going to kiss her when I see her next.

"Thank you," I say out loud, running my fingers along the row of the suits. "This is great. But now..."

There are butterflies in my tummy and a smirk on my face. This is forbidden. This is *wonderful.*

Snooping seems necessary. It's one tiny revenge in the much larger-scale revenge I need to exact on Lyle for handing me over to my father so easily, despite knowing about me being his regina.

I practically skip out of the wardrobe, making Henry jostle on my shoulder. It's then that I notice Eugene hasn't followed us. Frowning, I retrace my steps back outside the bedroom and find Eugene standing stiff by the fireplace door. It's almost like he doesn't want to come in. No doubt some innate instinct telling him that this is the domain of a territorial predator. "Go stand guard by Eugene," I say to Henry. "You two make a sound if someone comes in, I need to concentrate."

Henry zips off with an affirmative chirp.

Heart pounding, I return to the bedroom. Scanning the space, I note the two matte black side tables. I hurry to the closest set and yank the top drawer open, keen to learn Lyle's secrets, because so far, his apartment is just as stuck up as him.

The blue rectangular box hits my eyes like a sledgehammer. I grab it up and open it to count the foil packets. It's mostly full.

Meaning some of them have been used.

Fire lights up my veins. Heat surges through my stomach.

Asshole. Fucking asshole prick.

There is a box of tissues in there as well as a small blue tube of lip balm. I hold each item up to my nose and sniff them suspiciously, but I only sense Lyle's scent. There are a couple of books too, all crime non-fiction, including a memoir by a human gangland crime boss. I snort, it was definitely something Lyle would be into.

In the second drawer, on a bed of purple silk, is a heavy navy blue box that looks very special. On the top it's labelled with gold letters: "Scent Safe Technology TM." My eyebrows shoot up as I examine the tiny lock that secures it. But when I test the lid, I find it unlocked. Excitement bubbles within me. What is Lyle hiding in here? Scent Safe boxes are super expensive, and needing to use one only means a great precious thing must need hiding. I ease open the lid, holding my breath for the revelation.

What I find in there has me choking on my own saliva.

I recognise my underwear instantly. Six pairs of cheap pink, purple, and yellow bikini briefs I'd packed into my bag when I ran away from home. The same undies Savage stole right from my dorm. It was the sort of thing a territorial, dominant animus couldn't help but do to a protesting regina. I told Lyle about it, embarrassed that I needed early access to the student village to buy underwear and then... I'd heard nothing more about it from him.

And yet here they are, each neatly folded and stacked, in a special box in his bedside table. He clearly confiscated them from Savage. But then why not give them back to me as per the rules he so loved?

The possible reason has me flushing. Has my stomach

clenching. I close the box, set it down on the bedside table and cross my arms, staring at it.

Everything I know about Lyle will now have to be re-evaluated.

He's keeping my knickers as if they're talismans. Coveting them.

My anima roils alongside me, irritated and restless. His scent that coats this place fills my nose, my head, my body.

My intense attraction to him from the first time I met him can now be explained. At the time, I just thought I was attracted to him in the same way that *everyone* is attracted to Lyle Pardalia, the dangerous, dominant beast in a suit.

But now it's different.

And he's keeping my underwear like it's precious.

Something wild takes me over and I yank open the top drawer again, pull out the box of condoms and storm into his bathroom behind me. I toss it into his rubbish bin, glaring suspiciously at his shower as I do. It's all shiny black tile, and lining the shower recess are bottles of high-end brands of shampoo and conditioner marketed towards male lions. There's also body wash, soap, and nothing else. Nothing to suggest a woman has been here.

I feel marginally better.

But it's not enough. With my heart pounding unevenly, I slowly sit on his bed. The exhale I let out is more of a sigh and I try to tell my horny anima to calm down.

But it's too much to be here in his personal space where there is only his scent and his sheets and his pillows.

The need to feel them against my skin overwhelms me. The need to play a little with him overwhelms me.

Before I know it, I'm lying on his bed with my fingers brushing my pussy over my thong.

His fresh parchment and sunlight scent is even stronger now that my nose is closer to this pillow. I imagine Lyle making his bed every morning with the flair of his signature male arrogance. This morning in his office, those amber eyes had assessingly flicked down my body and I'd enjoyed every second of being observed so closely by him. I suddenly crave more of that. More of his bold looks, however cursory or disapproving, more of that snarky, irritated voice directed at *me*.

Even when he's filled with anger, I now know what's under it all. This whole time he's been fighting this just as much as I have. He wants to touch me. That's evident in how much he pointedly *avoids* touching me.

Eventually, he'll have to give in.

I imagine those huge lion's hands trailing over my body, that mouth, following with kisses, sucking and licking every part of me like he can't help it...

It takes all of sixty seconds for me to come—enveloped in Lyle's heady, delicious scent.

I gasp, my back arching under an orgasm that brings moisture to the corners of my eyes... and all over my thong. Panting in the wake of the fact I just came in Lyle's bed, rather illegally, I stare at the chandelier hanging from the ceiling, wondering at his reaction when he gets into bed tonight.

I extract myself from his bed and, with a smirk, take off my underwear. I leave it on top of the scent safe box and just to annoy him further, artfully arrange it so it looks like I've carelessly dumped it there. A quick hunt through his kitchen drawers and I've written a note in messy cursive:

Another one for your collection
xoxo

I smack it right on top of my underwear. He'll see it as soon as he walks into his room tonight. Take *that*, deputy headmaster.

As I stalk back outside to where Henry is perched on

Eugene's back, waiting for me, I'm still irritated and wired. Me, coming by myself, will never be enough. Now that I've been here, seen Lyle's things, come on his bed, it's going to be forever etched at the back of my mind. How, in another world, this space would rightfully be mine. That my place is in his bed. At his dining table. Preferably being fed by him as was a regina's right.

And the sight of my underwear kept in his special drawer has permanently altered something in my mind.

Did he actually think he would get away with that?

* * *

Upon shutting the new door in my room, it seals itself seamlessly shut, blending back into the wall like it was never there. The only thing that's left is a tiny metal dragon head that, once touched, lets me open the door back up. You can't see it from the entry to our room, so the others will be none the wiser.

I now have private access to Lyle's apartment.

Grinning like the Cheshire Cat, I peer through my window in time to hear Christine say, "Off you go then, boss!"

Bless that gargoyle.

I suddenly feel quite well. Rather happy, even.

Lyle's blonde head disappears through the dorm doors and everyone else stays put, clearly having been instructed to stay outside. Savage stalks up and down the same patch of grass, obviously irritated. I rush into my bathroom and wash my hands. "Can't believe you shut down the entire dorm for that," I say to the school. "But I'm bloody grateful right now."

I'm stepping out of the bathroom by the time Lyle steps into my room—without knocking, I might add.

I suddenly realise that this is the first time he's been in *my* room as well. A day for firsts, apparently.

The boss lion completely dwarfs the doorway as he stands there, staring at me with two tiny lines appearing between his dark blonde brows. His angelic face is pale and tight, his mouth pressed into a thin, hard line. My breath catches as I stare at him in return.

Goddess, he's so perfect in that navy blue suit and the way it hugs his broad shoulders and tapers down to those hips. His tailor needs a raise. But what I would give to see him cast it off and give in to the urges I now know are in there.

His gaze flicks quickly down to assess my body before glancing about the room. I enjoy that cursory look so much that I sigh and casually lean against the doorframe next to me.

Then his nostrils flare, and I calmly watch as his pupils dilate.

Yup, he still smells my arousal. I demurely fold my hands behind my back, knowing perfectly well that the movement pushes my braless tits out. His eyes slide to Eugene perched at the end of my bed.

The bird squarks a sombre greeting.

Lyle's eyes slide back to me. "Are you well, Miss Aquinas?" he asks tightly.

So much restraint, Lyle, I want to say. *Let go a little. Show me more of what I just saw in your room.*

Those clenched fists by his sides are giving him away, and I wonder if I should tell him I'm not buying any of his noble teacher act. Not anymore.

My voice is blessedly light as I purr. "Oh, I'm quite well, Mr. Pardalia." I can't keep the grin off my face and he regards me with justified suspicion. "Thank you for asking."

There's a moment of silence, like he's waiting for me to say more. I allow the space between us to become taut and heated as I just gaze into his amber eyes, thinking about those condoms.

"Savage wants to see you," he says.

"Tell him I'll see him tomorrow." I smile sweetly. "That's an order from his regina."

He stares at me with what looks like a *"don't test me, Miss*

Aquinas" warning look before he stalks back out, shoulders tight and his gait oh-so-controlled. I restrain myself from following him and throwing myself into his arms. He probably wouldn't even catch me and I'd be left to slide down to his legs, fully embarrassing myself.

After a minute, Minnie thunders in, throwing me from my musings. She fusses over me like a mother cat, but Gertie, Eugene and Henry calm her down. I don't tell her about the door or about the incident on my stomach. She clearly has her secrets about Titus, so I take that as permission for me to keep my secret about the door.

My little secret is to be between me and the school. And I really don't want to worry her about the attack. As long as I keep my cool, I won't have to worry about any breaches. I'm in such a good mood that I'm not even upset when Minnie prances off to spend the night with Titus.

Chapter 25

Lyle

Ten years ago

One spring evening when I was seventeen, Skye Ulman is bringing me and my siblings our nightly teacup of Milo when she whispers to me, "Dad got a tip-off from PETA. The animal rights group. I've never seen him so furious! They're going to make us hand over all the lions. Even the cubs."

Happiness whirls through me like a carnival carousel. The thought of my siblings and my parents living a normal life in a house, with normal bedrooms, where we can walk around freely? Just like the Ulman's? Only in my wildest dreams did I think that was possible. No cattle prods. No cages. No stupid shows.

I press the "when" button, followed by the "question mark" button.

"They're coming back in two weeks to give us time to close up," she scoffs, strawberry blond plaits swaying. "Like Dad is going to give up his *life's* work? Like any of us are? They're fucking stupid. All of 'em."

I press the "what" button, then "now" and then "question mark". The electronic voice forms the sentence and I hold my breath.

She smiles sadly at me, and for some reason it makes me uneasy. "I'm not allowed to talk about it outside the house. But Dad says we'll be set for life with the amount of money it'll bring. It's gonna be, like, *millions*. So I can go to uni and be a scientist just like my parents. But yeah. I'll miss ya." She scratches me behind the ear, just where my almost-adult mane grows, puts her bush hat on and scurries back toward her house. I press my head against the cool bars off the cage and listen to the crickets chirp their nightly song. For the first time in years, a little spark of hope lights up my chest.

* * *

Seven days later, men and women arrive at the park. They speak with different accents. They bring wooden crates that smell like new metal. Skye comes to see me.

"I wanted to give you this." She opens her fist to reveal a pile of the jelly babies I love but get so infrequently, and I eagerly lap them up from her hand. She takes a deep breath. "Bye, Lyle. I'll really miss you. But this is the way it has to be."

We were leaving. Finally leaving this place. The PETA people must be on the other side, coming to save us. One of my litter-sisters comes up to rub her face against mine. She's excited too. I nuzzle her back before the sliding door at the side of our cage opens up. Eagerly, everyone grabs their favourite toys. Mine is a blue-painted wooden carved angel that I snatch up with my jaws. I charge through the open door, my siblings right on my tail.

When I reach the end of the tunnel, the shiny bars are down on this side, locking me in. It's newly built from the fresh, metallic smell and the new silver shine. Outside, there is no cage. It's out in the open. My heart leaps in my chest. This is it. Freedom.

Outside, metal glints in the sunlight and I turn to see another tunnel with other lions waiting to exit. My mother stands on the other side, staring at me with wide, alert eyes. Behind her, I can make out my two fathers and my second mum.

Our parents are here with us. I'm shocked for a moment because we've never even been allowed to share a cage with our mother before. My heart thuds in my chest. This is amazing. We'll all be together for the first time.

Heavy engines sound in the distance, and I know they're the open safari trucks Ulman likes to use to transport guests around the sanctuary. All four of them appear. Ulman drives one, Mrs. Ulman drives another, and Skye and her brother drive the other two. They're full of passengers.

Passengers who hold rifles.

The scent of human excitement is thick in the air. Are they going to dart us to move us to our new home? If so, why did they put us out in the open?

Ulman is smirking, his ruddy red beard twitching. He's really happy with himself for some reason and it makes my skin crawl. I strain my ears to hear what they're chattering about.

"Will we get to keep their pelts?" one human female asks.

"Sure, but it'll be extra," Ulman replies.

My heart becomes a hammer against my ribs.

There are excited murmurs from the humans.

My breath catches in my throat and I paw uncertainly at the tunnel's exit. I suddenly don't want to leave.

"On my mark!" Ulman shouts. "Now!" He fires a shot into the air.

The long walls of two tunnels fall outward, slamming into the dust. We're out. We're free. But where are we supposed to go?

I turn to look at my mother, confused. There is nothing between us but open air. I want to run to her, but—

She shifts.

And it's the first time in my life I see her in her human form.

She is so beautiful it makes my heart hurt. Wild blonde hair, long down to her waist, rich brown eyes, and a face of wild beauty. But it is contorted in fear. In outrage.

The first human word I ever hear her utter comes out of her mouth in a scream. "Run!"

Shots are fired. Many of them. The sound vibrates the very air. My mother falls to the ground, bullet holes appearing in her abdomen. Her chest. My head whips around. It's Ulman who has the smoking rifle in hand, his black eyes filled with anger. The humans in the jeeps are screaming.

It hits me then. He would rather us dead than free.

"Shoot!" Mrs. Ulman cries.

My litter-mates flee in all directions, led by instinct. Shots are fired but I stay still. A heavy thud sounds from behind me. One of my brothers snarls before another shot cuts him off midway.

And then I'm screaming and roaring and all I know is a terrible, violent rage that burns through my marrow and sets my soul on fire.

Everything turns black. And I know I'm alive and I know I'm conscious, but something is caging me where it is deep and dark. There are faint screams. My body is moving, but it does not feel like mine. And yet I *know* it is mine.

The faint smell of guns being fired tingles in my nose. There is a taste in my mouth. Something burns. All I can do is wait as a power that is bigger than me, stronger than me, holds me tight in its grasp.

* * *

Blood. There's so much blood. It's on my human hands, lining my human palms, and caked under my human fingernails. My naked body is sticky with it, the hot, dry air of the arid desert congealing it onto my skin. The metallic tang of it fills my nose. But it's not just blood that I sense.

I rub at my eyes, trying to understand. Trying to clear the fog that engulfs my brain. The four jeeps are scattered around in the distance, as if their owners left them in a hurry.

But there is blood splashed on the side of the vehicles as well. I look back down. Chunks of flesh lie about me. Like a giant tore through humans and only left their parts behind.

Terror chokes me as my vision clears and I understand what I am seeing.

I'm standing amongst bodies. Bodies that lie still and silent. Lions with bullet holes and humans eviscerated by some merciless monster of nightmares who chased them down one by one and tore them apart one by one—

These are people I know. My family. And my enemies.

This is a massacre.

The dusty wildlife sanctuary of my home has become a killing ground, and somehow, the only soul left standing is me.

I fall to my human knees with a thud and a cloud of red dust billows around my waist.

A gurgling sound makes me snap my head left. A bloody body the size of a grown man lies choking on his own lifeblood. I scramble towards him. His face and throat have been torn open, as if a claw slashed right through one eye all the way across to his mouth, twisting it down. But he has a bald head and a red beard...

"Ulman?" I choke, not used to using my human mouth. To my own ears, my voice sounds a hundred years old. Haggard and rusty.

The man who murdered my family gurgles on his words.

"You..."

Ulman tries so hard to speak and I don't want to look at him any more. Next to him is Mrs Ulman, by the long hair. And a girl with strawberry blonde plaits, a bush hat lying a few steps away.

Frank Ulman finally gets it out what he's been trying to say. "Fucking *animal. Monster.*"

The words condemn me. Sharpen my mind.

I stumble back from Ulman's dying body. A roar, broken and beastly, erupts from my bloody throat.

I did this?

And I remember none of it.

Horror is a machete, shredding my heart to pieces.

Chapter 26

Aurelia

I wake up from my dream of Lyle's past with my heart pounding, covered in sweat.

Sheer terror fades into a low fizzing in my skull as I realise that I'm not in the dry heat of the outback, but inside my dorm room at Animus Academy.

A quick check of my new phone tells me it's only one a.m. Henry chirps a question and I pat him on the head.

"I'm alright," I whisper, "just a..."

A mate dream. It's a thing unique to serpent mating groups. A part of their psychic power that enables them to see into the pasts of members of their soul group, usually after intimate contact. It allows serpents to create strong, deep personal connections with each other and isn't spoken about outside the Serpent Court. My father's people are secretive beasts, and keeping their powers in the dark is a point of pride. I didn't want to admit it when it happened with Savage's past memories, but this time, with Lyle's, it's hard to ignore.

That primitive terror, that awful horror, was impossible to just push aside. My heart still thrashes in my chest from the traumatising vision of all those shredded bodies.

I wonder if the others know I have these dreams, or if they too have them because of me. Wiping a fine layer of sweat off my forehead, I push my covers back and head to the balcony to open the doors. Fresh, cool air caresses my skin as I open one of them, and I breathe in the nighttime stillness like it's a balm that will soothe the old wounds of my past. And the visions of Lyle's past.

My eldest mate lives with a terrible history fraught with horrors. And if my suspicions are correct, they all do. *We* all do. But this vision of Lyle's past...only leads to more questions. I would never have guessed that he grew up in an illegal wildlife reserve. That his mother was forced to give birth in beast form, with her litter being tortured until they forgot how to shift into a human. It was unthinkable. How after all that, did Lyle end up here?

Staring out at the quiet academy grounds, a prickle on the back of my neck demands my attention. I scan the hunting games field and the eucalypts that border it on three sides, employing my eagle eyes to see better through the dark. If there is a threat out there, I want to be able to see it straight away. If there is a chance my father breached the academy's security and is physically coming to get me, I need to know straight away. I can sense my shields around the school well enough, but I don't get good visuals from them.

At least four pairs of academy guards always patrol the night, but they're usually not visible as they stick close to the buildings or to the perimeter of the academy.

But then I see the cause of my unease.

There is one guard who stands on the concrete path before the anima dorm, the red cherry flame of a cigarette glowing through the dark. He's looking up at the building. Looking right up at me.

My heart leaps as I look down at his utterly still form. He's tall, broad-shouldered and dressed from top to toe in all black, just like the other guards. An automatic weapon rests in his arms, just like the others.

Except he is not like the others at all.

The only thing different that I can see is a slight red gleam coming from his eye area, probably a reflection of the cigarette in the shades they all wear in the daytime. Perhaps he's a raptor and can see through them at night?

As I watch, he seems to fade into the shadows. And then he really does; the shadows beneath him rise up, swallowing him whole, that red gleam the only thing remaining visible. Between one blink and the next, he's gone entirely. As if he was never there.

I rub my eyes. Then rub them again. A shiver creeps over my skin, biting and cold. Tiredness suddenly weighs my body down. Now, nothing at all stands beneath the anima dorm. It's likely my tired mind, seeing things where there are none.

I check my protections again and remind myself that if people were to breach the school's natural protections, I would know about it. All my energy is going into defending the school and that is the entire point. I couldn't simply have stayed down in that cavern without... resources.

The food is working to help me. But I will definitely need more.

I tumble back into bed, and within seconds, I'm asleep.

The next morning, I wake up, cosy and deliciously warm, wrapped up in my blankets. My neck is wet.

My eyes fly open, thinking that Henry has shat on my neck in the night.

The scent of ancient forests and fresh grass strokes my nose.

Those are not blankets keeping me warm, but a heavy, muscular arm and torso curled around my back.

"Wakey wakey, regina." Between his kisses along my neck, Savage's morning voice is a deep purr in my ear.

I sit bolt upright.

The first thing I see is that the double doors leading to the balcony are open, letting cool morning air billow in. There are no signs of breaking and entering.

"They were open," Savage says.

Did the school *let* him in? Because those doors were definitely locked when I closed them last night.

I stare down at Savage, lying fully naked in my bed. He smiles lazily at me, stretching his body. My eyes find the curve of those tanned abdominals and I can't look away.

"You're a deep sleeper, regina." He reaches out to trail a finger down my arm.

I gather my shit together.

"What makes you think you can just slip into my bed whenever you want?"

He puts his arms behind his head and smiles at me as if I'm the most lovely thing he's ever seen. There's a heavy amount of male satisfaction in that gaze. "What makes you think I would wait until morning to see you?" He frowns as his voice becomes accusatory. "And you never texted me."

"How many hours did I have that phone for, Savage?"

The wolf ignores that as a hungry expression flashes across his face, and slowly, he gets up. I scoot back in response, but he pursues me down the bed like a predator.

"You're going to have me in your bed every night, regina. You're going to have my face between your legs every fucking morning."

Trying to leap out of bed, it takes me a moment to disentangle my limbs from the sheets, and in that moment, Savage lunges for me, flattening me on the mattress. But instead of kissing me like I think he will, he rests his head on my chest, pinning my arms by my sides so I can't move.

"You're adorable when you sleep."

From the side of my eye, I see Henry raise his head from his donut bed on top of my chest of drawers.

All he'll sense is the heat that's rising in me from Savage's hard, naked body pressing against my thin pjs.

I've also come to the realisation that, for the first time in weeks, I feel rested. I haven't been sleeping properly, nor deeply. Something in me clenches at the realisation that Savage is likely responsible for that rest.

"Are you eating properly, regina?" His voice is stern. "Drinking enough water?"

I do need more energy. I need it for everyone's safety. Perhaps I could just give into the urge to fuck Savage a few times a week?

The school tablet pings loudly and Savage's head whips around to look at it sitting on my desk next to the balcony doors.

"You have a postal notification?" He frowns deeply. "Who's sending you things that's not me?"

I hastily push at his chest and he rears back so I can get off the bed and see what it says. "Not someone. I'm just shopping. And how can you read that, anyway?"

"It has a box emoji next to it. Regina, if you need things, you come to me."

I scan the notification and find that my *Eggplant Emporium* shipment has arrived. "I can buy my own stuff."

"You should also know Scythe knows everything that comes in and out of this school. So does Lyle."

I stiffen at the low meaning in his voice. Do they know what I bought with this shipment? I even arranged for express delivery via courier. That's how desperate I am to deal with my... situation.

"What?" I say in disbelief.

He nods. "Yeah. Why, what did you buy?" He tries to peer at the tablet.

How embarrassing. Fuck. Them.

"You need to go, Savage."

"What?"

"You heard me. I need to get ready for the day."

He gives me a very unimpressed look and drags himself off my bed in the slowest manner possible. I try not to look at the tall, perfect, mouthwatering expanse of his naked body as he straightens to standing.

Savage stalks towards me, eating up the space between us in a few long strides. Dear Goddess, this crazy wolf is supposed to be all mine.

Heat fills his hazel eyes as he holds my gaze, leans down, and with a possessive hand around the back of my neck, crushes his lips to mine. He bites my bottom lip just enough to cause a sting of pain before sweeping his tongue across it in apology.

I gasp in protest, but when he presses his forehead to mine, what he growls next stifles any argument from me.

"*Mine.*"

It's all my soul has *ever* wanted to hear. But dare I allow myself? Dare I allow him to make that a reality?

My body is all aquiver at the prospect. He's basically presenting himself to me. Basically throwing himself at me for my use.

Am I seriously saying no?

But I've spent all this money on these vibrators and the fact that those men know about it is sending me into a *rage*. Nope, I've got to try this method first. On principle.

"Bye," I blurt out.

He straightens and I try to meet his gaze, though I know he can probably hear the crazy beat of my poor heart. "I'll see you later, regina." And with one last look that promises hot, forbidden things, he saunters out of my room.

It's only after his naked ass disappears that I take a breath.

I have important things to do, after all.

* * *

Down at breakfast, I pass Eugene to Raquel, have a quick word with Stacey and Connor and leg it out of the dining room, giggling all the way to the student mail office. We have just enough time to take the massive box back to my room and check everything out. Connor and Stacey take their pick, and I quickly snatch up the lion head one before Connor can and stash it safely in my bottom drawer.

We pinky promise to give them a whirl tonight, and the two of them hurry out of my room to their first class.

I'm about to leave when another *ping* goes off in my room. But it's not from our academy tablet. Excitedly, I leap for my chest of drawers and pluck out my new phone. But my excitement fades as I read a message from an unknown number.

I know what you did, snakelet.

My heart stutters in my chest. Who is this? Quickly, I check the numbers Savage put into the contacts. There are numbers for Scythe, Xander and Savage and also... Lyle Pardalia. This number, then, can't be any one of them.

I succumb and type back.

Who is this?

The reply comes back straight away.

A long-time admirer.

What does that even mean?

My heart wants to leap out of my chest, but the first bell is about to go off and I need to get to class.

I make sure I'm wearing clothes in which I can conceal my new phone. Stacey keeps hers in her bra and I decide it's worth the annoyance if it means I can have my phone on me at all times. This new... *admirer* might want to message me again, and I want to know right away if they do. But what were they referring to with their first message? I've done many things since I've arrived here. I have to reply.

> And what was it that I did?

> My my. How does a pretty snakelet forget a dead body in her bed?

My heart stops in my chest. I hadn't forgotten the night before my trial at all. How I'd found a murdered snake in my bed and a message from my father. How that was what had led me to Savage, Scythe and Xander's dorm. But how the fuck did this guy know about that?

> I don't know what you're talking about.

> Poor snakelet. You can't hide anything from me. Not even if you tried your hardest.

> I'm getting rid of this phone. Don't bother contacting me again.

> Careful with the lies. It'll make your snout grow.

Well if it turned me into a fucking toucan, then I was all for it. I decide that's quite enough and shove the phone into my bra. If someone wants to play games with me then that's their problem.

Xander burned that serpent's body to ashes so there was no proof. No body no crime... right?

* * *

We've been separated into two groups to begin a new class. And it's not until I walk into a new classroom with a fancy electronic whiteboard and I read what it says in bold cursive that I realise what this is.

"Regina classes?" Minnie pipes from my elbow.

Startled, I pull her into a hug. She ate breakfast with Titus and his seven rare steaks this morning. Minnie laughs and takes my hand, leading me to a group table near Savage, Xander and Yeti. But before I can protest about table choices, I realise Sabrina and Raquel are behind us, too.

Minnie says it before I do. "Wait, we're all reginas? How did we not know this before?"

But we know why; most animas are too superstitious to talk about their phoenix prophecy or mating group and your position in one before you find your pack. And it was considered a taboo thing to ask.

As we take a seat at our table, excitedly chattering about what we're possibly here to learn, I cast an eye around to see who's here from the first and second-year students.

The first thing I note is that Scythe isn't here.

Does he think it will ruin his reputation if people think he has a regina? Does he think it *lessens* him to have a regina?

Minnie's taking out her array of pencils and rainbow notepad when she notices me looking around. She also casts her eye about and understands what I'm fussing over.

To my surprise, she grins at me. "You know..." Her voice is sly. "Shark daddy already knows this stuff."

I gape at her as Sabrina snorts, but Raquel nods in agreement.

"What?" Minnie asks. "He's almost too old to even be here. He's clearly just conned his way in to keep an eye on you."

"H-He knows sh-shit," Raquel agrees. "Like h-he knows e-everything."

Shit. I think they're both right. Animus Academy only accepts eighteen to twenty-five-year-olds and Scythe is a few years older than Savage.

Sabrina grabs my arm. "You lucky bitch. If it were me, I'd be in shark daddy's bed every night! You know he doesn't even let anyone touch him. Like at all."

"Yeah, well, Savage was in my bed last night," I hiss back, fully aware that the wolf is grinning from ear to ear, unabashedly listening in to our conversation.

"They c-can hear you," Raquel deadpans.

"Let 'em." Sabrina rolls her eyes and waves at Yeti.

"Quieten down." Lyle's voice is *cold* this morning as he strides into the classroom and we all shut up and sit straighter at his tone.

Well there you fucking go. I guess he found my little present last night.

My stomach flops on itself. I fucking hate how he makes me feel like a giddy teenager. But it wasn't a giddy teenager who *consecrated* his bed, was it?

I try really hard to hide my smirk, but I don't think I'm successful.

Lyle glances around the room and his purely icy gaze lands on me... and heats up. "Do you have something funny you want to share with the class, Miss Aquinas?"

His tone would send any other beast running in the other direction. Someone in the back even gasps.

"Uh oh," Minnie mutters under her breath.

My voice is super, duper sweet and I bless him with my prettiest smile. "No, sir. Nothing's funny. I'm just really looking forward to this class with you."

And boy am I.

Chapter 27

Xander

The Boneweaver girl is smug as shit and it's irritating as all hell. Apparently, it's irritating Lyle just as much because he's practically white-lipped with rage.

She has this grin on her face that tells me she's done something she shouldn't have.

"Your regina is looking suspiciously happy," I tell Savage mind-to-mind, letting Scythe in on the conversation, too.

Savage can't take his eyes off her. *"Isn't she sexy in that little dress? She wouldn't let me eat her out this morning, but I'm sure as fuck going to get her later."*

I'm not the only one scanning the animas—nay, reginas. Fancy my surprise when Minnie, Sabrina and Raquel revealed themselves as reginas when we separated into groups this morning. In Raquel's case, that made them a regus, since they're nonbinary. The rexes were sent to their own group, along with anyone who has a rex as the leader of their pack. While the reginas and anyone with a regina in their pack was sent here to be taught by Lyle.

Minnie being here isn't a complete surprise. The fact that

Titus wants her in his bed means he detects her power and it lures him in.

This classroom is full, with every beast staring at the reginas who naturally placed themselves in the middle of the room.

A gaggle of attention seekers.

As always, they're dressed to please their inner promiscuous anima. Aurelia is in a baby pink dress that highlights the olive skin given to her by her father. It's the type that sticks to your body and shows all of a woman's curves. It's short, and sliding to her upper thigh as she sits. Bonus points: she's actually wearing a bra today, with a little lace peeking over the neckline of her dress.

When we first arrived, her breasts *bounced* as she scooted forward on her chair and I barely contained the urge to leave right then and there. She ties up her long, black hair with an elastic. It's a wavy sort of mess, and as she puts it up, it exposes the golden column of her neck.

My dragon snorts and licks his lips.

Down, boy, I mutter to him. *He's* been acting up lately, and it's setting me on edge.

I wouldn't put it past some of these animals to sniff the anima's seats after they leave. Thirsty fuckers. If Savage knew what disinfectant wipes were, he'd have them on hand all at times to get rid of her scent from public furniture. He's always been a jealous bastard when it comes to his women, and now he's openly claiming his regina, *openly* calling her by the title, it's given him a licence to show his true self: a proper menace.

It's the entire reason Scythe and I were so keen to get rid of her. A single woman in control of males like us, let alone five, is a dangerous thing. So much for plans well laid. Aurelia has proven herself to be more conniving and manipulative than we thought with her little escape plan.

But this morning, her breathing is a little fast, probably because she's thirsting after Lyle like everyone else. As a result, there is an obvious, fiery rope of tension between the two of them.

The lion, for his part, is barely holding on, which is my new entertainment at this sorry excuse of a school. He's sort of pale under his tan, and I know exactly where his blood is rushing. All because Aurelia's keeping her legs a little open, angled right at him.

"Scythe, you really ought to be here to see this," I send to my shark brother, who's busy looking at some documents Marduk gave him.

A dark chuckle rumbles down our bond. *"I'll be there next time."*

Lyle starts up his slideshow. "Alright, if you are here, you're either a regina or regus." He nods at Raquel, who nods back. "Or an animus who belongs to a regina, whether you have met them or not."

There are some annoyed grumbles from those who haven't met the central member of their pack yet.

If only I was so lucky.

"So," Lyle continues, "this begins a series of classes where I'm going to teach you the proper way to conduct yourself around a regina and the challenges you'll face." He gestures to the middle table. " And the common issues reginas come across. We'll also talk about the instincts that all animalia have inborn within them and how to deal with those instincts in a modern context."

The irony of this isn't lost on me—or Aurelia, for that matter—as she sits back in her seat, toying with her pen as that smirk grows wider on her face.

Savage has positioned himself so he's got her in his sight at all times.

"So, today we're going to talk about base instincts," Lyle continues, "which is what comes up most obviously when you meet each other for the first time. Who remembers meeting their regina for the first time?"

Savage crosses his arms and a lion from behind me puts up his hand. We all know him from our first day when he dived at his regina during the lineup. A few of his friends snigger.

"Yes, Dion. What was that like for you?" Lyle asks, seriously.

"It was overwhelming," Dion admits. "It was like my animus took over and I just... had to have her. I wanted to be inside of her. I wanted to fuck her and lick her and kiss her and feed her all at the same time. I didn't know what to do first."

Savage and a few others chuckle. Aurelia is biting her lip and Minnie and Raquel have turned pink.

Lyle's face turns serious. "That first meeting can be over-whelming. And this is where we talk about consent. The animus is a hungry beast, and the urge to claim your regina is perhaps one of our strongest instincts. Stronger than our urge for food or water, in many cases. It's important that we learn about this before it happens so we can control our animus and don't injure our regina."

"That's what I was worried about," said Dion. "When I leapt on her, I could have knocked her out."

"Exactly," Lyle says with approval. "Males have more muscle mass than females. We're heavier and generally stronger, so we need to know our strength around them."

"But sir?" To my surprise, Minnie puts her hand up. "We're sort of built for that, aren't we? Reginas are normally a bit stronger than other animas."

"Correct. Stronger physically as well as with your order's given power. That's why reginas have an allure that all beasts can sense, whether they are in their pack or not. It's why, we think, reginas have stubborn personalities. To be able to handle a pack of beasts and lead them is no easy task."

Minnie discreetly elbows Aurelia, but I still see it.

Savage chuckles under his breath. "*I wouldn't have her any other fucking way.*"

"So, then we come to the question," Lyle continues, "what is the *role* of a regina?"

I'm surprised when Aurelia answers quietly. "To lead."

"What was that, Miss Aquinas?" Lyle's voice is as sharp as a slap on the ass.

Savage stiffens next to me, practically on the edge of his seat.

But Aurelia is undeterred and replies with all the sass she can muster. "I *said* a regina's job is to lead her pack. To be their reliable centre." She sounds like she's reciting it from a textbook, and knowing her proclivity to read, she might actually be. "To *hold* the pack together."

"That's right." Minnie nods firmly, like she's helping Aurelia fight an invisible argument. "A regina's job is to keep the peace between the personalities of the group. And she doesn't even have to do anything to do that sometimes. Her very presence will calm them down and sate their beastly urges. She... She makes them into a family."

There's a silence after that. A little bit of it is longing, plenty of it is lust.

A muscle clenches in Lyle's jaw, and I see a little of Scythe in him. They both hold their emotions in a steel fist. Savage prefers to knock people down. I prefer to let my music and smoke drown my emotions away. Today's choice: Britney Spears.

Lyle is definitely in a mood because he snaps, "Next time, put up your hand to speak. Both of you."

Minnie purses her lips and Aurelia rolls her eyes as Lyle stares her down.

Our deputy headmaster stiffens, and suddenly, the temperature in the room goes up. A dark thread of delight winds through me as I sense Lyle's dominance spread through the room. A couple of hyenas at the back let out involuntary, appeasing whines.

With a voice of such quiet menace that even my dragon raises his head, Lyle says, "Did you just roll your eyes at me, Miss Aquinas?"

To everyone's surprise, Aurelia tilts her chin upwards and stares him down. But her purring voice is not physical when it responds. It resounds within our pack's telepathic group chat. "*I believe I did, Lyle.*"

Lyle's pupils dilate, and the hairs on the back of my arms stand on end at the way I see his animus flash behind that cold gaze. Any male who takes one look at Lyle knows that he has the worst sort of animus, but I got the impression he has a death grip on it. And by the collective sucking in of breaths in the classroom, nobody has seen that dangerous, unhinged flash of his animus before. The dominance of his regina is forcing Lyle's beast to come forth and meet her. I'm about to warn the group when Scythe's voice enters the minds of just me and Savage.

"*Let it play out,*" he says. "*Let's see what our lion-brother is made of.*"

Savage gives a soft growl of begrudging acceptance.

No one is moving in the classroom. I don't think anyone is breathing, either. It's the natural response of less dominant males to avoid setting off the clearly lethal male before them.

But my dragon? He wants to play. I tell him to stand the fuck down though, because I'm more interested in seeing Lyle's interaction with Aurelia.

The two of them engage in a heated stare-off, neither allowing themselves to stand down. Minnie gulps. Sabrina licks her lips. Raquel looks like they want to intervene and clenches their fists instead. Smart anim. On my other side, Yeti shifts, just a little, his dominant tiger probably wondering if he could take Lyle on.

And then something happens that has me glaring at the Boneweaver girl. She raises her hand and asks, "I have another question, sir. Why does a pack naturally want to question their regina's dominance? What makes them want to test her so badly?"

The fucking audacity.

Lyle stares unblinking at Aurelia for a moment longer before rising to his feet. One glance at Savage tells me that his wolf has come out to listen, his eyes blown out, his energy simmering with primitive power.

"You're right, Miss Aquinas," Lyle says so calmly that it makes a thrill run down my spine. "A regina is tested by her pack." He rounds his desk to stalk towards her. "Again and again. She needs to prove her worth. Her strength." He stands before their group table now, staring down the reginas one by one, and my magical sight can see his power spreading out over them in a show of overt domination. "Her pack needs to see that they are in good hands. That this anima can handle them. Only then does she gain their respect. And their submission." The animas at the table collectively shiver. Lyle continues, and a lick of his power reaches for Aurelia like he can't help it. "The animus does not like to submit. It is not natural for them. To get one to submit requires..." Lyle blinks then, as if he realises where he is, who he's talking to, and his power snaps back into his body. He frowns, almost at himself. "Something special."

Lyle turns on his heel and goes back to his desk, stiff-backed.

All Aurelia's sass, attitude, and audacity are gone. She sits in her seat, staring at Lyle as if she's looking at a ghost.

I could really use a joint right about now.

Whatever spell the two of them cast over the rest of the class is broken and Dion raises his hand again. "Sir, what about food? I always have this strong urge to bring food to my regina, but I never know how much. She doesn't like waking up covered in potato chips."

And like that entire thing didn't just happen, the class continues. "The urge to feed is so primitive that it's a hard one to control," Lyle says. "It's best to let your regina lead you on that one. Have you even asked her what she wants?"

Dion's ears turn pink under his mane of blonde hair. "Yeah, I probably shouldn't wait for her to tell me off afterwards, should I?"

"Again, I come back to consent," Lyle says firmly. "When your animus has an urge, you must wait and ask your regina permission first. If I want to stress anything, that is your golden rule. When it comes to food, intimacy, sex, anything. You must ask her. Use your words. If you are a wolf, you have it easier than the rest of the orders, but the rest of us need to open our mouths and ask the question."

"Sometimes it ruins the moment, sir," a serpent whines.

The urge to extract his fangs and snap his neck almost makes me whirl around. But I take a leaf out of Lyle's book and tell myself that this is a classroom and murder is not meant for classrooms.

Suddenly, Raquel throws a plastic water bottle at the snake, hitting him hard, right in the nose. His head snaps back with a satisfying *oof*.

Everyone sniggers.

"I'll let that one go because it was in good spirit," Lyle says. "But no throwing, Raquel." The wolf nods. Lyle points at the vermin. "Robert. A quiet, 'may I?' or 'can I?' works well and ruins nothing."

"I mean, unless you have an agreement in place *already*," Sabrina drawls. "One that *says* 'fuck me any time, any place, unless I say my safe word' then it's okay. I think everyone should have a safe word. An amber one and a red one."

"Like a written legal contract?" Minnie asks, cocking her head like a puppy.

"Yeah," Sabrina says enthusiastically. "And you can write on it all the things you like and all the things you don't. So that"— she casts a disapproving look behind her as if indicating to the rest of us dirty bastards—"the animals don't get confused. Animuses need clear instructions, don't they, Mr Pardalia?"

The barest amusement shows on Lyle's face as he nods seriously. "Indeed, Sabrina. There are even apps you can get these days, but paper works fine."

Minnie violently scribbles her notes down as the animuses burst out into chatter at this fantastic revelation.

I turn *Toxic* up louder.

But Aurelia. Aurelia is slowly sliding the end of her pen in and out of her mouth.

"Holy, Wild Mother," Savage groans in my mind.

Her expression is thoughtful as she sucks on it, staring unblinkingly at Lyle, and I'd *almost* believe she's not aware of what she's doing. Lyle's attention slides to her, and he's staring, transfixed. I watch while his eyes turn glazed.

"Regina, *stop* giving that pen a blow job," Savage barks out loud.

Everyone is shocked into silence as Aurelia's pen drops out of her mouth, her hand poised mid-air as if she's in just as much shock.

All at once, the animas burst into laughter. Sabrina tilts her head back and chortles. Minnie hoots into Aurelia's shoulder, and even Raquel covers a smile.

"Settle down," Lyle drones like he's not got a semi hard-on that he's now hiding behind his desk. "Felix, come and hand these worksheets out." A small puma with orange hair hastily obeys as Lyle explains, "I want you to spend the remaining twenty minutes filling out these sheets about what you aren't familiar with. It'll give me an idea about what this group needs to work on the most."

These animals sit in as much silence as they can manage as we all fill out our forms. I write in hard, slashing dot points about not wanting to know anything, then wait for the twenty minutes to be up.

At the end, Lyle instructs for someone from each table to bring the sheets up. Savage snorts because Lyle is still not getting up from his desk.

"I'll take them." Aurelia's voice is laced with sickly sweet poison as she gathers up the papers from her table.

Every male behind her stares at her round ass as she gets up, the impressions of a thong are visible.

Are those diamantes I can see? Fucking hell.

Savage growls in pleasure until she reaches Lyle's desk. The lion is determinedly not looking at her, typing something on his laptop instead.

She leans down, unnecessarily close, her breasts not a millimetre away from his shoulder, giving everyone a view of her cleavage. Henry holds on to her shoulder for dear life.

I clench the edge of my desk.

"Here you go, sir," she purrs, placing the papers in front of him, her hand brushing his arm on the way back up. "Another one for your... *collection*."

Lyle stops typing. His jaw tics again and again as arousal pulses through his power, thick and heavy. Her words have the cadence of an inside joke, and I wonder why it's making the most lethal lion in this place blush.

Yeti shifts in his seat next to me.

A hyena in the back clears his throat. More than a few adjust themselves. If I didn't hate her, I'd find this display hilarious.

"Where are your shoes?" Lyle barks so sharply that almost everyone jumps.

"Oh!" Aurelia huffs a laugh and looks around as if she'll find them there. Henry fluffs his wings, startled. "I suppose I forgot."

"Another detention for you, then, Miss Aquinas. It's literally my easiest rule to follow." His eyes flick down to her tiny dress as if it's an affront to his sensitivities.

She gapes at him, but then shuts her jaw. "If that's what you want," she says primly.

"It is," he grits out.

"Oh, he wants a lot more than that," Savage growls into my head.

When Aurelia gets back to her table, Minnie takes her hand and whispers, "You're fucking playing with fire and I love it."

Wild God, they're all nuts.

"Do you know what I'm gonna call it?" Minnie nods like she's happy with her choice and sweeps her open palm out in front of her. "Aurelia's Reign of Terror."

"I need a fucking smoke," I mutter to Savage and stride right out of there.

I have ten vibrators of different models and types, and after a week of trying, they all fail to hit the spot. Even when I use the clit sucky one, all I can think of is how much I want Savage's tongue there instead. Or his fingers. Or his... anything, really.

The way I'm craving his earthy, old forest scent is driving me feral. Every night, I try to go to sleep after another round with a new vibrator. Every morning, I wake up to Savage kissing my neck. After that tiny moment of vulnerability, I'm keeping him at arm's length.

But he can't stay away, and even his kisses give my power a tiny oomph. Each morning he slips out, striding down the hall naked, to the delight of the animas leaving their rooms for breakfast. He never pushes me. Never demands anything other than my presence.

I'm actually starting to believe that he just wants... me.

It's lucky that with Minnie's absence I have some privacy to try and pleasure myself, but it's real power I need to keep my shields up, and while my own orgasms are getting me by, I'm feeling worse and worse as each day passes. For forgetting to wear shoes, Lyle has me scrubbing communal toilets for the week, and the bending over only makes the injury on my stomach hurt all the more.

* * *

Burn. Burn. Burn.

One morning, I hiss in pain as phantom fangs punch through my shields.

My father is relentless in his pursuit of me, and I know this is just the beginning of what he's capable of. He doesn't want to murder me through these attacks, but will gladly do serious damage. He wants me running scared back to him.

But I'll die before I do that.

I've wrapped a layer of pilfered bandages around my stomach to protect them, but I just know they'll be bleeding through now.

"What's wrong?" Savage's husky morning voice in my ear sends shivers down my spine. He brushes a strand of hair off my neck so he can go back to kissing the skin there, and I allow myself to let out a tiny whimper.

Savage's head snaps up. It's the first time I've responded with a noise to his kisses.

"Regina, baby, is this you letting me eat you out?" He looks at me with bright, excited eyes.

Fuck it. Fuck everything, including this pain.

"Yes," I whisper.

A wicked grin spreads across his lips before his wolf comes out to play. I know it by the way his pupils dilate and the air around him becomes charged with wild, feral intensity. Adrenaline courses through my blood and my anima keens with glee.

Savage trails kisses down my arm as he slides down my body. My top has ridden up just below my stomach wounds, and he kisses me just above my sleep shorts, sucking gently on the sensitive skin.

I hiss at the tingle that spreads into my core. "Oh Goddess."

Savage growls, hooking his fingers into my shorts and gently tugging them down and throwing them aside. "I've waited so long for this, princess. You made me wait *so fucking* long."

I flop on my back to give him permission, spreading my legs for him. Those bloody vibrators never had me this excited. I'm already—

"So wet, regina," he says in awe. Were you thinking about me?" His eyes darken as they look up at me from between my legs. "You better have been."

Him and Lyle and Scythe. Maybe Xander too.

Over my underwear, he runs a finger down the seam of me and I cry out, arching my back.

"So reactive," he says in wonder. "And what about if I do this?" He presses his lips and nose to my sex, inhaling deeply. "Wild Mother." He groans into me and grabs the top of my panties and rips them in two.

"Savage!" I say in protest, looking at the torn pink cotton.

"*Don't,*" he growls in that deep guttural voice of his wolf, his pupils now covering his irises completely. The hairs on the back of my arms stand on end and I'm in a dazed sort of shock as a stare at him.

"Let me eat from you," he growls. "Let me *devour* you."

The breathy whisper is out of my mouth before I even think. "Do it."

He blinks as he registers the words before his eyes slide back down to my core, completely open to him.

Closing his eyes like he's savouring this moment, he surges forward, tongue stroking gently first. His large hands grip my thighs as he flicks my clit with the tip of his tongue.

"Fuck!" I cry.

This is better than I ever could have dreamed.

My power is surging already, all but *purring* as Savage serves me with his lips, and his tongue swirling sweet circles over my most delicate places. He's inquiring, but demanding, as if he's trying to learn all the parts of me and committing them to memory. Tendrils of pleasure rise up through my legs into my stomach and I'm in a golden haze within seconds.

"Regina," he groans into my pussy, and the vibration of his voice is a sweet tingle through my core.

I swear out loud and he makes a sound of approval. Burying my hands in his dark waves, I get lost in the feel of him, finally, *finally*, giving my anima and I what we've always wanted. My hips move in small circles, grinding against his face as liquid pleasure rises in spirals from my very centre. From this moment on, there's no way I'm going to look at his lips and think of anything else.

There is no way I could have *replaced* him with mechanical toys.

I look down at him and his eyes flick up to me, those pupils burning with need. He laps noisily at my swollen clit before sucking that tender nub and growling deep.

My back bows and I cry his name, pulling on his hair like they're reins and I explode onto his face. He's relentless, moving with me, almost chasing me as I grind against his moving tongue, wringing out each and every shockwave of utter, delicious pleasure.

It's golden, when my power rises like a mountain spring being refilled from beneath. I feel his power trickling into me from where we're connected, like Savage is opening up to me and giving me what I need on a deeper level.

So this is what it's like to be *filled* by your mate.

I lie there in wonder, panting, as Savage gently gives me gentle, sweet kisses across my labia, then my clit.

I shiver as he lays his head on one of my thighs, his eyes half lowered.

"I'm drunk on your pussy," he whispers up at me, the entire lower half of his face glistening. "I *refuse* to move from here."

"Well, you're gonna have to," Minnie pipes as she prances into our room. "We have class soon. Titus and I..." She blushes and shrugs at us as if Savage isn't lying between my legs. "We did a similar thing this morning." She's beaming to herself, sighing dreamily. "He never goes *down* on me, per se, but he's great in bed."

I gasp, pushing away from Savage, who lets himself go tumbling dramatically to the floor. "What do you mean he never goes down on you?"

Sabrina was right, after all.

"Um, well..." Minnie adjusts the purple scarf on her neck as we both ignore Savage's grumbling. "He's great in bed, but he says... I mean, like, I don't *need* to be eaten out."

"He says that you don't need it?" I ask suspiciously.

"Red flag," Savage chokes from behind me.

"Out!" I shout at him, pointing to the door.

He gives me a hot look and licks his lips before leaving. The picture of his naked ass sauntering away will never get old.

Minnie's too busy lighting incense at her altar of the Wild Goddess to notice. "It's alright, Aurelia," she says softly. "I really love him, and he's so *passionate* about things. I know he'll tell me he loves me back any day now. Oh!" she laughs, finally turning to look at me. "Aurelia, put some panties on!"

I hastily comply and make my bed while Minnie fusses with her scarf and then her laundry bag. Frowning, I straighten from my bed.

"Min?" I inquire.

She turns around with infinite slowness and something like dread winds its way through my heart.

"Don't freak out," she says, not meeting my eye.

I hurry over to her. "Goddess, Min, what is it?"

Her brown eyes look up to me, almost pleading. She touches

the thin purple material wound around her neck. "Can you please heal me before class? I've just got a little hickey." She unwinds the material and finally shows me what's on her neck.

My stomach hollows out. My breath comes out in a gasp.

"You have to leave him," I whisper. Because a chunk of my best friend's neck is missing. A clear bite mark slants across her delicate brown skin. There are impressions of sharp teeth and pink, shiny skin oozes blood where her skin has been torn clean off.

"Aurelia, please do this for me?" Minnie's voice wavers a little but her stance is firm.

"Min," I repeat. "You have to leave him." Even as I say it my magic powers toward her, as if my anima can't look at the awful bite. My own stomach burns in solidarity as my power soaks through the wound and cuts off the bleeding and encourages new tissue to grow. "The Academy won't stand for this."

"No I don't," Minnie says evenly. Closing her eyes as she feels the skin growing anew.

"You do!" I say. "This isn't right. Your flesh is *missing*."

The furniture in the room trembles. Gertie squeaks in urgency from Minnie's other shoulder. My tigress takes a deep breath and the furniture goes still again. "When you were with Savage, I never tried to tell you—"

"This is different!" I exclaim.

"No, it's not." She says firmly, turning around and grabbing her makeup case. "I don't want to hear another word, Lia."

It's the tone in her voice that gives me pause. A firm, unyielding sort of cadence that I've never heard from Minnie. It's a tone that brooks no argument.

"Thank you for healing me," she says quietly, before hurrying into the bathroom.

I sink onto my bed as she takes her turn in the shower. Worrying about Minnie is a new thing for our friendship. She's always had such a positive way about her, but I'm worried that

Titus is taking advantage of that. Scrap that. I'm worried that Titus is a monster that will harm her further.

Inspiration strikes me and I snatch up my phone from where I've hidden it in my underwear drawer.

At first, Savage tries to knock on my mental shields for telepathic conversation, but I can't let him. His replies are a little slow due to his use of text-to-voice to listen and then voice-to-text to reply.

> I want a phone for Minnie as well.

And what do I get in return?

> I thought you said I could ask for whatever I wanted.

I never said it would be for free.

> Asshole.

Yup

> It needs to have a pink glitter case

You're taking advantage of me.

> Am I though?

I want to renegotiate

> Alright, what do you want?

I want you in my bed on weekends

> But you sleep in a room with the other two

> Scythe and Xander, yes. They won't care if we make love

Make love? Something flutters in my stomach, but I turn it away and take out clothes that will hide a phone.

> What do you know about Titus?

> Stay away from him regina

> Why?

I don't get a reply.

But at least I'll have a way for Minnie to contact me or even Stacey if something bad happens.

* * *

It still feels odd that Savage has finally outed me as his regina, but none of the other students make a comment. For fear of him, certainly. It still spikes my adrenaline, though, anytime it comes up, especially in class, where Lyle feels the need to probe everyone about their thoughts.

Savage and I have to work together, so I swap chairs with Xander. We're filling out an exercise sheet on our expectations from each other, which means *I'm* filling it out while Savage smiles at me and offers helpful titbits.

"Write down that I expect you to spread your legs and take my tongue every morning and every night."

Sabrina sniggers from the other table. I give him a warning look.

"And write down that I expect you to never give any of my presents away--don't raise your brow at me, it turns me on."

But I'm thinking of my pink handbag, still safe in my chest of drawers. "Well, same goes for me," I mutter.

"I have it in a glass jar."

"What?"

"The wrapper from the chocolate you gave me."

Something in my gut uncoils at his words.

"You still have it?" I murmur in disbelief. He took my gifts after all.

Carefully, he takes my left hand and kisses the back of it. "Of course."

"Order traitor," someone mutters from the table behind us.

It's in moments like these I realise that not only do I have zero control over Savage, but that he's a volatile wolf in human clothing. For an infinitesimal unit of time, Savage and I stare at each other. Alarmed blue eyes into burning hazel ones. I see the exact moment his wolf takes over.

And then everything turns into mad, bloody chaos.

Savage whips around and lunges for a stocky eagle with blonde hair called Dante. They both go tumbling back with the chair Dante's sitting on as Savage rains blows to Dante's head.

"Stop!" Lyle commands. I dart him a look and see that he has his hands out, but his telekinesis is *not working* on Savage.

Fuck. One on one, my mating group has roughly the same strength.

"Xander!" I shout.

But the dragon just closes his eyes and shrugs. "Not my circus, not my monkey."

I could punch him in his perfect dragon face.

"Should we do something?" one wolf animus asks in a shrill, frightened voice as Savage pummels his fists into Dante's face and shoulders.

"No." Yeti's reply is harsh. "When he gets like this, it's best to let him finish, otherwise no one's safe."

There's so much blood and the sound of bone crunching.

"He's going to kill him!" Minnie cries.

Dante is fully limp as Lyle strides up and hauls Savage off

him by the neck of his black tank top. Savage aims a punch at Lyle that catches him square on the left side of his jaw. Lyle's head flips to the other side. Everyone in the room gasps.

But that movement seems to trigger something in the lion. Quicker than I thought was possible, Lyle punches Savage back.

My wolf's head snaps back with a faint *oof*.

I'm simultaneously aroused and horrified.

But Savage is laughing and gestures to Lyle to come at him. "Again!"

The entire room becomes charged with an electric force as Lyle and Savage stare at each other, their violent animuses clearly in control and challenging each other's dominance.

Lyle looks like he's about to punch Savage again—

"Lyle." The word is out of my mouth before I can stop it. It's sort of husky. It's sort of a warning.

Lyle's head snaps towards me and I'm taken aback by his eyes and the lion he never lets come to the surface. I'm stricken by the sight of him and the sheer force of his will behind it. His irises *tremble*, as if Lyle is actively battling his animus and his animus is saying *no*.

But in a flash, it's gone, and Lyle is in control and prodding at Savage. "Calm down," he snaps. He turns around and gestures to a couple of lions. "Rush Dante to the medical centre."

Savage growls as we all watch Dante levitate upwards, his face nothing more than a bloody mess. I see white bone peeking through. My stomach clenches and I hope he's not dead, but the medical centre is close by, so I think he'll make it.

"Guess who's spending the weekend in solitary," Lyle grits out. "That was not necessary, Sav."

Sav? Since when are they on friendly nickname terms?

"He insulted *my* regina," Savage snarls, "Aurelia can't help being fated to us. Fuck you, Lyle."

"Get in fucking line."

Okay, so maybe not on friendly terms.

"Go quietly, Savage," I say, worried he'll say more in this angry haze of his.

Savage sighs like this is a great inconvenience, but his body goes lax and his shoulders droop as he allows Lyle to steer him out. Just when they go out of view, Savage's tattooed hand grips the doorway and his head appears. He blows me a kiss and says quickly, "I love you, Aurelia," before Lyle snatches him away once again.

Sabrina snorts as Minnie bats a chiding hand at her.

My own hand flies to my stomach, not because of the nasty, burning wounds etched there, but because my insides are suddenly full with a dainty fluttery feeling.

Minnie takes my hand and leans her pink curls on my shoulder. "I'm so happy for you, Lia."

And by the Goddess, I think I'm happy too.

Chapter 29

Lyle

"Here's your list of appointments tomorrow," Georgia says, sliding the neatly typed A4 sheet of paper across my desk.

"Thank you," I say, not looking at her but at my computer screen, where I've pulled up six security camera feeds from around the school. Five are only there as a pretence, because I'm only interested in one.

Aurelia is sitting between Beak and Eugene in an avian specific class. They're watching Theresa demonstrate how to check for wing health with one of the bearded vultures sitting patiently on her desk.

Beak leans down from his much taller height to whisper something in Aurelia's ear. She chuckles under her breath.

I stare at Beak and the minute distance between the two of them. Beak is careful not to get his scent on Aurelia's skin, but there are barely centimetres between them. The eagle reaches up to stretch his arms, flexing the biceps bulging out of the white T-shirt he's wearing. The cassowary on the other side of Eugene glances at Aurelia and runs a tattooed hand through his shoulder-length blue-tipped brown hair.

A red coil of anger twists through my chest as I stare at their posturing.

Aurelia, who was absently twirling her pen, loses her grip on the biro and it falls, skittering under her table. Suddenly, all the males in her vicinity dive under the table, beside themselves as they try to be the first to retrieve the pen... and no doubt get a look up her dress while they're at it.

Aurelia hastily pushes her chair back and shakes her head as the winning hawk proudly presents her the biro, still on his knees before her.

Fucking idiots.

"Pardon?"

With alarm, I come back into my office and realise that I've spoken out loud.

I glance at Georgia and hastily point to another camera feed showing the front of the academy grounds and the colony of white birds on the Hunting Games oval. "The cockatoos are back."

She clears her throat and laughs.

Sitting back in my chair and trying to relax the muscles that were coiled in readiness, I chide myself at my own behaviour. I've become addicted to watching Aurelia through the security cameras. I watch her in class; I watch her in the dining hall, and I even find myself watching her walk through campus on the way to her dorms at the end of the day. Even in meetings, my attention wanders and I resort to getting out my phone and bringing up the camera feed. I have her timetable memorised so I always find her quickly.

And if for some reason she's not where she's supposed to be, I find myself urgently flicking through each camera, my heart pounding until I lay my eyes on her again. With the closeness with which I stalk her, I should have been able to find out how she'd gotten into my apartment and left her...little *gift*.

She played a dangerous game, putting her scent all over my

bed like that. I'd been caught out, and I didn't know how to feel about it. But if she'd thought it would make me embarrassed, she was wrong. It only made me more fixated on her.

Heat gathers in my veins and I crack my neck to try and relieve some of the tension as I stare at Beak's arm, where it rests on the table, far too close to Aurelia for my liking.

I tear my eyes off them before I punch a hole in my screen.

"I'm going to stay around this weekend," Georgia says, loitering by the side of my desk. "Might visit my parents next week."

"Great," I say faintly. Because we're a couple of hours out from the city, most of the staff and guards choose to live in accommodations in the small township twenty minutes away during the school week. Most often go home on the weekends.

"What are you getting up to tomorrow night?" she probes.

"Working," I reply, scrolling through my emails to see five new ones in the last ten minutes. One of them is yet another meeting request from Serpent Court. It's not until my phone case creaks, threatening to crack, that I consciously loosen my grip.

Georgia laughs and the cadence of it streaks down my spine in all the wrong ways. "You work so hard, Lyle. You should come to the movies with me. There's that new one—"

I look up, regarding her seriously, and she immediately shuts her mouth. Georgia has her pick of feline males any day of the week, but has not yet found her pack. For the protection of my students, I only hire staff who are already in mating groups. Georgia was not my choice for a secretary, but as the niece of the feline king, I was forced to take her on board when she applied last year.

She'd set about trying to get me into her bed straight away. With limited options out here in the central hinterland, I'd accepted her offer.

Until, that is, I met Aurelia. And suddenly even looking at

my secretary gave me a feeling of profound revulsion. If this kept up, I was going to have to fire her.

"Have a good evening, Georgia," I say flatly.

She stiffly nods at my clear dismissal and strides out of my office. With fire still flooding my veins, I decide I need to blow off some steam.

* * *

When Celeste started working with me at the age of seventeen, she made it clear everything in her training program was non-negotiable. I needed to keep calm. I needed to maintain control. So, it was a strict daily regimen of meditation, essay writing, talking about my feelings, hard physical exercise, mixed martial arts, and general schooling. Once I turned eighteen, I also had to make sure I had sex regularly. One of the different things about an animalia prison compared to a human prison was the need for beasts to have sex to temper their volatility. Blackwater had a huge roster of sex workers, so it was never difficult for me to sate my carnal urges. Once I started working here, however, I had to make my own roster, and Georgia was a convenient regular.

Now that my roster is non-existent, it becomes more important for me to focus on the rest of my daily disciplines.

All animus males need to exert physical energy every day to remain stable. It was why we invested so much in both the jungle gym and traditional gym equipment in the warehouse at the back of the school.

With students only just finishing up their final class of the day, the gym is empty. After changing in the locker rooms, I head straight to the boxing equipment. We have a line of animalia-strength punching bags, speed-balls, and even a boxing ring, which I've forbidden Savage from entering.

I head towards the same boxing bag I've been hitting every

other day for the past four years and set to work, finding stability in a familiar rhythm.

My mind wanders back to Aurelia. Back to Beak and the males surrounding her in every. Fucking. Class. To the way Savage puts a possessive arm around her at every chance. To the way every male rakes their eyes down her face, her body, her legs.

The way she licks her lips and bites her pen. The way she looks at me with those big mythical blue eyes that make my cock harden and every cell in my body jealous of anyone who gets to touch her and laugh with her and speak with her as an equal—

But then I'm hitting air and I stumble back, my vision clearing.

Where there was a punching bag, now stands a shredded mess of leather and padding. I don't even have to glance to my left to know there is a line of students staring at me, still and silent, the scent of their fear and lust strong in the air.

From the side of my eye, one of them slowly approaches me, keeping his movements slow and predictable in the way of beasts not wanting to trigger a predator. I remain still, waiting for him to make himself known.

"Um, sir?"

It's a third-year panther I accompanied to court last year on a couple of manslaughter charges. I still see him for monthly sessions to work on the anger management issues, so I know him well.

It takes conscious effort for my voice to emerge calmly. "What is it, Maddox?"

He tentatively holds out something, his hand trembling a little. "You can keep it."

I turn to take the object from his palm and, upon recognising it, sigh through my nose. It's an academy stress ball some of the students designed as a project. Printed on the front in bubble letters, it says: 'Squeeze me, baby'. On the back: 'I like it hard'.

"Thanks," I say dryly.

"No worries, boss."

I exit the gym, ignoring the many wary glances before shooting an email to Ruben to order a new boxing bag.

Chapter 30

Scythe

In the dark of the night, by a gibbous moon, Xander lands a discreet distance away from the city centre, at one of our regular landing spots. Two cars wait for me fifty paces away.

"See you in a few days, brother," he says.

"Happy hunting," I reply as I climb off his back and jump onto the field.

I watch him leave, his powerful body launching into the sky, a sheer defiance of physics that's always a magnificent sight to see. His scales gleam blue-black under the moon until the sky swallows him whole.

It's low tide out on the coast of the country, and though I long to see it, I don't have the time. Rufus steps out of the first car and shakes my hand. We exchange a few words before he passes me the keys to the second car and leaves.

I put myself into the driver's seat of the second, my favourite black Maserati, and take off to find the road. After dragon flight, driving a car should be child's play, except the ghost that forever haunts me now has a reason to be close.

He appears in the passenger seat, glistening wet blue-grey skin, with stringy black hair and a mouth full of razor-like teeth.

Find them, stalk them, tear them to pieces, it whispers into my head. *Drive the car off the road, crash it, steal it, choke it.*

I exhale a long-suffering breath. Land-psychosis is something I can usually work around. It's always with me, but being away from my brothers always lengthens its leash. Xander asked to come with me, but I persuaded him not to this time. I have to be gone for a few days for my inquiries and we cannot push Lyle so far as for *both* of us to disappear completely. So I push the whisperings aside with something else.

Reaching out to the academy, I locate that familiar golden energy that will distract my roaring brain.

Irritation floods my arteries as I come up against a barrier. There is that new bubble around the academy that protects all within from external forces and will not permit me entry. It's old magic, no doubt awoken when the latent dragon power within it came into full force. But the timing of it is extremely interesting. For some reason, the school has recognised Aurelia as a kindred spirit.

But then, there is my dragon-brother. I know he feels newly untethered. Like the mythical creature at the base of him is retaliating against these new powers.

He doesn't know what to make of it and neither do I. Dragons have a slightly different way of forming mating bonds. It's a process that's even more primitive than for the rest of us. So primitive that dragons typically only mate one to one.

It's one of the many reasons Xander was cast out of his family. Not the main one, but it was one more thing to add to the situation.

I arrive in the main city two hours later, at the peak of the nighttime rush, and it almost helps distract from the ghost. There are too many things to see and smell and taste. Too much blood coursing around me in a cocktail of drugs, alcohol, lust, and adrenaline.

The humans are stumbling and noisy, dressed in their best, or worst, as they make the most of their Saturday night. There are some animalia-only clubs, but even the human clubs have done away with human bouncers and opted for bears and lions. Then there are those strip clubs who hire unmated reginas to lure in beasts and rake in the cash. A couple of these are mine. Each of us who play the big game has a territory in the main city. A couple of streets that we have under our sole jurisdiction, with scouts and guards to monitor for illegal activity. This city is way too big for just one beast to rule and might have led to great bloodshed if not for this arrangement. This way, we're about as happy as we can be.

I weave my way into my territory and the hotel I've agreed to meet Marduk in. As an unmated, virile tiger, he's restless, never staying in one place for long in the hopes that he'll find his mating group.

This hotel is one of my bigger ones, and I hand my keys to the valet, a scrawny young wolf who almost trips at the sight of me.

I pretend not to notice and he stammers a greeting, promising to look after my car.

"You'd better," I tell him. "It's my favourite one."

He almost shits his pants, so I give him a smile. He almost shits his pants yet again, so I hand him a fifty to make up for it. I make my way inside, cutting left at the atrium to head into the club.

Savage changed its name to *Bouncing Bazookas* when I took it over, and I shake my head every time I see the neon yellow sign emblazoned above the entrance. We keep things classy for the richer clientele who like to come here.

"A pleasure to see you, sir." Ragnar, the burly lion at the

front, unclips the red corded band and lets me in. I nod in acknowledgement as I stride past.

In the front, some new RnB plays and the dance floor is full of bouncing younger millennials in their Saturday night best. The bartenders nod at me as I pass, heading to the VIP area at the rear. Adonis, a handsome, flirtatious lion in the club uniform —a black suit and tie—grins at me, gesturing aside a pair of brave she-wolves, trying to get through.

More than tipsy, they gaze open-mouthed at me as I pass.

The club music becomes muffled as the door closes behind me and the ghost begins its incessant mutterings once again. There are many rooms branching from a wide, red-patterned corridor. Some of these rooms and alcoves are curtained, others have glass doors, so you can see exactly what debauchery goes on inside.

Some of that debauchery brings back unpleasant memories and makes the ghost's whispers grow even darker, so I don't bother with these doors.

But I do go through a door right at the end of the corridor.

The first thing I see is Blair and Blade, a pair of cheetah twins Eiffel Tower-ing a willowy brunette in red lingerie, on her hands and knees on the red leather couch. Both males are completely naked, their powerful bodies thrusting in unison. The jaguar female moans around Blair's cock while Blade fucks her asshole from behind. He slaps her ass and then waves at me with the same hand, hips never missing a beat. His tongue was severed many years back, so he can't talk.

"Sir," Blair says, nodding formally at me. "Always a pleasure."

The fine sheen of sweat glistening on both their toned chests under the dim, mood light, and the strong smell of arousal saturating the air tells me they've been at it an hour or more already.

I happily pay for this high-end sex worker and her discretion because these cheetahs are the best assassins I've had the pleasure of hiring. They're efficient, effective, and best of all, quiet. The only tell that they get any stress from their work is that they like to fuck their women to exhaustion, hence why I get them the best sex workers in the city.

Virile, unmated animuses like these need to fuck regularly to keep calm and focused on their jobs. Frustrated males are far too happy to take uncalculated risks and wild decisions are usually bad decisions. I won't have that on my team.

Marduk sits on a red armchair adjacent to them, watching the threesome with a clinical, narrow-eyed assessment, his long, tattooed fingers steepled. He rises as I approach him, sweeping a bow. The Caspian tiger looks fine in a black suit with his shoulder length black hair gleaming. Those dark piercing eyes assess me with their typical cut-throat precision, before gesturing for me to follow him into an adjacent room.

I enter and he shuts the door, cutting off every sound. Before us is a one-way glass, showing the dance floor of the club and two stylish armchairs, a small round table between them.

"Thank you for the information on Titus Clawson," I say, taking a seat and lighting up a joint.

"You are welcome," Marduk replies in his slightly accented, old world baritone. "The Clawson family's alliance with the Halfeathers and the Nagas may prove to be a problem."

Problem indeed. Titus' father owned the territory bordering my newly occupied one. He also turned both his sons purposefully rabid, responding only to him for his use as hitmen.

And I have no doubt Titus' appearance at Animus Academy while I was there was not at all a coincidence. While they have a truce with Halfeather and the Serpent Court, they certainly do not have a truce with *me.*

"Next business." Marduk hands me a slip of paper with printed text. "This is the address where she is located."

After I've read it, I raise my brows at him.

"I know," he says dryly. "It'll be a dangerous operation. And with the monster that guards it? Almost impossible."

A monster indeed. "Would you be willing?"

"Yes, of course." He says it like it should have been obvious to me.

A rare smile twitches my lips.

"All pack members are accounted for?" he asks seriously.

"Lady Celeste has confirmed the three of them."

"I would like to meet Aurelia," he muses.

My response is instant—a primitive growl that tears unbidden from my throat.

The Caspian tiger shakes his head, black hair catching the multicoloured lights from the dance floor. "You know what I mean, shark-friend. She and I are both the last of our kind. Perhaps she has some wisdom to share with me."

"She's only twenty, Marduk," I mutter. "And only just coming to terms with the fact that she is... what she is."

"And what were you doing at twenty? You had already made a name for yourself amongst those of us who walk in the dark. You must teach her," he says that last part incredulously. "Are you not?"

No, I've been trying to do the exact opposite. I'd been using my enemies against themselves for far too long. There was something so inherently satisfying in twisting an offensive attack right back onto them. And yet...

"You do not think of her as an ally," he deadpans. "This is not good."

Even now, I feel a need to return to her and have her blood close to my nose. The various flashes I got from Savage and his *time* with her were torture enough—in more ways than one.

"You have not met her," I say, getting out my lighter and setting the paper aflame. We both watch it curl upon itself.

"I, for one, cannot wait to meet my regina." Marduk steeples his fingers and stares unblinkingly through the glass at the writing dancers. Strobe lights dance across his aristocratic features. "She could very well be a bald, bare-breasted harpy with fangs and I would happily lie prostrate at her feet. That is our responsibility. The *only* responsibility. I have been collecting far too many trinkets with neither female nor harpy to gift them to." His gaze flicks back to me. "There is nothing you can see in my blood?"

The impression I get off Marduk's blood makes my head ache, but there is a certain glimmer there I cannot place. Like a thought just out of reach.

I tell him so, and for the first time since I've known him, his eyebrows raise in a faint almost-expression.

"Interesting," he murmurs.

As Marduk leads me back out of both rooms and into the corridor, we pass a room in which I hear a male screaming. Orange and black, desperate energy emanates through the door. Marduk saunters behind me to calmly open the door.

The screaming abruptly stops.

"Shhh," he says, pressing a finger to his lips. "People are trying to copulate, among other things." He clicks it shut. "Sorry about that, friend. It seems our latest prisoner has no manners. But he will give me access to the blueprints before the end."

I offer him a rare smile.

Marduk smiles mildly back.

Chapter 31

Aurelia

On Sunday night, I'm in the student village with Minnie and Stacey, getting hot chocolates at a cutesy little cafe run by a pair of artsy wolf sisters. It's almost closing time and we're the last ones left to leave the cafe.

"So how many beasts can you turn into?" Stacey whispers excitedly.

I finish the last of my hot chocolate. "I have to touch them to be able to turn into them." I say quietly. "But in primary school we had a petting zoo and I got to touch an alpaca, some mice, chickens, sheep—"

"Oh come on!" Minnie whispers. "Farm animals, Lia?"

I grin at them. "Well one time I got to touch this saltwater—"

Stacey makes googly eyes and I shut my mouth just in time to see a guard swaggering down the cobblestoned laneway. He stops before our little outside table and silently presents me with a black appointment envelope.

I take it from him, frowning up at his incredible height.

A tingle runs down my spine.

He wears a black gaiter and sunnies, covering his face and identity, like all the other guards, but I can't help but feel that there is something different about him. He's pretty tall, the same height as Savage, and the black combat uniform hugs a clearly muscled figure.

"Are you new?" Stacey purrs, ogling him.

The fairylights strung above us glint along his dark sunglasses as he says nothing and just gestures to me with a gloved hand to open the envelope.

"You look new," Minnie agrees, sniffing delicately.

I clear my throat and open the notice.

This time, it's not written in Lyle's hand like I expect, but a very feminine, confident cursive.

"Oh shit," I whisper.

I show the girls.

"The headmistress?" Minnie whispers. "She wants to see you?"

"It's about time," Stacey says.

"I think she was giving you time to settle back in." Minnie nods. "And maybe coming up with a plan for the council."

Goosebumps erupt all over me. "I hope so. I don't know how long a phoenix injunction lasts for."

We asked Theresa a few times and she didn't know; even looked up cases in the library, but couldn't find anything in recent history. But, to my chagrin, it *was* all over the news. The first thing I did when Savage gave me my phone was download the *Animalia Today* news app. It was now relegated to the middle of the hot news lists, but it was still very much present.

"It's curfew, let's go," Stacey says. "And you're dropping me off at the animus dorm."

But as I look up, I realise that the guard still towers over us, listening carefully.

What a snoop.

He gestures for us to go ahead of him, as if he means to escort us out. We look the guy up and down again, casting looks over our shoulders before sauntering forward. As much as I wished my friends found their mates so we could complain about it together, at least they know how to distract themselves in the meantime. More than one anima tussled with a guard, we all knew that collective secret, but there were so many animuses in the dorm to choose from it usually wasn't an issue.

Just one of those distractions prowled out of one of the men's clothing stores, black shopping bag in hand.

"Ladies." Yeti, the white-haired Siberian tiger, nods at us, though his blue-eyed gaze is hot on Minnie alone. He was *the* menacing tiger of the school before Titus came along and is loyal to Scythe. He is one of the biggest males around here, and when not with Scythe's group is always alone. I imagine his pelt is the exact same colour as his hair: bone white.

"Hi, criminal," Minnie drones like he's an irritation. "Off to beat someone up again?"

"Bangles." He leans down and flicks the silver jewellery around her left wrist. "You get prettier every time I see you."

Minnie scoffs and covers her bangles with one hand. "And *you* get ruder every time I see you!" She stomps past him and Stacey and I follow, giggling.

"Geez, Min!" I hiss excitedly as we leave the village, showing our bags to the guards at the exit. "You've got the two baddest tigers in the place lusting after you!"

"Yeti is a dick," she says, though I note her cheeks are definitely flushed.

As we leave, that same tall guard follows us at a distance. I suppose I appreciate the extra security, but I find it odd because they usually walk in pairs.

The back of my neck prickles and I cast another look at him. He saunters behind us like he has all the time in the world. My eyes are drawn to the long line of his legs and the breadth of his shoulders, lit behind by the village fairy lights. His silhouette is intimidating, and it makes me uneasy.

I know that a lot of the guards here are under Scythe's

payroll, but would it be so hard for my father to sneak one of his own in here? My heart races as I consider this. But to nab me from inside the school directly would be almost impossible, considering all the protections I've put in place myself.

Henry clucks softly under his breath from where he sits on my shoulder, reminding me that he's another form of protection as well. And a single animus? I can handle the bastard if he tries anything dumb.

We pass the animus dorm and both of my friends halt.

"This is my stop too," Minnie admits softly. She points to her rainbow overnight bag to indicate her things are in there. "See you after your meeting tomorrow morning?"

"Yup!" I try to hide my unease as I hug the two of them, then watch as they practically skip into the animus dorm. Rock music pumps from the stereo system in the rec room and the urge to follow them makes me take an actual step towards the door. Two of my mates are no doubt up in their rooms while Savage lies in solitary. I wonder what they're doing. Do they jerk off thinking about me at night?

With Savage still in the shu, I've got no possible action tonight. Looks like it's just me and my vibrator of choice, and I'm really keen to get out that lion's head one.

Only once Minnie and Stacey are safely inside do I sigh and hurry to the anima dorm, looking behind me and shivering in the cool nighttime breeze. Cicadas chirp in the night and the fresh smell of eucalyptus sharpens my mind.

And that lone guard is still following.

Frowning, I make it to my dorm, get out my ID card and practically bash it against the sensor.

"Aurelia!" Christine says happily, not unlocking the door. "We've not chatted today."

"Let me in, Christine," I say, tapping my card again. "It's late."

And dark.

"Oh, hello friend!" Christine says cheerily.

I whip around to see the intimidating guard right behind me. He raises a gloved hand to Christine in greeting but says nothing.

My heart pounds in my head.

"Why are you following me?" I demand. "I'm here now. You can go."

In the dark of the night, he's nothing but a lurking beast staring down at me from his great height. He must be as tall as Xander. I break out into a sweat. I can literally see nothing of him, his own skin, or features. Not even his eyes. Every inch of him is covered by his uniform. His hands rest on his automatic rifle strapped in front of him with the ease of someone who's held one for many years.

He cocks his head as if asking me a question. I shake my own, unclear of what the hell is going on. But the way he is staring at me has my body quivering.

Wait a minute.

"You can go now," I repeat, trying not to show my panic.

"Goodnight, good sir!" Christine pipes. "We can chat about your dating life tomorrow night!"

With no other option, he inclines his head and strolls off. I watch him until the shadows of the night swallow his body.

I feel him leave like a physical sensation. It makes my shoulders sag in relief.

"Creepy," I say to the gargoyle, trying to hide my trembling and the sudden suspicion I have.

"Oh, I dunno," she says, gazing after him. "I'd be tempted by that death stare he's got going on."

It's my turn to stare at Christine. "What did you say?"

She sniffs. "Can you blame me? I'm the spirit of a dragon-manor. The mythic orders get me all excited. Makes me want to help them. Like I help you."

I all but leap inside.

When I get back into the room, I'm greeted by a loud squawk that immediately distracts me.

I let out a scream on reflex.

Startled, I switch on the lights to find Eugene fluffing his wings on my headboard.

"By the Goddess, Eugene!" I say in relief as Henry zips over to say hello. They knock beaks and cluck at each other before Henry plops himself on his donut bed. Eugene was following me around everywhere but tonight he'd wanted to stay in. I had a feeling his little legs got tired running after me all day. "We'll make a party for ourselves, us three birds, won't we?" I say happily.

Even after years of sleeping alone, without Minnie or Savage's company, I'm suddenly left bereft.

I take out some sugar cubes that I saved for Henry from my side table. Feeding some to Eugene, he lets me pet him softly. "I wonder what you're doing with Savage," I say suddenly. His feathers are as black as shadows, and the frill on the top of his head is scarlet. "You're quite pretty, if I may say."

He ducks his head like he understands, and I suddenly see that Eugene is *not* a normal rooster by any stretch of the imagination. "I do hope Savage is not holding you captive." He ducks his head again, and then seems to change his mind and shakes it. "I can't tell if that's a yes or no. But, well, if you ever wanted to escape, you'll let me know, won't you?" Eugene makes a sound, and it's sort of sad.

* * *

The next morning, Eugene insists on following me out the door. I think he's just going to relieve himself or eat something, but he follows me all the way to the dining hall and remains by my side like a little protector. The girls love him and he ends up being sat in Raquel's lap while Stacey feeds him titbits from her plate.

I eat a quick breakfast before bidding my friends goodbye and showing the two *normal*, regular looking, non-creepy guards outside the dining hall my appointment note with the headmistress.

"Must be important, Aquinas," the female one says, leading me in the direction of Lyle's office. She's the chattiest of the guards in the dining hall and ends up holding Eugene because some of the animuses are eyeing him hungrily. "The headmistress doesn't see anyone. Didn't even meet her when I got my job here."

"Really?" I ask in surprise. "How odd."

I want to ask more questions, but I don't think that's a good idea. The fact that our headmistress is a phoenix is something that would be spoken about a lot, and yet it isn't. Does anyone even know about it?

We get to the elevator that leads to the senior offices, but instead of pressing for level 3 like we normally do to see Lyle, the guard uses a key to open a compartment in the elevator's button panel that reveals another three floors. She presses 5 and off we go.

I have a sneaking suspicion that Lyle's apartment is on level 4, judging by how far up I had to climb in my secret doorway to get there. I haven't tried to get back in since that first time, but I don't want to risk it while Lyle's actually around. I might have to convince Christine to come up with another distraction of some kind.

The elevator doors open to reveal a space almost identical to Lyle's office level, with plush maroon carpet and fancy oil portraits of likely long-dead people on the walls. But instead of only being occupied by a receptionist's desk, this room is a boardroom, complete with ten carved chairs on a long black table. To the left is a sideboard with water and a jug, along with a fat little gargoyle in the shape of a long-necked dragon, his obsidian scales glinting orange under the warm downlights. The dragon's mouth opens up.

"Name?" He has a heavy rasp through his snout.

"Aurelia Aquinas," states the female guard, looking curiously around.

"Leave her here and get out," the gargoyle orders in a superior tone.

The two guards nod at me before stepping back into the elevator.

Only when the doors close and we are alone does the gargoyle rasp, "You are about to enter the presence of the Lady Celeste Agra, warden of Draykaris House. Appoint her due respect, Lady Boneweaver."

A little shock zings through me at his address... and due warning.

"Yes, of course," I murmur, straightening my spine. I look down at my bodycon mini dress and denim jacket, suddenly feeling incredibly underdressed. I smooth down my hair and blow out a breath. Henry preens himself as if he also feels the same.

"Present to the door on the far side. Knock twice. The cock stays here."

I give Eugene a little pat before I obey, striding past the intimidating-looking chairs, my heart pounding an unsteady rhythm as I knock.

Minnie described the headmistress as beautiful. Sabrina called her sexy. Connor called her powerful, with great fashion sense. But the woman who opens the door physically knocks the breath from my lungs.

A memory comes back, bold and biting. I sat in an office with her, and she tore my world apart with dark, rhythmic words.

"Aurelia." Her voice is a quiet, husky purr. "I want to tell you how much of a joy it is to see you again." She smiles at me, brilliant white teeth flashing.

She appears to be in her fifties, and it's been seven years since I saw her last, but her beauty hasn't faded at all. If anything, her crimson hair appears brighter, her wise, siren eyes have even more depth, and her red-lipped smile is kinder. The flash of a memory reminds me that she wore a white pantsuit when she came to see me in my cavern. Today, she wears black. There is a gravity to her presence I can't explain; something the mythic orders definitely share. It's as if the majestic fire that defines her kind pulses around her in a wave of not heat, but energy. She contains it under skin, making her glow from the inside.

Quite suddenly, I don't feel like I'm just a plebian student here. My posture straightens.

"The joy is mine, Headmistress."

She smiles and something clenches in my chest. "Please come in, Aurelia."

I start when I see that, behind her, Lyle rises from one of the two chairs in front of her ancient black desk.

"Oh, don't worry about him," she coos. "He'll behave."

I shake myself and turn back to her.

"I'm really glad I could meet you again, too," I manage to croak out. "I always wondered, if... you knew about me... that day."

She closes the door and strides around to her desk, not sitting down but perching on the side of it.

Lyle sits down and I take the seat next to him, trying to ignore his general aura of menace and ice and wondering why he has to be here and craving his presence all the same.

I feel his eyes burning on the side of my head as Lady Celeste speaks with a knowing smile. "I did know that day," she confirms. "And your father has hounded me ever since. Unfortunately, he got two names from me at the time." She gives me a sympathetic look. "But I was shaken from what I'd seen when I took your hand. Four faces were clear to me."

I'm shaken by this because my father outright lied to me. That day, which is seared in my memory, he stormed out of her office with cold anger oozing from every pore, telling me he found nothing.

But he was given two names. And I can guess which two.

But... *four* faces were clear to her?

My brows shoot up. "And the fifth?"

"Covered in shadow; the prophecy was quite literal about that."

I exhale slowly. So my fifth is going to be a problem after all.

But she also takes a deep breath, and from this confident, striking woman, that worries me.

"Aurelia, I want to ask you something very serious," she says, golden eyes boring into mine and holding me there. "I want you to consider it carefully. I've been able to buy you some time to stay your sentence, however, these things have a time limit. The Council will want a reason for the injunction. They'll want a very good one."

Dread winds its way like an anaconda around my body, squeezing tight. This room suddenly feels very small. Some part of me knew this was coming.

I swallow through a thick throat. "What are you suggesting?"

Those golden eyes flick to Lyle and I turn to him.

The lion says carefully, "We believe, Miss Aquinas, that it will be in your best interests to reveal that you are a Boneweaver."

Old, black-wreathed terror grips my heart.

"No!" The words are out of my mouth on pure instinct. I'm gripping my armrests hard enough to bruise. Panic lashes through me and the wound on my stomach pulses a low, steady throb. The sudden urge to shift into my eagle form rises up—and I slam my anima back down.

Celeste says, "Aurelia, your father instilled a great fear in you—"

"It will do nothing but put a target on my back!" Wings rustle in my head and I shove the feathers back down. "Every beast with an agenda will come for me."

Henry croons softly in my ear and I grab him from my shoulder to hold him with shaking hands.

"But it will also stop your execution." Lyle's words are a knife cutting through my terror. Focusing me.

My head whips around to stare at him. The words sink in and silence stretches out between us.

He leans forward infinitesimally, amber eyes intent. "We won't do it if you do not consent," he says gently, as if to a frightened deer. "But I need you to consider that we do not have many other options."

The world is quiet as Lyle and I stare at each other. Something flickers in his amber irises. Something that's not entirely cold.

"For now, we will proceed with Plan B," Celeste says, breaking the spell between the lion and me, "and ask for an extension. That's the best we can do."

Relief pours through me, a wash of warm summer rain. I almost sag in my seat. My secret can *never* be out in the world. Not for any reason.

I clear my throat. "The other phoenixes will agree?"

"They are aware of the... delicacy of this situation."

Cool relief. So I have time. There's time yet.

"So, what do I do?" I look between her and Lyle and am surprised to find Celeste waiting for him to respond.

He looks at me with eyes that search my own. Like he's trying to look for something very particular within me. I'm afraid he won't find what he's looking for. I'm afraid the only thing he'll find is a girl who got herself off on his bed for revenge. A girl with a death sentence hanging like a waiting noose. Does he see me as a lost cause?

His jaw clenches. "We'll do what we can, Aurelia."

Disappointment floods me. I don't know why I was expecting a declaration of love or something similar. Seeing into his past and thinking that he might find some kindred spirit in me was delusional thinking. Savage, I can believe might love me, or try to. But *this* lion? He's fighting his animus and winning each battle.

But I know all about fighting. Especially fighting invisible forces.

"We leave now," Lyle says. "Celeste and I will attend the meeting with the Council and we'll do what we can."

"Great," I say tightly, glancing quickly at Lyle and then away again. "Thank you."

"Hm." Celeste makes a sound that's somewhere between interest and disappointment. But when I look at her, she's smiling at me.

And I get the feeling that it's not *me* she's disappointed in.

Chapter 32

Lyle

Terror. Sheer, raw-boned terror is what I saw in Aurelia's stunning blue eyes. Pupils dilated, trembling with adrenaline. I've never in my life seen terror so profound in the eyes of another. I almost reached a hand out to her.

I swear under my breath. I almost touched her bare skin. Sure, it's all I crave every time she comes within my line of sight, but to do that would be a terrible mistake.

As Celeste and I silently walk out of her office to head to the academy's underground garage, I sense her disapproval. She's been my mentor for long enough for me to know what she thought of me without her saying so.

I send my awareness out in a newfound skill.

"Scythe?"

"Yes, Lyle," comes the cool, but faint reply. He's not in the academy, I realise. As much as that would irritate me about any other student blatantly leaving my school, Scythe has never really been a student here. I'm man enough to admit that.

"She was not willing to declare herself openly."

"I thought as much. She has been taught silence and discretion since the cradle. That is the way of the Serpent Court. You know that."

I do. We all do. But the fact that it sat so... primal in her. That need to keep away. To keep quiet. I'm sure it's part of the reason she succumbed to that strange rabidity.

"She seemed to think it would put a target on her back."

"It will."

"But the alternative is to go to her father for supposed breeding. Why is this not the better option?"

There's a pause and then, *"I'll see you at the meeting, Lyle."*

Scythe's presence fades away, hanging up the telepathic phone line. I have to admit that, despite my initial shock, these telepathic chats are convenient. Despite this, I've made it clear I am not a part of the Boneweaver pack, which currently has its members standing at the grand total of two. And yet Aurelia is not alone in her battle. The issue she faces is about more than just her. It's about doing what's right.

Celeste, too, was coming out of the protection of secrecy, putting herself at risk by presenting to the Council of Beasts as the Headmistress of Animus Academy for the first time. If she was nervous, she gave no sign of it. When he'd brought it up with her, she'd only smiled and said, "It's time, Lyle. Long past time." She could protect herself, of course. But...she'd never found her mate. She put it down to the dwindling population of phoenixes. There were only ten left in this state alone and only one mating pair had children.

If they were not careful, their species would end up like the Boneweavers. With a single survivor carrying the torch in frightened, trembling hands.

My animus rattles his chains, growling low and deep in the way of rabid beasts. Old fear comes rising to the surface, the flash of blood on my hands, flesh under my nails. A bleeding sky, a dry heat.

Never again. I'd made a promise to myself long ago in the bowels of Blackwater Penitentiary. Never again will I let my rabid animus out. And to ensure that, I needed to keep away from Aurelia.

Chapter 33

Aurelia

Celeste and Lyle bid me goodbye and I leave level five in a hurry, Eugene in tow.

It makes my blood roar in my head to think of where they are going. To, essentially, convince the Council of Beasts not to send me to my father for a fake execution.

To instead be forced to breed with the highest bidder to maintain old family lines.

An actual execution would be a mercy.

And yet, what they ask of me to fix this, is impossible. They think it'll stop the execution order, but all I know is that it will make everything one hundred times worse. And in a school full of budding criminals, many from crime families and gangs, I'm a rabbit in a wolves' den.

I need to find Minnie. I need to see what other options I have. Revealing myself is a stupid idea and there just *has* to be another way. We just need to sniff it out.

I'm so engrossed in my frantic thoughts and clutching Henry so tightly that we both miss it.

The silence in the air. The tiny inkling that a predator stalks behind us. The fact that Eugene has not been following me for the last ten seconds.

The black hood snaps over my head like an adder's strike, faster than I can compute. My hands and ankles are snatched up and bound. My power blinks out, snuffed like a candle. With horror, I realise that means they've put tourmaline shackles on me. Henry is suddenly not in my hands. Eugene is nowhere to be seen.

This is it. He's come for me.

Panic consumes my mind, and I descend. Becoming nothing but that rabid animal, bucking and thrashing my entire body. If I had power, it would be shifting or lashing out left and right, but all I have now is my human muscle and flesh.

Somebody swears, but the hands are firm, strong enough to tell me that multiple animuses have me in steel grips. I scream out for Henry, but it just makes the cloth suck into my mouth.

Something pricks me in the shoulder and I recognise the sting of a snake's fangs, just as a nasty female voice, vaguely familiar, slithers into my ear.

"The King Cobra says hello, bird shit."

Venom burns my bloodstream. Panic turns into terror, but it only makes my heart beat faster. Three seconds later, the venom shoots up my neck, reaches my brain, and everything turns dark.

* * *

Cold water splashes on my face and I return to consciousness with a gasp, blinking away tears and the blurry vision.

"He said it wouldn't affect her," that husky female voice chides. "See? She's fine."

"I've never seen someone do that with my venom." A quiet male voice sounds disturbed and I recognise him as well.

Suddenly my mind clocks in, working rapidly to assess my situation in the way my father trained me from toddlerhood.

I'm tied to a chair, arms bound behind me, ankles bound to each leg of the chair. The rope is so tight that I can't even wriggle an inch. I reach for my power again, but there's still nothing. My phone is tucked securely in my bra, but I have no way to get to it.

We're in an underground cave—the air is humid and it's dark, the only light coming from a soft orange lamp in the corner. A quick glance at the dirt floor confirms my suspicion that this is a shedding cave as old, dead snake skins are littered in the corners. It was nice of Lyle to give the serpent students a place to shed during the year. I'll have to congratulate him when I see him next.

Five figures loom over me, all dressed in ripped black jeans and black t-shirts and hoodies. These are serpent students from the academy. Not any of the generals from my father's inner circle. A small part of me relaxes.

Someone steps in front of me and tight fingers lash around my throat. A voice growls in my ear. "What the fuck is your secret, Aquinas?"

I grit my teeth against the digging fingers restricting my air supply.

My father knows about my venom trick because my mother was the same. We're immune to the venom of any creature, probably because we can turn into any of them. Those fingers squeeze my airway further and I wheeze audibly. But it makes my vision narrow. A wave of fresh panic clears my eyes and I recognise the face—

"Stop it, Thaddis," hisses the lone female anima, dragging out the *s* like the feral she is.

Thaddis, a blonde, muscular anaconda, lets go and I gasp in the damp air, each breath painful and strained. As he removes his grip I notice, on the back of his hand, the same black and green tattoo that had been etched on Thomas Krait's hand. A stylistic 'B' encircled by a black snake with long, serrated fangs and startling crimson eyes.

"What the fuck do you want?" I wheeze out. I need to find out their plan. Get them talking.

The only female, Natalia, steps around Thaddis and I mark the five of their faces. Natalia is a cobra, there are two pythons, a black mamba, and Thaddis the anaconda. I know Thaddis and Natalia from my father's court. The other three didn't grow up near me or I didn't see them around as children.

"Tali," I say smoothly. There's water still dripping down my face and it slides down my forehead, getting in my eye. I blink irritably against it. "Didn't you come to my tenth birthday party? I thought we had a good time."

She's a waifish brunette with a venom identification number along her cheek and as a child, she was a whining, meek sort of girl. How times have changed.

"We were all forced to come to your stupid party," she sneers down at me. The black eyeliner under her eyes accentuates her green irises, making her look predatory and cruel. Her black leggings are strategically ripped, and the black hoodie she wears dwarfs her frame. By the way the two pythons possessively flank her, I take them to be a mating group. "You never had any real friends."

"It was a great party, though," I muse. I will not give this bitch the upper hand by showing fear. "That pink cake tasted so good."

Natalia spits at my feet and points at me. It's then that I see she has the same 'B' tattoo on her hand. "You didn't deserve any of it, you ugly whore. Especially not after what you did to Theo."

That cuts deeper than any other thing she could have said. My heart sinks, but I don't lower my gaze from hers as I say quietly. "What does my dad want?"

There's a collective hiss that echoes around the chambers of the cavern walls. How did they even find this place? I don't know how far they've moved me, but if it's in the school, then help will not be far.

Of course, they spent weeks planning this. They must have been waiting for the one day both the headmistress *and* the deputy headmaster were gone from the academy.

"*His Majesty,* is not your dad," Thaddis snaps. "You're just property. Livestock." He gestures to the black mamba with the inky comb-over. He's short and slender, with lip and brow piercings, and takes out a roll of material from a backpack.

He gets down on his knees before me.

My heart thunders in my chest and I try to kick out of the rope and shackles tying me to my chair. I try summoning my power once again... but it's like trying to draw breath in a vacuum--there's nothing to pull.

"Yuran has a special talent," Natalia says smugly. "He was taught by his father."

The name rings a bell. I wrack my brain, trying to remember the serpents on my father's payroll.

"For you," Yuran's voice is barely above a whisper, "we'll do something special."

It's the thump of the roll of fabric falling open that triggers the memory for me.

Metal instruments gleaming in the moody light of my father's throne room, knives of different lengths and widths, metal pliers, screws, a tiny, jagged saw...

All the blood drains from my face.

He's the son of one of my father's six masked generals. They called him the—

"So she remembers the Serpent Charmer," sneers Natalia.

Fuck.

Yuran smiles faintly as he lovingly gazes down at his torture set and then selects a black knife as wide as one of my fingers. "His Majesty knows everything. There is no point trying to hide."

"If he knows everything, then why bother questioning me?" I say quickly, my eyes on all that lethal metal.

"Who said anything about questioning?" Yuran regards the knife, holding it up as if he's checking it for his sharpness. "This is a message."

My stomach plummets into my nether regions. "Really," I deadpan. "And what does daddy dearest want to tell me?"

Yuran lunges, grabbing my chin with iron fingers and angling his knife at the right side of my neck.

My mating mark side.

And I'm really not ready for the flash of hot pain that sears across my skin.

I scream and he lets me go immediately. Warm liquid trickles down my neck as I stare at them all in shock.

All five serpents are sniggering at me, like it gives them pleasure to see me bleed.

Yuran takes out a bleached white cloth and casually cleans his blade. "Honour your sentence. Surrender yourself to the King."

His words hang in the air like a guillotine.

"Or?" I grit out, blinking away the burning in my eyes.

"Hold her head," Yuran whispers.

Primal terror grips me, but I refuse to beg or plead or ask questions. Annoyingly, tears leak from my eyes, blood slides down my collarbone, and my skin *burns*.

But my efforts at self-restraint only seem to egg them on. Natalia strides behind me with nothing but her best customer service smile and grips my head in both hands, wrenching it to the side to present the bleeding skin to Yuran once more.

"If we cut off the mark completely," says Thaddis, excitedly looking on, "will it grow back?"

"Yes. But it will hurt," Yuran murmurs, back at my feet, selecting another tool. It makes me shiver at the confidence in his voice. He's done this before. Or seen it. I know my father tortures beasts, but *this*?

Natalia is shutting my jaw with her hand on my chin, but I manage to grit out, "My father really told you to do this?"

The cobra is in my face, and upside down she looks like a monster. "Yeah, His Majesty did. And what he wants, he gets."

"Eagle," Yuran says, standing before me. "Surrender yourself to the King Cobra in two Saturdays' time, or he will take your mates down, one by one. He knows exactly who they are."

"I'd like to see him try," I spit.

"He said you'd say that," Yuran nods. "So he also said, we'll take your *friends* down, one by one. He also knows who *they* are. The little pink-haired tiger. That slutty leopard. That nerd lioness and the wolf anim."

Dread forms a living snake around my ribs. I can't believe this is happening.

"Don't forget Connor," Thaddis offers. "He'll be the easiest to get since he lives in our dorm."

Yuran stares down at me, black eyes wide and fixed at my bleeding neck like he's getting off at the sight of it. He's creepy as hell and I half expect the guy to adjust himself at any second.

Suddenly, pain erupts across my abdomen as old, necrotic wounds burst open anew.

For the second time, a scream rips from my throat before I clamp my mouth closed.

I squeeze my eyes shut and suppress a whimper as violent fangs slowly scrape across my stomach, tearing skin, searing muscle, infiltrating with venom. It feels like he's really here, gouging deep wounds with his massive king cobra fangs. A laugh resounds in my head, low and macabre.

They've coordinated this attack.

Sweat drips down my spine, my brain seizes at the sheer blinding pain. I want to faint, I want it to stop, I need it to stop.

I'm completely powerless here. My muscles strain, wanting to shift, wanting fangs to descend, wanting claws to tear and wings to sprout. But I can't and instead I'm splayed on a psychic torture table, unbearably open for my father's full use of my body.

Natalia laughs and it's the ugliest sound I've ever heard. "His Majesty is getting her, isn't he?"

Yuran prods my stomach with a finger. Pain hits the fresh wounds and both me and my anima scream in pure agony. As I clamp my mouth shut, my eyes water and I fight my bonds once again, kicking out so hard it rocks the chair backwards. Natalia swears but I barely hear it. I need to get away. I need to find Minnie. My *friends*. He's going to go after the people who've become my family. It's a worse punishment than death. I won't be able to live with myself.

"Just think," Yuran whispers in awe. "If he's powerful enough to cast an attack from so far, what else is he capable of? He doesn't even have to be here to hurt your friends."

Minnie. Oh God, *Minnie*. Not again, please not again.

"He'll be here in two Saturdays," Natalia says, yanking my neck for emphasis. "Present yourself for collection or your friends will suffer. You're not allowed to be a martyr, but the rest of them can be."

I thrash again, protesting against her words, at the implication. The serpents laugh.

"Well, well, well," a deep voice sneers in disgust, "look what we have here."

My eyes snap open just as a set of white glowing eyes appear through the dark.

Chapter 34

Xander

How many vermin does it take to kidnap a Boneweaver?

Five, apparently.

The first thing I see is *that* heinous glowing symbol shining through the low light. A skull with five beams of curling light.

It's the third time I'm seeing the so-called "mating mark" and it feels like I'm digging up an old, rotting corpse.

I almost gag.

Eugene squawks a question from the shadows behind me.

"Yeah, yeah," I assure him. He came to me frantic and cock-a-doodle-do-ing to high heaven. I had to calm him down with some fumes from my joint before he told me what was going on.

Most people think chickens are too stupid to make use of the healing powers other avians have. Instead, the Wild Gods gave them a little something to help them survive with their low intellect. It's barely useful, but if something unexpected is about to happen, they can see five seconds into the future.

So, Eugene had been able to see the vermin jumping out and gotten out of the way in the nick of time. I'd dragged myself out of bed and had to put clothes on just for the stroll over here.

They have her tied to a chair with power dampening shackles, and have her surrounded like five filthy, towering worms.

I announce my presence and the worms whip around, mouths gaping open.

Sighing, I take out my headphones and put them in my pocket. The Red Hot Chili Peppers will have to wait.

The five worms recoil and terror sparkles around them like feverish, red stars.

I wait for it to hit—the killing rage that turns my vision red and means death to all in the room.

But— Wait, what?

It doesn't come. My vision doesn't bleed like it usually does when my headphones are out.

I'm still... calm. All executive functions intact.

And then everyone in the room seems to realise it.

They rush at me all at once and I don't have time to think about it. I don't *need* to use the fire, but I rather like the smell of charred meat. I chuck a crimson fireball from each hand, and they blast into the first two worms in the chest so fast they don't have time to try and dodge them. The flames engulf their writhing bodies. They shriek and drop to the ground, rolling around, arms flailing like cockroaches.

"Mmm. Roast snake," I rasp. My dragon likes to watch when it comes to killing. He doesn't want to miss out on the fun, and I can't blame him.

The next two worms bring out knives from their pockets, throwing them at my head in unison, but I dodge both and they clatter uselessly to the dust.

As the screams of their friends die out and the two balls of flame become funeral pyres, some primal fear takes over the remaining three. They shift into their vermin forms, clothes falling into piles on the floor as two giant worms, an anaconda and a Black Mamba, slither right at me while the female tries to escape.

But they don't know that I love them most in this form.

Really, I cherish it.

I lash out with two ropes of orange fire, catching them lasso-like around their necks. They screech for all of two seconds as their throats burn all the way through and then drop to the ground. The cobra anima, no doubt their filthy leader, is now rearing up, baring her fangs at me and doing that weird growling hiss that cobras do.

"Go on," I taunt softly, walking around the Boneweaver to see the cobra better. "Give us a little bite."

A foul, forked tongue slithers out and tastes the air. It's like nails on a chalkboard for me, so I flick a hand out and snag her around the throat with a thin band of low heat flame. This one I want alive.

The anaconda now lies dead under my fire lasso. I allow the flames to engulf him completely to make a third funeral pyre. It'll be cleaner if we just burn the carcases to ash and leave no evidence.

The Black Mamba, however, still thrashes against his lasso. A roll of black fabric lies open with various tools for slicing, opening, and just good old pain.

Anger rises in me, hot and fiery like my own living flames.

Before I know it, my hand has lashed out and blood and guts go exploding in every direction. My magic is not like feline telekinesis. It's pure power, and in this case, pure pressure. I don't use it often because it's usually not necessary or fun.

Four vermin down, one left.

I increase the pressure on the cobra anima's airway until it goes unconscious.

Then there's only the sound of flames from the pyres consuming the four corpses.

No, that's not correct, there is a certain... melody in the air. It's pure and crisp. Like ankle bells chiming under moonlight. It's seductive, wild, alluring—

I shove my headphones back in.

Aurelia stares at me almost blankly, as if she doesn't quite believe what she just saw in the last five minutes. Then her nostrils flare as she takes in a breath and smells the burning corpses.

That face that haunts my nightmares contorts in outrage. "You killed them!"

Her stupidity knows no bounds.

So, I explain it to her like she's a child. "I had to leave one for Savage, otherwise he'd be upset." I gesture a dismissive hand at the cobra, lying unconscious by my feet.

My dragon self sends me smoke and cinders in a mighty, threatening puff. *Settle down,* I snap to it. *Can't you see I'm saving her sorry ass?*

Hurry up, cretin, it snaps back. *Get her back to our room so we can soothe her wounds with our tongue.*

Nope, not in this lifetime.

The cobra anima seemed to be the leader, so I kick her clothes around until keys chime, and return to the Boneweaver girl.

Blood trickles from the glowing mark on her neck, but it's clotted, so it wasn't deep. She's scared out of her wits, sweating, trembling and stuttering with adrenaline like a hatchling. She smells of fear and pain and something heady that's just as offensive.

Crouching down before her, I roughly release her ankle shackles, first the left and then the right, and now her bare legs are in my face. "Why is there so much drama everywhere you go?"

"I'm the drama?" she splutters, holding back tears. "*You're* the one *murdering* left and right."

"I don't need much of a reason to do that, really," I reassure her. "Might be you next."

"You already tried that, remember? Didn't work."

She's blubbering, trying to be brave, but her constant tremor gives her away.

"Barely. You escaped by the skin of your venomous fangs."

"How did you know I was here?" she demands.

"Tip off."

Eugene squawks behind me, putting in his two cents worth. Although I should probably thank him for the opportunity.

I need to get away. I don't bother untying her ropes and instead collect the torture instruments and obsidian shackles. "Scythe won't like this. Not at all."

"Why? Because he didn't know about them?"

"A mundane assumption," I snort, rising to my feet. She thinks I mean the torture instruments, but I knew exactly who Yuran Black was before I killed him.

Eugene, sensing it's now safe, comes bumbling around the corner. He makes for the ball of blue fluff that is Henry, lying unconscious against the cavern wall.

I take the loose end of my thin fire lasso and proceed to drag the giant tapeworm that's the cobra anima out with me. What have I become? A courier? An errand boy? By the Gods.

Aurelia, still bound to the chair with the rope, starts to blubber something again, so I cut her off. "You can get yourself out now that the vermin are gone."

"W-Won't you get in trouble for this?" she stammers, pretending she cares about me.

I throw her a smirk over my shoulder and stalk out.

How many dragons does it take to kill a den of vermin?

One, apparently.

Chapter 35

Aurelia

It takes me half an hour to telekinetically untie each of the ropes around my four limbs, swearing at that giant reptile under my breath the entire time. I'm not great at telekinesis yet because I've not had all that much practise. I'd been forbidden to use powers other than my shields for so long that I practically forgot that I had them until I got here and saw Minnie and the other felines use them frequently.

But that dragon-sized asshole Xander Drakos just left me here without a second glance, like I'm rubbish for disposal. And the way he *killed* those serpents with hate in his eyes... It was chilling. Until, of course, he all but lit the place on fire. Four mounds of licking flames are piled around me, and the heat from them is turning this cave into a kiln. My clothes are saturated with sweat by the time I get myself out.

As soon as I'm free, I rush to Henry, where Eugene is trying to rouse my baby's tiny body. I scan Henry right away, checking for any injuries. He's breathing and his little heart is beating normally under my index finger, so he looks like he's been knocked out by something. Did they envenomate him? I panic, but I can't find any fang marks and he's not symptomatic. I send my healing into him, but my magic can't sense anything to heal.

Cursing under my breath, I cast a look at the four mounds of dragon fire. Sure, they'd held me captive, but did they deserve to die for it? Bile rises in my throat, as I think of Natalia's two mates, now dead and how Xander executed them without so much as a blink.

That was a bad turn of phrase because Xander doesn't actually use his eyelids, but he executed these people like they were nothing.

Eugene squawks with urgency and I look down at him. "I suppose I have you to thank for this," I murmur.

He bobs his head.

"Come on," I say. He clucks in affirmation, ready to follow me. Cradling Henry to my chest, I race out of this blasted cavern, wondering how I'm going to explain this to anyone.

It's best if no one knows, isn't it? I don't want people knowing I was stupid enough to get kidnapped and I don't want my friends to flap out. But at the same time, they need to be on the lookout for murder attempts.

Fucking murder attempts! All because of me. I need to reconsider my shields. I need to consider the fact that my father's threats are very real and that after he hears word of four of his own being murdered, he'll have no qualms murdering for revenge.

And what Xander is going to do with Natalia, I have a terrible feeling about. But there are more snakes in the academy and all of them are loyal to my father.

I pant as I jog up a long set of stairs and eventually have to slow to a walk when I become lightheaded and shaky. Venom must still be in my system, and while it won't kill me, it's certainly compromising my body.

When I do finally come up to ground level, I find that I don't know where I am. I have to wander around until I see a set of guards patrolling the corridor.

I raise a bloody hand. "Help, please."

"What the hell, Aquinas?" One of them says, rushing towards me.

Confirmation that I look like shite. "Yeah, I got jumped. Where's the medical centre?"

By the time they rush us to the emergency room, I'm a breath away from crying. My neck hurts and is sticky with blood, my stomach burns like an absolute bitch, and that venom is burning through my entire circulatory system. I heal myself, but with my power being taken up by all my shields, it takes a sweaty, near-fainting toll.

The worst part? No matter how hard I tried to stop the guards, they phone Lyle.

The even worse part? I'm *glad* they've called him and realise with a sort of numb shock that I'm *missing* Savage.

I wish he was here to put his large arm around me. He'd probably make a joke to make me feel better. He'd also probably kill every serpent on sight.

The only good thing is that my favourite nurse Hope is on duty at Emergency. She rushes towards me, her eyes wide as she takes in the guards, me, Henry, and Eugene.

She steers me right inside and sits me down on a bed. Eugene evades the guards and rushes to follow us in.

"I'm not here for me, but for Henry." I hold him out for her inspection and she frowns before taking the tiny ball of fur and setting him on the rolling table. "Someone did something to him," I explain, getting to my feet to carefully watch her work. "His heart rate is steady at one hundred and twenty, his breathing is sixty, and there are no signs of fang marks or injury, but I wasn't sure about needles."

She gives me a look and glances at my neck and bloody clothes. "Calm down, Aurelia. Take a breath. You look like you're going to pass out. Did you get into a fight? You've lost blood."

I plonk myself down on the bed again and it makes that sad *poof* sound all hospital mattresses do; an echo of how I feel.

My head is spinning and I clutch my hands tightly together to stop them from shaking. Eugene perches himself on the equipment counter, watching over us through his funny brown goggles. *Pull your shit together, Lia,* I tell myself. *Pull your fucking shit together.*

"Lia?" Hope's voice brings me back to the present. What had she asked me? It wasn't even a fight. Not bloody close.

"No. I mean yes."

"Which is it?"

I sigh, rubbing my neck. My hand comes away sticky and I almost gag. Not at the metallic smell of my own blood but what they'd been about to do.

They tried to cut my mating mark off. They were literally going to flay my skin off my body like I was being prepared for cooking.

My vision blurs at the realisation that comes crashing into me like a freight train. I barely hear Hope get out her phone to rattle instructions to someone about giving Henry an opiate reversal, plus IV and fluids.

A tiny bit of relief. Henry is one friend that will be okay. One friend that won't be killed by being associated with me.

I'm sobbing into dirty hands within seconds; vicious, shoulder-wracking sobs. My anima is asking if we want to shift and I really want to shift into feathers and talons, head back into my nest under the school to curl up and hide away from this mess. But I can't do that. I need to stay here and keep alert. I can put up with my father's shit if it means my friends are safe from injury. I re-route my shields with a shift in my power. Any psychic attacks inflicted upon the school will be re-directed to me. For my friends' safety, it's the least I can do.

A tissue box lands into my lap and a cup of water is set next to me as Henry is taken away. That makes me sob even more because now no one is here to tell me when to breathe or how to breathe or even *why* I should breathe.

A storm rages within me and all I have is a rickety dingy that I just keep paddling in. Holes litter the sides and it fills with water and yet I still keep paddling.

In my darkest times after my father abandoned me, I remembered my mother. Imagined her ghost was with me in my little boat, a second paddle gracing her slender hands. She kept me company. She kept me strong. But now I'm older, I ask questions that cannot be answered. Why is it that we both spent our lives fighting so hard for life? Is her fate my fate, too? Do I keep going now, only to succumb in the future?

My heart hurts so badly and so does everything else. I let my heavy body fall onto the mattress, falling short of the pillow entirely, but I don't care.

But my life is nothing like my mother's was.

For a few golden moments these past few months, I had a glimpse of a future that could be beautiful. A place that is as bright as the sun. That is filled with friends. Kind, compassionate creatures like my Henry, Eugene and Minnie, Sabrina, Raquel, Stacey and Connor. Savage. I have to fight for that hope. For the memory of my mum gone too soon. I fight to make her proud and do our bloodline justice. Boneweavers were kings and queens once. I have their spirit in my veins. They fight with me, too.

Warmth envelops me as a heated blanket is draped over me. I roll into it and pull the edges around my body, cocooning myself in with my misery, because the last thing I need to do is spread it around. I can almost imagine the blanket is my set of wings, folding around me, secure and safe.

I make sure all my shields are back up, all seven of them, and the extra one that I have around *everything* to keep us all safe.

Perhaps it's that, but I fall into a deep sleep and can't even control it.

* * *

The sound of a familiar baritone wakes me up from a sea of murkiness. That voice is deep and whole, like a bass drum, and it strikes up a memory. Of soft hands under dim light. A gentle, soothing voice. But today, there is an undercurrent of violent power in that deep drum. Like a volcano moments away from erupting.

Something primitive inside of me preens at that terrible, profound anger.

I force my eyes open to see the curtain is drawn all the way around my cubicle and Eugene is sitting on the rolling table, watching over me. Large, perfectly polished business shoes stand under the curtain, opposite a worn pair of blue crocs. The feline in me stretches and yawns lazily. I whisper his name, to no one or nothing in particular, but just because I want to *feel* the sound of it in and around my mouth.

The curtain snatches open and I frown, blinking in annoyance at the new, harsh light. But it's him standing there alright. A towering figure of power and—

"Miss Aquinas?"

Oh, for fuck's sake, he really needs to stop calling me that. I want to hear *my* name in his mouth. But for the first time, there is an uncertainty in the way he says it. Like he's not so sure about it anymore.

The lion strides in and I remain curled up in my blanket, unmoving, because my body feels like a boulder. Looming over me, his massive body blocks out the harsh medical lights. Suddenly I'm in line with his crotch and the large hands that hang by his sides, veined and beautiful.

Those hands stroked my fur at one time. I remember that now.

Alright, so I might have enough energy for *something* after all.

I manage to find my hand in my blanket cocoon and reach out and take one of those beautiful, inviting hands. For some reason, he lets me. It's warm. Oh Goddess, warm enough to send the chill in my bones scuttling away. His skin is golden and tanned and *yup*, those veins are the stuff of dreams. Without thinking, I bring the utter perfection of anatomy to my face and press my lips and nose softly against his skin. I inhale deeply, and it's like the first breath I've ever taken. It's the dawn sun and fresh leaves of paper, hot off the press.

My moan is faint and wanton. "*Need*," I whisper against his skin, my lips brushing across the back of his hand, unwilling to give up contact. I want to scent the beast underneath. The wild, broken lion that I *know* is under all that self-righteous control. I want to taste it, taste *him* and every part of his naked body. His cock is so close to me. Close enough to my face that I could lick that, too.

His hand tightens around my own.

Permission? Perfection.

So I do.

The tip of my tongue darts out and I give his hand a tiny lick. He's musk and man and *lion*. I growl softly against him.

"That's Miss Boneweaver to you," I whisper faintly.

"Sleep," he commands, all sharp edges again. But alas, he still holds my hand! A victory.

Because I have no willpower to disobey, I do close my eyes. And it gives me a strange, delicious sense of satisfaction.

Chapter 36

Lyle

Celeste and I left the Council meeting and called it a success. We were begrudgingly given more time. Mace Naga's reaction was confusing when it was decided. I thought he'd be angry or at least irritated, but instead, he looked me right in the eyes and smirked.

Like he knew something we didn't. It unsettled me, Scythe too, and I wanted to throttle the serpent for it. But then it was time for us to depart and Scythe, Celeste and I parted ways, with the lady phoenix going to a meeting with the rest of her order and me coming back here. Scythe went wherever it was he needed to go and I wasn't going to be asking him where.

I got the call from Ruben half an hour out from the academy and, on pure instinct, my telepathy lifted my BMW off the ground and shot it down the bitumen.

In *my* school? They attacked her on *my* territory? Only focusing on the empty regional road kept the hot-blooded rage at bay.

That is, until I got here and saw Aurelia curled up in the fetal position, drained and covered in blood.

Her blood.

They tried to cut her mating mark off, and I realise it with a murderous abandon.

Eugene squawks loudly and I shake my head, trying to clear the red, the burning need to tear into someone's throat.

"Thank you," I tell him stiffly.

Of all the guards and beasts in this place, it was the rooster that saved Aurelia in the end. Lucky for Savage and his paranoia about the fifth member of the Boneweaver mating group.

I run a hand through my hair and breathe in heavily.

The scent of her blood and pain fills my nose and drives me near mad. Adrenaline heats my veins as two hearts pound in my head.

Colours change, my vision narrows and chains creak. Even with her skin ashen, her eyes closed in sleep and covered in blood and sweat, she is achingly beautiful.

Protect her.

It is a command deep and primitive, coming from the dark depths of my being. Beneath any pride, any ego, beneath everything I thought made me who I am. A distant roar shatters one layer of chains.

Fuck.

Panic makes every muscle in my body go rigid.

Alright, I quickly say to my animus. *Alright.*

I know what he wants.

Giving in to that mating instinct, I let that aspect control me.

Gathering Aurelia into my arms, my animus lies back down behind his door. The scent of the hospital blanket invades my head and momentarily stops me from licking her blood clean off her skin.

A low rumble tears from my throat, as Hope walks in.

"Mr Pardalia—"

"I will take her." The words are out of my mouth in a guttural timbre I barely recognise.

The eagle anima takes an instinctive step back, her eyes wide and assessing. I know what she sees: a barely controlled animus far more powerful than her, making a claim over a female.

Her eyes flick to where the guards are stationed at the entrance to the emergency bay. She's wondering if she should call them. But intelligence overtakes her primitive instinct, and she decides against doing anything. She inclines her head and moves her body to the side to show me she is not in my way. "Of course, sir."

She is perfectly trained. I would know because I trained her. And that is the only thing saving her now.

With Aurelia bundled safely in my arms, I stride out of the emergency bay. Ruben is talking with three of his team in the corridor outside. His eyes dart between me and Aurelia and a frown flashes across his face before it smooths out to neutrality. He is one of the rare males that I have to physically look *up* to when talking.

When I don't stop walking, Ruben falls into stride with me. My feet are working on autopilot; I need to get Aurelia out of here and into a safe place.

I start rattling orders. "Scout the serpent's shedding cave and the surrounding areas. Send me footage."

Ruben nods and I'm pleased to see he leaves a metre's distance between us. "Has she been questioned?"

"She's asleep," I snap. I didn't mean to, and something tightens in me at the awareness of it.

Whether Ruben registers this as unlike me, he doesn't say, only strokes his beard. I hired him for his discretion as well as his power over other beasts. He understands that's the end of the conversation and veers off at an intersecting corridor.

I power through the corridors, right into the executive building and into the lift. Opening the hidden panel, I press number four with my power, tapping my foot as I wait for the lift to take us up at its snail's pace.

The first time I saw Aurelia, it was in the dark of her

bedroom and I was nothing more than a spectre, called forth by a power greater than me. I fought it, at first, before realising that fighting was bringing my animus out and turning me half mad. So I let her regina's song carry me to her bungalow, deep in serpent territory. She lay on her bed, in this tiny, barely there nightie, and it hit me like a lightning bolt. The centre of my gravity shifted, and I was unable to look away as she writhed and moaned, lost to her own pleasure.

It felt depraved and lecherous. And, against my better judgement, I'd craved it ever since.

Men like me are allowed to crave, to want. But to *have*? To have Aurelia like a regular animus would have his regina in body and soul?

Impossible.

I shiver at the thought as I arrive in my apartment and kick open the door to my bedroom. Aurelia snuggles into me, nuzzling my chest affectionately, and I suddenly have the intense urge to wrap her up in my bedcovers and keep her here forever.

I gently lay her down in the middle of the bed and she doesn't stir.

And I don't pull away. I can't.

Her scent is too strong, that blood is too vibrant on her skin and the primitive sense that tells me she is vulnerable refuses to let my arms release her.

Clenching my teeth, I lie down next to her, curving my body around her smaller one as if I can protect her with the sheer bulk of my muscle. Somewhere between the meeting in Celeste's office and the emergency bay, she's lost her denim jacket, leaving her only in this thin dress. Her dark hair is wild and strewn messily about, and I can't resist the urge to set it into order. I gently sweep it off her face, my fingers brushing the skin of her forehead and cheeks.

My hand tingles from the contact and I pause for a breath

before leaning down to sniff the delicate, smooth olive skin of her cheek. Her scent is like a sweet flower, but more heady than floral. It calms the lethal beast behind that door and makes him settle down to rumble a soft purr. Perhaps if I scent her for a bit longer, I will calm enough to return to my normal self. I lower my face to hers, brushing my nose against the line of her jaw. So soft. So beautiful.

What the fuck am I doing?

Aurelia murmurs in her sleep and the sound is like a siren song that holds me in its grasp. I have no choice but to lay my head back down and hold her tight, inhaling her scent and remembering that one fateful night when I first laid my eyes upon her and then just a few days later when she ran from me in the daylight.

More than one part of me stiffens.

I'd killed for her. After years of abstaining from murder, keeping my promise, on pure instinct, at the sight of her being chased by someone other than me, I killed. Five serpent souls returned to the Wild Goddess because my animus is a rabid fucking beast triggered by her.

It's the blood. It has to be the sight of her spilled blood pushing me to behave this way. Through a feat of sheer willpower, I remove my nose from her jaw. In one movement, I roll away from her, leap off the bed and stride into my bathroom.

When I return, Aurelia doesn't wake under the friction of the wet washcloth and the primal bastard in me is purring low and hard, satisfied to be cleaning our regina. He loves that we're touching her, caressing her in the gentle way she deserves.

It's just hygiene, like we keep teaching the students. A part of the syllabus. It's the first rule of the academy. The students must keep clean.

I'm covering her back up when the video call comes through and it's Ruben, his face sombre. "Boss, take a look at this."

He switches to the outward facing camera and what I see turns my vision red.

"It smells like dragon," Ruben says, as if I can't see the three steaming mounds of ash, a few stray red flames licking upwards. I hang up on him before I can throw my phone through the wall.

I'm so riled up I can't bear to use the new telepathic connection we have. I dial Scythe and he picks up on the second ring. He should be back by now.

"Put me on the phone to Xander right now or by the Wild God, you're all fucking dead."

Chapter 37

—

Aurelia

When I wake, it's in a large, luxurious bed with silken sheets that are *definitely* not mine. None of this is mine.

My eyes snap open to see black. Black sheets on a king bed and a lion who sits in an armchair close to his bedroom door and as far away from me as possible.

"What?" I ask myself.

Lyle sighs and it's a strained, self-punishing sound.

"I brought you here," he admits, not looking at me and gripping his armrests hard enough to turn his knuckles white. It has the feel of a man seeking contrition. "I slept next to you for a time. I... held you." Suddenly, he stands, like he's furious, staring hard at the wall like he's thinking hateful thoughts. "I don't know what madness possessed me."

My eye catches on the fluidity of that motion, how he moves through the world like his body is not strong, rigid muscle, but silk.

"We both know what possessed you," I say softly, my own hand tightening on the soft material that encloses me. "The same thing that possessed me to come in here the other day."

Me, on the other hand? I don't regret my actions at all. I let the knowledge of that sit there in the gaping void between us.

"I knew Christine was up to something." He runs his hand through his hair, uncharacteristically loose, staring at his bedroom door like it's his worst enemy. I've never seen him like this. Not when he casually murdered my father's retrieval serpents before I got here. Not in the many times I've seen him furious and irritated by me. Never have I seen him at a loss for words. Never have I seen him... lost.

Something else is out of place, and I look down to find myself covered in one of his shirts. My dress is on underneath, so he thankfully didn't remove it and see my wounds, but I smell of masculine body wash and the skin of my face, neck and chest is soft and clean, like—

"Did you..." I whisper in shock. "Did you..."

He nods stiffly. "Bathe you? Yes."

A tingle shoots up my legs. "Why?" I whisper, clutching his shirt to my chest and wondering if it would be inappropriate to sniff it.

And then I remember that I *licked* this man's hand.

"You were covered in blood," he replies. "Your own. And it wasn't helping... things."

He turns to look at me, amber eyes flicking down to my neck as if he's seeing it all over again. I realise it with a jolt to the stomach. It was unbearable for him to look at my blood. He wasn't able to resist the urge to bring me here, to a private place, cover me up and clean me. Heat pours through my chest, as well as something a little scarier.

"Thank you."

His face says, *are you serious?*

Mine says, *yes, I fucking am.*

I would not have had the energy to do it myself, after all. Although right now my power is still depleted, my desperate exhaustion from before has receded.

"Where is Henry?" I ask.

"He is being admitted for investigation," Lyle says, still not looking at me. "Eugene is with him."

Relieved that both my babies are okay, I try to comb down the bird's nest that is now my hair.

Lyle continues, "I want to know what they used to incapacitate him. And—"

His eyes follow the movements of my hands as I comb through the knots in my long, black locks. "And?" I prompt.

Lyle blinks like he's coming out of a reverie and I can't help but feel some satisfaction. His face becomes stormy, almost scary in its rage. But it's not directed at me. I know that, in my bones, Lyle is raging at the fact that his regina was attacked.

My anima flutters in my belly. Arousal prowls through my veins, slow and intense.

"And I need to know what happened, Aurelia," Lyle says with barely repressed anger. "Xander will not tell me much more than the obvious."

"That bastard." I haven't forgotten that he *left* me there. Probably the reason why he didn't want to tell Lyle anything.

My lion frowns like he wants to tell me off for using a bad word.

Try me, my face tells him.

I'll let you have this one, he says with his.

God, he's hot when he's angry. And angry on my behalf? I rub my thighs together as my clit pulses. I wonder if he can see my hard nipples through the shirt.

His shirt.

This is starting to make up for that time he sent me to my execution. 'Starting to' being the operative phrase.

My anima coos for him, and suddenly I can't stand the distance between us.

I kick back the sheets and swing my legs onto the plush

carpet. Carefully, I ease to my feet and, finding myself not at all dizzy, but warm and tingly, saunter away from the bed.

He never takes his eyes off me as I close the gap between us and it feels like electricity funnels between our bodies, sharp and biting, but also delicious and sweet. It only heightens as I stop mere inches from him and look up at his face. I stay the urge to reach up and touch him, gripping the bottom of the shirt hanging by my thighs instead.

"You are something else when you're angry," I say softly.

My body sways towards him, giving in to his powerful lure.

Hands grab my biceps, squeezing firmly to stop my advance. Perhaps to stop himself too. I love looking at him and I know the desire is clear on my face. In my scent. But wait. All my shields are up and he won't be able to scent me at all.

So I let my scent shield down.

Lyle Pardalia's pupils dilate and he licks his lips, his eyes dragging down to my mouth. And by the Goddess, the pleasure I feel knowing he really is turned on by me.

"Tell me what happened down there, Aurelia," he says firmly, not looking at my eyes but my lips. "All we found were piles of ashes."

And a chair with rope. Though he can't even say it out loud.

"Lyle." I state his name softly. It's a caress. It's skin sliding against satin. I suddenly can't remember why I've never touched him. Why we've never kissed. "I'll tell you if you kiss me."

His face changes. Pure agony flashes across it for the barest moment before it's replaced by frustration.

"Stop it, Aurelia." His jaw grinds forwards and backwards.

"Why?" I ask gently, completely enamoured by his jaw, his scent. His hands are firm on my arms and I crave more of it. I want his firm hands on every part of me. I want him to ravage me with the same intensity he's using to deny me. I inhale deeply. "You smell so good."

"It's only natural for you to feel that way," he says, grimacing.

But I can't help but notice his restraining hands loosen just a touch.

"I want to touch you," I whisper, trying to implore him with my eyes.

"You cannot." But those hands loosen a fraction further, and now they're just holding me gently as he stares hard into my eyes.

His lips are a perfect shade of pink, not too thin, not too full, with a perfectly formed cupid's bow. I suddenly need to run my tongue along it.

I can't take my eyes off those lips as I say, "I thought you looked like an archangel the first time I saw you, did you know that? Handsome, and so stern."

His hands drop off me. "What?" His voice is strained and taut, like he's holding onto his own leash so tightly it might snap completely. But his power surrounds me then, like it did in the classroom that day during regina class. It strokes my arms, my shoulders. My neck.

Even the way he forms words is fascinating. Whether sharp or soft, his mouth is always perfect. My hand comes up to touch his lip and nothing but pleasure fills me at the soft feel of his skin.

Lyle goes so still, and I think he's not breathing either. I can't help but touch him more, allowing my fingers to brush the strong plane of his jaw, his chin, his throat. But something is missing there. I touch my own neck and hiss, the cut still stinging. I reach back for his throat, but he catches my hand in his own. A warning.

But I want to see it again. I've only seen it the once, and I need to see that it's real.

I drop my mating mark shield. Casting it away like old clothes.

Celestial light pops to life on the side of his neck, neither gold nor silver. That skull with five beams of light. My anima caws with joy.

Lyle drops my hand and steps back, his eyes widening in a sort of horror mixed with awe. The corners of his eyes glisten.

"Oh Goddess," I whisper. I've always thought the mark was beautiful. I've always thought Lyle was beautiful.

And both together? The vision is devastating.

I can't help it. Gently, I step forward and put my arms around his neck. I go up on my tip-toes. Whether he wants it to or not, his power reaches for me.

"Lyle," I whisper.

His face lowers, meeting mine. Our breaths mingle.

"We can't, Aurelia," he whispers.

I brush my lips across his. "I know."

His arms come around my hips and I let out a whimper at the contact I've craved for so fucking long.

"We—"

But I don't let him finish, sweeping my tongue over his lower lip, tasting that masculine arrogance. Licking away his reluctance.

He groans, crushing my body to his and, in a way that seems like the heavens have opened, captures my mouth with his own.

I invade his mouth with my tongue, burying my hands at the nape of his neck amongst all his loose, glorious hair.

He groans into my mouth and it's a terrifying, dominant sound. He bites down on my upper lip before sweeping his tongue past my lips to claim me. I moan in my throat, my breath haggard and needy as I claw at his shoulders, his chest.

But whatever aggressive need I have, Lyle has more.

A regina claiming a mate this powerful can never hope to maintain dominance for more than a moment.

Nor do I want to.

I want to be devoured by him; I want to be invaded by him.

His power shifts, overwhelming me and making the hair on the backs of my arms rise.

Lyle shoves me off him and I stumble backwards, shocked and enraged that he would *dare*. He pants, wiping his mouth with the back of his hand and staring at me with searing heat and anger in his eyes. I swear I can see that rabid animal beneath his skin, trying to claw out and come to me.

His gaze flicks down to my chest, where a few buttons have come loose, revealing the curves of my breasts.

He closes his eyes as if fighting it, the pain in his face softening me, calming my anger, before his eyes flash open and the pure hot burn of his gaze makes me want to run.

And be chased.

A sly smile curves across my lips.

"Don't," he warns, but his voice is barely human.

I turn for the door handle, but he's so fucking fast. He grabs me, spins me around and thrusts me up against the bedroom wall, his body hard against my back. With my cheek pressed against the wall, Lyle leans down to whisper in my ear.

"You know what your *running* does to me." He forces it out like it's a swear word. "You've tried to run from me *three times* now, Aurelia."

In one smooth motion, he rips the shirt in half. Buttons go bouncing in all directions.

"Three times?" I pant. Is he including the time *he* sent me to my father?

"Yes," he growls, pulling the shirt down my arms and tossing it to the floor. The left spaghetti strap of my dress slips off my shoulder.

My back is pressed against him, the softness of his shirt a great contrast to the hard body beneath it. And the even harder cock pressed against my ass. I shove my dress up and hook my fingers in my panties to drag them down, but he places his large hands over mine, engulfing them completely and stopping them in their important work.

His breath brushes hot against my ear. "I should spank your ass for what you did in my bed last week."

I laugh until one of his hands comes around my throat.

"You think that was funny?" His voice is low and dangerous. A dominant male demanding for submission.

Well, I'm not laughing anymore. His second hand slides down past my left breast, following the dip and curve of my side until it comes to rest at my panty line. I shiver under his touch, wiggling my hips to try and get him to move lower.

"It was funny at the time," I offer, breathlessly.

He grunts, finally sliding his hand under my underwear. His two fingers find my slit and slide between them.

There's a sharp intake of breath before he slides his fingers through the moisture and murmurs, "Why are you so wet?"

I lean back into him in answer, a high-pitched moan breaking from my throat. One of his thumbs strokes over my mating mark as his other circles my *very* swollen, wet clit.

His cock twitches behind me and he presses closer.

"What the fuck are you doing to me?" he whispers, pressing his lips to my mating mark, *our* mating mark, while his fingers slide down and into my needy entrance.

I'm reduced to a stammering, trembling mess.

"Fuck, Lyle," I gasp as he strokes a big finger in, then out. I'm so wet that we can both hear it as he adds a second finger and moves in slow, languid motions like he's savouring the feel of me.

He growls low, and suddenly, his hand is gone. The sound of his zipper coming down sends me into a frenzy and I try to turn around, but he keeps me in place with his massive body.

"You were not what I expected," he grits out through clenched teeth. "This is not what was supposed to happen."

His fingers find my entrance again and he stretches me out like he's testing my ability to have him.

"I need this," I pant, pressing my palms against the wall. "I've needed it for so long. Just give *in to me*."

A hand snakes around my throat and he tilts my chin up to force me to look back at him. His beautiful face glows with strain. Like he's about to combust.

"Lyle—"

He leans down and captures my mouth roughly and the possession in it makes me swoon.

"I'm not small, Aurelia," he pants out. "I hope Savage has prepared you for me."

He's still in his suit, his bare cock straining against my ass, and I somehow know it wouldn't have happened any other way. I spread my legs and reach back to grip his cock.

A sharp intake of breath, but he allows me to touch him, watching me as I feel him for the first time. Such a big perfect cock, thick and long, and immediately I know I'll need him in my mouth soon. He *is* huge, bigger than I thought, but not so big that I'm worried. I took Savage, after all.

I watch Lyle's face. It's flushed with tension, restrained aggression, and I know he's still fighting his animus and losing the battle. I position his cock at my entrance, whimpering at the way the wet crown of him demands entry.

"I'm your regina, Lyle. I was made for your cock."

His hot eyes flick back to mine in surprise before he flexes his hips forward to enter me.

I cry out, breathing him in.

Lyle also lets out a strangled moan as he eases his way inside, stretching me open slowly because my pussy wants to grip onto him.

Goddess, it burns, and I see stars, but it's a sweet torture to be *had* by him, to feel his girth claiming my most intimate place.

Then he's sheathed all the way in, and we just listen to each other's breaths, feeling the intensity of it. I'm so full of him that it makes me lightheaded. The only thing keeping me up is the hand he has around my neck and his other around my waist. He withdraws and I whimper in protest, immediately craving to be full of him again.

He's shaking with the force of his own desire when he says, "You didn't consent, Aurelia."

"What?" I whisper in confusion.

He's poised at the entrance of me, and I'm so annoyed that he's not in me again that I look back at him with a frown.

His amber eyes burn a heavy gold. "You need to consent to this."

Are my grinding ass and needy moans not enough?

"Say it," he breathes in my ear. "Tell me with your words that you want me inside you."

I'm silent in my shock. That he needs to hear this. But he's Lyle. Of course he does.

Then I grin and say in a low, breathy voice, "Lyle Pardalia, I need you to fuck me with your bare cock and come inside me right fucking now."

He closes his eyes as if it's all he wanted to hear, and giving in to the force of his desire, sheathes himself inside me once more.

I moan as light dances inside of me, fractals coming together to form something new.

In that moment, something seems to change within my lion, too.

"Is this what you wanted?" His voice is ragged as he growls by my ear and thrusts into me again. "Is this what you fucking wanted? Me uncontrollable, begging to be inside of you? *Needing* to be inside you over and over again?"

"Yes," I moan. "Holy shit, Lyle, *yes*."

He makes a sound of pure male pleasure in reply, holding me tight, burying his face against our mating mark and fucking me. I tremble and whimper under the force of his cock, the intensity threatening to send me under, but also filling me up, my power stroking his as it enjoys being united with one of the pieces of my soul.

I whisper his name, and it makes him shudder, filling me with profound, golden satisfaction. His grunts are angry and forceful, but he instinctively protects me with his arms, with the careful movement of his hips. Flesh slaps on flesh, and pleasure builds in me like a ball of light just waiting to make me come undone.

"Angel," he whispers.

It's this new name for me that makes me explode. Light bursts through my body, starting at my pussy and rushing through my stomach, my lungs. I scream his name as pleasure gleams and gilds every particle in my being and it's the only thing in this world that feels good and right and true.

Chapter 38

Lyle

"**A**ngel." That word slips from my throat against my will, borne from a part of me I've long kept shut. There is a reverence in the way the beast holds her against my body. Clings to her as if she is my clear oasis in a bleak, desolate plain.

But then Aurelia is spasming around my cock, her inner walls pulsing, gripping, *fluttering*.

I completely lose myself in her. There is only her. My regina, my light in the dark. Her power surrounds mine, caressing, keening for me with desperate, absolute need. It happens within seconds, but her power is laid naked before me. It's golden, brilliant and so vast that I can only marvel. It pulses around us, around the room—around the entire school. It pulses to the beat of a song that resounds deep in my regina's primal being.

I've never beheld a beast with power like this.

More than an equal.

That is a terrifying concept. My own animus is a monster that requires chaining for me to survive in a civilised world.

And yet, her power strokes that half-mad, lethal power within me as if it is kin. There is no fear, only quiet, gentle confidence. *Come here*, her power whispers. *We have run alongside each other for many lifetimes.*

In reply, I come with that soul-shattering awareness, the thrusting of my cock filling her most intimate place.

Aurelia moans loudly as I fill her with hot bursts of my cum, receiving it, receiving *me* with a face of utter pleasure. I hold her close and she leans back into me like she trusts me. It makes my hips stutter to watch her go limp and take my seed, my animus pleased we are giving her a piece of us. Pleased that she is submitting.

For the first time in a decade, my animus does not pull at his chains. For the first time since my animus woke up on a blood-soaked desert plain, I do not need to fight him.

This feels infinitely *right*. I hold her in my arms, and for moments, we pant against one another, still joined.

But the memory of Aurelia's latent power reminds me that we play a dangerous game. Eerily, it feels like looking in a mirror.

Gently, I slide out of her, and she lets out a little sound of disappointment. My cock twitches at that, but I step away, tucking myself back into my slacks.

She slowly turns to look at me, and for a moment, I can only stare at my regina. I don't think she knows how beautiful she is. How her face, even her gaze, affects me on a bone-deep level. How the softness of her mouth beckons to me even now, asking why we had to let her go. Asking why we deserve to have her when she was so perfect.

I deserve to burn in hell for touching her like this when I do not intend to keep her.

I can't keep her.

I can't keep her.

I can't keep her.

I don't want to leave her. Ever, if possible. My entire body screams for me to bundle her into bed so we can curl up next to her and help heal her wounds. So she can sleep and be safe where we can protect her forever.

But I need to leave this woman before I succumb again.

"Aurelia." Even her name in my mouth affects me. But I clench my teeth and rely upon the resolve that once saved me from madness. "Come here." I can't help but hold out a hand. The bastard in me wants her skin on mine again.

Audibly swallowing, she complies and places her hand in mine. A tingle shoots up my arm, but I ignore it and lead her over to my bed.

My bed. The one she's already slept in. The one I want to give her.

"Lie down," I instruct.

She happily complies. And it feels so good.

May my soul be cast into darkness and sent to rot in the depths of the blackest night. It's the only fate worthy of a man like me. A man who sees perfection and must cast it aside.

I reach into the third drawer of my bedside table and shield the view from her. Inside is a set of purple fluffy handcuffs that Celeste gifted me last Christmas as a joke. I clasp her hand and secure one cuff around it.

She blinks at it in disbelief for a moment before trying to get up. Quick as a flash, I secure the other cuff to the inside of one of the cast iron scrolls in my headboard.

"I need to know you're safe here," I say stiffly. "Otherwise, I won't be able to leave you." Otherwise, I won't be able to stop scenting her.

She gapes up at me, still in a sort of glassy-eyed daze from her orgasm. Her skin glows from our union. Her lips are still swollen from the force of my desire. Her pussy is still full of my cum.

I hate myself for what I'm about to say. What I *have* to say. This is to keep her safe. From me and from everything else. But I get it out and almost fall to my knees when I see her bubble shatter completely. "Aurelia, we can never do that again."

I stride away from her, even as my soul bucks and screams and beats against my insides, promising death and destruction.

"*Scythe,*" I call out into the ether. Three powers of awareness perk their head up. "*We need to talk about Aurelia.*"

"*You called her angel,*" comes the reply. There is no malice in his normally icy voice. Only curiosity.

They'd all seen.

I stop in my living room. Then I turn around, pick up one of the black dining chairs and smash it against the top of the ancient wood. It splits the table in two. The two halves crashing into each other like enemies on an old battlefield, both tired from an eternity of fighting.

The vision does not abate any of my agony.

Chapter 39

Xander

Scythe and I are sitting outside the Moonlight Stroll cafe in the student village, smoking some good quality cigars to process our meeting with an unhinged Lyle, when we see something unusual.

Minnie is skipping down the path, pink curls bouncing, ballet flats prancing and completely by herself, no other animas in tow. This cafe is operated by one of Savage's wolves, who turns a blind eye when we smoke so we come here more often than not. It's well made, with fairy lights, tiny tea-light holders, and hand-painted wolves running under a full moon along the drywall.

Minnie's been leaving Aurelia for her own adventures these days. Leaving the Boneweaver girl all alone at night.

My stomach does a weird turn and I take another drag to try and make it go away. Scythe raises a brow when he sees the tigress because she's clearly dressed for a date in a long, flowing pink dress that shows her shoulders and her makeup is done all extra nice with glittery eyeshadow. My shark brother and I both scan the vicinity to see if anyone is going to join her because an anima wandering around unaccompanied at night is not normal around here. But there's no one else running to join her as Minnie does a double take when she sees us, takes an obvious breath, pointedly ignores us, and goes inside to sit down at a two-seater table. She orders an iced tea when the student server comes to ask, then starts swinging her short legs and humming under her breath.

The whole thing sort of looks *romantic*.

Fifteen minutes pass by and still she sits there alone and tries not to look outside. Her annoyingly positive attitude falters, perhaps for the first time that I've been observing her at this academy, and she starts nervously fidgeting with the many silver bangles she wears on both wrists. The dragon in me assesses them for the quality and I know on instinct that they're pure platinum and white gold. Minnie comes from a wealthy family, according to our research. Her father is state manager for a chain of animalia-owned banks. It makes sense that she's here on the down-low, considering it was white collar crime that got her in pretty bad trouble in the first place.

"The fires are all out." Yeti pulls up a chair next to me and sits his large self down. His white hair has a dusting of black ash and he smells like power and soot. I offer him a cigar and he takes it with tattooed fingers. "We collected the ashes in separate boxes."

"Good," I say, lighting his cigar with a finger flame. "And the one left is secure?"

His powder-blue eyes dance. Merciless bastard, just like the rest of us. "Yes. She's out cold."

Yeti's plume of smoke adds to ours, and I relish the silvery cloud. Natalia fought to keep her vermin secrets, but with a little dose of her own medicine and Scythe's ruthless hand, we got a little more information out. It's lucky Savage is locked in isolation, because he would've torn her apart so quickly we wouldn't have been able to get anything from her.

Yeti mutters some more news under his breath while Scythe and I listen quietly, making small comments as he goes.

Eventually, the tea-light in front of Minnie goes out, the wax all used up. She stares at it with a small frown and it's not until I see her bottom lip tremble that I sigh and re-light the thing on my power alone. It splutters to life and Minnie flinches in surprise, then stares at it, confused.

Clara, the student-owner of the cafe, brings her a sympathy cupcake, which Minnie tries to decline, but the wolf only smiles and leaves it on the table. The tigress blinks at it a few times before defiantly pushing it away. She sniffs softly.

Yeti has suddenly gone very still next to me.

Silently, he stands, puts out his cigar and strides inside. I'd like to think I have some sort of manners, given my upbringing, but I want to hear this and plan to eavesdrop on the entire thing.

"Bangles," Yeti greets, pulling out the seat opposite her and seating his large frame.

"Criminal," greets Minnie says tightly. "What are you doing here? Helping to dispose of someone annoying?"

"I'm done for the day, actually." He grabs her cupcake and tears into it with his teeth.

"Hey, that was mine!" she says in outrage. Her cheeks are bright pink, but I can't read her aura. I haven't been able to for months. Yeti's energy, however, pulses pink the same colour as Minnie's hair, then red, then green.

"Didn't look like you wanted it."

She glares at him with all her might, little fists clenched tightly in her lap.

"What are you doing here alone?"

"None of your business, *animus*."

"So that's how it is." Yeti's eyes roam over her. With his pupils blown out, he doesn't miss any detail. This power pulses grey.

Minnie presses her lips together.

"Think you're gonna kill me with that stare?"

"Maybe."

"Won't work. Your eyes are too pretty."

"Screw you."

"I wish."

Minnie scoffs and shifts in her seat.

Yeti stuffs the rest of the cupcake into his mouth, staring Minnie down as he chews. The tigress just glares back at him, never breaking eye contact. Heat dances between them—and a surprising amount of lust. "You owe me a cupcake now."

Yeti's voice suddenly turns so vicious it's half feral. "I'll give you five hundred fucking cupcakes if you tell me which mother-fucker stood you up tonight."

Minnie flushes and she breaks eye contact to play with the pink glitter phone Aurelia demanded we give her. But Yeti is nothing if not ruthless. Quick as a whip, he lashes out and snatches the phone right out of her hand. Minnie yelps, but can't do anything as Yeti scrolls through what's probably her messaging app.

His face becomes increasingly enraged and even if I can't see the violence in plumes of black and grey with my special sight, my dragon can feel it rolling off him. Suddenly, he puts down the phone, crosses his large arms and stares at Minnie, his mouth forming a hard line.

She's bright red like she's been caught doing something wrong and snaps viciously, "*What?*"

Slowly, the Siberian tiger stands, unfurling all six foot five inches. He extends a hand to her in offer.

"No!" Minnie says incredulously.

He gives her back the phone and puts two hands on the table, leaning across into her personal space. Most animas might be frightened by this show of overt dominance, but Minnie, the stupid kit, actually licks her lips. I might have laughed if this wasn't so interesting.

"*Then*, kitten," growls Yeti, "go back to your dorm." A direct order from the order leader of the felines at this school can't be denied by one of his own, and there's nothing but pure command in his voice.

Any other feline would be running.

But Minnie just sits there and I chuckle under my breath at the look of confusion and anger mixed on her round face. Just when I think she's going to obey, as she should, she crosses her arms and narrows her eyes at him.

"*No,* you oversized snow cat," she sneers. "*You* go back to your dorm and pretend you didn't see anything here." She gestures to her phone.

They stare at each other, neither one of them backing down. The largest tiger in the academy versus the smallest.

To my giant fucking surprise, Yeti straightens. Heat rolls off him in arousal and Scythe makes an amused noise. Yeti runs a hand over his clean-shaven jaw before stalking out of the cafe and down the cobblestoned path... clearly going back to his dorm... as ordered.

Well, I'll be.

"That's... rather interesting," I murmur, glancing over at Scythe.

My shark brother is clinically focused on Minnie, like she's a particularly interesting type of starfish.

Finally, he rasps, getting to his feet. "It sure is, brother."

Chapter 40

Lyle

Ten years ago

The Animalia Police Chief, a powerful, bald-headed tiger, stares at me in disbelief. "You're… giving yourself in?"

"Yes," I say earnestly. "I need to be locked up."

"I don't understand," he says flatly, looking me up and down. "What crime are you confessing to?"

I swallow. "Crimes I don't even remember. My memory goes blank. I don't even know. The beastly murders I see on the news. I think I did them, but I can't be sure."

He sighs. "Son, we get people confessing to things they didn't do all the time. For attention, for fame, for—"

"I need to show you," I press. "What happens when I…" I can't even say it anymore.

"Shift?"

"Yes."

"Alright, son. We have doctors for this type of thing. Specialists. I'll arrange for a unit to meet us."

And they do. True to his word, the police chief arranges for a team. They put me in a padded room with six animalia guards dressed in prison riot gear. Heavy plastic shields, helmets, batons. Cattle prods.

It happens again. My world turns dark and it's like I'm hearing through a tunnel, with people screaming from very far away. When I come back around, I'm covered in hot, sticky liquids and there is nothing but torn bodies, cloth and plastic lying on the floor.

"What did I do?" I scream, staring at my red hands, my red legs. "What did I do?"

Through a sliding panel, a set of obsidian shackles are thrown into the room. "Put these on, boy."

"Please," I whisper, wiping at my face, "tell me what I did."

Silence.

Then a door opens, and a woman in white walks in. I've never met a beast like her before. Like golden fire made into a human.

"Your animus is damaged, Lyle." Her smooth voice is kind but not weak. "We think he might be mad. When he comes out to protect you, he... does not *see*. He only fights."

I look her right in her golden eyes. "Will you put me down?"

"I will not lie to you. It is a consideration."

Still, I do not look away from her eyes. Her judgement. "I deserve it."

When she considers my face carefully I do not feel like an insect under glass. I do not feel like an animal in a cage. I feel like a boy. A person. "The thing is, Lyle, *you* don't deserve it. The human side of you is very self-aware. Clinically so."

I know that it's another way to call me *cold*. "I don't want my animus. I hate it. Is there a way to take it away?" I'd rip it to pieces if I could.

"That is asking to take your soul away. But we *can* do something else."

My mind is awash with images of electrocution, of waterboarding, of torture. All the things I've researched since I ran away from Ulman's property into the city. "And what's that?"

"We make your human side stronger than your animus."

My scoff is loud. "Impossible."

But she shakes her head. "Just very difficult. If you want to do this, it will take everything you have. It might even break you. Are you willing?"

"Already broken," I say softly. I have nothing left. "Let's do this."

She smiles at me. "I will see you in Blackwater Penitentiary, Mr. Pardalia. And we will begin."

She calls me by my new name. The one given to lions who do not know their family. Even so, *'mister'* sounds human.

It sounds like someone I could be one day.

Chapter 41

Aurelia

That bastard lion actually handcuffed me to his bed.

As soon as his apartment door slams closed, I tug at the fluffy cuff. Although last year, Sabrina taught me to pick locks for my grand escape after my trial, I have no bobby pins or lock picks to use.

After that crazy, intense, mind-blowing sex, the wounds on my stomach burn all the more. I need painkillers and... I need to pee.

Lyle is clearly losing it if he smashed whatever it was in his living room and then planned to keep me here for an unknown amount of time. I consider my options, but the thing is, I'm incredibly tired. Post sex with one of my mates is leaving my insides overwhelmed. I can still feel him inside of me, that ghost of a burn that reminds me that Lyle has been inside my body.

I sigh contentedly, and even with my arm up in the air, I begin to doze.

* * *

Minnie. Hours later, I wake up with a rough start, gasping for air as panic chokes me once more.

Keep them safe. Keep them safe. Keep them safe.

It's an infinite hymn my power has been singing since the day I went into hiding under the academy. I need to make sure Minnie or any of my friends have not been attacked by my father like he promised to if I didn't comply with his order.

Natalia said he'd be here in two Saturdays' time. Typical serpent dramatics. Everything has to be threes or sevens, doesn't it? But knowing my father, he'll make his point with more than just idle threats. He'll want to show me he means business.

Lyle would have surely said something if someone wasn't okay, but then again, I don't think he left his room at all while I was here.

I need to get out of this fucking cuff.

Tugging at it does nothing.

With an angry scream, I blast the cuff with every last dreg of power afforded to me by Lyle's tortured fucking.

We can never do that again.

Like hell.

The metal trembles, shudders, then explodes into pieces.

Angrily, I leap out of bed, and run straight for the fireplace door. But halfway, I halt in my tracks.

Lyle's dining room table lies broken. As if a giant took it in both hands and snapped it in half. One of the dining chairs lies destroyed, too.

So that was the terrible sound I heard. I swallow as I survey the evidence of Lyle's anger at having had me. I know he hadn't intended to fuck me, but this reaction is a bit extreme. My anima keens at the sight. He had *this* much distress at being with me?

But then my anima caws at me. She smells no regret here. It's something else. Something more painful and sinister than that. A memory that's not mine flashes in my internal eye. A memory of self-hate.

Anger burns anew along the lines of my veins.

Slowly, carefully, I walk to the fireplace.

I stand there, staring furiously at it. I'm furious at a cruel world that hurts young children so badly they become monsters. "Open," I growl.

Metal and wood let out a tired groan before a crack on the side of the mantelpiece appears and I pull it open and rush down the cold stone stairs.

Emerging in my room, I don't bother changing or cleaning up. But I do need to delay a minute to empty my bladder with happy relief. After that, I hurry right out of my dorm and straight outside.

It's after dark, no doubt I missed dinner, but now I feel physically *energised*, like I could run a whole marathon and not be tired. Rage does that to a person. So does fear.

Lyle and I need to have sex more. Not '*never again*'.

Right now, my heart pumps for Minnie... and Yuran's sadistic voice in my head. Minnie has *already* been attacked once when I was weak, and even though I've redirected any psychic attack to myself, my father knows Minnie's special to me and there are many wounds not so easily fixed by an avian's healing magic. I can't rest until I see she's okay with my own eyes.

I duck in to check the dining hall and don't see her pink curls anywhere, so I move on to the animus dorm. She's always with that bastard Titus after class these days, so that's where she must be.

I rush down the paved path to the dorms, my bare feet pelting on the bare concrete until I skid to a stop at the towering animus dorms.

"My lady!" Bastian the gargoyle calls, waving his stick fingers at me.

"I'm in a hurry. Can you please let me in?"

"Any anima may be allowed in the animus dorms, my lady.

However, I cannot guarantee an unmolested exit. It's rather rowdy in there tonight, are you sure—"

"Yes! Yes, please!"

"Very well." He sweeps his hand as both doors dramatically swing open and I rush in. There are males milling about everywhere. Five of them are playing cards in the ground floor foyer.

"I need to find Titus!" I blurt at them. "Where is he?"

A feline with perfectly coifed hair to rival Elvis scoffs, "Why are all the animas after him? You need someone more refined, Aurelia birdy."

The fact that he knows my name and I don't know his is unnerving, but there's so few of us animas that the males know all of us whether we like it or not.

"Just tell me where he is," I demand.

They look me up and down and I'm suddenly aware that I'm not actually wearing any shoes, only the blood-stained mini dress and probably a dishevelled bed-head. I swear under my breath at my hastiness, but there's no point in going back now.

"He's got company," one of the wolves drawls. "Try someone else. We're all available."

"I don't want to see *him*," I cry out. "I'm looking for Minnie."

The felines make grumpy faces before one of them says, "Second floor, third door on the right."

Without thanks, I jog up the stairs to the second floor. There are felines and birds of prey on this level, and there's a moment of silence before I'm called out by name.

"Hey, Flight Risk, come into my room!" someone shouts.

Urgh, not that name again.

But I ignore the stares and hollers and count down three doors on the right with a pointed finger. I form a fist to get ready to knock, but find it already open.

Titus is starkers, sitting on a bed while an also naked anima bounces up and down on his cock. She cries out with exaggerated pleasure as he thrusts to meet her. There is a huge tattoo of a serpent coiling around her breasts. It smells of weed and sweat.

"Fuck off, Aquinas," she pants.

Titus bares his teeth over her shoulder. "Birdy can join if she likes."

The serpent stops her bouncing to glare at me.

"I was looking for Minnie," I said pointedly, glaring back at the both of them, not moving an inch.

They both laugh and it makes the hairs on the back of my neck stand on end. "She didn't want to join in," Titus says, his eyes suddenly hard on me. "It's her own fault."

The look he's giving me is making me shiver in a bad way. It makes the dominant regina in me want to wring his throat to teach him a lesson. Frowning, I turn away.

It's normal for animalia to be in relationships with multiple people, given the fact that we're fated into mating groups. It's not surprising that Titus is fucking multiple animas. What *is* surprising is that there's no condom being used. STDs are rampant here, and he's putting them all at risk. I wonder if Minnie knows. Dejected, I cross my arms and make to leave. Did they break up, and I didn't know about it?

I'm brought out of my reverie when a few animuses whoop and whistle in my direction. More emerge out of their dorms, half-clothed, trying to see what the fuss is about. The scent of male, soap, cologne and sex is heavy in the air as I quicken my pace.

But just as I reach the stairwell, a group of felines walk up from below, cutting off my path. They appraise me with dilated pupils and licking their lips.

I swear under my breath.

"Hello, little tweety," comes a deep voice from behind me. I whirl around to find a group of eagles gathered on the landing, as if watching a very exciting movie. "Looks like you're stuck with us instead of Titus."

"Um, no," I laugh nervously as one of them actually has the audacity to rub his hands together. "That's not gonna happen."

"Naw," chirps one, stroking his chin. They're flushed and jittery, no doubt feeling the arousal from the other animas fucking in this place. Stacey, Sabrina and Connor are no doubt around here somewhere as well. "Don't be like that, baby. We haven't had a new eagle anima in here in ages. We'll show you a good time. We have food and everything."

A part of me feels sorry for them. Their instinct tells them to look after a female, to bring her food... but also to fuck.

"Savage had you all to himself, but he's still in the shu." The first one leans forward to look me up and down.

I take a step back, only to bump into a hard, sweaty torso. I whirl around, only to find the felines crowding me in from behind. I bare my teeth but they only laugh.

Suddenly I'm back in a chair, tied with obsidian shackles with five serpents towering over me. Panic surges through my veins as my heart rate pounds in my head. The world seems to tilt.

Escape. Escape. I have to escape before they kill me. Before they flay my skin and cut off my mating mark. Primitive darkness opens up in a deep lake at my core. I whirl around again, trying to calculate how much damage I can do in a short space of time—

Just as someone begins singing from down the stairwell, his voice echoing up in a rhythmic, sing-song chant.

Chapter 12

Aurelia

"Seven little birdies sitting on a fence. One falls off and breaks his neck. Now there's *six* little birdies sitting on the fence—" The birds of prey scatter back down the hall without so much as a backwards glance, while the felines hastily skirt past me, trying to escape without getting their scents on my skin and clothes.

Complete idiots.

I close my eyes as a sensation of pure, utter relief floods through my chest and booted feet pound up the stairs, getting closer and closer. I could've used my telekinesis, but I really shouldn't be using my powers so openly.

"And then there's *one* little birdy sitting on the fence!" Savage appears, leaping over the staircase railing and landing neatly in a crouch in front of me.

It's almost in slow motion that I watch him. He rises to his considerable height, the muscles of his glorious naked abdominals rippling. Shirtless, with his hair tousled and his tattooed chest gleaming with sweat, he's a sight for sore eyes. His voice is low and serious as he regards me. "Great acoustics in here, don't you think, regina?"

The sob tears out of my throat as I fling myself at him, and he catches me in his strong arms, swinging me around in a circle like I'm a princess in a Disney movie. "I'm so glad to see you," I murmur into his neck. Underneath the sweat, he smells like pine and far away forests and... *mine*.

"Now what was that?" Savage puts me down to look at me, his eyes fever-bright. "Say it again."

I hide my smile by looking at my feet, but he tilts my chin up so I'm forced to look at him and those cunning, hazel eyes. They shimmer with heat and his voice drops into a dangerous command. "Say it again, regina."

I swallow. "I'm glad to see you, Savage."

He whoops and seizes me by my waist, hoisting me over his shoulder like I weigh nothing and slapping a hand on my ass to keep my dress from riding up. He begins chatting non-stop, clearly having been bursting at the seams to see me while in isolation. "I'm never letting you out of my sight again. I was ready to snap necks as soon as I got out and heard what happened, but Lyle stopped me. He had four urns in his hands and said it was already done and he was going to send their remains back to their parents. For some reason, I thought to myself, 'is this what it's going to be like when we're a full pack?' Because he fits right in, you know, regina. Lyle is as nuts as the rest of us. His animus might even be the worst of us. I don't know, we'll have to see. He sees this academy as *his* territory, possessive bastard, and so he's taken it all very personally. He might have even been annoyed at Xander for taking care of it. Anyway, as soon as I got out, I hunted you all the way here, and now we're going to go and make love so I can get their snakey scents off you."

My head is swimming, mostly with the blood that's rushing to my head by virtue of being upside down, but also from Savage being... Savage and telling the brutal truth. The fact that those snakes died because of my father's orders. The fact that Lyle sees this land as his territory and he has a right to deal with insubordination in the way he pleases. According to the Old Laws, the archaic ways of beast kind, death or torture are the only fair solution to a transgression that big.

But I wonder if my father will care. If he'll retaliate worse because of it. Because on the other hand, the school is supposed to have a truce. The young animalia of the community are supposed to be safe here.

Guilt swirls through my stomach and bile rises in my throat as I think about the consequences of my father's actions because of me. I can't help but feel the blame for all of this.

I bite back my tears because they won't help me fix anything.

"I need to find Minnie," I protest, slapping him on the hard muscles of his lower back.

But as he walks down the corridor, he's too busy sniffing at my hip and growling.

"After we fuck, I'm going to pull the fangs out of every serpent here."

I gulp because that's literally the worst torture you can do to a serpent. My father only reserved it for extra special transgressions and I've never seen it used in person.

"You can't do that Savage," I say quickly. "It's not right. There's too much death already."

He just growls again like he doesn't agree. We make it up to the hidden floor at a rapid pace and I just make out Scythe's slacks and business shoes before Savage reverently sets me down, sliding me down his front until I'm on my feet.

"Wait a minute!" Savage leans down and sniffs my neck, rapidly moving to the other side and then down beneath my breasts. He drops to his knees and presses his face right against my crotch, inhaling deeply. His nose rubbing against my slit sends a pang of pleasure through my core, but I realise there are other people in the room.

As well as Scythe and Xander sitting down, Beak, Yeti and a few wolves are also scattered around, drinking and smoking.

"Um, Savage—"

"Lyle," Savage growls into my vulva, his voice muffled. "Fucking *Lyle* was here."

"I'm a person, not a place!" I say, slapping him on the shoulder and darting a look at the other males. They are all averting their eyes. Apparently Savage trusts them enough to speak openly.

Savage looks up at me, hugging me around my ass and resting his chin on my pubic bone. "I know, you're *my* person."

My stomach does a little flop and blood rushes to my face. I didn't expect him to make me feel this way. Not at all.

"So he finally gave in." Scythe says it like he already knew. His rasp is a pleasant sound against my eardrums, and my head snaps up of its own accord to stare at him. My heart aches like I haven't seen him in years. He never came down to see me in my cave and he's been missing more than a few classes.

He sits like a king, one arm draped across the back of the black leather couch, whiskey glass in the other hand. His business shirt has three buttons open, letting me see a glorious slither of his elaborately tattooed chest. There are flowers there as well as a skull. Under the tattoos, his skin is almost luminous, like it's lit from within, and I wonder if he's been for a swim recently.

Those glacial eyes bore into mine, before darting to my left as if he's looking at something there, before they dart back.

"Are you trying to make me jealous, regina?" Savage growls, clambering to his feet. "Well, it's fucking working."

"I need to find Minnie," I press. "Has anyone seen her?"

"Why are you worried about her?" It's Scythe who asks me and I'm taken aback by the question because he sounds genuinely interested.

"I just need to see her."

"She was down in the village," Yeti grumbles, lounging in an armchair and looking very disgruntled. "In her usual snippy form."

Scythe smirks at him, but then he's back to looking at me and the smile is gone. He's assessing me, and I don't like it. I don't look my best right now, and I'm not feeling my best either.

"Where have you been?" My voice comes out more accusatory than I intend.

"You don't get to ask," Xander snaps.

"Well, yeah I do, actually," I snap. "If it's anything to do with me."

"Not everything is to do with you."

I clench my jaw and glare at the dragon. Did he forget I was kidnapped today?

Scythe makes a gesture and Beak, Yeti and the others make their way out. I'm surprised they talk so openly with those males. They must really trust them.

I step away from the stairs to give them space to leave. Savage jumps up to sit on the dining table, swinging his legs and beaming at me like I'm his saviour.

"Come here," Scythe says.

My body stills like I'm at gunpoint and I blink like a stunned idiot. Today has been... too much. Too fucking much already, and now this. Now... Scythe.

The Great White shark crooks a finger at me like I'm a naughty hatchling in primary school. "Come here, Aurelia."

I glance at Savage, and he's still beaming. Well, that means nothing bad is about to happen, surely?

But I can't just do whatever Scythe says. These other two tried to hand me over to my death not all that long ago and are now acting like nothing happened today.

Scythe's voice drops low, and he's stopped blinking as he says, "If you want an answer, Aurelia, come here."

Well, I *do* want an answer, don't I? Scythe has an irresistible, innate lure, and the way he's staring at me is like there is nothing and no one else in the room but us. His silver hair sparkles under the chandelier's light, and his skin is a tempting wonder that begs to be touched. I don't blame the other animas for wantonly offering themselves to him.

More curious than anything, I allow his lure to draw me in and I take tentative steps forward. Savage won't let anything bad happen to me, but is his loyalty to his brother stronger than his loyalty to me?

I'm standing right before Scythe, who's leaning forward now, intent on my face. I can smell him from here, even through my shields. That vast current of power. Like the sea under the full moon. Salt and moonlight.

His rasp cuts through my reverie. "Kneel."

By the Goddess, I drop to my knees without question, my eyes never leaving his, focused on that cold, cold blue.

I shiver, just before he grabs my face in one hand, squeezing my cheeks together and making my lips pucker. I'm caught so unawares that I do nothing but stare.

"You don't get to ask me questions, Aurelia Boneweaver," he rasps.

My shock spans multiple levels of my stupefied brain, but it also stirs something in me. Something wild and raw, borne of weeks of rabidity protecting my friends and family. Something that took flight the moment a serpent tried to cut my mating mark off.

I wrench my face out of his grip and he allows it, before I lean forward, getting right into his face, nose-to nose in a show of full authority. He doesn't move an inch, but his eyes drop down to my mouth before darting back up. It's all the leverage I need.

My voice emerges deep and venomous, like fangs ripping through tender flesh. "I am *'regina'* to you, Scythe Kharkorous, or *nothing* else."

His gaze turns knife sharp, narrowing on me, and I barely hear Savage chuckling under his breath.

But it's Xander who sneers. "Stand down, Boneweaver girl, or you'll regret it."

I tilt my head back to regard the Great White shark who sits before me, achingly beautiful and unashamedly dangerous. On the outside, he looks undisturbed, but I can sense that he's now... tense, and his aura of danger has only increased.

As slowly as I can, to show that I'm not perturbed by any of them, I rise to my feet and say in a sweet, measured voice, "See you in class tomorrow."

With that, I turn on my heel and leave.

As I do, a frantic clucking follows me down the stairs. Eugene is rushing behind me, his feathers all askew. Silently, I open my arms and he leaps into them, black wings flapping. The poor bird must've been terrified of Lyle's animus when he took me from the hospital and came here to wait until I reappeared. Eugene's heart beats in a rapid pace against my own, and together, we leave the animus dorm.

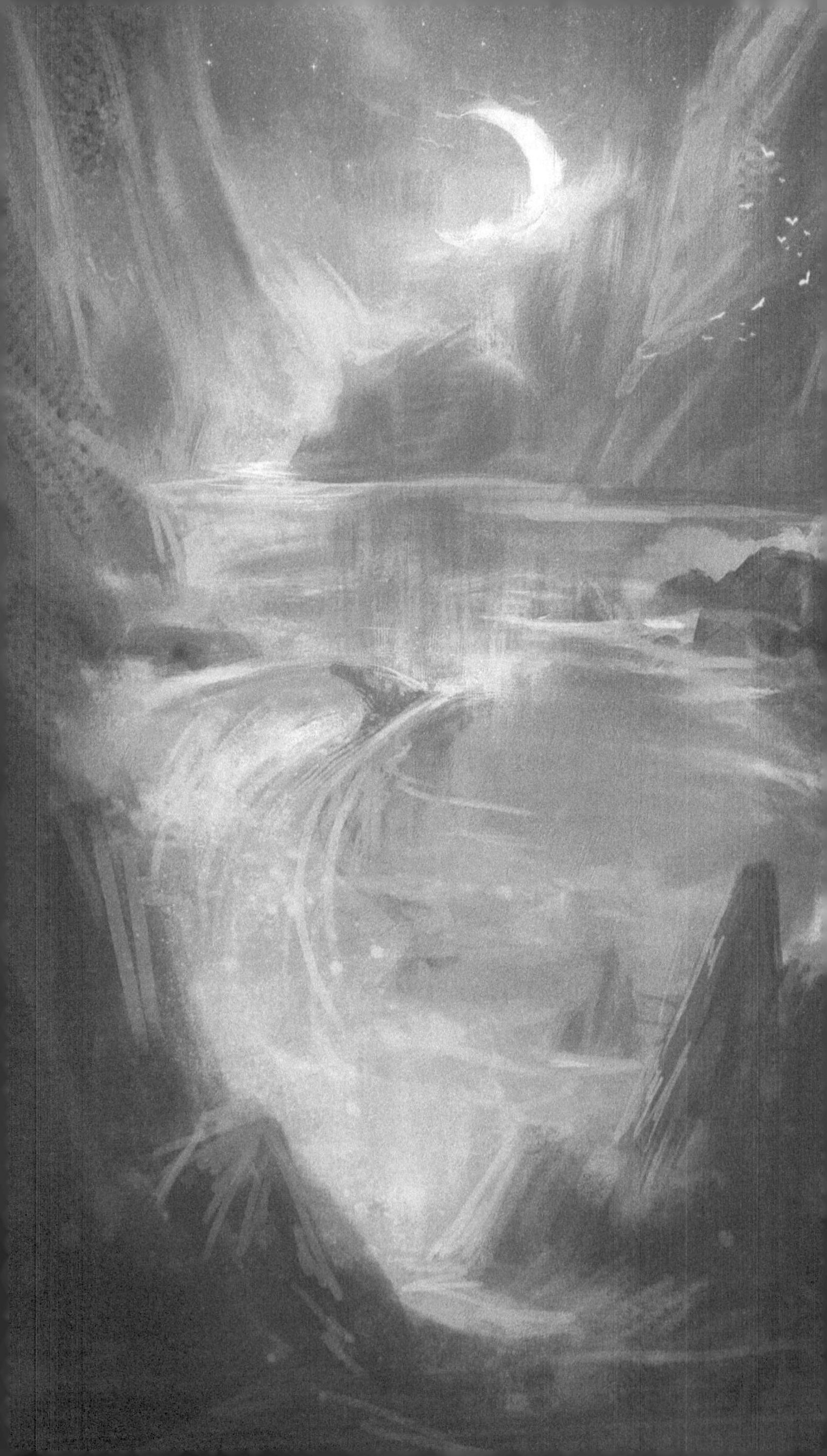

Chapter 13

Scythe

I should have thrown Aurelia to the floor and smacked her ass for speaking to me like that. An attempt at showing dominance from any other beast would have them bleeding and lifeless on the floor.

But *her* outright dominance... by the moon, she might actually end me. I sit back on the couch, swirling my whiskey as the ghost kneels on the floor, dripping wet and praying to some dark god in the ether.

"Her regina-ness is growing," Savage quips, knocking back more water and smacking his lips loudly. "You can actually see it!"

"That's not even a word," Xander snaps back. "And you need a shower. You smell like a stray dog."

"I'm not a stray dog anymore," Savage says faintly, staring at the stairs as if he can still see her. "Not at all."

Xander mutters expletives under his breath as he lights up a new joint. The past five minutes replay in my mind over and over again. The way she turned up here with Lyle's cum still dripping out of her, looking for Minnie. The way she looked to Savage for reassurance when I called her to me. Some part of her trusts him now. That surprises me. It does something unwanted to my cold, black heart.

But some part of her also wants to claim me.

A large part of *me* also wants to claim her. To compete with the brothers who've already claimed her, to fuck their cum out of her and drench her cunt, her womb with my seed instead.

The whiskey glass in my hand shatters.

I don't actually want that, but neither did Lyle and the bastard lion gave in. It's natural for pack mates as dominant as we are to compete against one another. And if she grows more confident, how long do we all have before we're under her thumb? I've been right to stay away. And I was right to send her back to her dad when we thought it was for her execution.

"I love her," Savage says quietly.

Xander splutters around his whiskey. "You keep saying that! Again and again, but you don't even know what it means. It's just her manipulation. It's just your fucking hormones—"

But Savage is shaking his head back and forth, with a sure smile on his face as if he won't be swayed. "No, I do. You don't know her like I do. She's sweet, and kind, and even innocent in many ways." Xander scoffs in disbelief. "And when I found out that she'd been taken, I—"

I can barely breathe as my brother's eyes glisten in a way I haven't seen since we were children. Since the night I killed our father and his mother—

"You'd think I would have been in a rage," Savage continues. "But it wasn't the first thing I felt. The first thing I felt was"—he gulps—"fear. That she'd been hurt, or wounded, or scared."

Xander smashes his whiskey glass on the ground, almost as if to try and shock Savage out of his stupidity.

"See!" the dragon cries, pointing a finger at Savage. Heat rolls off our dragon-brother in a wave of harsh anger. "This is exactly what we were avoiding. This is exactly what's going to happen. Sav, you need to snap out of her spell. She's going to control you with her pussy and then we're all fucked. You need to control your fucking wolf's cock!"

But my brother, the most unhinged and out-of-control member of my entire organisation, shakes his head as if he pities Xander. "I don't feel it here." He points to his dick. "I feel it here." He moves his finger up to his chest. His heart.

Xander snarls and turns his head back on him, crosses his arms, and stares out the window into the gathering night.

The shark at the base of me thrashes around, protesting, raging and refusing to grieve for a lost cause. I knew Savage might succumb, but I didn't think it would be this quick. My little brother is not the type of wolf who can be swayed from his urges. I've tried my best over the years—not to tame him, but to re-direct him.

But there is nothing to re-direct him to.

There is no *equivalent* to his regina.

"I won't let them take her, Scythe," Savage says, unblinking eyes boring into me. "You know I'll tear apart every court one by one if they take her away for... *breeding*."

We all know it. We would have a rabid wolf on our hands, who wouldn't care for the consequences of any amount of slaughter. It would be a massacre.

But it is that one triggering word that sets off a dangerous, psychotic bloodlust in me. *Breeding*.

I refuse to let her be bred by anyone but me or one of her mates. Only *we* have that fucking right. In this life, in any lifetime.

Even the thought of *others* makes me want to drag Aurelia back here and chain her to my bed and covet her.

Seeing Mace Naga's smug face today at the council meeting sent my shark on high alert. I gave my vote to extend the phoenix court's injunction, but I had to go for a swim in the underground pool afterwards just to calm myself down. I didn't think I'd been so affected until she turned up here.

With that stunning, ferocious face and wild power that plucked an ancient thread right in my marrow. She awoke something in me today. Something dangerous, potentially disastrous, but true.

I value many things in my life. The truth, most of all.

Suddenly, my fingers crave the feel of her. Suddenly, my retinas crave the sight of her. I crave the sound of heartbeat, her breath. I need to know what she'd look like being fucked on a beach amongst crashing waves or in the water itself. By my cock. By my...

"Brother..." Savage's voice is almost drowned out by my thoughts, but there is caution in his tone.

Caution?

I come back to reality.

"Uh-oh." Savage grins at me with all his teeth, his eyes flicking down to my bleeding hand and the glass shattered all over my lap. Xander turns, staring at me, though there is disappointment in his glowing orbs.

"Don't say it," I say, my voice low and dangerous. "Don't fucking start."

Savage holds his hands up in a way he knows will placate the Great White.

"Do I need to get the fucking chains out, Scythe?" Xander snarls. "Do I need to get you away from her?"

"*No,*" I reply with a pulse of bloodthirsty power.

Xander shuts his mouth, sensing that I mean it.

I can't be away from her. Not anymore.

Chapter 14

Aurelia

When I get back to the anima dorm, I get the scent of steam and Minnie's shower gel. Eagerly, I rush into our room, only to find it dark and Minnie only a small, round figure curled up like a kitten in bed, facing the wall on her side. Setting Eugene down to roost in the purple armchair at the end of Minnie's bed, I creep up to my friend and find her breathing is deep and even. Gertie is asleep against Minnie's forehead, which means that Minnie needed her comfort tonight. My heart pangs with sadness and guilt. My best friend is under her covers, so I can't see her body and need to make do with sniffing the air around her.

I scent no blood or anything that might indicate she's been physically harmed.

Relieved, I head to the bathroom. I consider taking a shower, but the fact is, Lyle's scent is still over me. I want it to last as long as possible, so I end up just washing the dirt off my bare feet and washing my haggard face before brushing out the tangles in my long hair and hopping into bed for the night. I turn to check Henry's little bed out of habit and, finding it empty, my heart sinks. I'm sure he's being looked after, but I really miss him. At least I have Eugene's occasional sleepy clucking from where he settles himself down to sleep in the armchair.

My phone goes off and I snatch it up. There's a goodnight message with a whole bunch of kissy emojis from Savage and a second from that unknown number.

> Lock up, snakelet. You wouldn't want any stalkers getting to you in the middle of the night.

I get up and double check the lock on the balcony doors, then check the automatic lock of our main door has been acti-vated for the curfew. Heart pounding, I crawl back into bed and watch as three dots flash on the screen before disappearing. I watch, captivated by the dots, but they appear only to disappear again. Cursing this unknown guy, I toss my phone under my bed where I won't be tempted to check it at odd hours and settle in to sleep.

* * *

In the middle of the night, I wake up with a start, my instincts screaming. My heart feels like it never stopped pounding and my neck burns from the wound I haven't had the energy to heal. Gasping for air, I stare at the dark ceiling and work to centre myself, but my senses are on high alert.

A whisper of something more than me demands my attention.

With careful, slow movement, I turn my head towards Minnie's side of the room.

My heart turns to ice.

I'm in a living nightmare.

Because sitting in Minnie's purple armchair is a monster that could only haunt a person's most terrifying dreams.

Veiled in pulsing, roiling shadows, sitting in a casual position, is a large man. Glowing red pinpricks of light where his eyes should be burn through the dark, *fixed* on me like the laser beams of military firearms.

I scramble off my back, scoot into my headboard, managing to choke out, "Who are you?"

He doesn't answer, merely sits there, staring at me with awful, hair-raising focus.

Those shadows move around him, coiling up his legs, torso, large forearms, biceps, flowing up his shoulders and neck to surround his head. My heart pounds in an unsteady rhythm. It's like looking into the void. It's like looking into true death.

There is something familiar about the dark rhythm of them. And they call to me in a terrifying hymn.

Then it hits me.

I've seen shadows like this before.

"Oh dear Gods." My voice breaks as cold realisation pummels through me with the force of a steel door in a dark dungeon banging open. A shadow in the shape of a snake coiled around a spinal cord calls to my memory.

In the dark of a cold dungeon, owned by Charles Halfeather.

As shocked as I am, in my heart, I know what this means. Only one person can walk through my protections around the school and not be detected by me. Only five men can elicit this heart-wrenching, soul-screaming response from my anima.

Holding my breath, my skin tingling incessantly, I let down my mating mark shield.

The air around me grows a little colder.

It appears on the right side of his neck, glowing with ancient celestial light. A skull with five curling beams of light.

My fifth mate. The final piece of my soul group. The same unknown beast I healed in Halfeather's dungeon all those months ago.

A quick glance tells me that Minnie is still fast asleep in her bed. Swallowing, I allow my eyes to shift into their eagle form. Through my improved vision, I can now see... not much more.

He's covered in moving shadows, like he is a man made of nothing else. My mating prophesy from seven years ago comes to mind, spoken in Lady Celeste's deep, dusky cadence:

"Five black devils are approaching
Five black hearts are wanting
It is five who cry a dark and lonely song, calling for their queen.
Lion, shark, dragon, wolf and... shadow."

"Show yourself," I whisper. I hadn't been privy to a visual of his human form in Halfeather's dungeon either.

He shakes his head slowly like he's disappointed in me. Those red glowing dots seem to see through my skin. My anima commands me to move forward. To see him better. To brush my fingers through those obsidian shadows and find out what manner of monster lies beneath.

But deep-seated instinct tells me this monster is dangerous beyond imagination. Perhaps it's the way he sits, impossibly still yet with a casual, almost nonchalant grace, with one foot crossed over one knee. Though he bears the form of a man, I know he is anything but.

"What are you?" I whisper.

There is movement and his hand lifts. In it is something that lights up.

A phone. The glow from the screen should illuminate the thick shadows that make up his face, but nothing is revealed by it. It only demonstrates that the roiling darkness is a black so deep it sucks in all the surrounding light.

A shadow no light can penetrate? I shiver, suddenly chilled to the bone.

The red laser beams disappear for a moment as he looks down, then they reappear, making me shiver all over again.

The phone under my bed vibrates. Alarmed, I reach down

and grab it. I don't really want to take my eyes off this monster, but I need to see what he's saying.

I raise my phone to my face.

I am damned

My breath catches and I look back up at him. And then my phone pings again.

You are more beautiful than reality when you sleep. Even more beautiful now, with your mark visible to me

It makes my toes curl. But then I remember myself. I glare at him, wondering if he can see it through the dark. But if he is a creature of the dark, his night vision is probably perfect.

Are your eyes as big as a possum's? Is that why you don't show your face?

Shadowy fingers move and the reply comes within seconds.

Careful, pretty snakelet. People tend to die when I show my face.

"Why are you here?" I whisper irritably. And what I don't ask out loud is: why are all five of my mates A-grade assholes? "What happened to you to land you in Halfeather's dungeon?"

Perhaps I wanted to see my regina. Perhaps I want to hear you moan again.

That shadow around his spine I freed him from looked much the same as these shadows. Had he... He couldn't have done it to himself, could he?

I flush at the memory of the five astral forms of my mates looking down at me while I first pleasured myself and then Savage took over.

"I learn from my mistakes, apparently," I hiss back at him. I'm worried we'll wake Minnie, but she seems to be in a deep enough sleep. "You're not here to kidnap me or anything, are you?" I whisper-shout. "Because I will fuck you up if so."

He raises his phone again, and seconds later:

> If I want to take you, I will. You would not be able to stop me.

The fucking nerve! I want to throw something at the guy, but I actually think that would be a *bad* idea. The power that emanates from him like a toxic wind actually makes me think he's right.

"Well, if you're going to kidnap me, then do it now, because I'm tired of this conversation." I kick my blankets off to illustrate my challenge.

He doesn't reply or move to text me again, just stares at me with those eyes that give Xander a run for his money.

I sigh long and loud. I've had quite enough of this.

"Well, if that's all, I'm going back to bed," I hiss, setting my phone aside and preparing to huddle back under the blankets. Honestly, fuck him. "In case you haven't heard, I've had *quite* a traumatic day on *multiple* fronts."

So slowly that it makes my eyes water, he uncrosses his legs and rises from the chair. The way he rises reminds me of a cobra rearing up and spreading its hood out.

I try to keep calm. And fail.

It's easy to see that he's as tall as Xander. He's a giant in the room. A scary, nightmarish giant who's making my heart pound and... my nipples harden.

Laser beam eyes move. They lazily peruse my body from my toes to my face. I can barely breathe as I watch him watch me.

Without warning, this monster of shadow lunges towards me. I go to scream, but then he's *on top* of me, his weight pinning me down, those red points of light hovering inches from my face. A calloused hand clamps over my mouth.

I let down one of my psychic shields and blast him telepathically. *"You fucker!"* I thrash under him.

But my anima recognises that this is our mate and is purring and preening like the hussy she is. The thrashing turns into wiggling under his obviously hard, muscular body.

A low, rumbling chuckle enters my brain in a seductive caress. His voice is barely human and I think he's sunken into his animus. Or perhaps this has been his animus the entire time.

"My animus and I are one, snakelet," he whispers into my mind. *"I am the monster and the monster is me, unfortunately for my beautiful little regina."*

"What does that even mean?" I reply into his mind as he still covers my mouth with that one cool hand.

"It means..." He lowers his head and removes his hand from my mouth. Featherlight lips brush my own as he talks into my head with a low, seductive drawl. *"That I've waited far too long to come and steal a kiss."*

My toes curl at the overt power and lust in his deep voice.

I let my scent shield down then, desperate to sense more of this monster. *My* monster. He flinches, almost in surprise, before lowering his nose to skim my cheek, inhaling with his full chest. Tingles flood the length of my body. I clench my legs together. His scent is deep and dark like the night. As if all the powerful, seductive things that stalk in the dark culminate in a single, divine caress through my nose.

"What do I call you?" I ask, trying not to succumb to my own wanton desire. But I want to know everything there is to know about this creature.

His nose skims down the side of my face until he tilts his head upward and brushes his lips down my neck. He opens his mouth and sharp, *sharp* teeth scrape gently across my skin. It's like a sharp, primal kiss and I sense the restraint behind it.

Oh dear Goddess.

"I am known by many names, snakelet. Boogeyman, devil, king... snake eater..." I can feel him smirking as more of those teeth kiss down the line of my neck, his breath searing me. *"What name would you give me?"*

"Irritant," I whisper. *"Deviant. An all-round nuisance."*

A rumbling chuckle sends shivers right down to my pussy. *"Tell me you need me and I will take you right here."*

By all the Gods known and unknown, I want to scream yes. But I keep my lips tightly sealed. I'm playing a fucking dangerous game with someone who feels like he could destroy this entire building in an instant.

"You reek of lesser serpent. It makes me want to fuck the smell off you. It makes me want to wash it off you with my tongue."

Stay calm, Aurelia. Stay fucking calm. The more he speaks, the more he reveals. So he hates snakes? And kills them? And yet he has fangs. Is he a type of dragon? But a lot of orders hate snakes, not just dragons.

When I don't reply, he raises his head to look down at me. This close the red pupils hurt my eyes.

"I can smell your arousal, my pretty, pretty snakelet. Give me what I want and say it."

This is my mate. His scent fills my brain, heady and luxurious. It makes my body languid and pliant. I bow into his hard body, pressing my breasts into his hard chest. He works out. He's strong. The words leave my mouth in a wanton moan. "I need you inside me."

That mouth stops their delicious movement, and his whole body goes still. The words hang in the quiet, dark place that lies between us.

"They call me Ghoul, regina. You have not earned my real name."

The name rings a bell in my distant memory, but I cannot place it. But before I can ask another question, his weight eases off me and those red pinpricks are overcome by shadow. His entire body dissolves into darkness, dissipating into the room like smoke. It fades into nothing, disappearing completely.

Like he was never here. Like he never even existed.

That bastard. He comes here, gets me all worked up, and then leaves?

Breathing hard, I glance over at Minnie, but my eyes are pulled back into her purple armchair. Eugene sits in it, sleeping soundly, by his even breathing.

Quietly, I get out one of my vibrators. I need to dispel the crazy level of arousal Ghoul just brought out in me.

But one part of me is grateful because the sheer power rolling off him in cold waves tells me he's so dangerous that sex with him might make me implode completely.

I have a feeling that I've just met my most dangerous mate.

Chapter 15

Aurelia

The next morning, I wake up to Savage curled tightly around my back and Minnie ducking into the shower. Eugene is still on the purple armchair. I don't know what happened to him when Ghoul was here last night, but he seems fine except for a thin golden bow tied around his beak. I frown, staring at the curled ribbon, that type that my nanny used to use on my birthday and Christmas presents. It's shiny and has been tightened into a bow, keeping his beak shut. But Eugene slept peacefully, and with no other signs of Ghoul hurting him.

Ghoul.

As if he knows my thoughts are on another mate, Savage growls softly into my neck, tickling me with the vibration. "Regina," he murmurs sleepily.

I sigh in contentment, turning around to kiss my wolf on the mouth. With his eyes still closed, he grumbles against my lips, "He was here last night, wasn't he?" I go still. "I can smell him on you."

I sit up and push him, excitedly wanting information. "You *know* Ghoul? What is he? What are all those shadows? Why are his eyes like that?"

Savage rubs his eyes as he blinks them open. "Did you recognise him from Halfeather's dungeon?"

"I sensed it. But I didn't see him in person then."

He rolls off my bed and lands on his feet, straightening to look down on me. "He's dangerous. I don't like that he's here. But we can't stop him."

Savage calling someone dangerous piques my interest.

"No one can stop him?"

Savage shrugs. "He's... a real piece of work."

The irony of this makes me laugh. "Alright, I'll have to see you later. I need to talk to Minnie in private about her love life."

He leans down to kiss me and I'm surprised when it's a forehead kiss. "I just can't have you out of my sight after what happened." He snags my chin with his thumb and forefinger. "That's *never* going to happen again. Not on my watch."

"Eugene saved me."

Savage smiles faintly. "But I should have been there. I'm sorry, my princess."

I doubt those words have ever come out of his mouth as many times as in the past few weeks.

"I know," I reply softly. "It's okay. I forgive you."

He landed himself in confinement after defending my ass, after all.

Savage leans down and presses a series of kisses on the left side of my neck, opposite to my mating mark side. Ghoul kissed me in the same place last night and I wonder if this is the wolf's way of replacing the scent with his. The skin burns a little.

"Cover this up," he says, his voice husky. "It'll set the others off. Fuck, it's setting *me* off."

I watch him saunter out of my room, pointing threateningly at Eugene as he does. Venomous fangs still loom over me, poised and ready to strike. I have to be on alert at all times.

I grab the small mirror I use to pluck my eyebrows and check my neck for hickeys. But when I see the skin of my neck, I gasp in annoyance. There are no bruises, but something worse. Two long lines of deep red stretch all the way down the side of my neck. Fang marks. That bastard *marked* me—given me fang hickeys! I'll have to cover it up with concealer before everyone sees.

When Minnie gets out of the shower, I observe her carefully. Her eyes are puffy, and when she looks at me, I just run over and wrap my arms around her. "We need to talk, Min."

She sniffs loudly. "Yup." Then she looks up at me with a wild expression. "But you need a shower first. You smell strange, Lia. There's a dangerous mix of scents." She frowns. "Mr Pardalia being one of them. And are those *fang* marks? Holy Goddess almighty."

"Oh, shit. Yeah." I bite my lip. "Lyle's one of my mates, Minnie. I found out that night my father came."

"I surmised as much," she says quietly. "Four Lia? I thought me having *three* was intense. But I suppose it makes sense with you being an all-powerful Boneweaver. That's one from every type of order!"

"Five."

"Pardon?"

"I have five mates. That's the *other* scent you're getting off me."

She stares at me goggle-eyed. "I think you'll need therapy, Lia."

"Lucky Lyle's trained for it."

She snorts before sobering to the situation. "Go and wash them both off you. We have a whole lot of feline shit to deal with today."

Stupid, selfish me wants his scent to linger on my skin, which would only mean that every animus would be aware I've been cosy with him. I ran through the animus dorm last night, but hopefully they were too enamoured by my own scent to notice?

Within half an hour, I'm freshly scrubbed and Stacey, Raquel, Sabrina, Connor, Minnie and I meet in the library for an emergency meeting before breakfast. The only one of us missing is Henry, who is still admitted for investigations at the vet. But Eugene insists on sitting in my lap, apparently taking Savage's threats seriously.

"Where the hell were you yesterday, Lia?" Sabrina demands. "I was worried, and Connor heard you and Henry were admitted to the hospital but we didn't know why! We weren't allowed to visit or anything."

"And!" Connor points a long, red-tipped nail at me. "Then I hear Savage was carrying you through the animus dorm!"

The entire table turns to look at me.

I lean back in my chair, needlessly adjusting Eugene's little goggles. "I was jumped by five serpents."

Connor nods like he guessed this. Raquel swears as Minnie grabs my arm. Stacey gasps loudly before Sabrina makes the sign of the cross.

I raise my brows at Sabrina, but she shrugs. "My grandma is Catholic. Don't change the subject."

"Look, Henry and I are fine because Eugene found help and saved me," I say quickly, patting my little rooster on the back. "My dad was trying to get to me and he's threatened to use serpents here to get to my friends. *You* guys." I take a deep breath as they all cast glances over their shoulders. But this early in the morning, the library is empty. "I will understand completely if you don't want to associate with me anymore. To be friends with me is going to be dangerous from now on."

Minnie's hand comes to her stomach like she remembers the injury that brought me out of my hibernation. Bile rises in my throat. Not again. Never again.

"Serpents are skilled at psychic warfare," I continue. "I'm doing my best to stop them, but—"

"But use of those powers is illegal," Stacey says pointedly. "Really illegal, Lia! Since the Purge!"

Raquel scoffs. "They d-don't c-care about that."

"Exactly," I say, preparing myself for the worst. "So no hard feelings if you want to divorce me, alright?"

Sabrina blows a raspberry. "I live for the drama, Lia, you know that. I'm not going anywhere."

"Me too," Stacey pipes. "Otherwise, my skills and good looks will go to waste."

Raquel gives me a wry grin and shrugs like it's no bother.

Connor rolls his eyes. "And you're forgetting the psycho mates sitting in the animus dorm will protect you, Lia! Savage is literally declaring his love for you to anyone who'll listen! And there's Mr. Pardalia." There's a mischievous glint in Connor's perfectly lined eyes that makes me bite my lip.

My friends are smarter than I gave them credit for.

"Geez, I didn't know my friends were such badasses," I say. I didn't expect this at all. I thought they'd bow out given the chance.

"You didn't?" Sabrina asks me, feigning great offence. "We followed you down into a mysterious dark cavern after you escaped from something worse than death and found out that you're from a mythical order not seen in decades! We're *in this*, woman. We're going to make history with you!"

My heart swells. But shit, I really don't want them to get hurt. If they put obsidian shackles on me again, my power would be cut off, and then it would be free game for my father. I need to be really careful. There are still plenty of serpents around here, and all of them are loyal to my father.

"And look how brave Eugene is!" Stacey says, stroking our rooster with the back of one finger. "He deserves to be our club mascot for saving you."

We all coo over Eugene for a moment, needlessly adjusting his goggles and petting his feathers.

"Alright, now that's out of the way," Sabrina says, sitting straighter in her seat. "My news is that I've broken up with Ashton and I'm currently fucking a tiger in second year. That's it." She sits back in her seat to signal she's done. "Now Minnie's business."

"Right," Minnie says, her voice thick. Tears well up in her eyes.

"What happened?" I whisper, reaching for her hand and dreading what's coming.

In answer, she buries her face in my shoulder. All I can do is hold her.

"No, I'm okay," she whispers, separating herself from me and dabbing at her eyes. "I don't want to make it worse by getting all emotional."

"Good girl," Connor says. "Show him he can't hurt you."

"Titus?" I hiss at her. "I saw him yesterday when I went looking for you and I saw him..." I try to tell her with my eyes. "I know you're in love with him, Min. I'm sorry."

"I can't bear to hear it, Lia," she says. "But I can guess what you saw."

"He's pretty obvious about his sex life, that Titus," Connor says wryly.

"A-Asshole," Raquel mutters. "We a-all called it."

"Well, that's the thing," says Minnie darkly. "I suppose I was a bit blinded. Yesterday, he was supposed to meet me for a little date." She looks down at her hands. "He never showed."

Connor slaps the table in disgust.

"I'd been telling him how I thought we should do more than just sit in his room and he was like 'yeah, sure, fine.' But when he didn't come, I went to find him and tell him how I felt, but—" She shudders. "I can't even say it."

"He was fucking that serpent with the tattoo around her tits," Connor says. "She was bragging about it all night."

"And then?" Sabrina presses.

"And then he asked me to fuck one of his followers so he could watch. Shelby was super keen but—"

"Shelby?" Connor shrieks at the top of his lungs. "He did *not!*"

"Who's Shelby?" I demand, pounding on the table.

"An oily little hyena who likes to pick his nose," Stacey says snidely. "He tried to get me to hack into the school's kitchen ordering system to buy him raw pigeon meat."

We all shudder. Eugene squawks in disgust.

We all let this sink in.

"And what did you say, Minnie?"

"Of course I said no," she said. "But then I think that really pissed him off because he texted me—"

"You've been texting him?" I say, grabbing her arm. With the phone I had Savage get her.

She turns her face up to mine and nods like she's guilty. "Titus saw that phone you gave me and I've been texting him. He has a laptop he uses for messages that the school gave him."

Guilt is poison in my stomach. "Okay, and?"

"Oh, Minnie, no!" Stacey suddenly covers her mouth in horror.

"Yeah, Stace. I'm a complete idiot."

Connor slaps his own forehead.

"What am I missing?" I look between the felines.

Sabrina gives me a droll look. "What Minnie is too polite to say is that she's been *sexting* with Titus."

"Nudes," Stacey adds.

"You couldn't pay me any amount of money to send that tiger nudes," Sabrina says snidely.

"I trusted him!" Minnie's voice is high-pitched with strain. "I should have been able to trust him! My—" She cuts herself off and wipes angrily at her cheeks.

"He's going to share them, isn't he?" Connor deadpans, going ashen.

I stare at my friend, horrified.

Minnie shakes her head. "Not *yet*. But he's going to, if I don't do what he asks."

"That shit-eating vermin," Sabrina swears. "What does he want?"

Our friend wrings her hands while Gertie chirps softly in her ear. The other nimpins cluck in awareness of the high emotions.

"Minnie," I say gently, "I think it's time you told us how you got in here. It's because of Titus, isn't it?"

She nods and takes a deep breath. "Yeah. Alright. Well, it all started at my first university ball. He came with another girl and brought some of his friends. He caught my eye and I suppose I caught his. My parents were really strict and didn't let me do anything outside of uni, so when he came along with his fancy car, and was super nice to me, I thought my white knight had come."

"Yeah," Sabrina says darkly. "We get that all too well."

It was the same with me and Theo Krait. He came along at the right place, at the right time, and I *fell* into him. Except Minnie hadn't been responsible for Titus' death.

"So when he asked me to 'transport some money'"—Minnie makes air quotes—"I really wanted to help, you know? I wanted to be useful, not just go to university and study boring banking and finance. I wanted to do something that *mattered*. And I really wanted to show him I was dedicated to him and a responsible... adult. So I got the money he gave me and drove it across the border, but I got stopped by police on the way, and, well..." Minnie's cheeks go red. "The bag was full of counterfeit money."

Sabrina groans into the air, while Raquel and Stacey shake their heads with dismay. I just feel sick to my stomach.

"Since it put my dad's banking job at risk," Minnie says, "he had to pay the council to keep this quiet. They just said as long as I enrolled at Animus Academy, I would have all the charges dropped."

"That scumbag," Connor sighs. "Why are the hot ones always evil?"

"Yeah, that's why no one can know about it. And look, I know how it sounds, but Titus felt really bad afterward, and look at the state he was in when he got here! He was rabid and had to have rehab and everything. It really affected him, you know? There was a misunderstanding with the bags. He didn't intend for that to happen."

Alarm bells are going off in my head. I can't reconcile my intelligent, book-loving friend with this girl who has fallen head over heels for someone who's manipulating her. But Titus has an allure. A huge seductive draw to all the animas, so much so that even the serpents are fucking him, and they rarely step outside their order. The whole thing screams that something is off about this.

"So what does he want you to do now?" I ask.

"He wants to set up a meeting with my dad," she admits. "Talk about finance or something. But I can't have him and my dad in the same room *at all*. He might want to blackmail him too! I need to protect my dad from this. He's so embarrassed about me already."

"So if you don't?" I dread the answer. "What will he do?"

Minnie's face crumples. "He's going to leak the nudes."

Fury like I've never known strikes me. And half of this is my fault for giving her that phone.

Minnie tugs at her hair. "This'll kill my parents! Literally, it will kill them! And probably destroy my dad's reputation too. They'll never forgive me."

We sit in silence for a moment, processing all of this. Minnie's honour is on the line here. She deserves so much more than this.

"We need some dirt on him," Sabrina says. "That's the first thing we need to do. Blackmail him right back."

"What?" Minnie gasps. "No, that's cruel."

Silence descends, heavy and unforgiving.

My kind, loving, beautiful tigress lowers her head. "Oh, right."

We all look at Connor.

"I don't know much more than anyone else," he admits. "He's not talkative, you know?"

Inspiration hits me. "So we need information, right? Where is all the student info kept? Like the files with all our details."

Minnie stares at me wide eyed. "Lia, you're not thinking what I think you're thinking?"

"Yes, I am B-two," I say with a smirk. "It's snooping time. Except Sabrina will need to teach me how to pick a certain lock."

Sabrina removes the set of lock picks she keeps in her pocket like a talisman. "Bitches, we've got this."

* * *

When we head to breakfast, it's already packed with everyone eating. I feel Scythe, Xander and Savage's eyes on me the entire time I'm standing in the queue for my ham and cheese croissants. I fill Minnie's plate for her, and listless, she lets me. As we grab our coffees and head to our table, I sneak a glance at the serpent's corner. They sit there minus five members, looking grim. Thomas Krait also sits with a coffee, pointedly ignoring me. It's then that I notice every single one of them except him has a pair of obsidian shackles on their ankles. I glance at Savage and he winks at me, though he doesn't smile.

Swallowing, I look to my left.

Titus sits at one of the feline's tables, and there's a new girl in his lap. The fact that he's openly flaunting this in Minnie's face just makes me hate him even more.

Minnie comes around the table to sit opposite me, so she doesn't have to look at Titus and his cronies.

And then something happens that makes every cell in my body go still.

Someone at the hyena table makes an oinking, snorting sound. The others take up the cause, and a chorus of oinks thunder through the back of the hall.

They point at my best-friend, chortling through the oinks.

Minnie stiffens as she goes to sit, blinking rapidly as if she's trying to contain herself. Gertie huddles up to her ear, clucking to keep her breathing even.

Sabrina, Stacey and Raquel also pause before our table.

My blood *boils*, fire scorching my arteries, my anima demanding vengeance with talons and claws.

I slam my bamboo tray down hard enough to crack it.

Scanning the back of the hall for the culprits, my eagle-sharp vision narrows as I find them: oily, scummy males, all with matching curling black eyebrow tattoos. I mark my prey and stalk down the hall, my power pulsing around me in heat and ice and electricity. My anima begs me to shift and leap down to snap necks and gouge out eyes, but I leash her for the moment.

I sense Sabrina and Raquel are behind me, flanking me like guards. The hyenas see us coming and laugh even harder, doubling over and continuing to oink.

We come to a stop in front of their table.

When I point at them, my finger is steady. They're seized by the violent force of my barely restrained telekinesis. Stuck in their positions, feeling the pressure of my power, they have no choice but to remain silent, staring at me with bug-eyed expressions.

And when I speak, my voice is a deep, vicious growl I barely recognise. "If you so much as make a *single* noise towards my friend, I will *rip* out your motherfucking throats and *eat* them."

They stare at me, stricken. The entire hall is now silent.

"Do. You. Understand. Me?" I squeeze all eight throats for emphasis before releasing them.

They wheeze and nod frantically.

Hopefully, they put the throat squeezing down to an eagle healing-adjacent power.

"Good," I growl, releasing them.

They all sag in their seats.

I turn on my heel and walk back to our table, Raquel and Sabrina stopping to glare at them before stomping behind me.

Minnie remains frozen in her seat; Stacey has a comforting arm around her.

Then Savage's faint voice sails over the choked silence. "She's the Goddess of my black heart, my regina. Isn't she perfect?" I'm breathing hard after my rage, but my gaze flicks to Savage. He beckons to me before tucking a napkin into his black T-shirt and planting a knife and fork down on the table as if he's ready to eat. "Come here and let me eat your pussy for dessert, regina!"

"Later," I say roughly. Though it seems to calm my anima down and she starts mewling for our wolf.

"I love her more and more every day," he sighs.

We all sit down at our table, both Sabrina and Stacey trying hard not to laugh.

"This evening," I mutter to our table. "We're doing it this fucking evening."

Chapter 46

Aurelia

During group counselling this morning, Savage surprises me by putting his arms around me and dragging my ass into his lap. He plants a gentle kiss on my lips. "Regina." He smiles and proceeds to cuddle me to his chest. I discreetly adjust Savage's arms so they don't quite press on the painful wounds still marring my stomach. I also have to ignore the sniggers of Sabrina and Connor because this means I'm right next to Scythe, who turns his icicle eyes towards me. I suppress the way my entire body wants to shiver under those lethal, predatory eyes—as if what I said to him yesterday, with my face all but pressed up against his, is still fresh in his mind. It's sure as hell fresh in *my* mind too.

"Savage," Theresa scolds, making me tear my gaze off Scythe. "This is a classroom. You may be able to do whatever you like in your spare time, but we need to sit in our own chairs."

I nod and attempt to get up, but Savage's arms tighten around me, a low growl vibrating through his chest.

Theresa sighs.

But something draws me back to Savage and I draw a soft finger down his cheek before leaning in to whisper against his lips, "Boundaries." And then into his head, *"I promise we can cuddle as much as you want tonight."*

His arms reluctantly loosen around me, and I slide off him and back into my seat. He's still angry about the serpent incident and ready to jump at anyone who gives him so much as a side-eye. So, I scoot my seat closer to his and take his hand in mine, holding it tight. He squeezes my hand back.

Savage is my moody, growling, over-the-top bodyguard the entire day until classes are over and I tell him I need to attend to my own business. Xander resorts to putting my wolf in a head-lock and wrestles him back to their dorm, demanding that they go to the gym. Scythe follows with his usual unbothered walk behind them.

"They're so adorable." Minnie grins at me.

"They're murderous and psycho," I mumble, but really, my anima and I *love* Savage's open claiming of me.

Minnie, Eugene and I go to collect Henry from the veterinary clinic. He's awake and being kept in a large tank with butterflies for entertainment and other insects for him to eat, but when he sees me and Eugene, he plasters himself to the glass and squeaks in annoyance.

"I'm sorry, Hen," I sniff, holding up my hand to the glass. "But you're alive, that's the main thing."

The nurse unlocks the tank and my favourite blue fluffball zips out, hurtling himself into my face, licking me and chittering like I abandoned him in a desert for months on end.

The nurse gives me the rundown. The serpents used a low dose of anaesthetic that could have gone wrong very easily. Henry was basically lucky to be alive. I cried, then Henry cried, and I fed him fresh, plump blueberries that I brought with me from the dining hall.

It's a happy reunion back in our dorms, with my animas and the other nimpins. Connor comes to join us and we give all five nimpins a bubble bath and a grooming with tiny brushes.

We wait until after business hours are over when neither Georgia nor Lyle are likely to be in office. It will take a little toll on me, but I'm boosted after that last round of sex with Lyle, so it's not too much trouble to envelop myself and Henry in my invisible eighth shield and scuttle off to the management building. Eugene doesn't want to be left behind, but Raquel has taken a liking to him and cuddles him to their chest to watch us leave.

Henry is excited to be out and about, and I give him his own bubble of invisibility so he can zip around corners and let me know if anyone's approaching.

We make it into the elevator and, to my surprise, it lets us up without trouble. When the doors slide smoothly open on the third level, the floor is dark and Georgia's desk is unoccupied. As soon as I step out of the lift, the lights blink on and I jump back, heart pounding.

But Henry does a lap of the space to show me no one is there. It's just the automatic lights.

Blowing out my nerves in a huff, I hurry to Lyle's office door and video call Minnie's phone. At first, all I can see are Sabrina's tits in her new push-up bra as I kneel before the door.

"Alright, I'm here," I say, taking out her second set of lock picks from my bra.

"Okay, show me the goods," she cackles, like this is great fun.

Sabrina and Minnie squabble in the background as Sabrina squints down at the phone. I show her the lock.

It's as lovely as the rest of the finishings of the old dragon mansion. Heavy yellow gold, with the doorknob itself moulded into a dragon's head. The attached lock is that same gold, but it has been modified into the modern style.

"Alright," Sabrina purrs, "go in like I showed you. Real nice and slow."

Stacey snorts behind her. "You forgot the lube Lia!"

"Dirty animas," I mutter. Henry picks up one of my tools with his beak and offers it to me. I take it, blowing him a kiss because it's the right one. I insert the first pick to hold back the lock's tumblers and then grab the second one to make my manoeuvres.

Sabrina guides me through the process, just like we practised on her training locks. After five minutes of jiggling the pick around, nothing happens. "Shit, I think you're gonna have to come here and do it for me," I say. I have one eye on the elevator the whole time to make sure there's no one on the way up. At least I'll get a warning if the elevator pings downstairs.

Sabrina swears. "I *really* don't want anything else on my record."

She's right. Our leopard friend has a number of small felonies on her record for breaking and entering as well as theft. She called herself one of the best jewellery thieves in the state and only got caught because various boyfriends snitched on her.

"Open, you bastard!" I mutter, smacking the golden handle.

The lock clicks and the door swings wide open, revealing the dark, empty office inside.

"What happened?" Stacey shouts.

"Gotta go!" I end the call.

Grinning madly, Henry and I inspect the door. There's no hiss of magic as we peer in through the doorway, because I sure learned my lesson that time I got caught in Xander's trap. When I detect nothing, Henry and I bolt into the room.

This is like being in Lyle's bedroom, only it feels more devious because I'm actually here doing something illegal. Adrenaline and excitement make me near-giddy as, for the first time ever, I freely cast my gaze around the space without the boss man to distract me.

Every time I've been to Lyle's office, it's been the same: super clean and organised, with not a paper or pen out of place. On the right and back sides are his set of wall-to-wall bookshelves, and snooping at the titles reveals they're only academic texts and manuals for the school.

But the student files are what I'm after, specifically about the rabid students. He has to keep them around here where it's easy for him to access. Eagerly, I plonk myself down in his chair and wiggle around, checking out the view from this angle before looking at the desktop. His computer monitor sits to the left side and I notice with chagrin that even his keyboard is squeaky clean. Honestly, it's unnatural. Tapping one of the keys, the screen comes on to the login page. I have no chance of guessing the password, so I move on. There's a pen cup with a couple of the fancy fountain pens he uses, and next to that is a carved piece of wood I recognise with a jolt.

The peeling blue paint has faded to a near-white, and it's carved with clumsy hands into the shape of an angel. The wings are round and small. You can barely make out the female shape because it's worn from over handling.

I hold it gently in both hands, cradling it like a baby. The backs of my eyes burn as I register an old memory that's not mine.

Quickly, I put it back in its place.

"Focus, Aurelia," I mutter.

Henry squeaks in agreement, tapping his beak on the set of drawers on the right of the desk. I try to yank it open, only to find it locked.

Henry and I get down on the floor, and this modern, silver lock I can actually crack. It comes open with a satisfying click and I congratulate myself on a job well done. There are student files in the drawer, arranged according to year level and then alphabetically. I run my finger down them, checking the names. But they're arranged by surname. I pass my own file, and when I see Titus' first name, I quickly pull it out.

It's huge, with over a hundred pages of documents, all detailing his daily activities while he was in the rabid unit, presumably Lyle's special cages underground. It's detailed right down to every bowel movement.

My face flushes as a brief thought of Lyle monitoring my own bowel movements enters my mind. I shake the thought off and scan the rest of Titus' details.

It's his surname that makes me stare. That makes the back of my neck prickle and recognition twist through my bones.

Titus Clawson.

I know that name. My hands tremble as I brush a finger over his surname and realise why I thought Titus looked familiar. Quickly thumbing through to the first page where his personal details are listed, I run my finger down his age and address until I get to his next of kin.

Next of Kin: Cain Clawson

Relationship: Father

I stare and stare at the paper. At the memory of a tiger who I once saw stalking up the stairs to my father's manor. I'd just returned from kindergarten and was riding my tricycle through the foyer at full speed. He appeared on the threshold and I rammed right into his bare feet, hitting his shins before my tricycle rolled backwards. I'd looked up... and up... and up. He was tall. As dark and wild as Titus, but his eyes weren't nearly so hard.

I thought the sight of him would offend my father because he was sort of feral, with dirt on his chest and rumpled, dirty track pants. Humans might have thought the guy looked homeless if not for the arrogant swagger, the obvious threat he posed.

But he knew my name. "Aurelia," he greeted far more gently than I expected. "You have beautiful eyes, like your mother. I wonder if your father has noticed."

"Cassius?" My usually gentle mother's voice was sharp as she strode into the foyer. I remember being scared by that tone. "Since when is it commonplace for territory leaders to wander into foreign land unannounced?"

"Athena." When the tiger replied, I had to stare. I didn't

know the word for the way he spoke to her then, but I do now. Reverent. There is no other descriptor for it.

I don't remember what happened after that, except that my nanny Rosalina ushered me away. But a part of me had sensed who he was. What he was to my mother.

I'm very tempted to take this file and run so I can study everything completely, but Lyle would probably tear the school down until he found the perpetrator, and I don't want to implicate my friends. Sighing, I leaf through each page of boring notes by vets, nurses, and the zookeeper, Rick. Lyle's notes are handwritten in long detailed paragraphs. I leaf through them faster and faster until I hear a sound that makes me and Henry freeze.

The pinging of the elevator.

"Henry!" I breathe. My nimpin is hovering by Lyle's computer and whips around, zipping up to me in alarm.

Slowly, I grab the file and close the drawer, retreating into the corner of the office and enveloping both Henry and I in my invisible shield. If I stay super still, then—

But it's not Lyle who peaks his head around the wood panelled door. It's a head full of dark waves and hazel eyes that gleam with mischief.

"*Regina*," Savage sings softly. "I've been tracking you all over the school. Are we playing a game?"

"Fuck," I say it out loud.

Savage's head snaps to my corner, his face lighting up. "Caught you!"

He steps in, kicks the door closed and prowls right up to me. "I'm thinking we make love in here to fuck with Lyle."

Henry makes to go over to Savage, but I grab the nimpin and shake my head at him. But that's all the distraction Savage needs to bound right over to me and press me up against the wall.

"Regina," he coos.

Henry coos back.

Savage makes a face.

I sigh, and lower my invisibility shield, revealing the both of us squashed against the wall.

"You're up to no good," Savage tuts. "Naughty girl."

I push at his hard chest. "Get out of here. I'm busy."

His gaze narrows on me. Then he sees the files I'm clutching to my chest like treasure. "What's this?" He grabs the Titus file out of my hands, but of course, he can't read it.

"Tuh," he says, trying to sound out the letters. "Tie—" He frowns.

"I really need to teach you to read," I mutter. "Anyway, you don't need to know what it says."

"Then you don't get it back." He steps out of my reach.

"You're ruining my plans," I snap. "Give it back before we get caught."

"Too late for that." Savage cocks his head, his eyes glittering with excitement. "Lyle just got out of the elevator... but he's with people."

I grab at Savage and throw the shield around the both of us. "Who's the second person?" I whisper.

We both go silent as muffled voices sound from the other side of the door.

He shakes his head like he can't make it out. Then sniffs the air purposefully. "Georgia and a serpent."

My brows shoot up. Serpents can see heat! Which I *can't* shield from.

"Shit!" Making wide eyes, I drag Savage and look around the room, but there's nowhere to hide.

My eyes fall on the massive oak desk.

Dragging Savage towards it, I push him down and under the massive frame just in time for the office door to open.

Savage is grinning from ear to ear like he's having the time of his life and the only way we fit is to put Savage's big body in the farthest corner, with his legs stretched out and for me to sit on top of him, bent forward so that my head doesn't hit the underside of the desk. Savage takes the opportunity to wrap his arms around me and hold me close. Henry huddles into the shadows of the opposite side, his liquid eyes glistening in the dark as we all listen to the two voices.

"Well, I appreciate your time, Mr Pardalia," says a slippery, sugary sweet female voice.

That *voice*.

I turn and grab Savage's face in one hand to try and make him understand without words. He gazes back at me with that breezy smile before he frowns. I press my finger to my lips and he rolls his eyes to say, *as if I didn't know to keep quiet.*

"You and your brother have been rather persistent, Mrs Naga." Lyle's voice tells me he's smiling. "I suppose we've delayed this long enough."

"Oh, please, call me Charlotte."

My aunt laughs, and it's a sultry, fawny sound. What the hell is she doing here? I can just imagine her in her best cleavage-showing blouse, fluttering her freshly done eyelashes and smiling with her extra bright red lipstick.

Lyle comes to sit at his desk and I fixate on his big shiny shoes and the slacks covering his long legs. I'm suddenly desperate to touch him. To lay my claim on him. I squeeze Savage's hand to help contain my anima.

"Charlotte," Lyle says, and I know there's *definitely* a smile in his voice. Is he... fucking *flirting* with my Aunt Charlotte?

Chapter 47

Aurelia

Rage ignites my blood.

"Well, with the family visitation day coming up," Aunt Charlotte says, "I was hoping you might put in a good word for me with Aurelia?"

Oh, she's good. She barely hides the usual sneer in her voice when she says my name. And the fact that my father is trying to get communication with me through her makes me furious. He thinks Charlotte can *seduce* Lyle? I have to hold my breath as we listen.

"Well," Lyle says seriously, "I'm afraid if Miss Aquinas doesn't consent to see you, there's not much I can do." Hell yes. I wrote a big fat *NO* on my visitation consent form when we first arrived here.

"Surely, an allowance can be made for her mental health plan?" Charlotte purrs. "I know she's never been all that great in that department." She chuckles like it's a joke they have between the two of them.

"She is making progress, even if it is slow," Lyle says.

I direct a disgusted face towards his lap. His legs are spread wide under the desk, and I can't help but glare at his crotch.

"She has little cousins who miss her," Charlotte sighs wistfully. "And I just know if she saw them, she might feel a bit better. I'm all alone at home right now with my two husbands away for work in the mines."

Fire floods my veins at the *overt* implication in her voice. My anima shrieks in my head, the need to claim our dominance over this situation, demanding that I get out from under this desk and lay my claim on Lyle in an obvious way.

Mine. This lion is *mine.* Savage rubs tiny circles on the back of my hand as if he's trying to comfort me. It's not working to soothe me at all, and instead, it's only fuelling the need screaming in my lower belly. I tremble from the force of it.

"Aurelia has many surprising skills," Lyle says slowly, purposefully. Both Savage and I go still. "But she's also very good at *hiding* things right under my nose."

He knows we're under here. Shit.

Charlotte laughs, completely oblivious. "Oh, yes. She lived with me for seven years and I barely know the girl."

"But she didn't live *with* you, did she?" Lyle says quietly. Even from the other side of the wood, I feel Aunt Charlotte go still. Can feel the accusation in Lyle's voice. "She lived in a barely weatherproof, ramshackle dwelling, with a paltry allowance for food and hot water. Isn't that right, Charlotte?"

My heart is beating a scary rhythm and I think I'm going to pass out from disbelief. Lyle sounds like he's chastising a student.

Aunt Charlotte lets out a chiming, high-pitched laugh. "Oh, that's a bit dramatic, Lyle," she coos. "It was a quaint little thing that she rather loved, actually. It was just her style."

"I treat my rabid beasts better than that." Lyle's voice is dangerously quiet. "I will put forth your proposition to her and if she does not wish to meet you, she will not."

Hope and gratitude rise in my chest. I'm going to climb this man like a tree when we get out of here.

There are a few tense beats of silence where I imagine them staring each other off.

I wonder if my aunt will dare to try to dominate him. She is sister to the serpent king, after all—a high-ranking member of his court.

Charlotte speaks just as softly. "You were not held accountable for the five serpent lives you took from our court four months ago."

She's threatening him. I can't breathe. I can't help but reach forward and gently touch Lyle's outstretched leg. He gives no indication of noticing. Savage squeezes my thigh in warning, but I ignore him.

Lyle leans forward in his chair. "They were given merciful deaths. They were trespassing *on what is mine.*"

Am I imagining it? But no, I'm not. That gravelly voice is talking about *me.*

I can't help it. Overwhelmed, I drag my hand up his leg, my mouth watering, heat spearing up my spine. In gratitude, in lust... in everything.

"They were valued members of our court," Charlotte says accusingly. "It's not a good look for you."

Lyle chuckles and it's a cold sound. "If it goes to trial, I will gladly mention my observations about the serpents under my care here. The evidence of venom harvesting, the interesting torture techniques, the PTSD that is oddly unexplained... Shall I go on, Mrs. Naga?"

I'm wet and shaking with need, my breaths heavy and hard as I listen to him outing serpent court for the awful things that go on there. Led by a mad need for him, I remove the invisibility shield and ease away from Savage. He lets me and I position myself between Lyle's legs. I *want* him to see me. I *need* his skin in my mouth. I need his voice whispering in my ear. I need to see those cold amber eyes succumbing to me. I drag my nails up his thick, muscular thighs. He lets out a little shiver.

That pleases me to no end, and I quiver in response, barely able to hold back. I can see him now. The square cut of his beautiful, perfect jaw as he stares my aunt down with overt, cold dominance. His eyelashes are long and a lovely shade of dark blonde from this angle and they don't move, don't even blink.

I gently brush my fingers across the bulge between his legs. He gets harder as I stroke him up and down his thick length. Oh dear Goddess, he's straining against his slacks. The only sign of him being affected by me is that his hands form fists on the armrests of his expensive leather swivel chair.

Charlotte's chair gets pushed back as she stands and says pertly, "You'll be hearing from us again, Mr Pardalia."

"I'm sure, Mrs. Naga. Georgia will escort you out."

There's a moment of Aunt Charlotte's disbelieving silence before stilettos thud on the carpet, and the door opens.

"Oh, and Lyle?" Aunt Charlotte says.

I unbutton Lyle's pants and pull the zip down, leaning forward and giving a lick to the sliver of hard, perfect cock I can see.

"Yes, Mrs. Naga?" Lyle's voice is blissfully tight.

"We know." A beat of silence. "About you."

Oh shit. Does she mean that I'm his regina?

"Very well," comes the tight reply.

The door clicks shut.

There are five seconds until the elevator door pings open and it's so quiet that we all hear the faint whirring of it descending.

Savage lets out a huff and Henry zips out like he's desperate for air.

Lyle pushes back a little from the desk, but I'm still between his legs, my hands still on his cock. He looks down at me. Though his face is deathly serious, his gaze is simmering, pupils blown out in gold irises.

"What are you doing, Aurelia?" he asks, his voice gravelly and restrained.

"I don't even know," I reply faintly, my eyes dropping back to his lap. "But I want this." I squeeze his straining cock, remembering the feel of it inside of me. His girth. Gods, I wanted— "I need it in my mouth," I breathe.

Savage's hands find my bare thighs, stroking his fingers up and down like he can't help himself either.

Lyle's scary gaze shifts towards Savage before cutting back to me. There's a beat of silence in which we simply stare at each other. I can't even explain what I feel for him, but I hope my eyes communicate it. No one has ever stood up for me against my serpent family. Not ever. It makes me want to kiss him. Everywhere.

Savage's fingers go up and down my bare skin, skimming my ass.

"I'm so wet," I murmur.

Lyle's eyes darken.

"Say less, princess," Savage roughly yanks my panties down in one go and shoves his face into my pussy so hard my face is shoved forward into Lyle's lap. I moan out loud, gripping Lyle's cock harder, rubbing my face against him.

I drop my mating mark shield and my scent shield in one fell swoop. When I have him, I want him to experience all of me. I look up at him, our mating marks gleaming, letting the pleasure from Savage's tongue soak into my eyes.

Lyle is clenching his teeth, a muscle in his jaw feathering out.

"Let me have it," I desperately whisper. "Please, Lyle."

Lyle's face changes as he looks down at me, heat turning those amber eyes molten. Although his fists never leave his armrests, the zipper on his pants magically slides down the rest of the way. He's using his telekinesis. I've never seen anything hotter in my life.

He commands me with a single word of dominance. "Suck."

In one swift movement, his massive cock springs free, beautiful, long and thick. Gods, was it this huge last time? His crown is glistening with his arousal, thick blue veins begging for my tongue.

It feels so *right* to comply with his demand. I surge forward, taking his length with a moan. I come back up and release him with a satisfying pop. He tastes like salt and power and something so uniquely Lyle it makes my mouth water. I take him again, as far as I can, wanting all of him inside me this way. He hits the back of my throat, making me choke a little.

My lion tilts his head back and lets out a strangled moan. Savage devours my ass, pushing a big finger into my pussy as he licks the tight band of muscle.

"Fuck, you taste so good," I tell Lyle through telepathy as I come back up to suck on his head and look at him.

His eyes widen with pleasure. He grabs my face in both hands, stroking my cheeks with his thumbs and staring down at me like it's the first time. I grin around his cock as Savage chuckles darkly into my pussy.

"Regina, you really are dripping," Savage mumbles between my cheeks.

I hiss at the vibration it sends through my core. Gods, these men might actually kill me with pleasure.

I grind into Savage's face while I trace one of Lyle's thick veins down his cock with my wet lips. I wantonly moan, licking his cock from base to tip before swallowing his crown again and sucking hard. His pre-cum is liquid heaven on my tongue and I suck harder, drawing more of it from him. Lyle only has eyes for me as I bob up and down, groaning at the feel of his taste and how Savage licks and pumps that glorious finger inside of me. A little part of me knows what Savage is doing. That he's preparing me for something that might come to pass in the future. Something I would *love* to do. Something I thought would never be possible until this exact moment.

My anima screams in pleasure at the possibility.

"Do you know how long I've wanted to do this?" I ask Lyle mind to mind. *"Do you know how long I've thought about your cock in my mouth?"*

Lyle growls, long and low. Or is that a purr?

Lost in the sensation of both men, I suck hard as I come back up, releasing his cock with another pop. I lap at the sensitive area on the underside of his crown and my lion shivers, flexing his hips to send his cock back into my mouth. I make a sound of immense satisfaction, imagining the hard, powerful body flexing underneath this suit.

Not stopping my rhythm, I reach up, unbuttoning his shirt so I can see more of that golden skin. He lets me, letting out a heavy breath. I undo as many buttons as I can reach, pulling his shirt out of his pants and making a happy sound at the stunning flesh I see underneath. His golden torso is a little paler than his face, a six-pack of hard abs flexing and contracting as he strains.

As *I* make him strain.

I can't help but run a hand down those beautiful, rigid muscles as Savage growls behind me, descended into his animus. I grind my pussy onto his face, making him growl louder and Lyle pushes my hair off my own face with a gentle hand.

"Mine," I growl into his head.

"Aurelia," he whispers, looking down at where we're joined.

I suck harder and faster, keen to see him undone and out of control. I need to taste his cum on my tongue and I need to hear him say *that* name again.

Lyle responds to my increased pressure. His hips buck upwards, and he groans into the air before looking down at me. I know he's out of control when he whispers, his entire body straining, "You look so beautiful sucking my cock, angel. So fucking beautiful."

That does it.

Savage crooks his finger in my pussy and I come hard, gripping Lyle's thighs as I see stars. The sound I make is a strangled, husky scream. Savage doesn't stop, pumping his finger and lapping mercilessly at my core, relentless in his claim.

"You're going to take my cum, angel," Lyle grits out, fucking my mouth in a way that keeps me moaning with pleasure. "And you're going to swallow all of it, do you understand?"

I cry out in agreement, letting him take his pleasure from me, so content that he's claiming my mouth in this way. Tears stream out of my eyes.

Lyle grips my face, and he roars into the air as his power pulses in a massive wave through the room and he explodes.

Hot cum spurts into my mouth as he cries out, gripping my face with firm but careful hands. I swallow every burst because this is what I've been waiting for. This is the only real way to quench my thirst for this lion. Savage and Lyle groan at the same time, and I come yet again as I swallow a final gulp.

When Lyle is done, he rests his hips back on the chair and looks down at me, heavy-lidded. He pulls his cock from my mouth and I give it a playful lick, making him shiver. I stroke his thighs possessively.

Some of his cum dribbles down my chin, and before I can reach up to wipe it, Lyle's thumb is there, pushing it back into my mouth. "All of it," he rumbles. I take his thumb in my mouth, sucking on it with relish. He pops it out of my mouth, skimming my swollen lower lip with a sort of heavy-lidded wonder.

Savage peppers kisses over both my ass cheeks and Lyle licks his lips. I follow the movement like an eagle.

"Come here," he orders me, but it's gentle.

Savage releases my ass and I rise up Lyle's body to straddle his lap, running my hands up his arms and shoulders. He rests his forehead against mine before capturing my mouth in his dominating one. Growling, he tastes first my upper lip, then my lower lip, running his tongue along the seam of both before invading me with his tongue.

I whimper around him, and he holds me tight in his arms.

That single movement tells me what his words dare not. That he wants me. That he's claiming me for himself. That he... needs me in his lap and on his body as much as I need him to be in mine. He pulls back just enough to let us both breathe, panting softly.

I murmur against his lips, "I thought you said never again."

He pulls back to see me properly, stroking my cheek so gently with a thumb, his eyes ever so soft on mine. And it's such a new, beautiful thing, that gaze, that I can't help but get lost in it. His lips quirk up into a blinding smile before he murmurs, "I suppose I lied."

My heart swells ten times the size.

Lying spread-eagle on the floor under Lyle's desk like he's eaten the biggest meal he's ever had, Savage chuckles, "Scythe is gonna be so mad."

Chapter 48

Lyle

Aurelia sitting safe on my lap, soft and warm, just having swallowed my cock whole calms the roaring, raging beast inside of me like a sweet song sung to a weary heart.

It shouldn't have pleased me so much to see her on her knees before my desk, but one look at her gorgeous figure, staring at me with such overt, wanton need, sent me into a crazed frenzy.

My very bones couldn't deny her.

I sensed the two of them in here before I even opened my office door. Savage's unhinged, erratic scent trailing through here was obvious. And now that I've been inside the source of Aurelia's power, as her mate, I can sense that golden lick of heaven wherever she is on campus. It tortured me with its latent promises. It set my skin on fire and damned me to hell.

Dazzling blue eyes smile down at me, content and sated. As she should be. The need to claim her, to dominate her, was a wound that only she could heal. Her lips were a balm on my own, soothing my red-hot aggression. That sly monster slid down my spine now, content that our regina is in our arms, safe and glowing with happiness.

During her time at my academy, I haven't seen her close to happy. With her friends, she came close, but it was incomparable to the golden power that emanated from her now.

I sigh, skimming my knuckles across her olive skin, flushed with her exertion. She wants to please me, I realise. She got off on obeying me, just as much as I got off on commanding her and seeing her obey.

Heat fills my chest and I'm compelled to say it. "I want to see you happy," I murmur, tucking a strand of her long midnight hair behind her ear. The need to groom her is over-powering.

Surprise flashes across her face before she smiles shyly.

That smile makes me go still. It makes me stare at her, this creature granted to me by fate.

Her aunt set me off and made me unreasonable. With her words, with her obvious flirtation. Every second conversing with her was a poisoned fang tearing at my calm exterior. That woman caused harm to Aurelia. My mate had lost her mother, just as I had. And when she could have looked to her aunt as a mother, Charlotte Naga had rejected her completely. Such a wound only came from a truly malevolent person.

But it brings me back to why we are here in the first place. I glance at Savage, lying flat on his back, half under my desk, our regina's cum shining all over his face.

I ask, "Why were you two in here?"

The swiftness with which Aurelia's face goes from smiling to nervous makes my lion growl behind his door. But the man in me raises a brow. She glances behind her and tries to get off me, but I capture her neck in one gentle hand. She goes limp, succumbing completely.

Nothing makes me happier than to see that. It makes me go hard again.

"What were you doing here, Aurelia?" I repeat quietly.

Savage snorts when I glance at him, and he mimes zipping

his mouth shut and throwing away the key. I wonder if Scythe knows where his brother's loyalties now lie.

Blue eyes fix on my own. "I, um... Does it matter?" She licks her lips and I know I have to let her go before I bend her over my desk.

I release her neck and gesture for her to stand. She quickly obliges.

It's then that I see the student file under the desk with them.

"You two make for poor criminals," I mutter, using my telekinesis to shoot it towards me. When I read whose file it is, I frown at Aurelia.

"I was just interested in the other rabids," she says quickly.

I lean back in my chair and study her. The way the lie shot out of her lips.

"Your nose is growing," I remark.

She blushes prettily under my gaze and it pleases me to know I have that effect on her, but... does she not know her power rivals mine? Or does she know, but our physical size difference makes for a successful illusion? Her father might not be in physical possession of her, but he's still there, in her mind. Still there in the way she fears.

"I'll just be going now," she says. Henry zips for her out of nowhere. The nimpins are trained to make themselves discreet during sexual activity. Rick and I didn't want to risk them getting hurt.

Savage rolls gracefully to his feet. "I'll walk you back to your dorm, regina."

Every instinct I have tells me to bundle Aurelia in my arms and take her up to my bed where we should spank her for her audacity and then dress her in warmer clothes.

I give a resigned sigh. Any relationship with Aurelia can't work. Not with me here as one of her teachers. There were procedures made for cases of packs being found with the members being in a teacher-student dynamic or healthcare worker-patient. But those procedures meant removing one or both parties from their position before their union. Our kind are particularly forgiving when it comes to mating groups as we hold them sacred—a priority above all things.

Since Aurelia is adamant she doesn't want to reveal her secret, we can't reveal me as one of her mates. People would start to wonder how she, an eagle, had a wolf and a lion in her pack. Without the sanctity of matehood, any other public relationship with her is rightfully illegal.

My hands are, therefore, tied.

But my animus is already sending me after her.

"I'll walk you back as well," I growl. "And you're going to tell me why you're interested in Titus. He is not one of yours."

Celeste told me who he belonged to. As a phoenix, she's aware of all the bonds in the academy.

"He's not," Aurelia agrees hastily. I stalk after her as she hurries out of my office with Savage. I have to suppress my hunting instinct to take her to the ground. "I just thought I could find out more information about my condition."

Another lie.

"Why didn't you just ask me?"

She casts a doubtful look over her shoulder and I realise she doesn't feel like I'm someone she can reveal things to.

It wounds my primal self, and I frown at her back as the lift pings and the doors slide open.

Aurelia visibly flinches as Georgia is revealed.

My secretary's eyes flick from Savage, to Aurelia and her mouth twists before she looks at me.

"Move, feline," Savage growls impatiently.

Her brows shoot up, but she stalks out of the lift, brushing her arm across mine as she does. "I'm almost done for the day, Lyle," she says stiffly. "But I can stay if you need me."

"I don't." The growl is out of my mouth on pure reflex.

Georgia blinks in surprise. Then her nostrils flare. Her eyes flick to Aurelia again.

As Savage tugs Aurelia into the lift, I have the sudden urge to hide my regina. I step into the lift and press for the doors to close.

Georgia turns to follow my movements and I stare her down in warning.

Once the doors are safely closed, I take Aurelia's small hand in mine. "I want you to come to me if you have questions," I say gently.

Her cheeks flush under my attention, but she nods. I sense she's still uncertain. My animus makes me stroke her cheek. She leans into my hand and a purr bubbles up from the depths of my being.

The lift descends.

"You are entitled to your secrets," I murmur, even as my animus screams in protest. "But I am not here to hurt you. I *want* to help you."

She looks at her hands. "I know."

But her words are telling me one thing and her body language is telling me another. She doesn't quite trust me.

Perhaps it was the fact that I handcuffed her to my—

I suddenly go still with horror. I found the pieces of the cuffs lying in the bed when I returned, but sensed her with Savage at the time and hadn't rushed after her. But... her entire life, she feared being sent away to be bred. And I *chained* her to my bed.

Savage is staring at me and frowning as the lift door opens. "What is it?" he growls.

Aurelia looks back up at me. I take her face in my hands and let my power softly brush over her. She blinks, feeling me around her and in her mind. *"I'm sorry I cuffed you to my bed."*

Her eyes shutter in memory and something in me tears anew at the sight.

"I am so sorry. I'll never do that again. Ever."

She bites her lip before replying. *"I never thought I'd see the day when you would apologise to me."*

I shake my head. *"I'm not above it. Not when it comes to you."*

She sucks in a shocked breath, before leaning up to press her lips against mine.

"My job is to protect you," I say possessively. "No one is taking you away from my academy."

"Away from us," Savage growls.

The elevator chimes from being kept open for too long by Savage's finger on the open button. I suddenly remember we're out in the open and step away from her.

I deserve every ounce of agony that tears through my chest at the hurt I see on her face. But Savage lunges for her, tucking her under his arm before throwing me a dark look. Together, the two of them leave me standing there like a fool. A fool headed to the lowest rung of hell.

Chapter 19

Aurelia

"So, what did you find?" Stacey asks eagerly.

I towel dry my hair and glance at Minnie sitting on her bed, nervously chewing her thumb nail. As soon as Savage dropped me back here, I jumped in the shower to get as much of Lyle's scent off me as possible. My scent shields are good, but I have a tendency to slip up these days with how much I'm using my powers all the time. I can't chance Lyle getting in trouble because of me and Georgia almost catching us only hammers that home. I know that's why he stepped away from me back in the elevator, but it hurt to see his face realise it and then purposefully move away from me. It felt like the worst type of rejection.

"I got caught," I say dryly. "Just as I had the file in hand, Lyle walked in with my bitch of an aunt."

Raquel swears where they stand, peering out of the glass of our balcony doors. Eugene parades around the room with the little keychain Stacey made for him to wear around his neck. She's drawn a picture of him with the words, "Eugene Appreciation Club" curved around it in fancy letters. Now all the nimpins are sitting in front of the lioness, watching her make more for the rest of us to wear on our lanyards.

"How much of a bitch are we talking?" Sabrina sneers with her arms crossed.

"She kept Lia in a leaky hut at the back of their big house and starved her to death, so the biggest sort of bitch," Minnie says darkly before looking at me with wide eyes. "I knew we shouldn't have risked you like that, Lia. You're already on everyone's watch list."

"I mean," I shrug, "it could've gone worse. Luckily, Savage came in time to prevent anything awful from happening." I can't look at them while I'm lying so I settle for staring outside as well. Sabrina is watching me closely, but says nothing more. With a sigh, Minnie heads into our bathroom for a shower, taking Gertie with her for support.

I watch them go with a sick feeling in my stomach.

The truth is that I'm a bit shaken by finding out that Titus is a Clawson. It's dredging up old memories I thought were long buried. In a place that hurts too much to go digging.

"So... plan B," Sabrina sighs.

Raquel groans. "N-Not this, p-please."

"You up for it, Lia?" Sabrina rises from Minnie's bed. "'Cuz I am."

"Are y-you sure, Sabrina?" Raquel asks darkly.

"I know you didn't want to add to your record," I say.

For the first time since I've known the leopard, I see a glimmer of uncertainty in Sabrina's fierce brown eyes. Almost to assure herself, she reaches into her shorts pocket, fingering what I'm sure is the set of lock picks she always keeps on her person. If she doesn't have pockets, she keeps them in her bra. It has the cadence of a security blanket. Given her history of being locked up in a cupboard when she was a child, and with my own fear of a similar thing, I understand why she keeps them like a talisman.

Lyle's eyes when he realised he might have hurt me by

cuffing me to his bed will always be seared into my memory. There was real horror there. And the fact he had the ability to realise it... I shivered. He cared about me and seemed to regret everything that happened the day I found out he was my mate. Perhaps that was the scariest thing of all.

But Sabrina is now nodding in determination. "After stealing an entire diamond chain from a *Jaguar Jewellers* right in the middle of the CBD, Titus' laptop should be a piece of cake. I won't get caught. Besides, it's time you guys understood the extent of my brilliance."

Stacey snaps her fingers. "Then let's hack this bitch."

"On Saturday afternoon," Sabrina says firmly, "when he'll least expect it."

* * *

That night, alone in my dorm, because Titus summoned Minnie and she *wanted* to go, or so she told me, Savage slips into my room and climbs into my bed. I move to the side to make room, but instead, he pulls me on top of his chest.

"You smell like the most perfect piece of cake in the universe," he whispers, running a gentle palm down the length of my back.

I snort as I settle down to sleep. "You smell like an old, dirty forest."

He chuckles. "You promised you'd be in my bed on weekends," Savage says. "I can't wait for tomorrow night."

Am I nervous about spending weekend nights in Savage, Xander and Scythe's room? Hell yes, I am. There's just so much happening right now that I need to focus on and being distracted by being there is the worst sort of torture. How do they sleep? Is Scythe a side-sleeper? Does Xander use an eye mask? I want the answers to so many questions.

"What was your mum like?" Savage suddenly asks. "My mum was nice sometimes."

I startle at the question because we've never spoken about this. Hell, I avoid thinking too much about my past. I've seen his mum in his memories. A pale, skinny sort of woman who never treated Savage well and seemed to favour Scythe.

"When I'm upset, I imagine she's with me." The backs of my eyes start to burn, and suddenly I don't want to continue. But Savage rubs the length of my back in long, slow strokes and it helps me feel better.

"I'm sorry, you don't have to talk about it," Savage whispers. "It's just, Ruben told me that when you love someone, you should try and get to know all about them."

Well, I can hardly fault that, can I? Something loosens in my stomach and I trace a finger along the black ink that makes the edge of the wolf's ear tattooed on his chest.

"It's okay," I say after a gulp. "I was five when she died, so I don't have a whole heap of memories. I had a nanny who looked after me, Rosalina, but I would cook with mum. She was really great at baking and we'd make the most wonderful muffins and cakes. She'd let me lick the bowl and wouldn't get upset if I made a mess or spilled something by accident. I always thought that was such a funny difference between my father and her. My mum didn't care if things were a bit... wild, but my dad wanted everything spotless and in order."

"Kind of like Lyle," Savage says.

"*Not* like Lyle," I say firmly. "My dad could be... cruel when things didn't go his way. I was always a little scared of him. It made learning my powers a not-so-pleasant process. I became really good at them, but I didn't like the classes."

Most animalia gain their powers when their beast appears at puberty, except neither me nor my mates are most animalia. Wolves can do telepathy as children but the other orders have to wait. "I've always had my powers. Since I was a little kid. My mum started to teach me shields when I was, like, three. It must be a Boneweaver thing."

Savage makes a pleased noise. "No wonder you're so good at them. Those invisibility ones."

I chuckle. "Yeah. The one time I used it to sneak around the house, my dad..." I trail off because that *one time* I used my invisibility shield to sneak around the house unseen, it was to steal a chocolate Easter bunny from the pantry. But I saw my mother crying. It upset me so much that I ran in to comfort her, not realising my dad was watching her from the shadows too, and saw me emerge from my shield. It was the first time in my life I remember feeling uneasy about him.

Savage's voice is tight. "What did he do, regina?"

I take a deep breath to try and control myself. "I don't want to talk about it, Savage." I feel Henry fly over to me and he lands on Savage's chest. I snuggle the nimpin close to my cheek and Henry clucks in that comforting way of his. I sniff back sudden, annoying tears.

To my surprise, Savage brushes a finger over Henry's tiny head, before squeezing me tight. "You'll always be safe with me, regina," he whispers. "Always."

I cry properly then, all over Savage's bare chest, getting snot and tears all over his skin. But Savage doesn't care one bit.

The next morning, when I meet Sabrina and the other animas for breakfast, my blood thrums with energy. I flex my fingers in wonder and marvel at how my stomach doesn't hurt so much today. Having two of my mates at the same time felt like a dream, and I might've put it down to exactly that if it wasn't for the fact that I could still taste Lyle on my tongue. I feel so good that even this morning's text (*Unknown: Don't do anything stupid, snakelet*), couldn't tear me down.

"You're glowing this morning," Stacey says accusingly, though there's a wry smile on her face. Raquel hides a grin.

"I thought you were fretting about *something*," Sabrina says, cutting into her stack of pancakes. "Did you finally seduce Xander? I heard dragons have to *stay inside* a female the entire night to claim their mate. Can you ask him if it's true?"

Raquel, sitting next to me, sniffs discreetly in my direction and I hope I scrubbed myself thoroughly enough yet again this morning. Raquel would never say anything if they did sense my lion, but it would certainly complicate things for everyone if they all knew.

Meanwhile, I choke on my coffee. "No, I didn't seduce the giant reptile. He hates me, and, well... I'm not so keen on him either."

The others roll their eyes.

"When's our opening?" Stacey hisses excitedly. "I've not fiddled with someone's tech in a long time."

"I can't believe you're excited," Raquel scolds into our collective minds. *"Connor warned us against this for a reason."*

Last night, we decided to make use of my being able to use telepathy. And with Raquel able to broadcast back to any one of us as well, we were able to communicate from a distance in case something happened. Because our other friends are felines, any conversation could only be one way.

"Relax." Sabrina waves her fork at our wolf anim. "We've got Sneaky McSneak sitting next to you. We'll be in and out with no problem."

We haven't told Connor or Minnie that we've activated plan B, but when we mentioned it as a possibility initially, both of them outright told us it would get us killed and that they'd stop us if we tried. Since Sabrina, Stacey and I thought it was a good plan, and we had no other ideas, we convinced Raquel not to tell them we were going ahead with it.

It feels pretty shitty of us to do so, but as far as I'm

concerned, Minnie needs us to do this for her. She's too sweet and kind to come up with something this cunning.

Once I'd revealed my extra Boneweaver powers of invisibility and telepathy, even Raquel seemed more content that we could pull this off.

"He comes down for lunch on Saturdays," Sabrina continues. "Min will probably be with him."

"You two need to act normally," I say around my blueberry Danish, "so we don't arouse suspicion."

We spend our morning in our dorm, where Stacey and Sabrina help me practise my telekinetic skills. It's actually really hard to be able to manipulate objects from afar, especially if they're moving already, but I find that because of my massive boost in energy, I don't tire from it. By the time lunch comes around, I'm able to bat away the bra that Sabrina throws at me with little bother. Raquel's leather boot, however, hits me square in the face.

We leave before lunch begins so we can get a good table and watch Titus and Minnie arrive.

I'm sitting so that I'm facing the outside door, tearing into my second danish, when they come in. My hackles rise immediately. Titus prowls through first, his arm around the shoulders of his serpent girlfriend, who is in full goth regalia: black eyeshadow, lipstick and a black dress and boots.

Raquel lets out a low, unhappy growl next to me as Minnie shuffles in next. Her chin is raised in dignity, her makeup is perfectly done and her pink hair is pulled up into a cute ponytail, but the thing that makes me rage is that she walks alone and behind them.

In our world, this is a language that speaks volumes.

"She's his fucking girlfriend," Raquel grits out without stuttering. "And he puts her behind them!"

We watch with bated breath as she lines up at the buffet

behind the pair and Titus doesn't even spare her a glance. He's even feeding her last.

"Fucker," Stacey chokes out.

"That limp-dicked neanderthal," Sabrina sneers. "I hope he catches salmonella from all that raw chicken he eats."

Eugene caws in agreement from where he sits between me and Raquel.

My blood is boiling, my heart is racing, and my fists are tight around the edges of my chair. I don't know why Minnie is insistent on following Titus around when he's treating her like this. Surely this is not what love is supposed to look like. It's through clenched teeth that I say into Sabrina's head, *"Let's get this bastard."*

Chapter 50

Aurelia

Sabrina nods, her body also taut with anger as the two of us exit the dining hall. Minnie doesn't look around as we pass her for the doors, but her body is stiff right up to her shoulders and she's still in the way of someone trying to keep themselves together. She's in a simple, loose black dress and Gertie is like a tiny ball of sunshine that is clucking in her ear.

Black is Minnie's least favourite colour. And apparently, it's Titus' favourite.

"You can hear me?" Raquel projects.

"Loud and clear," I reply.

Outside, the autumn sun beams down on us, warming my cold veins. We walk down the path towards the anima dorms before slipping into the gap between the central building and one of the wings. There are no guards around, nor anyone to watch us as I slip a bubble of my invisible eighth shield around my leopard friend and me.

With yesterday afternoon's *activities* under Lyle's desk, I'm powered up and feeling confident that the shield will hold all the way in and out.

"Fast walk," I instruct Sabrina. "And remember, it doesn't block sound."

"Got it."

With my arm looped through her slender one, we leg it back out and head right for the animus dorm, weaving through the steady stream of animuses heading in the opposite direction for lunch. Luckily, I don't see any of my mates, which surely would have spelled disaster. Scythe can hear my heart beat, so there is no escaping him, and Savage can just... well, bloody *feel* my presence, can't he? He's the best tracker out of all them. Hopefully, they're cosied up in their secret level eating all the fun food the rest of us don't get. For once, that benefits me.

The second thing I'm nervous about is Bastian, the animus dorm gargoyle, leering down at everyone through his monocle. I don't know how far his magic goes, but it turns out he's too busy ogling animus asses as they leave their dorm to notice two invisible girls. Sabrina huffs as we hear a slyly muttered, "Buttocks as firm as a fresh peach on that one, ripe for the plucking!" before we slip inside after two spikey-haired hawks.

In the cool of the dorm foyer, we find a corner and catch our breaths because I don't want anyone to stalk us from our panting. When our breaths are slow and even once again, we tip-toe our way up the stairs and to the first floor.

The corridor is empty, bar a few stragglers at the end who appear to be on cleaning duty, steadily mopping the floor around their rooms.

"It's the third door on the right," I mutter.

Sabrina grunts and gets out her lock picks. "Shouldn't take me long."

We reach the door and both press our ears against the black wood to sense if anyone is still in there. After hearing nothing, Sabrina sets to it with her lips puckered adorably. It's fascinating to watch. She doesn't even use her hands, just her telekinesis as the picks make tiny adjustments I can barely see. Her ability to handle tiny delicate things would come in handy for many different things. In another life, Sabrina might have made a great animalia scientist, handling dangerous chemicals.

With a *snick,* the lock opens. We both cast a look around before Sabrina pushes the door open. A shout from the end of the corridor gives us both pause. I grab Sabrina's arm.

"You can't collect rat bones in your room, Ray!" Savage bellows loud and clear from a room at the very end of the corridor.

"Why not, sir?" whines a male, presumably a wolf. "I'm saving them up for when I meet my regina—"

"It's not hygienic!" Savage cries.

"I'm torching it." Xander's dry voice makes both Sabrina and I stare at each other. "It's downright offensive to my nose."

I split my invisibility shield in two, right down the middle. It takes a moment of intense concentration, but I manage it, and it enables me to step away from Sabrina.

"Go in," I say telepathically. *"We haven't got long. I'll guard at the door."*

Sabrina nods and slips inside Titus' room.

"Please don't, my lord!" the wolf begs, whining without shame. "I'll tidy them up into neat piles and—"

Light erupts from the room as the wolf shouts in dismay. There's a crackling, whooshing sound. An awful burnt smell hits my nose and I almost gag, but it's gone in seconds, replaced by only the scent of burning.

"Done," Xander snaps. "No point crying about it, wolf. Clean this up or I'm torching your ass next. Savage, we have an eavesdropper."

My heart drops into my nether regions, and for a full second, I contemplate turning around and purely running. But my anima firmly refuses. The regina in me straight out *refuses* to run from my mates and that tone of contempt Xander just used.

So when Xander and Savage stalk out of the room right at

the end—guess which one has a malevolent sneer and which one is beaming?—I cross my arms and drop my invisibility.

"How did you know I was here?" I snap at Xander.

Although I can't tell where exactly his glowing white eyes are focused at any one time, I just know the dragon is looking at me suspiciously up and down. I don't care, I just need to give Sabrina time to find that laptop and leave at the same time as I do. I can't put a shield precisely around her if I can't see her.

It's Savage who whoops with joy and jogs up to me, explaining, "Dragon-magic. Xander can do all sorts of nifty things."

"Sorts of things I don't like known," Xander says disapprovingly as Savage bends down to wrap his arms around my waist. He straightens, bringing me up with him so my feet dangle and the length of my body is pressed right up against his rock hard one. I press my lips against his, half because I need to hide my grimace of pain, and half because I'm delaying to give Sabrina time.

"Are you here for me?" Savage asks, not letting me go and swinging me back and forth. "I missed you too."

Inconveniently, Xander lingers, looking down at us with disapproval. His hair is loose today, the silken lengths hanging over both shoulders, the cords of his headphones just peeking through.

"Actually, no!" I say loudly, hoping Sabrina can hear me.

Savage grimaces and puts me down, sticking a finger in his ear and wiggling it around. "My hearing is very good, you know."

"Sorry," I say. "I'm looking for Minnie actually."

"I'm not surprised she's hiding from you with all your neediness," Xander says snidely. "She's not here anyway. Get out of the animus dorm."

My heart drops a little at his swift dismissal, but I have to give it right back to him. "Animas are allowed in these dorms, Xander Drakos, though I'm sure none of them are here for the likes of your scaled ass. I've always meant to ask you about that actually."

Savage intervenes just as Xander opens his mouth. "Ask him what?"

"If his ass is scaled," I say smoothly. "Maybe that's why nobody wants to see it, you know? They're scared it's super weird looking. Sort of like psoriasis."

"They throw themselves at my feet," Xander says, almost in disgust. "All fucking day and night. Both animas and animuses."

I suddenly do remember the girl he set on fire when we first got to the academy. "The ones into sadists, maybe?" I shrug. "It's the only plausible explanation."

Xander leans down to get closer to me and growls with restrained anger, "You ever heard the phrase, 'don't poke the dragon?'"

"You ever heard the phrase, 'don't be a cunt?'"

Xander's eyes flicker red for a moment before Savage chuckles and grabs my hand, tugging me down the corridor. "That's a rude word coming from a princess."

The dragon stalks after us, his mouth twisted in annoyance, his shoulders stiff.

"I know plenty more if you want to hear them," I say sweetly. "Lots of dirty words in my repertoire."

"Is that because you frequent unsavoury sort of places?" Xander drawls. "You'd fit right in with the bottom dwellers of this school, serpent girl."

"So would you, pretty boy." I smile at him and my silly anima preens her feathers.

The dragon makes a rude noise as we pass Titus' door.

"*Sabrina!*" I shoot out telepathically. "*Get out now, but quietly. You'll have to follow Savage, Xander and me out.*"

Savage halts mid-step. "Who are you talking to?"

Xander stops too.

Alarmed, I turn to look at him. "You could hear that?" But I'm now able to see the handle of Titus' door rotating slowly.

"I can tell when you're talking to someone using TP." Savage's eyes narrow in suspicion.

I put a sly smile on my mouth and begin walking backwards, putting my hands behind my back so my boobs are pushed out. I have to make sure I talk loudly to distract Xander's insane hearing. "Wouldn't you like to know? And also, you *do* know some of the alphabet. I've never heard it called 'TP' before, is it a wolf thing?"

"Yeah, it is. But who is it?" Savage demands, but he prowls after me as I walk backwards down the corridor, Xander following us. Two predators stalking a gazelle. Sabrina slips out of Titus' room, a silver laptop in hand. Her red nimpin, Cherry, bobs up and down in fear on her shoulder. I cloak them both in an invisible shield again.

"It's my secret," I say loudly, continuing to walk backwards. "You can have secrets and so can I."

"I don't have any secrets from you," Savage growls. "Tell me which of these beasts you're talking to. You should be talking to *me*."

Xander's glowing eyes flare and that red-orange glow returns.

"What?" I demand. We've reached the stairs and now I have no idea how I'm going to walk backwards down them.

Xander comes up behind Savage to stare down at me. "I'm thinking I don't trust a fanged, fucking thing you say, snake girl."

Savage rolls his eyes and, to my satisfaction, Xander heads *up* the stairs instead of down.

"Are you going up too?" I ask my wolf.

Savage yanks me against him once again. "Come with me, so I get my answers from you in more creative ways."

My laugh is genuine at the unrestricted promise in those words. "Maybe later. I need to find Min."

He steps away from me, heading up the stairs, though there's a firm frown on his face.

"She's in the dining hall. You should have just asked Raquel with your TP."

I feel bad, but I have to do this for Minnie.

"Yeah, I'll go there now. Thank you."

"You'll come to me tonight?"

I smile again. "Yes."

Once he's disappeared up the stairs with that grin on his face, I plod back down, my heart in my throat as I tell Sabrina it's now safe to come down after me.

When she's in my sight—holding up the laptop and shaking it like it's the grand final trophy, I surround us both with my invisibility shield, and breathless, we make our way down the stairs.

"I can't believe we fucking did it," Sabrina hisses in my ear as we reach the foyer of the animus dorm and the doors to our freedom.

We make it out into the fresh air of the great outdoors, and Sabrina shakes my arm with excitement. We hurry back to the anima dorm and I give Stacey the heads up that we'll be ready for her in mere minutes.

Giddy, I guide Sabrina back towards the alleyway we used the first time and take off the invisibility.

"We're on our way," Raquel replies into my head.

"Alright, we've got to be quick if we're gonna get this back soon," I say. But Sabrina grabs my arm, her eyes stricken in horror at something over my shoulder. I whirl around, heart pounding, to see a figure standing in the mouth of the alleyway, shadowed in darkness like something from a nightmare.

On instinct, my eagle eyes zoom in to see his face.

A narrow, lanky build, inky black hair that flops over his forehead and the hunched stance of a half-rabid serpent.

It's Thomas Krait.

With his slitted serpent's eyes narrowed at directly at us. His forked tongue darts out, tasting the air. Of course, he can't smell me. His pupils, however... dilate as they focus on my face.

He must've followed us here. Must've sensed our heat and vibration leaving the animus dorm and we'd been so caught up in victory we'd not noticed him stalking behind us.

I squeeze Sabrina's arm and talk into her mind. *"We need to walk very slowly out of here, or we're fucked."*

She can't reply to me, but I shriek out for Raquel. *"Mayday, mayday! Snake alert!"*

Raquel mutters expletives in my head before there's a growled, *"We're still leaving the dining hall. You have to take him out, Lia."*

Sabrina and I take a few steps towards him.

"Thomas," I say, faking a cheery accent, "what are you doing here?"

Thomas looks from me to Sabrina and what she has in her hands. I cringe internally. Like something from an awful dream, Thomas' voice is a rasping, hissing thing. "Thievessss." His fangs snap down and he snarls in warning.

We're almost at the mouth of the alley, but we freeze in front of him.

"Take him out, you two!" Raquel shouts in our heads.

While I would eventually be fine if Thomas attacked me, Sabrina wouldn't.

I step in front of my leopard friend.

"Shit," Sabrina mutters.

Thomas takes a single step forward and a clear drop of venom falls from one fang onto his lip. He licks it off. My heart thunders under my sternum.

Even one drop of that would kill Sabrina within minutes. Henry and Cherry both let out chirps of warning. But Thomas was once a rabid serpent—still is, to some extent. His psychic shields are in full force around him. The nimpins will be of no use here.

"Aurelia Aquinasssssss."

The hate I hear in that unused voice has my hackles raised. I clear my throat and try to sound as unbothered as I can. "Hey, Thomas, let us pass."

"Move aside, animus," Sabrina says haughtily.

Thomas doesn't move a muscle, nor do his fangs. He looks so much like Theo that my stomach twists at the sight.

A metal table under bright lights.

Obsidian shackles glimmering on hands and wrists.

A voice, scared and sobbing in agony. "Please," Theo gasped. "Please my king."

My own voice, shrill and hoarse from crying. *"Theo I'm sorry!"*

My hands ball into fists. The scars on my stomach burn. I deserved them, I fucking deserve all of this pain tenfold.

"Lia!" Raquel shouts in my head.

But I can't. I can't strike him. I can't hurt him or tell Henry to. There's only hate in Thomas' slitted eyes, and I deserve every inch of that. I—

Out of nowhere, Raquel appears behind Thomas and shoves him hard on the shoulder blades. A surprised Thomas tumbles to the ground with a choked breath.

"Run!" Raquel shouts, just as Thomas lets out this mad hiss and disappears into his T-shirt and shorts as he shifts. Sabrina is out of the alleyway first, hurtling for the dorm, Raquel and Stacey behind her. But I can't run. And I don't. I step out of the alley and watch as Thomas slithers out of his clothes at speed. The black scales have the series of white crossbars of his species, a pattern unique to their kind. Theo showed me his pattern once, and I called him beautiful. Thomas' markings are near-identical. A tear slips out of my eye as I watch him slither in the direction of the dining hall.

A sudden pain tears my heart anew.

I realise what it is. Because although the pain I experienced at Theo's death was great, it pales in comparison to the depth of grief I would feel if Savage was killed by my father.

Guilt winds around the aching chambers of my heart. And that is *terribly* confusing.

When I get back to the dorm, the animas and nimpins are in a state.

"Will he report us?" Sabrina asks as Cherry chirps softly in her ear.

I remember the hate in Thomas' voice as he said my name. The pure disgust on his features. And so it's with utter surety that I mutter a dark, "Yes."

Chapter 51

Aurelia

"What do we do? What do we do!" Sabrina paces back and forth between her bed and Raquel's, rubbing at her arms, while Stacey sits at the little shared desk, fingers moving rapidly over the black keyboard of Titus' laptop.

Five minutes later, Minnie walks through the door, closing it shut behind her. Her brown eyes dart between us all and we stare right back at her.

"What have you guys done?" she asks in a dark voice that I'm *not* used to my best friend using. "I saw you two rush out of the hall." She nods to Raquel and Stacey. Despite the concealer, I can still see the bluish bags marking my friend's brown skin. Can see the strain at the edges of her body. The way her nimpin trembles where she sits on her shoulder.

Raquel and Stacey are guiltily standing over Titus' laptop while I just limply stand there. "We did the right thing," I say numbly. "The right thing."

"Well, I'm getting rid of the nudes as we speak," Stacey says happily, tapping the special hacking device from the laptop and clearly in her element. "I just wiped his drive for good measure. There was mostly porn on it anyway. You're safe, Min."

My tigress' eyes widen in horror as she recognises the laptop.

"I can't believe you did this," she says faintly. Her lips are pressed together in a cold, hard line, but her eyes are shiny. I don't think she knows how to feel, and to be honest, the cold dread at the pit of my stomach coupled with the relief of our job getting done is also confusing me.

"I can't apologise, Minnie," I say. Even to me, my voice sounds distant.

Suddenly, Eugene flaps his wings and lets out a loud squawk. We all stare at him as a group.

Five seconds later, heavy-booted feet march up the dorm staircase outside.

"Sh-Shit," Raquel says nervously. "A-Animus i-incoming."

I grab Sabrina's hand and the look of pure terror in her eyes opens the part of me that lies buried beneath my common sense. It gapes wide open, threatening to swallow us both. My anima roars out, wanting to protect my friends, but before I can shift, a loud, heavy knock sounds on the door. A knock that rattles my bones.

We all just stare at it.

To my surprise, Minnie clears her throat and strides to the door. Tossing her pink curls, she opens it.

Four males tower in the doorway.

Yeti stands there with one leopard male, as well as Beak and another hawk animus.

The feline and bird order leaders of the academy.

"Aurelia," Beak says with exasperation, "what the fuck did you do?" The sheer unhappiness on his handsome face cements the fact that we're in deep shit. The fact that it's not Theresa who came to confront us. Or Lyle.

Yeti's pale eyes are only for Minnie, however, and he frowns at her. "Were you involved in this, Bangles?"

"She wasn't," I say quickly. "She had no idea."

"Involved in what?" Sabrina says, looking at me sharply.

Oops. Some crim I am.

Yeti levels both of us with a look that could have made a lesser beast shrivel. His wavy white hair is loose down to his shoulders and he runs his hand through it like he's really agitated. He points first at me, then Sabrina. "You two were seen leaving the animus dorm with a device. Titus has just reported his laptop as stolen."

The leopard and the eagle are truly out of the bag.

"It was just us two," Sabrina sighs, gesturing between me and herself. "No one else was involved."

I feel Raquel and Stacey shift uncomfortably behind me, but whatever comes of this, I *won't* be seeing any of my friends incriminated for doing the right thing.

"Where is it?" Yeti steps forward, his massive form completely dwarfing the room. He's even bigger than Beak and is nothing more than a menacing beast come to deal judgement.

"Where is what?" Minnie asks defiantly.

Us animas all look at her in surprise as she stares Yeti down—well, up—and doesn't move from her position at the door. They're almost touching. But he's so tall it doesn't matter; he just talks over her head to Sabrina. "The laptop. You were seen stealing Titus Clawson's laptop."

"Um, nope," Sabrina says. "Lies. He was rabid, remember? Maybe he doesn't understand what you're talking about."

"We will tear this room apart," Beak snarls, and I swear I see his eagle eyes flash. "Give it over. I can smell that tiger's scent."

"That could just be Minnie," Sabrina retorts, casting Minnie an apologetic look.

Everyone knows it's not.

There's a standoff between us two parties, the space heating up like a branding iron held over a fire.

"What do we do?" Raquel projects to us. *"It's under the bed. They'll fucking find it."*

Then Yeti raises a hand, and the entire room starts to *shake*. The floorboards tremble, and the beds start vibrating—the desk too. Sabrina's heart-shaped mirror trembles before crashing to the floor, shattering into a hundred tiny pieces.

"Alright!" I shout over the din. "Hand it over, Stace."

The furniture in the room abruptly go still.

"I would have held out longer, Lia," Sabrina grumbles. "I fucking *loved* that mirror."

"Girlfriend, there's no point and you know it," I reply.

"That's seven years of bad luck to you," Minnie sneers at Yeti.

To my surprise, he leans down and says straight to her face, "Does that include the part of this year I've already had or not?"

She blinks at him, almost in a daze, before turning her face away. I love her for not backing down from him.

"I've never seen more arrogant animas in my life," Beak says, shaking his head, his dark blonde mohawk shiny in the afternoon light.

"Well, you can't have met that many worth knowing," Stacey quips happily. "Besides, we were gonna give it back anyway." She tosses the laptop over our heads right for Yeti and it flips end over end before he catches it with a dark look at her. "Oops," she chirps. "So sorry, boss."

Beak snaps his fingers at us. "All of you, let's go."

"What, where?" Minnie demands.

Yeti steps back out of the door and sweeps a pale tattooed hand out. "To court for your judgement, your highnesses. Titus has demanded a trial."

Shit.

There's a moment of tense silence before Sabrina clears her throat. "Well, at least he knows what title to use," she says, before she struts out the door with her head held high, long ponytail swishing. The rest of us follow, marching between the two order leaders and trying not to look sheepish. Yeti instructs Eugene to stay behind and although the rooster clucks unhappily, he stays put on Raquel's bed.

I'm the last to exit the dorm building in front of Beak when the eagle commands my name like an army captain. "Lia."

"What?" I say over my shoulder.

He gives me a reproachful look, as if I shouldn't be speaking to him that way. Officially, he is my order leader and I should be giving him some respect.

"Sorry," I say more softly this time. "I'm just... nervous."

"You fucking should be, Lia. You're about to stand trial."

"Yeah, but it's not like the other guy, where Savage had to eat him. We just stole a thing." Or like my shitshow trial with the Council of Beasts.

Beak grabs my arm and spins me to face him. His tanned face says *are you kidding me?* "Lia, your father followed the Old Laws too. What would he have done if someone stole from him?"

The words are out of my mouth on autopilot. "He'd kill them."

Then it hits me. The blood drains from my face as I realise what Sabrina and I have done is theft. We've taken the property of a territorial, rabid male. And not just any property. An important item that was a bargaining chip for him.

The dread must show on my face because, satisfied that I've now understood, Beak lets my arm go and holds open the door to the anima dorm for me to exit.

Me and my animas are dead silent as we're marched behind the gathering crowd right into the animus dormitory, the autumn air casting a sudden chill over my skin.

Chapter 52

Aurelia

We walk into the animus recreation room with our heads held high. Why then, does it feel like I'm walking into my execution? The beams of sunlight cutting through the long windows are like slashes through the air, casting spotlights onto the old wooden floorboards. Dust motes swirl above the heads of the gathered crowd as they stare at us with brows raised.

"We did the right thing, girls," Raquel chants in our heads. *"Remember that."*

Titus is already waiting in the centre of the room with his posse of felines and serpents gathered behind him in solidarity. More than a few hiss at us, baring their teeth as we come to stand as a group at the edge of the ring of students. I spot Connor off to the side, looking frazzled, his dark eyes frantic as he pushes through the crowd to get to us.

"Oh my God," he whispers when he makes it to our small group. "Oh my God." He reaches for Minnie's hand and she takes his, her eyes glistening. Connor pulls her towards him and tucks her safe into his side. To his credit, he doesn't say "I told you so," but his nimpin, Trumpet, is huddled close to his neck.

I angle myself at the front of our group and Sabrina comes to stand shoulder to shoulder with me as the crowd's muttering grows louder as more students filter in. Beak is shouting at people behind us, animuses are snarling at each other, and there is a terrible, excited buzz in the air. Henry presses himself into my neck and Cherry does the same with Sabrina; the nimpins chitter at each other as if complaining about us.

Turning around to look at my tigress friend, I say, "I love you, Minnie. No matter what happens today. I don't regret a single thing."

Sabrina nods. "Yeah, I agree with that, Min."

Minnie just stares at us from Connor's side while Stacey nervously clasps her hands. Raquel stands protectively next to her and nods at me, piercings glinting in the afternoon sun.

"It'll be fine," they say firmly.

I turn back around to see Scythe, Xander and Savage walking onto the stage, much in the same way as they did at the last trial. Yeti and Beak come to stand at the edges of the raised platform, looking tense and stern.

Sabrina stiffens next to me because we notice the difference straight away. Savage's wolf eyes are in bloom, those massive hazel irises taking over, pupils dilated. His overt aggression is obvious, and it makes the many wolves in the audience shift in nervousness and excitement.

"*He won't let anything happen to you,*" Raquel says into my mind. "*You'll be fine.*"

But that's exactly what I'm worried about.

And then Xander assumes his position at his lectern, with that joint in his mouth, though he doesn't gift us with a suit today. Only a black shirt and chinos combo. He touches the phone in his pocket, either to turn the music up or down, I can't tell.

His voice suddenly appears in my head as he calls the crowd

to settle down. *"You stupid, stupid girl,"* Xander drawls. *"You don't even know who you've messed with."*

But I did. I do. I know the type of creature Titus is because I know the type of beast his father is.

The type of beast who would organise the killing of his own brother. His own blood. One of my mother's mates is dead because of the Clawsons. Now, Titus has hurt my friend. And those transgressions are something I will *never* forgive. Not in this lifetime, or all the lifetimes I get. It's only this that puts steel in my spine. Only this that stops the quiver in my hands.

The audience quietens at Xander's growled command.

My eyes find Scythe's and his irises are clear and cold. He shakes his head so infinitesimally that I'm probably the only one who saw it.

Disappointed.

Scythe is disappointed in me. I shake my head back because he doesn't understand. That makes those eyes go colder, sharper. They seem to cut at my own the longer I stare at him, so I look away.

"Titus Clawson," Xander snarls. "Why have you called this trial without giving due formal notice?"

Oh, so this wasn't supposed to come about like this?

"There has been a great transgression," a tiger standing next to Titus calls. "Valuable property has been stolen."

"Can he speak for himself or is he too stupid? Or Rabid? Which is it?" Xander asks loudly.

There's a hiss from the felines, but Titus steps forward and levels Xander a glare like he's not scared of him. Like he's trying to send a message. It's dominant and I'm surprised at his confidence when speaking to a dragon. He speaks slowly but in an equally confident cadence. "My laptop was stolen. I have a witness."

The serpents shuffle around and Thomas Krait is gently pushed forward.

"Tell them," Titus says, gesturing towards Xander.

Thomas' tongue flicks out once. "I sssaw them leaving the dorm. Followed their heat. Sssaw *them...*" He looks at me and I know he's trying to tell them about my invisibility, but doesn't have the words. "I sssaw them with the laptop. Thieving it and taking it to the anima dorm."

Everyone looks at the dragon truth-teller with bated breath.

"Truth," Xander declares in a deadpan. "*Who* did you see exactly? Point to them."

Thomas steps forward and points to me. "Aurelia Aquinas" —then he shifts his index finger to Sabrina—"and that one."

"My name is *Sabrina*," my leopard anima retorts, crossing her arms and glaring at Thomas.

"Speak only when spoken to," Xander snaps at her. Sabrina takes a step closer to me. But then Thomas moves his finger to Raquel. "Then that wolf hit me."

Savage's head snaps to stare at Raquel and my wolf anim seems to shrink back a little under that violent, withering gaze.

"Truth," Xander declares.

"May the three accused step forward," Xander calls, beckoning to us like we're children. We do, the three of us standing in a line. I'm happy that Stacey gets saved from this.

"Sabrina Panthara," Xander says. "You first. Tell the court what you were doing with Titus Clawson's laptop."

Sabrina opens her mouth.

"*Don't lie*," Raquel warns to our minds. "*You'll be punished for it.*"

"Nothing," Sabrina says snidely. "I didn't actually *do* anything with it. I just took it."

"Truth," Xander says slowly. "From where did you take it?"

"From Titus' room."

"How did you get in?"

"I picked the lock."

"Truth," Xander declares. "Raquel Loba, did you strike this here, Thomas Krait?"

"No," Raquel answers evenly. I try not to glance at them but they continue, enunciating carefully. "I just sh-shoved him. He fell over and g-got *scared*. Shifted and s-slithered away."

A couple of wolves laugh behind us. Not at Raquel's stutter but at the vision of what happened. I'm so proud of my wolf anim.

"Truth," Xander says, and I can tell he's trying not to smile. "Why did you do it?"

Raquel allows a dramatic beat of silence before their reply. "He had his fangs out."

There's a sharp intake of breath in the audience and everyone stares at Thomas in disgust.

Xander tuts and waggles his finger at the Krait as if that isn't a federal offence. "Truth."

Thomas is in real shit. He wasn't in danger and he wasn't defending himself at the time. With my own transgression, I'd forgotten all about *his*, but brilliant Raquel evidently hadn't.

And then Titus, clearly growing impatient, spits. "Ask *her*." He points an ugly finger at me, heavy black brows drawn together.

"Speak when spoken to!" Xander shouts at him. "Or I'll throw you out of here, Clawson."

"It's my own fucking trial," Titus shouts.

"I don't fucking care," Xander shouts back, and those eyes flash red for a moment.

The sight is enough to shut everyone up.

"Aurelia Aquinas. Finally, we come to you," Xander says out loud, voice dripping with disdain. In my head, he says. *"I fucking knew you were up to something."* Out loud, he says, "How were you involved in this vile thievery?"

"I was the mastermind," I say confidently. "I forced Sabrina to go with me to the animus dorm and steal Titus' laptop and take it back with us."

"Why am I not surprised?" Xander says, then frowns at me. He can't read my truth or lies through my shields and I allow myself to smirk a little at it.

"See!" Titus roars. "She's fucking smiling about it! No remorse at all. She'd do it again."

"Is that right?" Xander asks. "Do you feel any remorse for stealing another beast's property?"

I turn then, to look at Titus right in his terrible dark eyes. The tiger is panting, his pupils dilated, the rage in his body an obvious threat. He'd tear me apart if he got half the chance. I smile at that violence and match it with my own quiet dominance. "I don't feel any remorse, and in fact, if I went back in the past, I'd do it all again the exact same way."

Titus snarls and points a finger at me. "You'll get what you're owed, Aquinas."

"Lia, stop it," Minnie begs from somewhere behind me.

"Alright," Xander says, commanding our attention once again. I turn back to be in line with Sabina and Raquel.

"So the two of you"—he points to me and Sabrina only—"by your own admission are guilty of your crime. Raquel Loba?" He turns to Scythe.

"Innocent," Scythe rasps.

"Who's the serpent leader?" Xander drawls.

The serpents murmur amongst themselves, because I'm sure that Natalia was their order leader. A round-faced girl steps forwards. There's a venom registration number on her cheek and she wears ripped black jeans and a black singlet that shows elaborate serpent tattoos over both arms. She wears that strange 'B' cult tattoo as well.

"Are you content with that verdict?" Xander asks impatiently.

She has no choice but to say a quiet. "Yes. And does Raquel want to press charges?"

"Not worth it," Raquel growls.

There's a collective, low rumble of laughs from the males in the hall.

I almost feel sorry for Thomas, being publicly declared as weak, but he *was* the one who landed us here, so I can't feel too badly.

"Then, Sabrina Panthara and Aurelia Aquinas, you have been charged guilty—"

"No," I say quickly, stepping forward.

"Excuse me?" Xander's voice is a low, threatening rumble.

"I take full responsibility for the crime. It was my idea. I forced Sabrina. The only blame lies with me. It should be on my record. The punishment should go to *me* alone."

A few animas, including Minnie, gasp. Sabrina whirls around and stares at me with such a look of supreme shock that I have to smile at her. Gratitude fills her eyes, but the fear is still there as she reaches out for me.

"Lia, I..."

Over her shoulder, Scythe's eyes fix on me and I *almost* balk at that gaze of cold malice. He's furious, nose-flaring-preternaturally-still furious with me.

A small pulse of magic through the air tells me the bond-brothers are having a silent conversation. Savage crosses his arms as he stares me down with disapproval. Xander is confused by my words, because his hand hesitates as he reaches for the joint in his mouth.

Titus scoffs. "I don't fucking care if it's you or her. I want to see punishment for this, Scythe. I want to see the type of justice you serve in your *court*."

My anima roars at the overt challenge. I want to rip that bastard's throat for questioning my mate so openly. This is *not* the Clawson territory. A few of Scythe's henchmen cut Titus a sharp look for speaking so informally to their leader.

But the shark ignores him and says to me in that nightmarish rasp that skims my skin, "You are willing to take Sabrina's punishment?"

I shrug, trying to hide my trembling hands by clasping them in front of me. "It was my idea. It's only right that it's me." Jerking my head to Sabrina and Raquel to get behind me, they reluctantly obey, all but lurching back to Minnie.

"Lia, no," Minnie whispers. She sounds like she's about to cry and I don't blame her right now.

But as I step forward to make my guilt clear, I only have eyes for Scythe. And he only has eyes for me. Eye to eye, I silently challenge him. This is his court. Will he back down because it's me? Or will he be fair? What type of alpha is my shark, exactly?

"Whore of a bird will get her wings broken for this," Titus sneers. "That will be justice served in the Old Way. It's the only punishment for thieving and you all know it."

Scythe's eyes bore into mine and I swear he's staring right into my beating heart and weighing it. Weighing my mettle. My resolve. Challenging me right back.

It's almost as if he thinks I'm going to balk. That I'll run from here, that I'll cry and beg and plead. That I might even pull my regina card to get out of this. He and Xander want me to show them I'm weak. That I'm unworthy to have them. To prove to them I'm no more than the serpent girl they've always believed. Cunning but weak.

But I was *raised* watching pain and fear.

In doing this, I claim my power among these brutal, vicious males. Here and now, in a way that will broker no argument.

We all know the breaking of hands or paws or wings is the only punishment for theft. I've actually seen tails broken in my father's court over it.

I stare defiantly back at Scythe until he rasps a single word and my world threatens to slide from under me. "Shift." A command from our leader.

But he's not *my* leader.

I'm *his* regina.

I blink at him. I wanted to see how he would take my challenge. Hell, a part of me thought he'd laugh and send us animas away. But he's actually going to go through with it. So it's through gritted teeth I say, "I'll take it in human form."

There are more whispers from the crowd, and Beak is trying to call me stupid with his eyes.

We all know it'll hurt more. Human bones break harder than the delicate hollow bones of a bird's wings. But there's something about shifting here in front of all these animuses that makes me more vulnerable. I want to take this, standing tall, on my own two feet.

"Your sentence is the breaking of both arms, no healing for three days," Scythe rasps. He's not blinking. "You will be shackled so you don't use your own healing powers."

He's asking me if I really want to do this. Reminding me of how painful it will be.

Fucking hell. I thought I actually had healing up my sleeve. Looks like three days of hell for me.

"I understand. Do it," I say, nodding at Savage. Fuck, my heart is beating so damn fast.

But my wolf only stares at me. Xander says nothing.

Titus strides in my direction. "You're his regina. I'll fucking do it."

Beak moves forward. "No, it's my responsibility—"

"No," Savage's purely vicious snarl stops both Titus and Beak dead in their tracks.

The tiger throws his hands up in the air. "Then get it fucking done, wolf!"

But no one, not even Xander, moves. They just stare at me. I shake my head in dismay, trying to tell them with my eyes. *Your court has been challenged. We all know you need to follow through with this.*

"Do it," I say quietly, taking a protesting Henry from my shoulder and handing him to Raquel.

But when I turn back around, still not one of my three mates has moved.

My voice turns into a regina's snarl. "Fucking *do it.*"

The blast of my command is like a dark wind that hits both Savage and Xander right in the chest.

Savage stiffens, and his head ever so slightly cocks to the side.

Xander's glowing eyes turn a sheen of gold and a volcanic energy shimmers, distorting the air around him.

The dragon inside of him is awake.

As one, they both stalk towards me with a purely beastial gait that tells me their animuses have completely taken over. Unblinking, their voices resound in my head in unison, *"As you command, regina."*

Large, strong hands grip both my forearms.

I don't even get to take a breath before they snap my arms at the same time.

A strangled scream tears from my throat and I hate myself for showing weakness in public. But the pain threatens to split me open and my knees buckle, my mind wanting to shut off, to shift, to go back into a place that is dark and black.

I'm vaguely aware that, to the side, Minnie, Stacey and Sabrina are sobbing in each other's arms.

The combined strain of maintaining my protections and the pain makes my head swim and I know I'm about to faint. Someone—Xander, I think, from the smouldering scent—scoops me up.

"Terrible, ruthless, regina," Xander's dragon rasps inside my

head. *"In all our lives together, you have never, not once, asked me to hurt you."*

"Don't heal it," I mumble faintly. "That's the rule."

"By all rights I should take you to my den, lay you face down upon my treasure and remind you who owns you."

I can barely make a snarky reply of "Is *that* a *promise?*" before I let the darkness swallow me whole.

Chapter 53

Scythe

I should have known my regina would be just as insane as the rest of us. Hovering over Lyle's computer screen where I force myself to watch security camera footage of the event over and over again, I swear softly under my breath.

Lyle flinches. Visibly flinches at the sound of Aurelia's bones cracking in both arms at the same time.

The way she'd looked at me, defiantly, coldly. Trying to communicate with the sheer force of her gaze that I needed to hurt her. She'd understood the politics of the situation. She'd taken it upon herself to see it done.

The way she'd taken the full force of that pain for her friends. It was a rare thing to find a beast who was capable of that level of...self-sacrifice and determination.

I know what all beasts in my position know. That there is physical power...and *real* power. And today I'd realised that Aurelia has a dangerous, rare, alluring combination of both.

"Fuck." Lyle's voice is unusually haggard. He leans back from the screen and tries to control his fury, but a tremble runs through his hand as he rubs his eyes. "She's a nightmare."

He doesn't mean that.

"She's too beautiful to be a nightmare," I mutter.

He cuts me a surprised look and I return him a dark one. We both know it's true. That she has an inexplicable draw. That, if I was not her mate, I would still be drawn to her. Still... seek her out as fish seek out ocean currents.

Lyle is fighting that draw, but he's cracking. Deeply. What I saw of their time together has me certain of that. She has him by the cock now. Literally.

Right now, I fight her off like I fight off madness: just barely.

The lion's hands are curled into fists as Aurelia's cry of pain echoes around us. Under our skin and into our bones. I pat him sympathetically on the back, keeping close in case he wants to take out his aggression on me.

"I want to see her," he says through gritted teeth. But he doesn't rise from his desk.

Is he asking for advice?

To give him some privacy with his internal battle, I stride to the bay windows and look out at the gathering shadows of dusk over the academy oval. The floodlights come on one by one, illuminating the grounds for the guards to see at night. "Is that a good idea?"

"Is it a good idea," he repeats like it's a slur.

"If I smell her blood, I may not like the result."

"What do you mean?" Lyle's voice is suddenly sharp, as if he's glad I've given him something else to focus on.

"She hasn't bled while she's been here. Did you know that?"

He's silent, because of course he didn't fucking know. Of course I'm the only one who's monitoring that, waiting for that like I wait for a hunter's moon.

"You mean she hasn't menstruated? At all? But the heats—"

"She hasn't had a real heat either. Not here."

He swears, and I hear him bringing out his phone and sending a text. Probably to Theresa to start monitoring the female student's cycles.

"I've never seen a libido like hers. She's perfectly healthy—"

"Is she?" I turn around then and eye him, because he, more than anyone, should know that the state of a beast's mind is, in some cases, more important than their physical health.

He visibly pales under my stare. "She's too stressed for her body to even think about ovulating."

"I'm glad you've had the epiphany," I reply smoothly.

The knowledge settles between us like a sheet of ice and every instinct of mine, and I'm sure his, roars at us to help her, to heal her, to feed and hide and care for her until she's well again.

I think of her face as her bones were broken. That look of shock flashing briefly before being overcome by anguish. I could have broken Savage's neck for doing that. Xander's too.

That feeling of violence towards my brothers stuns me a little. Nothing comes above my brothers, not ever. Not until a few hours ago.

I have to blow out a cold, cold breath.

My psychotic ghost suddenly seizes. Standing, but having full tonic-clonic shakes until he starts to blur at the edges. He splits himself into two ghosts, and I turn around to stare at it. At them. They're both balding, stringy-haired, emaciated creatures with grey skin, identical in every way except for what they're doing. One is cackling madly, jumping up and down and chanting an evil song about death and decay.

While the other... just stares at me from beneath his black eyelashes. A hard, cold stare. A malevolent smile cuts along his thin lips as he fixates on me. Blood drips from his fingers.

"Stop," I rasp. My mouth is suddenly bone dry, and my hands are suddenly... sweating? No. No. No.

"What?" Lyle asks, dragging me back into the room and reminding me of the fact that these creatures I see are not real.

Not real. They never have been.

My name is Scythe Kharkorous. My brother is Savage

Fengari. My brother is Xander Drakos. My brother is Lyle Pardalia. I am real. The ghosts are not. I am real.

"Scythe." Lyle's voice is as sharp as a needle in the ass.

I tear my eyes away from the staring ghost and shake my head at the lion. "I want to see her too."

Lyle shoots up from his desk, pocketing his phone, clearly unable to contain his need to lay his eyes on his regina. I head out his office door behind him.

Outside, it's dark and quiet, which does nothing for my morbid mood. The automatic lights come on and when we pause before the elevator, Lyle's posture is strained.

"But when her real heat comes..."

I smile without humour. "Then you better have all the obsidian chains in the school ready for each one of us."

Chapter 54

Aurelia

A familiar beeping resounds in my ears, and then the scent hits me. Hand sanitiser, starched sheets, and under that, ancient forests, the deep earth, and something inherently mine. Obsidian shackles are cold on my ankles, neutralising my power.

I drag my eyes open with all the effort of pulling myself from unconsciousness. The lights are blinding above me and I groan as something cold runs up my left hand. The entirety of both arms throb with heat, but the burn is thickest in my forearms. Something is clutching my right hand.

Someone.

I turn my head to the right to see Savage sitting with one hand clutching mine and the other clutching his head as he stares at the medical wing linoleum between his legs, rocking slowly back and forth. I lift my hand reflexively, only to have a shooting pain fly up my arm. "Argh, that burns like a bitch on a stick," I groan.

Savage's head snaps up. His eyes are rimmed red, his cheeks wet.

"Why?" Savage's voice is a broken, shattered thing. "Why, Lia?"

I try to reach for him, but I realise that both my forearms are in casts. "I'm so sorry," I whisper.

"You made me do it," he whispers back. "You *made* me do it."

My heart is shattering into a million little pieces at the look of devastation on his face. I want to crawl into his lap and kiss it better. To tell him I'll never make him do something like that again.

But then his face turns dark with anger. "I told you to *never* regina-command me."

"You did," I agree faintly. "But you know why I had to make you do it. Better you than someone else."

He frowns and squeezes my hand as if to reassure himself that I'm okay. It sort of feels like a lobster's claw. A meaty lobster claw. With tattoos.

A giggle works its way up my throat, brushing past my lips and emerging into the air on manic wings. It sounds like a kookaburra's call.

Savage's frown deepens.

"What?" I giggle again. "You thought you were the only one allowed to be a little bit nuts around here?"

The corners of his mouth twitch like he wants to laugh. "Now I know how Scythe feels about me, I suppose."

"And," I say prissily, "*you* told me I could ask *anything* from you."

"I said you could ask. I never said anything about *doing* anything." He frowns up at the bag of IV medication running through my drip. "What is in that stuff?" he asks himself.

"*Um,*" I sing with a brilliant vibrato, twisting as far as I can to look up at the bag and flipping my feet side to side like windscreen wipers.

It's then that I see the second person sitting behind my bed.

Brooding in a corner seat with his glowing eyes narrowed on me is my big, scary dragon.

"Hi dragon-man!" I say cheerily. "I'd wave, but, well..." I glance back down at my two immobile arms. I pucker my lips and give him an air kiss. "You don't look happy to see me. And what *did* they put in that bag of IV fluid because I feel really, really, good." I look back up at the bag and squint. "What does it say, dragon-man? My wolf-man can't read."

"I'm only here because I want the answer to a single question," Xander says, leaning forward in his chair. His voice is infinitely low and dangerous.

I stare at him in awe because how does it do that? Look so sexy and scary at the same time? "Well, you can come around here and ask it because my neck hurts from twisting."

He rudely ignores me. "How long have you been talking to *my* dragon without *me* knowing?"

"Oopsie," I say sheepishly.

He sits back in his chair, waiting for an answer, all glary and growly.

I twist back into a neutral position, making wide eyes at Savage. "Is he angry at me? Why is he always angry at me? Even when he's mean, he's so pretty. That's why he gets away with it, you see. It's really not fair, is it?"

Savage is about to answer when the door opens. I didn't even realise they have me a private room until now. But I forget all questions, comments and jokes as Lyle prowls through the door, followed closely by an icy Scythe.

The sight of both men, in those clothes, with those faces, with those fantastic bodies, makes me heated in all sorts of pleasant ways.

"Goddess," I breathe giddily. What a lucky girl I am.

"Aurelia," Lyle growls, stalking right up to my bed, leaning down and putting his face right up to mine. "What the fuck were you thinking?"

Those amber eyes are simmering with such monumental anger that it transforms his face from beautiful to breathtaking. He has no pores that I can see. What type of magical toner does he use?

"Wow," I breathe, admiring his face. "Can we kiss now?"

His eyes flick down to my mouth before he pushes himself off my bed and whirls around to stride to the foot of my bed, his blond ponytail swishing prettily.

"Why did you go there?" I complain, pouting like the princess I am. Gods, I want to be Lyle's princess so badly.

But now I can see Scythe, leaning against the wall with his hands in his pockets. I grin at him. "*Daddy shark do-do-do*," I sing. "*Daddy shark do-do-do-do*." I lick my lips. "It's a children's song. Do you know it, gang boss?"

Somehow, an ice burn stings so much *better* than a fire one. His silvery hair always catches the light in the most perfect way. It's the closest thing to celestial light that isn't a mating mark I've ever seen. But then he prowls over to me and I suck in a breath because I also want him to kiss me so badly. And why is no one kissing me at all? But instead of placing those lips on my needy, pouty ones, he lifts a hand to examine the tiny IV pump hitched up next to the bigger one.

"Fentanyl," he mutters darkly. "They need to change her analgesic."

I gasp in surprise because how does Scythe know huge medical words like 'analgesic'? I'm so impressed right now. "No, but I like this one, daddy shark. I can't even feel the fractures! And besides, I feel all swirly in my head. Like my brain noodles have become butterflies." I hum a lovely tune to show them how nice it is up in here.

Lyle huffs and picks up my medical chart, flipping through it irritably. Xander heaves himself off his seat and strides around to stand next to Savage. Four mating marks burn before me, like pretty little jewels all in a row.

I giggle when I realise it. "This is the first time all five of us are in the same room together. You look like four scary giants." I giggle again. "Four scary, sexy giants. Who's gonna take their turn first? Because I'm ready!" I spread my legs wide to tell them what I want. "Or you can just do it at the same time, that might be best, actually."

Lyle gives me an exasperated look while Scythe glowers down at me. Xander simply shakes his head in disgust or dismay.

Savage groans and throws himself back in his chair. "By the Wolf Mother, she's completely off her face."

I grin at him. "Can you get me more of this stuff?" I turn to Scythe. "Shark daddy can, won't you, pretty please? You must know all the suppliers."

My shark just stares at me as Lyle leaves the room, probably to stop my fun. "Naw. Somebody scratch my nose, please?"

Savage leans over to do so, but then hesitates. "The last time I reached out to do something like this, you nearly tore my arm off."

I chomp my teeth at him. "Can't make any promises, baby."

He gives me a lopsided smile. "Did you just call me baby?"

"Yeah."

Savage grins at me and gently scratches the tip of my nose. I lean into him, enjoying his touch. "You're my favourite wolf!" I beam at him.

"Don't think that being this cute excuses what you did, regina," he chides, though he can't help his smile.

"Oh no," I say suddenly, and actual fear is a little spike through my stomach.

"What is it?" Lyle says as he comes back through the door.

I gulp again and squeak. "How am I supposed to pee?" My bladder is suddenly a pressing matter. I try to get up, but pain shoots through both arms and I cry out before thumping back on my pillow.

Lyle is by my side in an instant. "Aurelia, stop."

"I need to pee!" I exclaim. All at once, I become aware of *everything*. The fact that I can't use both of my arms. The fact that I need my arms to pee and get out of bed and do my hair and shower and I'm not allowed to heal myself for three days. "Oh shit!" I cry. "Oh fuck! Where's Minnie? Where's Sabrina? And where the fuck is Henry?"

"Calm down," Lyle commands.

I shut up instantly, pressing my lips shut to stop the tears from falling. So maybe I didn't think about *this* part of it when I planned it all in my head.

Lyle blows out a breath and his shoulders sort of sag as he leans down to cup my face. His gentle touch almost makes me break down further, but then he says, "We'll take care of you, angel. Don't worry."

I bite my lip as the words register. Lyle tucks a strand of hair behind my ear and straightens.

"Henry was quite upset," Scythe says. "We had to keep you separated. He's with Minnie."

I'm relieved at hearing Henry is with Minnie and Gertie and Eugene. All my favourites.

"Everyone is upset," Savage says through gritted teeth. "They wanted to come and see you, but I told them your mates get to see you first."

I blink at him and then blurt, "I'm really gonna pee my pants at any second."

Lyle ends up using his telekinesis to levitate me into the bathroom and onto the toilet. It's incredibly embarrassing, but Savage holds my hand the entire time. When both Lyle and Savage attempt to follow me into the bathroom, I snarl at them.

"Privacy, please."

"Ridiculous," Savage says. "How are you gonna wipe?"

"This is so fucking embarrassing, Savage!" I cry dramatically. I wish Scythe and Xander would leave, but they don't, talking quietly in the corner instead. At least they have sense enough not to watch me.

"I'll manage," I growl. "Lyle, set me down and get the hell out."

Lyle gently sets my feet down before the toilet and I have to keep my arms straight or it hurts. Savage crouches down next to me, and I glare at him.

"I've already been all up in there." He gestures to between my legs. "I'm not afraid of a little pee."

"Oh my God," I groan. But he has a point.

"Should I call a nurse?" Lyle asks.

"The fuck you will. I'm her mate," Savage growls. He puts his hands on my calves and rubs them gently up and down. "If you're a good girl, I'll eat you out while we're here."

"Really, Savage?" Lyle deadpans.

But the wolf only chuckles and I can't tell if the offer was serious or not. "I'll pull your knickers down and leave, okay?" he says, grinning up at me.

I can hardly deny Savage when he's kneeling before me with that eager face, so I nod.

He skims his fingers up my thighs and I suppress a shiver as he pulls my panties down to my ankles. He lifts my gown up and helps me sit down before he says, "Besides, how do you know I'm not into a nice golden shower? I'm sure one of us is."

I gape up at him.

Lyle makes a sound of great disappointment. "You heard her, Sav. Get out."

Cackling madly, Savage leaves the bathroom, blowing me an air kiss before shutting the door.

The breath I take feels like the longest one in history. I take a moment to centre myself, wondering how the fuck things ended up here and remembering the entire thing is my fault.

"Right," I say to myself. "Get your shit together."

By the time I'm back outside and sitting on my hospital bed,

I realise I've just been given a glimpse of what having a full pack feels like. Ghoul is missing, of course, but if I were a normal regina in hospital, it would be just like this, with my four mates fussing over me like they loved me, none of them wanting to leave the room.

Except, one of them is a dangerous mob boss, one is the deputy headmaster of this academy, one is a bad-tempered dragon, and one is an unhinged wolf.

"None of this is fucking normal," Xander mutters from the corner as we all watch in fascination as Lyle runs a brush through my tangled hair.

"Tell me about it," I mutter back. "Wait a minute!" I exclaim. "Are we agreeing on something for once, dragon-man?"

He sighs through his nose as if this irritates him.

Lyle gently detangles my hair and Savage watches him as if he'll pounce the moment Lyle pulls too hard. But my lion's hands are gentle and I find my muscles relaxing as he works. Eventually, he's done, and he ties it all into an efficient bun on the top of my head.

"Beautiful," Savage says, offering me a cup of water with a straw in it.

I raise my hand to reach for it, but a sharp pain under the cast stops me.

"Ow," I mutter. "This is fucking useless."

My power wants to surge forward to heal me, it wants to—

It's then that I realise it. I kick out my feet in horror and stare at the black obsidian cuffs that have been on me this whole time. "I need these off!" I shriek to Savage, my eyes pleading. "Right now, Savage, I need these off! I didn't realise— It's the drugs distracting me." I turn to Scythe. "Scythe, I need these off. Right now. Right fucking now!"

"Calm down, Aurelia," Lyle says, cupping my cheek.

I shake him off and try to get to my feet. To make them

realise. To make them understand. Minnie. I have to make sure they're all alright. My father might have already sensed—

"Please!" I scream.

I can't get enough air in, I can't breathe, I can't think, and my head is dizzy. The room swims and slides.

Keep them safe. Keep them safe. Keep them safe.

Someone shouts, but I don't know who. It might be me.

Hands are on me. On my face, my feet, my legs.

But then my magic splutters to life within me, burning through my veins. I send it back out, putting all seven of my shields back into place, and that eighth one that keeps *everyone* safe.

When everything is right in the world, I open my eyes to find that I'm cradled in someone's lap. Someone else is pressing a kiss to my cheek. By their scents, the first one is Lyle and Savage is before me, his face concerned.

"Breathe, Aurelia," Lyle says into my ear, making me shiver. "Just breathe, sweetheart."

I obey, inhaling through my nose as Scythe rises to his feet before me. He's the one who undid the shackles.

"Sorry," I say, thoroughly embarrassed. "I don't usually—"

"You wanted your power back," Scythe says, the black shackles dangling from his fingers. "Everyone in this room understands that."

But it's not for my own sake that I'm concerned.

"Someone needs to check on Minnie and my animas," I say thickly. "Please, I need—"

"Why are you always worried about them?" Lyle asks.

"Because," I say, "my father will come for them if I don't give myself up. That's what they told me when they took me that day."

The words sink into everyone's ears like heavy stones in water. It makes me feel lighter to tell them, but it's still an awful, ugly truth.

After a moment, Savage says, "Raquel says the animas are fine."

Relief washes through every artery, capillary, and vein in my body. Everyone is safe, and that's all that matters. To my great luck, my stomach bandages are still in place, keeping my wounds hidden from the healthcare staff.

Scythe exchanges a look with Lyle.

"You need to stay away from the other students for three days," Scythe says. "You'll have to pretend your shackles are on during that time. So—"

"She'll stay in my apartment," Lyle says quickly, his arms tightening possessively around me. "She won't go anywhere."

My heart swells, my pussy tingles, and I can't contain my excitement.

Scythe's lips twitch and he nods slowly. "Very well."

"What about the rules?" I ask tentatively. "The Old Laws."

"What gave you the impression that I don't make the rules, Aurelia?" Scythe asks. "And after what you did, you don't get a say either way."

"Wait, you *care* about me?" I say giddily. Despite Lyle having the nurse disconnect it, that fentanyl is clearly still having a party through my veins.

Scythe gives me a look I can't interpret. "I have one condition for this and you'll follow it. Do you understand me?"

The command makes my heart flutter. I still want his lips on mine, so I say quietly, "I'm listening."

"You keep your mating mark shield down and *never* put it back up ever again."

I swallow. Scythe sliced through all of my shields that one day they tried to kidnap me a few months ago. He saw every single one of my protections and apparently understood what each of them did. But— "Why?" I ask. "Why would you—"

"It's as good as a lie, Aurelia," he says firmly. "I won't have you lying to me. To us."

He glowers down at me and the room suddenly gets colder.

I blow out a breath in surprise. So Scythe finds a lie as offensive as slander against him. Alright, noted.

Slowly, I lower my mating mark shield.

Three marks blaze to life before me and one behind me. I'm going to have to get used to this. They're stunning to look at and the way each of them makes me feel all fuzzy and giddy--

Scythe's eyes fix on my neck with predatory interest until he nods. "Good girl."

My stomach flips on itself multiple times. I want to beam at him, but I bite my lip instead.

With that, Scythe gestures to Xander. "Make a door."

To my explicit surprise, the dragon strides to somewhere behind me and magic thrums through the air. The very wall groans for a moment before cold air sweeps through the room.

"I never get tired of watching that," Savage says happily and bounds around the bed.

The bed squeaks as Lyle gets off it, carrying me with him. And wouldn't you know it, Xander is leaning against the wall with his arms crossed, and next to him is a new dragon-trick door, the steps climbing up into the darkness.

Chapter 55

Savage

Aurelia is finally letting me look after her. Well, me and Lyle.

And it's getting my wolf madly excited. I'm with her on Lyle's bed, while Lyle putters about in his bathroom and Scythe and Xander are in the living room, probably raiding the kitchen or talking business.

I press a possessive kiss to my regina's forehead.

"I want these off," she sighs, looking down at her two forearm casts. "But I don't have the energy to heal the bones all the way just yet."

"Xander won't do it. He's sulking," I mutter. "He's upset about you talking to his dragon without his knowledge."

"He can heal?" she asks in surprise.

"Yeah, dragon magic can do lots of things. They just keep it secret."

"The more I hear about it, the more like serpents they sound."

"Don't let him hear you say that."

She sighs again, wiggling her fingers. "Well, I guess I'll have to wait a little. At least it doesn't hurt as much with the little I can heal. But what about Beak?"

I suppress a snarl, but it rips out of my throat anyway. "I won't have another male in here with us, regina. I—" Rubbing my thumb over the soft skin of the back of her hand, I wonder if I should tell her how much I need her to myself. "This is our first nest," I say slowly, indicating the room with my eyes. "The first time we're..."

"All together. Well, most of us."

"Ghoul doesn't count. He's a nutter."

"Uh-huh." She grins at me.

I lean down and kiss her mating mark, which glows a brilliant silvery-gold all the time now. I could practically kiss Scythe for making that deal with her. She shivers under my lips and I kiss her neck again.

"I think I smell," she complains so prettily that it makes me want to bite her. "I want a shower."

"Lyle's going to give you a sponge bath."

"Pardon?" her voice is a high-pitched birdy squeak. She goes to sit up but grimaces and lies back down, her cheeks turning a lovely watermelon pink.

"Oh, be a good girl and let us," I say, bopping her nose playfully. We both turn to look as Lyle comes out of the bathroom with a bowl of soapy water and washcloths. His sleeves are rolled up and he's got this look on his face that says he means business. Aurelia's cheeks go even more pink.

Lyle sets his things down on the bedside table and looks down at our regina.

"I don't think—" she starts.

But Lyle is shaking his head and the voice that comes out of him reminds me of the time we all spent together under the school when Aurelia was unwell. It's gentle and I try not to smirk at him being all matey. "Let me do it," Lyle says. "Let me look after you."

Something in his face makes Aurelia gulp. She seems to be doing that a lot lately. "Alright," she says quietly.

I reach for her hospital gown, but she stops me faster than any cobra striking. "Don't take it off."

"Princess, I've seen your body before and it's beautiful." I'm desperate to pepper her skin all over with kisses and get the smell of the medical wing off of her.

"You can keep it on," Lyle says firmly. "We can just move it around as we go."

"I've always wanted to do this," I say excitedly, jumping up to check the temperature of the water with my pinky finger. "Play doctors and nurses. Where's my rectal thermometer when I need it?"

It makes her giggle, and the sound makes my stomach do all sorts of nice things. I watch as Lyle submerges one washcloth into the soapy water and wrings it out. He sits on the side of the bed and folds the cloth over his hand and wipes at Aurelia's fore-head. She closes her eyes like it's pleasant. Lyle's eyes move over her face and his entire body seems to go soft as he cleans her cheeks, then her straight little nose.

But I won't be left out, so I take another washcloth, soak it, then wring it out like he did. I'm climbing onto the bed, aiming for her legs, when Lyle barks, "Shoes!"

Aurelia flinches, and I scowl at the lion before kicking my shoes off.

I lift up her gown to reveal her glorious thighs and start gently running the washcloth down one, then the other while Lyle does her arms.

"Does it feel nice?" I ask, lifting her leg to kiss her shin.

She clears her throat. "Yes."

I'm gently cleaning each of her toes, one at a time, when I smell the sweet, vanilla cupcake scent of her...and her arousal.

My cock twitches in response and I shuffle up the bed with a new cloth. Lyle is fussing over the dressing where the IV was inserted at the back of her hand. "Can I undo this, regina?" I ask gently, touching her neck where her hospital gown is tied up.

She looks up at me, her lips parted, and I just know that us both touching her is what's giving her pleasure. "Okay," she whispers, her eyes all droopy and sweet.

Barely containing myself, I undo the tie, then the buttons at her shoulders. I hold my breath as I pull the material down.

Creamy, olive-skinned breasts lie before me, just more than a handful. Her nipples are a lovely dark brown and erect in small points. I'm hard and drooling at the sight of my perfect, beautiful regina at our complete mercy.

"Somebody stole your bra," I say, after clearing my throat.

She chuckles, making her breasts bounce. "They probably took it off for an ECG."

Lyle has been silent for a while, but now he holds a fresh washcloth. "May I?" he asks quietly.

Aurelia swallows and nods. Lyle carefully runs the washcloth over the round of her breast and over her nipple. She inhales sharply and I suddenly can't help myself. I fall upon her other breast, closing my mouth over that delicious, taut bud.

My regina gasps and I swirl my tongue over her nipple, then suck.

"Oh Goddess," she moans, squirming where she lies.

I cup her breast, devouring her in the only way that I want right now. Slowly and completely. She's delicious on my skin, her skin tasting like sweet vanilla and woman and all mine.

Lyle is frozen next to me, staring, probably. I give him a side-eye and smirk. Just as I planned, it pisses him off and he growls and lunges forward onto our regina's other breast. He groans at the taste of her, as he should.

Aurelia makes a sound of utter feminine pleasure and I lose myself in her sound, her skin, in her perfect scent made just for me. It feels like worshipping the moon, sacred and right. I shoot a picture of her to Scythe, Xander and Ghoul because I know it'll drive them all crazy with jealousy.

"Fuck," Aurelia moans, arching back and turning her face up to the ceiling.

I chuckle around her nipple, releasing it to lick and kiss the rest of the soft mound. "God, I love the taste of you," I murmur, skimming a hand up her thigh and pushing her underwear aside, finding her sweet slit. I sit up, circling my middle finger over her centre. She opens her legs and I dive in deep. She's wet as fuck under my fingers and I growl in approval as I drag my fingers through the slick moisture. Lyle's kissing up her neck and devouring her mouth now, palming her breasts with both hands.

So I do the logical thing. I flip her gown up and lunge between her legs, devouring her pussy. I enclose my mouth around her clit, now swollen and pulsing and suck gently. And by the gods, I could eat her sweet cunt for days on end—

Aurelia comes, spasming and crying out, her whole body trembling with the force of her pleasure. The sound of her ecstasy almost makes me come in my pants like a teenager, but I squeeze the base of my cock hard and manage to stop just in time.

A door slams outside and I know Xander has left the apartment. I roll my eyes at his stupidity, because why anyone would want to miss out on this is beyond me. I flick my tongue over her clit over and over again, wringing every last bit of pleasure from her beautiful body as she moans. Lyle growls in approval, his face still buried in her neck.

"You came so fast, regina," I complain, setting her clothes right again. "I was barely getting started."

But Aurelia is limp and sleepy-eyed on her pillow, a tiny, satisfied smile on her perfect pink lips. "Sorry," she mumbles.

Lyle adjusts himself as he covers her back up, buttoning up the shoulders of the gown and pulling the blanket up. He strokes her cheek briefly, and she leans into his touch, looking up with tired blue eyes.

The lion clenches his jaw over and over again, that muscle working overtime. But his eyes are hooded as he looks down at her. I know he isn't going to be able to stay away from her now.

"Food," Lyle mutters, adjusting his cock again as he gets up. "We need to feed you."

He looks at me expectantly because the bastard really can't bear to leave the room. I wonder what his plan is, because it's pretty obvious he's besotted with her. Just as I am. Just as we all should be.

"I'll get it." I climb off the bed, licking my regina's juices off my lips.

He nods. "Thank you."

I stare at him in shock for a moment. Aurelia makes a sound and we both turn to her.

"You two are so cute," she murmurs before nodding off to sleep.

Chapter 56

Aurelia

Whatever I imagined staying in Lyle's apartment would be like, this is not it. Savage and Lyle never leave my side. One of them is always nearby, whether it's to feed me, bathe me, or doze next to me. Scythe and Xander seem to want to be near as well, though I think in Xander's case, he wants to keep a suspicious eye on me. The thing about all of it is that I bask in their attention. I've never had anyone pay such close attention to me before, and the fact that it's *these* dominant, powerful men is pretty crazy. I'm careful to keep my stomach covered and the first time I snapped at Savage for touching the bandages was the last time he went near them. I send healing energy to them to keep infection away whenever I can and the painkillers Lyle feeds me really helps to keep the pain away.

I suddenly get an insight into how they live their day-to-day lives. Scythe and Lyle are *busy*. Lyle is always on his laptop, sitting in an armchair by the bed, working on school-related things. He goes down to the school for meetings or a couple of classes and to check on his rabid students. But as soon as he's done, he races back to bathe me and brush a gentle hand over my cheek. He clearly can't help doing any of these things, and it's a wonder to watch him fuss over me.

When Lyle is gone, Scythe sits at the new, temporary dining table on a laptop. He often talks to people on his phone as well, and I can't help but listen to the rough cadence of his voice, talking in an even, measured tone. Even when something is clearly wrong, he never loses his temper, or raises his voice. It's always a low, icy depth that tells me he's not happy with someone.

I know that Xander is around, but he'll often come in when he thinks I'm asleep and he and Scythe will talk quietly amongst themselves.

Savage insists on stealing a kiss after every bite he feeds me, and I find myself craving his lips no matter how many times he peppers me with them.

I spend most of my time watching movies on a laptop Lyle loans me. Minnie and Stacey text me daily from their illegal phones. It's annoying that I can't send voice memos back without help, but at least I'm amused by the pictures they send me; usually funny candid photos of the nimpins or a scandalous outfit here and there. Savage won't let *anyone* in to see me, even Eugene, and Lyle seems to approve of this. They have a wild, possessive sort of energy right now and watch my every breath carefully.

By the time the third day comes around, I've managed to heal both broken bones entirely. I mention it to Lyle straight away after his return that night, and he smiles at me.

I feel like I've seen the sun for the first time in days when I see the happiness on his face and it makes me warm right to my very bones. That fades a little when he returns, not with the little cutting device they use to remove casts, but a stiff-backed, glowing eyed dragon.

"He'll probably burn my whole arm off," I say darkly.

"He won't," Savage says with a snarl, prowling in behind

them. "Or I'll rip out his fucking kidneys and wear them as earrings."

"Fashionable," Xander deadpans. "I've come on the condition that you'll tell me what you've been doing with my dragon."

It angers him that I've spoken to his dragon, and I can see it in the red flashes that flicker across the white glow of his eyes. But then Scythe enters the room and they're all standing before me like a group of smouldering beasts, mating marks lighting up the room like a constellation of stars in the night sky. It makes me heat up and I shift on the bed.

"Regina," Savage chides, but he's grinning. "Concentrate."

Shit, they can smell my arousal. I forwent my scent shield in favour of healing myself. Heat floods my face and I clear my throat. "Well, I didn't actually do it on purpose, you know," I say, tilting my chin upwards. "He came to me the day of my trial."

Xander narrows his eyes, making the glowing orbs become suspicious, glowing slits.

"Actually, I sort of thought you knew about it."

He remains silent, which tells me he hadn't known at all.

"You gave me some jewellery, and I asked you if you could open a dragon-trick door like the one you guys have and you... *he* said yes." He said some other pretty unbelievable, toe-curling things to me, but I'm not going to repeat that right now while the temperature in the room is literally sky rocketing. A plume of steam comes out of Xander's nostrils. "That was all."

Xander points his finger at me.

I stiffen as something sizzles and tears. Startled, I look down to see a perfectly straight line cut down one cast, and then the other. There's the faint smell of burning and a sour sort of smell from my skin being covered for three days.

Without another word, Xander turns on his heel and storms out of the room, leaving a smoky haze in his wake.

"I knew it wasn't him," I say softly to Savage, Scythe and Lyle. "I knew it wasn't him straight away."

* * *

Even though my arms are healed, Lyle bosses me into letting him wash my hair over the sink, with me in a chair leaning back. My intuition tells me he needs this control... over me and over the situation. I sense he's teetering on the edge of something here.

I get to stare up at him as he works shampoo, then conditioner into my locks with the same bold, intense concentration he seems to do everything. His hands on my scalp are soothing and his fingers are heaven as they massage me. I haven't been to a hairdresser to cut my hair since I left my father's house, so it's grown a considerable length with me just trimming the ends every so often.

"Are you staring at me, Aurelia?" he asks, a bemused smile on that sensual mouth.

Heat floods my cheeks because I'm remembering how that mouth felt on me on the first day he'd unleashed his mouth upon me like the best sort of weapon. I've had no action since, only small kisses here and there from my wolf. Both have kept a little sexual distance, as if they didn't want to push me while I healed. But in Lyle's case, I think he's pointedly keeping away. So naturally, I change the subject.

"I'm excited to see Henry and my friends," I say quickly.

But it also means that my time here is over. I'll have to go back to staying in my room without my mates. Without the privacy of this apartment or their scents in it. Without the privacy to be close to Lyle.

I realise Lyle is studying me carefully as he wrings my hair out. "You don't look that excited," he murmurs.

I wonder how much to say. How much I want to reveal to him. The truth is something petal soft in my chest, but it's also a scary, *dangerous* thing. I don't want to put Lyle in danger of being pulled up by the council. The regina in me wants to protect him from the trouble I would bring.

So instead of telling him the truth, I reach up and run my finger along a strand of his golden hair that's come across his shoulder as he leans over me. It's in perfect condition, soft and glowing. "You should let me do your hair," I say softly.

He braces his arms on either side of my head, his gaze softening as he examines my face. I think he's going to kiss me. I really want him to kiss me again. But he doesn't and instead says, "Would you like that?"

I try to blink away the sudden burning in my eyes, try to send away the burning in my weary heart. "I would."

"Aurelia, I—"

I feel the beginning of my face crumpling, a weakness gathering behind my sternum. I don't want to hear what he's going to say to me.

"Don't say it—" I breathe, looking at his chin because those eyes are too much. I see the beginning of the end in their deep, powerful amber hue. Like the last rays of sun as it sets. A herald of the darkness to come. "Please. Don't say it. I have one last night here." I gesture to the apartment beyond the bathroom. "Let me enjoy it while it lasts."

He leans down and kisses my forehead then, and I think it might very well kill me because I know his kisses are numbered.

How am I supposed to live the rest of my life, having known this side of him—his gentle tone, his soft touch, those intense eyes, only to... *leave?* Before I'd come here, I was going to live as far away as possible, and lead a life blissfully free of my mates. But to go back to that plan now I'd known them?

"I wish I had never met you," I murmur as something inside me breaks in the saying of it. "I wish I had never come here."

He blinks at me—in surprise, I think—before a terrible anger flashes across his features and he places a large, dominating hand around my throat. It's gentle but firm, made to elicit obedience. He snarls softly into my face. His scent wraps around me like wings, heady and overpowering. I breathe him in, desire and fear flooding my consciousness.

And what he says into my mind, his voice guttural and harsh, restraint made into a man, rattles my entire reality. *"I did not exist before you."*

He leaves me there, like a glass doll, her pieces sliding down to shatter onto the floor.

Chapter 57

Aurelia

On my final night in Lyle's apartment, Savage crawls into bed and pulls me onto his chest. It's the first time we can cuddle properly, now that my arms are healed and free from their casts. He pats my back and strokes my hair as I cry just a little bit, and though I fight sleep, pretty soon I succumb to its comfortable lull.

A little after midnight, I *feel* it.

That darkening of the room, the soft snick of the window latch. I blink open my eyes and stare at the window from Savage's chest, my heart pounding like in a nightmare as the glass pane swings smoothly open.

A voice, like the darkest things scuttling in the night, slithers into my brain. *"Pretty, broken, little snakelet. You didn't listen to me."*

A heartbeat later, a booted foot steps onto the carpet as my fifth mate saunters into the room. I keep forgetting how big he is —just as tall as Xander and broad through the shoulder. Covered in those moving, pulsing shadows, I can't see much of him except that raw athleticism. As he walks in, I follow his stride. He doesn't have the silken grace of an apex predator like Lyle or Scythe or Savage, but the bestial lope of an apex *monster*.

He settles himself in Lyle's armchair, opposite the bed, stretching one leg out and resting an elbow on the armrest. It's an arrogant pose, and he's in the perfect position to stare at me lying on Savage's chest. Those two red points of light are like laser beams through the dark of the room, and I can't help but shiver to be under their perfect, narrowed focus.

His presence seems to empty the air out of the room—out of the entire building. As if the spirit of the school knows a beast of nightmares has entered the premises and is drawing its breath.

"I don't follow commands from people I don't know," I say into his mind, but my reply does not have the bite I want it to. If anything, it just sounds sad.

His shoulders move up and down in a deep breath. *"But I know you quite well."*

"So you've been stalking me this whole time?" I accuse, allowing myself to get hypnotised by the pulsing shadows moving up and around his face. They're like dense storm clouds, only the blackest I've ever seen.

"It's my favourite thing to do."

I almost snort out loud. And he wasn't even the one to steal my panties. *"Well, I'm flattered."*

Those two red points don't move, don't blink. It's really unnerving, but somehow, I enjoy being under them. We stare at each other in silence for a moment, and though it very much shouldn't be, something in my heart settles at the fact that all five of my mates are in the same vicinity. Lyle, Scythe and Xander are in the apartment, eating a late second dinner, as I've learned they like to do.

"Why won't you show yourself to me?" I ask.

"Because it would ruin all the fun."

"I want to see you." I say it firmly, and for a moment I consider regina-commanding him.

He huffs a laugh, and it's a deep, cavernous sound.

Savage's breaths lose their rhythm under my cheek and his arms tighten around me. I can't tell if he's awake or just holding me in his sleep.

But then Ghoul says, *"I want to see you sitting on his face."*

My head snaps up so rapidly that I almost twist a muscle in my neck.

"I want nothing more than to see you writhing with pleasure while you lick the cum off my cock, snakelet."

Holy Goddess. Did he see what I did with Lyle and Savage the other day? Is he... *jealous?*

And then Savage's sleepy voice rumbles into my brain, husky with sleep. *"Climb on, princess. Don't leave a beast waiting."*

Excitement floods my stomach, golden and sparkly, but I'm frozen to the spot as another presence approaches the room on silent feet.

Ghoul rumbles, *"Oh, how fun, pretty snakelet. There's a lion on the prowl."*

"You think I wouldn't know when a predator has entered my den?" Lyle says snidely into our minds as he shoves open the bedroom door and steps in; a second, towering shadow in just the cotton pants he wears to sleep. His hair is out of its band, spilling gloriously over one shoulder.

"Why, thank you." Ghoul chuckles as Lyle advances on him in a lethal prowl like the angel of death himself.

It's then that I push off Savage and sit up, straddling the wolf. "Lyle," I warn over my shoulder. Lyle pauses and turns slightly, so he has both Ghoul and me in his line of sight. And then rather suddenly, I think it's funny to say, "Play nicely with your bond-brother."

Ghoul tilts his head back and laughs out loud. I have to stare at him because that deep, rumbling sound hits my clitoris with force.

Lyle cocks his head at me. "He's here with your consent?"

Savage stops me from moving off him with firm hands on my hips. I feel him grow hard under me and my pussy flushes with enough heat to make me clench.

"Well, he didn't enter with my consent," I say, my own voice surprisingly husky, "but he can stay with it."

Ghoul rises, slowly stretching out to his full height. Lyle and Savage never take their eyes off him as he says into our minds, *"I have a right to be wherever my regina is."*

Savage's hand roams over my hips, sliding around to cup my ass. I'm in a slip of a silk nightie he brought me from my dorm as I readjust myself on him.

Enough of this male *posturing*.

I grab the straps of the nightie and tug it down to show my breasts, making sure the bandages covering my stomach are still properly in place. Savage's response is immediate. My wolf groans and sits up, covering one breast with his hand and sucking the other into his mouth. I gasp, burying my hand in his dark waves as he plays with my nipples, his tongue teasing one and his fingers toying with the other.

The temperature of my skin rockets up. Lyle and Ghoul have gone still and they're quite suddenly too far away.

Reaching a hand out, I say softly, "Come here."

Lyle steps forward like he's in a trance, and I reach up to cup his face. He leans down, capturing my mouth with his. I groan at the contact as Savage's hands roam, featherlight touches over my breasts, my shoulders, my ass.

I suck on Lyle's lower lip, sensing Ghoul shifting. To get a better look or to participate, I don't know. Lyle pulls away to gesture at Savage and his voice is rough with command. "Move."

"Get fucked," Savage growls against the underside of my breast.

"I plan to do the fucking," Lyle snarls. A pang of excitement shoots through me. Quicker than any snake, Lyle's arms come around my hips and he yanks me right off Savage.

I cringe as he grazes my stomach, but they're scabbed over enough that it's not too painful.

"Hey!" I yelp as my legs dangle in midair. But surrounded by Lyle's warmth and scent, I'm not really that upset.

Savage makes a furious snarling growl and tries to make a leap for me, except Ghoul is cackling and tackles Savage right off the bed, right onto the floor next to us.

I giggle because it's hilarious to see Savage shocked that he's met his match and to be the one getting roughed up for once. Lyle carries me to his bed like I weigh nothing, settling himself down on his back, tearing my panties off at their sides, throwing them on top of the wrestling males and arranging me on my belly on top of himself.

Savage and Ghoul seem to be punching each other on the floor until Lyle shoves down his track pants and his cock springs free to hit my entrance and I let out a sweet hiss.

That sound grabs the attention of the two beasts and they sit up to watch.

Lyle grabs the nape of my neck and kisses me with demand, his tongue dominating my mouth in the roughest way possible as he growls with feline satisfaction.

It only serves to make me wetter and I writhe on top of him, enjoying the feel of his hard body against my soft one. I grind my bare pussy against his cock and Lyle reaches down to position himself at my soaking wet entrance. I slide down a little and his crown stretches me open. I gasp at his magnificent girth. Gods, I've been waiting for him to return to me for *so* long.

"Tell me if it's too much, angel," Lyle says, his whisper-soft voice in contrast to the large fingers dimpling my ass. With a flex of his hips, Lyle eases further into me.

"No, I love it," I moan around the words, getting lost in the feel of him.

I cast a look over my shoulder. The two males now standing, so still they could be predators waiting in long grass, simply stare at where Lyle and I are joined. It makes a sly smile stretch across my now swollen lips.

Ghoul chuckles. *"Our regina likes to be watched."*

Oh, yes I fucking do. I hadn't known it until that first night they all projected into my bungalow. It's then that I feel Scythe slip into the room, that cold, predatory power raking down my shoulders. Xander is probably outside, cursing us.

"I like this angle," Savage says, his voice husky. "Fuck."

I let out a strangled moan as Lyle sinks deeply into me. Suddenly, we're plunged into darkness. I gasp as Lyle stills and we look upwards at the dome of glittering shadow that now engulfs the room. Tiny red and white lights sparkle to give us light to see by, and under that glimmer, this entire thing could be a dream.

It makes me bolder than I have any right to be.

But it's Savage who says, "Fucking share, Lyle. You've always been an asshole."

I rise, allowing myself to settle down on Lyle's cock. Letting him sink into the hilt. I whimper and focus on my breathing as I accommodate his massive size to my full capacity. He fills me up so entirely that I feel lightheaded.

But it's still not enough.

Without all of them, it'll never be enough. Breathing hard, I say, "If you want something, Savage, *take it.*"

He cocks a brow at me and stalks towards the bed, all but tearing off his pants as he does. "Well fuck, princess, when you say it like that."

He comes up next to me and grabs the front of my neck, claiming my mouth with his. He swallows my moans with relish, and as Lyle flexes his hips up and down, Savage commands my mouth. Like generals at war trying to show dominance, they fight for my attention, one from beneath and one from above. I writhe and sigh, one hand on Lyle's hard abs and the other fisting Savage's thick hair.

But then two large, wet fingers find my clit and I almost come undone. I tear myself away from Savage to look into two red points of light entombed in shadow, standing shoulder to shoulder with my wolf.

Ghoul's shadows recede just enough so that I can see his face. Only it's not his face at all, but the white outlines of—is that *bone*? My stomach flops as he gently weaves his fingers through my wet core, circling my clit. I look down to see the skin of his hand, brown and large, tattooed, with a thick wrist. I can't make out the markings made in black ink, but I don't care right now because golden tendrils of pleasure spin from my pussy straight up to my head.

"Oh God," I whisper.

Then Savage's voice is whispering in my ear. He's positioned himself behind me, straddling Lyle's thighs. "Oh, my beautiful, perfect regina. *We* are your gods now."

Ghoul chuckles just as Lyle flexes his hips, making me bounce. He thrusts into me and I hold on to Ghoul's thick forearm for dear life as Lyle finds his pleasure in me. Golden heat coils through the void of my body as I relish being *had* by the three of them and being seen by the cold one, observing from the shadows.

But they really are. Three wild gods with the sole mission of worshipping me. Of making me come until I'm a puddle in their arms. I don't think I'm going to survive this. How the hell am I going to make it out of this apartment in one piece?

"Make yourself useful and pass me the lube, boogeyman." Savage points to Lyle's bedside table.

Ghoul opens the first drawer where I'm surprised to see a purple bottle of lube I never saw anyone put in there.

"Where'd that come from?" I demand breathlessly as Lyle thrusts in me in languid motions.

Savage kisses my mating mark as he accepts the bottle. "I've been thinking about this for a long time, regina."

"Be careful, wolf," Lyle growls.

Savage growls back and I turn around as far as I can to kiss him. He hungrily accepts my mouth and nips my lower lip.

"How do you know he wasn't trying to go for *your* asshole?" Ghoul says to Lyle.

"Because he doesn't have a death wish," Lyle says through gritted teeth, thrusting in me again.

Savage snorts. "Don't be so sure, lion."

But nervousness is flooding me as I hear Savage squirting lube onto his fingers. I'm already so very full and Savage is just as big. "I... don't know if I can—"

"Fingers only for my princess. We need to practise to get this right. If you're ever going to take Scythe *and* Xander as well, we'll need to."

Practise I can get on board with.

"Is what they say about dragon cock—"

Lyle lets out a vicious, almost rabid snarl and yanks me down to growl against my lips. "Do *not* talk about another beast's cock when I'm inside you."

I giggle and cup his jealous, angry face in one hand and press my lips to his. He holds my hips and fucks me relentlessly, making me throb and moan on top of him. My inner walls clench around my lion, flooding his cock with liquid pleasure.

"I didn't know you were the jealous sort," I moan.

"Well, now you know," he growls, before biting on my lower lip and wrapping his arms around me, thrusting deep.

Savage palms my ass before a slick thumb tickles against my asshole. I cry out and Lyle slows his pace, rocking my hips back and forth so my clit grinds against his pubic bone. Savage bends down and licks my ass, making pleasure shoot through my entire core. I clench around them both, making both wolf and lion grunt.

I turn to look at Ghoul, his eyes on my ass, and I reach out a hand to brush at his leg. He cocks his head.

Sitting back up, I pant, "Give it to me, boogeyman."

His voice is low and deeply husky, like boulders grinding in dark places. He grabs my chin. "Give you what, snakelet?"

"Your cock," I pant. "I want your cock in my mouth."

Savage eases his thumb into my ass, sending delightful vibrations fluttering all the way down to my clit.

Ever so slowly, Ghoul undoes the button and lowers the zip on his pants. The shadows fade away a little and I can now see he wears black pants that are neither jeans nor slacks or track pants. Silver rings glint on his fingers and I lick my lips as a thick cock with a deliciously wide head springs free. With a little alarm and a lot of excitement, I see that it's tattooed with black ink.

Black patterns whorl over his cock from base to tip, and some of it might be writing, others are symbols.

"Wow," I whisper in awe, reaching out to touch it.

Ghoul places a hand on my cheek and hisses as I make contact with his shaft. *"Let me see how pretty you can suck, snakelet."*

My mouth waters and my pussy clenches at his words and Lyle groans, thrusting gently into me as Savage's finger works its delicious way in and out of my ass.

Ghoul draws closer and I lick the slit of his cock where pre-cum already gleams. He rubs his cock against my lips and I open to take him in.

"Such a good girl," he rumbles with approval.

My belly flops on itself at his rough words. I moan around his crown, tasting him and taking him deeper, swirling my tongue around the rock-hard length. I marvel at his taste and scent. He smells like more than a man, like all my mates, but there is something familiar about it. His scent is like the dark poisonous places beneath the earth and ancient, brutal power.

The four of us find a new, enticing, seductive sort of rhythm. Their masculine groans mingle with my female sounds of pleasure and it's a song that I want etched upon my own skin.

Pleasure weaves through every dark crevice of my insides. It feels like my soul is being filled from every angle, filling me so completely that I just know when I burst, it'll be the most magnificent thing to ever happen to me.

I've gone years without being touched by a single person beyond the passing of change at my aunt's shop. Now, being touched reverently by three of my mates, like they hunger for my skin, heals something in me.

Fixes something in my broken soul.

I suck harder and Savage stretches me wider. I bob on Ghoul's dick and there's something about the fact that Lyle is watching me, heavy-lidded and thrusting, and that Ghoul's hips are stuttering as I pleasure him that gives me endless satisfaction.

Lyle's thumbs stroke reverent circles around my thighs and I bounce on him and Savage's thumb at the same time, finding a new sort of pleasure, a new dimension of intensity as I relish how deep I've taken them all. Ghoul's pre-cum tastes like salt and beast and I savour it with satisfied moans.

I work on his cock, devouring him, licking and swallowing and groaning until he's tilting his head back and making a low guttural sound I'm sure only a monster can make. I blink up at him and those red points of light flash violently. He comes with a shudder and I swallow every last hot burst, milking his cock with my hand and my mouth, excitedly swallowing the full taste of him—refined, sweet poison, pouring down my throat.

Ghoul's chest rumbles as he pops himself out of my mouth, leaning down to bite my neck and swirling a wet finger over my clit. His breath is warm against my pulse. "*I dreamed about you long before we met.*"

I come, screaming, bursting into a million fractals of light and sound. And it turns into a sob as I feel the totality of it. That we've found pleasure together, the four of us, and that there's still two parts of us missing. Lyle comes next from watching me. He whispers my name, thrusting hard and deep, his abs tensing, pouring his hot seed deep into me as Savage coaxes pleasure out of my ass.

When Lyle's last thrust is done, Savage snarls like an actual wolf and grabs me by the hips, pulling me off Lyle's cock and turning me over so that I'm lying right on top of Lyle's body. Savage lunges for me possessively, shoving his cock into me and kissing me deeply. I moan his name into his mouth and he growls something purely animalistic back. Lyle holds my thighs open with steady arms as if he's encouraging Savage while his own cum flows out of me as Savage pumps hard and fast. Like he's had enough of waiting and all his jealousy is coming out in his need to have me.

I let him claim me in that rough, possessive way his wolf craves, clutching onto his shoulders and crying out as our combined wetness makes me come again. "Never again," he gasps in my ear as he thrusts angrily, *desperately*, into me. "You'll never ask *that* of me again." Punishing thrusts of his hips tell me how much I hurt him when I made him break my arm. How much he cares for me.

I'm suddenly sobbing with overwhelm and guilt. "Never again," I gasp. "I promise, never again."

And when his cock explodes, Savage buries his face into my neck, and I feel the wetness of his tears as he whispers, "I love you with everything I have, Aurelia Boneweaver."

I sob into Savage's neck as I'm filled up with so much cum that Savage's stuttering thrusts make delightful wet sounds.

Savage possesses my mouth with his tongue, before bringing me up with him and rolling us off Lyle, settling me between the two of them.

We're sweaty and sated, a tangle of limbs and breaths as I glance around the room. Ghoul has disappeared, along with his dome of shadows, allowing moonlight to stream through the open window once again. The curtain billows in the cool breeze, and behind them, I just make out the gleam of glacial eyes, seemingly frozen in time and space.

"Scythe," I whisper.

But he doesn't reply—or move—for a long, long time, and by then, I'm dozing in my post-orgasm haze.

Chapter 58

Lyle

Ten years ago

The heavy obsidian shackles make a loud clanking noise as I'm marched through the bowels of Blackwater Federal Penitentiary for Animalia.

"Dangerous beast walking!" calls out one of my five prison guards in a heavy smoker's gruff. "Dangerous beast approaching!"

They all hold cattle prods like the one Ulman used to use when I was a cub. But these are bigger with an even higher voltage than what I'm used to. These leave marks.

The prison is loud. Beasts roar with their human voice boxes, guttural, snarling sounds that put my animus on alert. They bang on their metal cages with their cups and fists. They shout nasty, menacing words.

It smells like feral testosterone, sweat, and pure, lethal menace.

This is where I belong. With these creatures who hurt and maim others. And yet somehow, this place scrapes along my spine like sharp claws. Somehow, my animus gets *excited*.

They take me to see the warden first. A huge man with a long, long, white beard like Santa Claus. Only, Santa Claus isn't jacked with muscle and doesn't have a mean, hard-eyed stare that made my hackles rise. His size and scent tell me he's a bear, and probably a rex to a big, powerful pack.

He leans down to look into my eyes like he's searching for some defect. "Human or animal?"

I look down at my hands. "Monster."

He grunts and gruffly reads from the papers Lady Celeste sent with me. "'An animus so dangerous he has to be permanently locked away for the safety of all'. Well, cub, you'll fit right in. We're all monsters here."

The males around me chuckle darkly, and while the man in me doesn't like the sound, my animus gets excited.

"Lady Celeste is gonna teach me how to lock it away. To keep it safe," I grit out.

He laughs and the sound scrapes against my insides. "It will be fun to see her try. Take him to C Block."

"I'm supposed to be in confinement in case—"

"No space, cub. Let's see how you do in gen pop. Everyone's got obsidian on, don't worry."

"But—"

"You'll be right, cub," sniggers the guard who hauls me to my feet.

A cage is what I'm used to, I remind myself. A cage is where me and my animus belong.

"Dangerous beast walking!" they call again as I'm escorted out into the prison. "New, pretty meat!"

There's a large recreational area where inmates in orange prowl, lift weights, play soccer, or lean against the wall and smoke. When I come into view, everyone stops to stare.

My animus stares back.

My human heart sinks.

"Who's the handsome young man?" coos an inmate with tattoos all over his face. "Look at all dem big, purdy muscles." He elbows the inmate next to him. "Look at dem golden hairs."

"He's too pretty to be a monster," replies his friend with oily black hair. "What're the guards all talkin' about?"

They unlock the thick metal door and I'm thrust inside, my obsidian shackles clanking too loudly.

Males advance on me from all sides, staring, growling, hissing, and cornering me in a cage of man-flesh.

One of them—a huge, blond lion—grunts, beckoning to me with two fingers. His violent lust makes the air between us reek.

My animus growls and I shake my head in fear. "No, no, no!"

They laugh. They think I'm scared of *them*.

The guards dangle their arms through the bars, smoking and watching me with broad smiles.

"Rough him up a bit," one of the guards says through the speaking holes in the glass they all watch behind.

"Don't push him," another warns. "They told us he'd—"

"Fuck what they told us," snarls the first guard. "Come on, pretty boy, show us if it's true."

Once again, I can't stop my animus when he comes calling. When he growls and snaps and wants blood.

When it turns dark, I can't decipher whether the screaming is me or them. Whether the blood is theirs or mine. Whether the flesh in my teeth is lion, wolf, avian, or reptile.

Minutes, hours, an eternity later, putrid gas streams through the air and there's a choking sound as beasts around me fall. It makes my eyes burn, as my animus allows me to return to my human body, but I remain standing, staring at my crimson soaked hands.

"Didn't you have obsidian on him?" The warden's voice is terrible and loud as he storms up to the glass.

"The fucking obsidian didn't work!" The guards shout.

"I told you," I whisper.

Chapter 59

Aurelia

The next morning, when Lyle and Savage get ready to go down to the academy, so do I. Minnie helped Savage pack clothes for me a few days ago, and I head into Lyle's closet where he hung them all up.

Next to his.

It makes my heart quiver a little to see them neatly lined up next to his perfectly ordered shirts. I don't have the heart to collect them all and take them back down to my dorm. If he can keep my knickers in his bedside table, surely he won't mind if I leave these here for him too?

Lyle enters the wardrobe with only a towel slung low on his hips. I instantly heat up at the view of his naked, golden torso, the divots of his pecs and abs a clear indication of how hard he no doubt works in the animus gym. He's the only member of my mating group without any tattoos, and his body is a work of art all on its own. A work of art that thrust into me so possessively it took my breath away last night. I turn around quickly, trying hard not to feel his every movement as he takes off his towel and starts to get ready for the day.

It feels very domestic, all of a sudden, and my anima keens at how nice and normal this feels. But I swallow that rubbish back down and focus, selecting a bra and a lavender maxi dress for myself. I put them all on quickly, careful to keep my abdominal bandages in place. I've been so careful to hide my wounds this entire time, but every time either my wolf or lion brush past my stomach, I can't hide the cringe. I'm sure they put it down to self-consciousness. Although they don't hurt anymore, they don't look much better. The black tissue mars my skin in jagged lines, though there's new skin growing underneath where I've been plying with my healing magic... whatever I can spare here and there. The phenomenal sex last night boosted my power, but I don't know when we'll get another opportunity to be together. I don't want to waste my reserve on this dead tissue when I should be focusing on my shields.

I'm finishing putting a little mascara on when warm hands on my shoulders turn me around. Lyle is dressed in a navy-blue suit, complete with a matching vest and a white shirt. His hair is tied back neatly at his nape and his navy tie has a little golden pin with the head of a lion on it.

I did not exist before you.

Those heinous, beautiful words are stamped across the part of my heart allocated to this lion. Stamped, seared, *branded* there.

I swallow my misery, looking up at his face, trying not to breathe in the smell of soap and heady, musky male.

His voice is irritatingly even and calm. "Go to class as per normal, Aurelia."

He cares that I'm leaving. I know he does. But he holds his damn feelings back and doesn't show me anything of the truth. I want to say that his name for me is angel. I want to press my lips to his but I can't bear the thought of a goodbye kiss. And I don't trust myself not to cry if I know this touch, today will be the last. So instead, I let my stomach sink and nod stiffly. "I know... Mr Pardalia."

His face tightens a little at that, but in a flash, his features smooth back out to their regular handsome perfection. He reaches for me—

No, not me, but an item of clothing from the hanger behind me. "It's cold this morning," he says tightly, handing me a black jacket.

I take it silently. Those warm hands drop and he steps away. "Alright, then."

He strides out of the closet like I'm no one, taking a piece of my heart with him.

But another piece of my heart bounds through the door, beaming at me, freshly showered in a black T-shirt, shorts, and sneakers. "Let's go, regina," Savage says excitedly, taking my hand and leading me out.

Chapter 60

Lyle

Agony. That is the only word I can use to describe what it feels like to leave Aurelia. Those shimmering blue eyes barely contained the fact that she was upset by it. Perhaps she thought she could hide it. But now that I've been deep inside of her *twice*, she can't hide her true emotions from me anymore.

It was difficult every day I had to leave her to attend to my school duties. Duties that once sustained me, gave me purpose.

I did not exist before you.

I said it. Snarled it out of my possessive, black-hearted, accursed maw.

It was the truth. A truth so forbidden that the man in me had held onto it for the past decade.

But beasts cannot lie. And when those chains rattle in my brain, I can barely contain my need for her.

I stride out of my apartment and head down to the school, hating every step. But I have to go out early to check on the prisoners first. I promised my staff I would take up supervising breakfast duty in the academy dining hall to observe my rabid students, all three of which are trouble-makers of the worst sort.

A small smile threatens my lips as I think of my regina, defiant, even bound in two casts. Defiant, even when admitting the truth.

I wish I'd never met you.

Imagine my surprise when a pain like no other had struck me down like a lightning bolt, destroying the bubble of peace and security I placed us in. I knew this would have to come to an end. I also knew that to give myself what I wanted meant to acknowledge that it would be temporary.

And all I wanted was Aurelia safe, happy and tucked into my bed, preferably under me.

But it was a dream. Because what she told us four days ago—that her father is coming for her, whether anyone likes it or not—is a very real threat. I discussed it with Scythe immediately, and I'd begun formulating a plan.

Scythe gave me that hard, cold stare of his and called it a fool's plan. That if I thought I could defeat Mace Naga using *legal* means, I was an idiot.

I coolly asked him if he was going to launch an attack on the Serpent Court and if the Marine Court would back him. A regretful slip on my emotional leash.

When it comes to Aurelia, it feels as if we're all slipping. Savage alone remains unbothered, declaring that he would, in fact, blow up any serpent coming to take her from him. While the wolf might be the most feral of us, it meant that he was in tune with his animus. In spending time with him these past three days, I'd come to realise that Savage and his wolf were one and the same every moment of the day.

And I was jealous of that.

That instead of being two parts in one body, Savage was whole. A fully integrated animalia. Ferality was looked down upon in our community, but I was starting to think that we'd let the humans force us into an unnatural state of civility. Because at the heart of it, our beasts were powerful. And the suppression of our beasts made us not civilised, but *docile*.

More controllable.

For the first time in years, I doubt my work. I doubt my own teachings.

So, I'd carefully considered Scythe's perspective and agreed on a compromise to our situation. Celeste didn't like it, but she agreed that we have no other option.

I exit the elevator, take a short walk, and then go down another elevator and a set of stairs.

Ruben meets me at the first door, swiping his card to let me into the shadowy tunnel beyond.

"Any trouble this morning?"

"Only the usual," he gruffs. "But I did want to ask how long you were intending to keep them here."

I level him a look because he usually never questions my authority. Or my actions. Ruben looks down at me from his great height, the dark shadows creating harsh lines across his grey eyes and ruddy brown beard. I find myself wondering how long it would take me to decapitate him.

"As long as it takes to eliminate the threat," I reply evenly.

Ruben nods. "Roger that, boss."

Entering the tunnel, the automatic lights turn on, showing me the earthen cavern beyond. When I emerge into the circle of brighter lights, the shouting immediately begins.

From the serpent students we locked up in here two days ago.

"My father will hear about this!" one of them shouts.

"This is wrong!" a female voice screams. "This is fucking wrong and you know it, Mr Pardalia!"

The cells are carved into the rock itself, wide arches that are closed off with obsidian bars. There are not only serpents here, but a few hyenas too. Those Scythe informed me are friendly with Mace Naga's people.

There is a feral sort of satisfaction I get from seeing the enemies of my regina locked up. I know it's not healthy. I know my animus is leading me to do this.

But in this, I cannot stop the urge.

These serpents helped trap and torture my regina. They will try to do the same thing and worse once again to not only Aurelia but my other anima students.

They tried to cut off her mating mark. *Our* mating mark off her precious skin.

"You are being fed well," I say coldly to them. "You are receiving your classes. You are allowed outside." Under cover of darkness with a full guard, but I don't feel the need to mention that. "All your needs are fulfilled and more."

"How long?" someone cries. "Just tell us how long, Mr Pardalia."

I inhale, scenting fear and anger, human tears, and *serpent*. I exhale it all out. "Not long now," I say, before turning and leaving.

* * *

In the dining hall, I nod at an excited Sabrina and Stacey, waiting by the giant table they've made with Scythe's males at the back. Savage and Scythe felt the need to take Aurelia's animas under their wing. Savage saw them red-eyed and glum on that first day she didn't show up to breakfast and ordered the joining of tables. That cheered them right up.

Today, I allowed Stacey and Sabrina to set up a giant, multi-coloured banner across the back of the hall:

WELCOME BACK, AURELIA!

There's no name for the primal feeling I have at seeing her name emblazoned on my academy in gold and purple, as well as the illustration of an eagle, its wings surrounding the bubbled words in a hug.

Henry is jumping up and down on the table, zipping around Minnie's pink crown in jubilation while they all wait for her. Eugene is in Raquel's lap with a handmade necklace around his neck and brown goggles securely on.

On one of the feline tables, Titus is white-lipped, his nostrils flaring, eyes darting around the hall. A predator assessing prey. His eyes land on the two serpent's tables on the other side of the hall, the light from the stained-glass windows falling on all the empty seats.

The easiest option was to simply allow the students to think the serpents were sent home. No one would complain about it anyway.

I don't have to wait long before Savage and Aurelia arrive, hand in hand. The perpetual vise that forms around my chest every time I leave her loosens and I feel as if I can breathe freely again.

She is breathtaking, as usual. Glowing from sex with her mates last night. And more than that is the casually wild, heady power she oozes. The one that beckons to me with her every step and breath. I watch her, watch everything.

The hall activity lulls for a moment before it starts back up at double the decibels. I monitor the other students for their response to her presence. There is the usual male posturing and preening from the birds of prey and a general interest zoning in from the other males. A few from the feline and hyena orders actually stand up from their tables to get a look at her, before being pulled back down by their more socially aware friends.

They all wonder what I did. What I still wonder. At what type of female demands to have her arms broken for her friends.

Henry sees her next, almost sensing her at the door. He lets out an indignant chirp before shooting towards her like a fluffy blue missile. He's only a blur as he smacks into her chest, making her stumble back a step and then laugh; a brilliant, happy sound that makes me want to close my eyes and treasure it like a dragon.

"Settle down, hatchling," Savage chides like an alpha wolf telling off his pup. "Look at her, she's fine."

Henry chirps with his whole body, closing his eyes with the force of it.

"He's telling you off for keeping me," Aurelia says with a smile. "And he has every right."

A small growl rumbles out of my chest and Savage gives me a reproachful side-eye.

"Did you say something, Lyle?" a low female voice asks by my elbow.

I tear my eyes off Aurelia as her friends run towards her, surrounding her with exclamations and hugs.

"I was saying that the line is moving too slowly," I say loudly, pointing at a loitering tiger, who's too busy staring at Aurelia to realise the line has moved ahead. He hastily shuffles down the buffet with his tray. I glance at the cassowary anima I assigned to Aurelia as her female counsellor so many months ago. "How are you, Theresa? How are Felicity and Jess?"

"Were they keeping you in their dorm?" Sabrina asks Aurelia excitedly and *loudly*. "Were they *tending* to your wounds?"

"How was the sex?" Connor asks with equal volume. "Don't lie to me, girl, you glow!"

Theresa huffs a laugh at the sight of them. "I'm well, thank you. So are my women. I'm just happy to see Lia is back and looking healthier."

Felicity and Jess are Theresa's mates, a cassowary and emu shifter, respectively. I met Theresa during my training in psychology at Blackwater Penitentiary. There weren't enough males wanting to do the course in jail, so the few of us males were put in with the female cohort. It's one of the reasons I hire so many ex-cons. Theresa was in jail for manslaughter at the time. The so-called victim just so happened to be a human ex-boyfriend of Felicity's who'd been stalking them, but Theresa had a good lawyer and got a reduced sentence for her clean record and good behaviour.

I'm immediately aware that Theresa is looking between me and Aurelia. "Glad to hear it," I say. "We'll need to keep an eye on Titus."

She nods in understanding. I've already briefed the entire staff and guard roster on what happened on the day of Aurelia's student-run trial and the precautions we'd need to take. I have no intention of letting Titus get anywhere near my regina ever again.

Minnie, for her part, looks truly awful as she hugs Aurelia. All my male instincts are telling me she's not a female who's coping. I was hoping that with Aurelia's return, the tiny tigress would perk up and reengage with her classes and teachers. It's why I didn't insist on Aurelia moving in with Savage just yet. Her friends need her.

On that, I *can* fight my primitive urges.

My phone vibrates and I glance at it to see Georgia is taking sick leave for the next few days.

"I love you guys," Aurelia sniffs as she finally breaks free of her friends. Something vital in my gut tightens.

Her friends chorus, "We love you more!"

Savage and Aurelia get their food, both pointedly ignoring me.

"*Eat your vegetables,*" I say to Savage, mind-to-mind.

"*Prick,*" Savage replies in the same way. He loads up his plate with chicken thighs, bacon, eggs, and one thin slice of tomato.

"*I held her legs open for you, asshole,*" I reply.

He smirks as he turns around. "*And how sweet it was.*"

As Savage leads her to their new larger table, Aurelia's

mouth drops open upon seeing it. "Wait, what?" she says in shock.

"I've rearranged things," Savage says proudly.

"I'm not complaining." Sabrina shrugs, taking a seat beside a smirking Beak.

The rest of the day is worse than all the days preceding it. The first reason being because I know when I return to my bed tonight, Aurelia will not be in it. The second reason being that Aurelia's return to the general population of the academy stirs up Titus in the worst possible way.

Chapter 61

Aurelia

I never expected the massive welcome back party I was given, but it was the best thing ever to cheer me up after losing my perfect little nest. Minnie sticks close to my side at breakfast and everyone takes it upon themselves to try and distract her from Titus' malevolent, glass-cracking stare from a few tables down.

"I've been sleeping on the spare bed in Stacey's room," Minnie says to me as we sit down for sex-ed class.

"We thought it was best she wasn't alone," Connor says seriously, carrying Eugene in his arms. "Gertie has been amazing as usual, but sometimes you need a friend to remind you not to go sneaking about in the dark."

"I wanted to go see him," Minnie explains apologetically. "To"—her eyes shine, glimmering under the halogen lights of the academy classroom—"get an explanation, or just to get *something* from him, you know? To find out if it was just anger, or bad judgement, or—"

Sabrina snorts in disgust. "Girlfriend, we've been through this before. That animus knew exactly what he was doing."

A little dismay winds through my chest as I watch my best

friend grasp at straws. She's a girl besotted, and it's not normal. Something more than suspicion tugs at my gut. "His dad follows the Old Laws, Min," I say quietly. "He's just like my dad."

"You know his dad?" Minnie asks in shock.

I take a deep breath, glancing at Savage and Xander, who are clearly listening closely. "Yeah, Min. Titus' uncle was one of my mother's mates."

Raquel chokes on the water they were drinking and everyone stares at me. Savage tightens his grip around my waist.

"At first, I thought he looked familiar, but it wasn't until I saw his surname in his student file that I realised why."

Minnie reaches for my hand. "But Lia," she whispers, "Titus' uncle is dead."

I nod, unable to tell them any more than that. The rest of the horrible, awful truth I thought I put behind me.

Henry huddles closer into my neck, and noting this, my animas don't question me further. Savage keeps an arm around me at all times after that, in every class we have during the day, growling at anyone who so much as looks my way. But then he, Xander and Raquel reluctantly leave us to do some business with Scythe.

I drag the rest of my animas and Eugene into the library after our final class of the day: Communicating with Humans. We sign out a couple of laptops on the pretence of doing homework, but I take the time to tell my feline friends about Ulman's Wildlife Sanctuary. I don't tell them about how I've been seeing Lyle's memories, but once they hear about felines being abused, they're onto the cause like a rabid tiger on a deer's carcass.

It's difficult at first because those types of parks were closed down decades ago, but Stacey is nothing if not resourceful and finds newspaper articles from an online repository of newspapers.

"So, this is Frank Ulman," Minnie says, peering at Stacey's computer screen. "Looks like he owned the private wildlife sanctuary up in Darwin. There's a ton of articles talking about all the great work he did. But there's nothing recent."

It fits with the red earth and dry weather I saw in Lyle's memories.

"He's even written scholarly articles," Connor says, pulling up a scientific journal. "Look, this one's all about the mating patterns of animalia felines."

"And this one," I say darkly, "is about lion cubs and re-training them."

"I feel sick just looking at it," Minnie says. "What an awful guy."

"Does it say anything about what happened to the sanctuary?" I ask carefully. "About how it got shut down?"

But we find no articles on it. As if the whole thing was swept away.

"I've found a coroner's report," Stacey says quietly. "Looks like they were killed in an accident."

Darkness like I've never known opens.

"Lia, are you alright?" Minnie asks.

"Yeah, I just need a second." I get up from our table and walk to the window, trying to calm myself down. I take Henry in my hands and hold his cheek to mine.

Blood on human hands.

A blistering dry heat.

Screaming, broken and agonising, tearing through a raw throat.

Frank Ulman did that. However Lyle saw it, this human male had broken lion cubs down, and in Lyle's case, it turned his animus into something that would protect not only himself, but those around him. My mate suffered so greatly for... what? Entertainment. Curiosity. Power?

The window looks out to the back of the academy, where a group of wolves kick a football around on a green field. A couple of animas are making out on a picnic blanket at the edge of the field. This is Lyle's school, his pride and joy. He came from such a disaster, only to dedicate his life to helping young, lost beasts. It's only this that calms me down enough to return to the table.

"What does the rest of the report say?" I ask quietly.

My friends eye me warily. Minnie is chewing her lip.

Stacey shows me a highlighted paragraph. "The humans all showed signs of being ravaged. They were ripped apart so badly they couldn't even account for who was present. They only give educated guesses. But... the animals were all left intact. And..." She blows out a breath. "One male lion was missing."

I glance at Minnie. *"It was Lyle,"* I tell her mind to mind. *"That's where he grew up."*

My best friend's face turns ashen.

"There are always repercussions," Connor says quietly, "when dealing with dangerous males. Human or animalia."

Chapter 62

Scythe

I do not appreciate being summoned by Titus Clawson, but being the son of a fellow crime boss from a neighbouring territory, the tiger has every right to request an audience of me.

Me and apparently every other member of this academy.

After dinner, he commandeers Raquel in the animus dorm and pays the wolf anim in cash to broadcast a school-wide message. Loyal as Raquel is, they tell Savage first, giving me a five-minute allowance to assuage my irritation.

The message broadcasted to the rest of the school bears the cadence of black intention. I suspect what this is. And it's been a long time coming.

It's been all of four days since the previous trial, and this is Titus trying to regain his power. If he's going to be much more of a problem, he's going to be given a ticket out of here, whether his father wants that or not. Killing him would start a war. That's the only reason I've not pursued that beckoning path already.

"This is not going to be good," I say to Lyle, mind-to-mind. Since Aurelia's nesting in his apartment, the lion has been more forthcoming with these telepathic communications with me.

"*Is he—*"

"*It's not for Aurelia,*" I say quickly.

"*Do you need me there?*"

"No." I pause for a beat. "*But be nearby. And inform Lady Celeste.*"

The headmistress never gets involved in the day-to-day running of the school, no matter how severe it is. That's Lyle's job, and she's Lady of this land only.

The rec room is more crowded than any in previous trial as I enter to stand on the stage next to Xander and Savage, because even the guards, counsellors and teachers have been invited. The three chandeliers above us cast golden light against the gathering dusk and they make long, wavering shadows along the sides of the room.

Theresa, Aurelia's cassowary counsellor, waits along the walls behind the birds of prey, frowning as Connor leads Aurelia, Minnie, Raquel, Sabrina and Stacey through. The nimpins cower into their hosts' necks, tiny wings tight around their round bodies.

They can feel what's coming. Can feel its dark, unholy presence in the energy of the room. The breath the world takes before something truly devastating happens. Something that has every right to destroy a person.

Something that even I, in my darkest, most nightmarish states, would never even consider. It's a depth I *would never* consider. I'd come close to it with Aurelia when we first met, but I chose her death as the wiser path. The thought makes a shiver pass through me now. Makes my shark snap his jaws.

Titus stands in the centre of the room. Dramatic, proud, egotistical. His aura radiates black, grey, and dark green. It's oily and sharp as an executioner's axe.

Minnie is ghostly pale under her brown skin. Whether her human self realises it or not, her anima knows what's about to happen.

And when Titus points a long, thick finger to her, standing huddled in a shield of her confused friends, she begins to tremble like a newborn bird.

"Minnie Devi," Titus calls, his harsh voice dripping with disdain.

Gertie, Minnie's bright yellow nimpin, chirps in comfort into Minnie's ear, where she's perched on the tigress' shoulder.

This is the only time I'll permit myself to step in. "Remove the nimpin," I call.

I try to reduce collateral damage where I can. That has always been my rule.

Raquel quickly steps forward and cups their hands around Gertie, but the nimpin shrieks and clings onto Minnie's shoulder with her tiny feet. The sounds of distress and protest echo around the room and every anima cringes. Raquel prises Gertie off Minnie's skin, the nimpin crying out and squeaking as if her very life depends on staying with the tiny female.

It's only when Minnie says, "It's alright, Gertie," that Gertie croons low and allows herself to be taken back to the other animas.

Minnie seems to take a deep breath and steps forward. Her bubblegum pink hair is a mass of curls down her back and she wears a long black dress that doesn't suit her normally bubbly disposition. Her eyes are pink and puffy, probably for days now since Titus refused to let her see him. But she stands tall at all of her five foot three, her face a mask of noble bravery.

"Psychopathic motherfucking cunt," Savage snarls into my mind, sensing what's about to happen. *"We should've ground his living body into meat the moment he got here."*

"We don't have the right," I reply. *"Only Minnie does."*

"She's too sweet," Savage says irritably. *"She's too... gentle."*

I'm not so sure about either of those two things. I think Minnie has more mettle than anyone gives her credit for. I can see it in the power that hovers around her at all times.

Minnie steps into the centre of the hall, leaving a decent space between her and Titus. She gives him a small, hopeful smile.

Titus sneers down at her, the picture of dominant disapproval.

Minnie's smile falters.

"You are nothing to me," Titus announces his proclamation to the room.

That triggers Minnie because her anima bursts forth. Her mask of bravery bleeds into a snarl. "I am your *regina!*"

The revelation sweeps through the room in a crushing wave.

More than a few people gasp. Her friends, including Aurelia, stare at each other in shock. Savage frowns at Minnie. No one except Lady Celeste and Lyle know about the bonds in the school. I only knew because I could see their auras chasing each other every time they were in the same room.

Aurelia suspected it too. I can see it in the way she's concentrating; eyes darting between Minnie and Titus in an assessing, focused way. I watch her carefully, trying to figure out if what she did was on purpose or not. If my regina is as malevolent and cunning as I'd suspected from the very beginning.

What she'd done was something the daughter of Mace Naga, heir to the serpent throne would do.

But the more I watch Aurelia, the more my shark thrashes, trying to tell me something that I don't want to hear right now.

Minnie crosses her arms and juts her chin out, suddenly transformed into the dominant regina she was born to be. Suddenly given herself permission to be. "I kept it secret because you wanted me to, but I shouldn't have!"

Titus stomps up to her, a lethal beast in human skin. "If you were my regina, then where the fuck is your mating mark?"

The lights in the room seem to flicker. Aurelia's heartbeat skyrockets.

"You've seen it before!" Minnie says, touching the right side of her neck. "When we first met, it was there. We both saw it! It's just—"

"Just *what?*" snarls Titus, jabbing her in the chest. "You are an abomination. You are *wrong*. I let this go on for too fucking long. I should be a *rex*."

Titus isn't the only haughty male to protest fate not making him a rex. Of fate declaring that they bow to a regina. But eventually, males turn around. Eventually, they cannot deny their animus and the fact that their regina is stronger than them. Worthy of holding the position.

But Titus isn't a normal animus. Some males are born into psychopathy. Some males will never give in. It's rare, but I've seen it a handful of times. Most of those males end up at Blackwater or simply getting killed off by other males, usually members of their mating group.

"Titus," Minnie says, her voice suddenly small. "I—"

"Do *not* speak my name!" he snarls.

Like a skip in the melody, the song of Aurelia's power, the one she cast months ago, stutters.

Chapter 63

Aurelia

No.
No.
No.

I stare between my best friend and Titus Clawson. I stare harder.

Keep them safe. Keep them safe. Keep them safe. It's a hymn I've prayed into the aether for weeks now.

But Minnie can't see her own mating mark? Just in the same way I can't see my mating mark when I've hidden it? Except that's always on purpose.

A memory comes back to me, on old, dark, fearful wings.

On our first day at the academy, when Minnie and I stood side by side in front of the entire male population of the school for mating lines.

Against my better judgement, I grab Minnie's hand.

To my utter and profound relief, she doesn't shake me off and grips me tightly back. I hate that I look weak, but my blood is pounding in my ears and I can't breathe. I'm a predator. An apex predator, and there is nothing I fear.

I chanted it over and over again like a ritual mantra. I reenforced all seven of my shields to protect myself from the mates I thought were going to kill me.

Not realising that by clinging onto Minnie so fiercely, I extended one of those same shields to her.

I squint at my best friend, trying to feel it out... and finding it. A tiny tether. A tiny thread that enveloped her neck and kept her mating mark hidden.

Panic spears me through the gut.

Her mating mark is invisible because of me.

I only wanted safety. I only wanted to protect myself.

Why didn't she tell me she couldn't see her mark?

Fuck!

I frantically project to her, *"Minnie, I think this was me. I'm so sorry. I think this is my fault."*

Minnie whirls around to stare at me, her eyes wide. "What?"

Silently, I pull back on that tiny bite of power I shared with her. Not the psychic one that protects her from the serpents, but the mating mark one, so well disguised, nestled so tightly it was invisible even to me.

I can't see it, but I feel it come down.

Titus' eyes become dangerous as they flick down to Minnie's neck and he lets out a lethal sort of sound.

Minnie whirls back around and gasps. "Can you see it now?" she cries, reaching for her neck. "I can see it there on you!" She steps towards him, grabbing him by the forearms. "Do you see it?"

She can see his matching mark now too.

I want to tell her to get away from him. To run, to hide, to fucking just stop touching that monster. But she won't. She loves him. She's his regina. She won't ever let him go.

"Stupid snake girl," Xander says coolly in my head. *"You really fucked up."*

I take a step forward to run to Minnie, but Scythe's harsh

voice cuts through the racing panic in my brain. *"Let it go, Aurelia. You've done enough."*

It's only that last sentence that stops me in my tracks as Titus pushes Minnie back so hard she cries out.

Blood pours down her forearm from a long, thin laceration.

The tiger claw that is now Titus' right hand is tinged red with blood. "It's not enough," he snarls. "It never fucking was."

Chapter 64

Scythe

Blood spills, streaming down Minnie's arm. My shark stills in fascination at the sight of the crimson droplets as the little tigress stares in horror and disbelief.

And then Titus says the Old Words, snarling and hateful. "I officially reject you as my regina, Minnie Devi."

In my mad, sorry life, I have never seen a person shatter as Minnie does now. Her aura fractures in the same way bone does; it bleeds the same way a mortal laceration does.

Her face crumples at the same time as her knees.

This is a soul wound and it will live with her forever.

Aurelia cries out as Minnie collapses to the wooden floor, her body limp, her skin suddenly ashen. I take a step forward, but the one of the two ghosts beside me jumps up and down.

"*Unholy,*" he hisses excitedly. "*A black blade makes a black wound.*" He looks at me and points at Minnie. "*End her pain. End her. Mercy.*"

The second ghost just stares at me like he always does. That malevolent smile fixed on his ugly face.

I tear my gaze off him like I have every day since he appeared.

The limp tigress emits no physical cry, but the timbre of grief shatters through the astral plane, sharp as a knife, black as death. It makes me shiver. Pure shock sweeps through the crowd in hues of black, grey, and dull red.

I have seen and done many a dark thing in my life, but I've never witnessed the official ritual of rejection. It's a heinous act for our kind, worse than murder. Murder is *preferred* over this. We all turn towards Titus, who stands defiantly, with his chin in the air and his hands loose, as if he's completed some grand act. Something worthy of admiration.

Only a true psychopath would be so unaffected by an official rejection of his soul-group.

The shark in me levels him a new look. It marks him for his lack of emotion, marks him for the potential threat he poses to our family.

As Minnie was his regina, it was his right to reject her. But that didn't mean I couldn't slit his throat over it.

Minnie's friends hurry to surround her, but she doesn't move from her face down position. Theresa pushes through the crowd to kneel beside them and shake Minnie's shoulder. But the tigress is completely unresponsive. She could've been dead if I couldn't hear her heartbeat. A heart that will never beat quite the same.

Aurelia tries to turn her over, but Minnie is a dead weight.

"We have to get her out of here," she says to her friends, but they're all awkward hands and limbs.

Ernie, one of my own guards, steps forward, but I hold up a hand. "She shouldn't be touched by an animus. Not now." I gesture to Connor, likely the physically strongest of her friends. "Lion anima. Take your friend back to her room. Keep her warm."

Connor nods and puts his arms under Minnie's body. But I'm not watching him. I'm watching the Siberian tiger across from me, where he stands at the edge of the crowd, as pale as his white hair. Like a spectre. As if he's also left his body and staring at Minnie as if he's seen heaven and hell all at the same time.

"Everyone out!" I bark.

Everyone jumps out of their shocked stupor rushes to leave the rec room, as if they can't get away fast enough from the dark deed that was done here. The guards and counsellors herd them all along. Titus also leaves and doesn't so much as cast a glance back at his old regina. Eventually, only a few of our own remain, solemn and quiet.

But still, Yeti stands unmoving, his eyes unseeing his hand limp. It confirms everything for me. No doubt it's an agony worse than death to see your regina broken by a bond cutting. Let alone realising she's your regina at the same moment.

Xander steps up to Yeti.

"Do not touch him," I warn. "He will be unstable."

Yeti's mouth moves, forming words we can't hear. I listen to his heart. It beats in arrhythmia and I watch him carefully. I have heard a bond cutting can cause death for weaker beasts in the pack. But though Minnie succumbed, she didn't yield. And I know Yeti well enough to guess that he won't yield to this soul-wound either.

"Mine," Yeti's mouth makes the sound. A hoarse whisper, like the scrape of leaves across a tombstone. "She's always been mine."

"Yes," I say slowly, using my voice to ground him. "Minnie is yours. As you are hers. It was just hidden from you for a time."

He stares into space, his pale eyes glistening. "How?"

No one knew it to be possible. It's Boneweaver magic cast by someone who doesn't even know the extent of her power. I won't name her and put in her in potential danger. Savage cuts me a sharp look.

"Bigger powers," I say. "It wasn't intentional. You must trust fate."

Xander extracts his dragon-strength hand rolled weed from his pocket and holds it up as a question. I nod.

He lights it with a lick of a flame from his finger. "Come, my friend," Xander coos in a gentle, rare voice he only uses with his sister's children. "Smoke this and let us sit and talk."

Yeti opens his mouth only because he doesn't know what else to do. He takes a drag.

"Deeper," Xander instructs.

Yeti breathes in deeply and his pupils dilate. He blinks once, then twice. "I need to kill him," he says.

"You have your orders," I say sharply. "You took a blood oath to me. No one will touch that swine."

Despite my even, harsh tone, my shark thrashes in an awful, bitter realisation as we understand that all of Lyle's suspicions have been true.

Xander leads a catatonic Yeti away, Savage on his other side and the rest of our beasts following just in case.

"I felt it that first day," Lyle's voice comes careening into my head. *"Whenever I'm inside her, I feel her power. Going out and out. This is why she went into that state of fugue."*

I don't reply.

"You don't want to admit it, do you?"

Admit fucking what.

That Aurelia has been shielding more than herself? This entire time. That she has been psychically shielding the entire school?

Initially, I thought the school had awoken, and it was ancient dragon magic rising to protect the dwelling of the old dragon lords. The power is golden, vast and wild, like something old woken up. Like something beyond the rest of us.

But it was *her* Boneweaver power all along. Wild and strong and... protective. She was protecting us all from psychic attacks. The entire academy. Her friends. *Us.*

"*This is why she's always drained,*" is all I say. "*Why she is always unwell.*"

"*Fucking admit it, you cold bastard,*" Lyle says. "*She's been protecting us from the Serpent Court the entire time. Protecting you.*"

Chapter 65

Aurelia

Connor rushes Minnie back to our dorm.

"What the fuck?" Stacey sobs as we jog. "What the actual fuck just fucking happened?"

None of us, even Theresa, say anything because what is there left to say? Minnie is alive, but she doesn't look it. My fingers itch to heal her. But when my magic rushes into her, there is nothing to heal. I can't help her with this wound. That I caused. It makes bile rise in my throat in disgust at myself.

Lyle meets us on the way to our dorm, a serious, calculating expression on that angelic face.

"What—" He sees Minnie and his face softens.

We all begin to talk at once.

"I saw what happened," he says stiffly, cutting us off and putting out his arms. "Let me—"

"No!" all four of us bark at the same time.

"Use your telekinesis," Lyle says gently, bending down to look at Minnie's face. "It'll be gentler on her."

The four of us get our shit together and Sabrina, Stacey, Connor and I use our collective telekinesis to hover Minnie so we can gently manoeuvre her towards the dorm. Lyle follows us at a prowl, all the way up to our room where we put Minnie on her bed.

"Keep her warm," Lyle says from the door.

We don't say that Scythe has already told us that.

"Will she be okay?" asks Stacey, wringing her hands as I climb into Minnie's bed and pull her to my chest. Raquel kicks off their shoes and sits at the foot of the bed, pulling up the covers around us.

"She's shivering!" I exclaim, watching as my best friend curls into the fetal position against my body, trembling like she's freezing.

Theresa places a hand on Minnie's head like she's checking her temperature. "I've never seen this happen before."

Sabrina goes to the panel on the wall to turn up the heat of the room.

"That won't help," Lyle says softly. "Whether she wants to recover is up to her now." And with a gentleness that makes my heart weak, Lyle steps up to Minnie's altar and strikes up a match. He lights a candle and burns an incense stick, placing it in its crescent moon holder.

"Oh Goddess," Stacey cries, her voice thick. "Why didn't she ever tell us about being his regina?"

"I don't blame her at all," I say, my voice dead and empty. "Have you met the guy? I would've done—"

But I did the exact same thing. Am currently *doing* the exact same thing. Stacey goggles her wet eyes at me, nodding. "Yeah, I get it."

Lyle turns to look at me, desperately clinging onto Minnie's tiny shaking form. His amber eyes glow with something as they take me in and I wonder if he's ever considered it. If any of them have ever actually considered formally rejecting me.

Even though they tried to hand me over to my father with every intention to kill me, they've never struck me like Titus struck Minnie and made her bleed. Have never bitten me to cause damage. Nor have they humiliated me in public. They've been villains with… standards.

Then, to my surprise, the deputy headmaster comes up to where I lie on the bed. Theresa moves to the side.

Minnie unconsciously stiffens at the presence of another animus and I hold my breath. But Lyle only brushes a tender knuckle over my cheek, and his voice is a low rasp, almost as if he's talking to himself. "Keep her safe. Remind her what she needs to live for."

I turn back to my best friend, babbling and blubbering into her hair and hoping she can hear me. "You matter, Minnie. You matter to me and you matter to all of us. I even think you matter to Savage. He has a soft spot for you, did you know? It might have been the fairy bread incident, or maybe it was because of that time you tackled him to the ground to save me." Raquel and Connor laugh softly through their tears.

I clutch my friend tighter to my chest and pray.

Chapter 66

___

Lyle

Ten years ago

It's fitting that my mating mark arrived from the heavens bathed in blood, burning through it as if uninhibited and unrestrained despite the darkness around it.

I'm crawling through the red, dusty soil on my hands and knees, like an animal through the gathering death, when I see something glimmering. It's in a pool of blood, deep enough that it hasn't yet clotted or dried in the harsh heat of the outback. I drag myself to it and stare. Because there is the reflection not of some foreign thing, but my own self. Upon my own human flesh, freshly forged in the stars and now branded on new skin is a skull, wreathed in five beams of light.

"I am not alone," I whisper in wonder.

When a man has nothing left, he might become an animal. Teeth and claw, hate and fear. But he also might become something else. Something that yearns for a vision of more than just himself. I do not believe in a god anymore. But in that sacred symbol, I find belief in my regina. My own blue fairy. Because she's there, as real as the dawn on my skin and etched into my soul. Her heart beats alongside my own.

It is the only thing that makes me move away from that place of torture and grief. That urges me not to stay and die here with the rest of my slaughtered family, but to move on and find *her*. To become a man worthy of her and not an animal worthy of execution.

I had been ready to die but now I know that I'm not alone.

She kept me alive. Even when I didn't know her.

Yeti and I are sitting on the floor outside Aurelia and Minnie's dorm on the third day of Minnie's 'catatonia', as Lyle calls it. The white Siberian tiger leans against one wall and I on the opposite as we pass a joint back and forth. It's the usual kind. He doesn't need the dragon-strength anymore.

In the first hour after the worst thing to happen in a beast's life happened to him, Yeti was like a zombie, unable to talk or move or even blink. After about an hour, he fell into a deep, blind rage and it took me, Ruben, Lyle *and* Xander to wrestle him underground into a cage where he beat at the electric bars for hours. Eventually, with his skin melted through to the bone, he passed out. When he woke up, he did it again, demanding to see his regina. And demanding to see the demon who'd wounded her so badly.

He wouldn't see sense until the next day, when, dehydrated and covered in burns, he was sane enough to listen to Lyle's ultimatum.

Behave, and he could keep vigil outside his regina's door. Even then, he had to be supervised by one of us at all times.

An animus raging to protect his regina is a mighty thing. And Yeti raged better than anyone I know. I'm proud of my friend. He's also suffered as I have: not able to see his regina's mating mark, but wanting her anyway.

"She was mine this entire time," Yeti repeats for the millionth time as he stares holes at the closed wooden door, his voice so hoarse from roaring and screaming it's almost like Scythe's. It's like he still doesn't quite believe what he's saying.

"It's fucked up," I agree as I take a drag and blow blue smoke up into the air.

Yeti levitates the joint from my hand and it soars straight between his lips. He raises a now scarred hand to smoke it. A bag of chips crinkles by his elbow. We're surrounded by food Yeti brought up from the dining hall after threatening the boys who work there. There's, biscuits, scones, bags of chips, and a whole heap of cupcakes littered all around us, and I'm not allowed to touch any of it.

It's not for us, and it's not even for him. Yeti won't eat until he feeds his regina. That's always the proper way when an animus meets his regina. But I don't know how long Yeti will starve because Minnie hasn't given him a gift and accepted him yet. She's still asleep in there, recovering from the massive blow Titus gave her.

A tingle at the back of my neck tells me Xander has entered the anima dorm, and it takes a moment for us to see him stalking down the corridor. There's two bottles of whiskey and three glasses in his hands. Xander has always liked Yeti because they both share a general serious, grumpy attitude.

"Come to join the fun?" I ask.

Xander sits his big body opposite me, stretching his legs out and keeping a respectful distance from the volatile male and his horde of food.

"Something like that," he says through the joint between his own mouth as he pours each of us a measure of alcohol.

"Someone has to keep you two in line with all these reginas roaming about."

Yeti grunts his thanks as he accepts a glass. I down mine with relish and savour the sultry burn of animalia strength alcohol.

"Maybe we should check on her," Yeti says, still staring down the wood like he can see through the door. "Can you see through the door, Xan?"

"You know I don't do that."

"They could be changing clothes!" I say, affronted. "Or on the toilet. It's every beast's right to take a shit in peace by himself. Or herself." I slap my thigh for emphasis.

"Indeed." Xander clinks his glass to mine. "But no one is in the bathroom. I sense them still on Minnie's bed."

I can sense Aurelia isn't in the bathroom too, but I didn't want to hurt Yeti's feelings because he probably can't sense Minnie so well yet. I'm so excited for him though, now we can share ideas on regina things. Scythe and Xander won't talk to me about that stuff, and Lyle is always occupied with academy things.

Yeti growls low and deep. He wants to be in Minnie's bed. I know that because I want to be in Aurelia's bed, with my nose buried in her hair and our legs tangled together. I want her vanilla cupcake scent in my brain, on my cock, and her warmth nestled in my arms.

"Who would have thought our reginas would be best friends?" I say to try and lighten the mood. "But if you're one of the most powerful tigers we know, then that means Minnie is..."

There's another prickle on my skin.

"Very powerful, yes," Yeti says. "I could always smell it on her, it's just she looks so... sweet that I didn't pay it too much attention."

"Why do you think I put her in there?" Lyle's growling voice cuts through our conversation. I roll my eyes as we turn to see both the lion and Scythe stalking down the corridor like a pair of males who mean business. There's probably never been so many bossy animuses in this dorm.

Yeti leaps to his feet. "I want to go in there."

"I know you do," Lyle says evenly. "So do I. They've had enough time."

The door to my left opens a crack and I scent leopard and wolf, as well as wet hair and shampoo.

"We're coming too!" Sabrina says, stomping out of her dorm.

They've been taking turns cuddling with Minnie in bed. But we don't talk about it because it makes Yeti punch the wall to hear of his regina being shared with others, even if they're animas. Stacey made a glittery, colour-coded roster and stuck it on the dorm door so we can all see whose turn it is to be with Minnie while the others sleep and eat. They haven't been going to classes, which Lyle isn't happy about, but he lets it slide.

Lets it slide because this has never happened in his academy before. I also jump to my feet, pumped to finally see my regina again.

Chapter 68

Aurelia

Eugene's future-warning squawk from Minnie's purple armchair wakes me from my doze. I check on Minnie, who's nestled safely in my arms, when a soft but commanding knock comes at the door. They don't wait before opening it.

Light from the corridor spills into the darkened room. We've had the curtains closed the entire time because Minnie cringes whenever we open them.

"Let her grieve!" I bark hoarsely when I recognise the large figures outside.

Gertie and Henry chirp in agreement where they sit on the pillow above my head.

"It's been three days," Lyle says patiently as he stalks inside. His mating mark gleams through the dark and his scent fills my nose like perfume. "Minnie needs to eat. Her kidneys need water."

"Theresa and I have been monitoring that," I mutter, stroking Minnie's hair off her forehead where she rests against my chest. In truth, I *am* worried. Minnie won't drink water and her kidney function is starting to show signs of being affected. She hardly has any urine in her bladder.

"Then you know," Lyle says. "She needs to get up. That she needs her mate."

Something in my stomach lurches. Lyle told us all that Yeti is Minnie's mate. That whatever power suppressing Minnie's mating mark meant Yeti couldn't see it as well. The moment I took off Minnie's secret mating mark shield, Yeti knew. And then went through subsequent hell.

'Whatever power' being me and my good-for-nothing ass. I'm responsible for Yeti's torment, too. I owe him... Is an apology even good enough? No. It never will be. Nothing I can say will fix this mess I've made.

I deserve to rot in hell. I deserve the pain life has dealt me so far.

But Minnie stirs then. "Yeti?" Her coarse whisper almost breaks me.

It aches to hear her voice sound so fragile. She's been speaking in single words for the past day and I'm hoping that means she's almost ready to get up.

"I'm here!" Yeti calls. His deep voice sounds frantic and desperate, completely the opposite of the beast who escorted us for trial at Scythe's court. "Minnie!"

"Don't bring him in here," I call. "Until Minnie says."

"I can speak for myself now." Minnie's voice is barely a breath. She clears her throat. "Let us clean up," she says to Lyle, rubbing her eyes. "We will be out shortly."

Lyle nods and turns back around. The door clicks shut and I swear I hear more than one sigh of relief.

"Well, I'm impressed," I say, carefully extracting myself from Minnie's bed. "I would've—well, I don't even know what I would've done."

Minnie smiles without humour. "I need help with my hair. I... I want to look nice. Can you call Sabrina?"

"Girlfriend," I say gently, "you can have whatever the fuck you want. Let's call the team and we'll get right to it."

"Not you."

I freeze, cold fingers raking through my stomach. Through my spine. Through my world. "What?"

"You heard me," Minnie says quietly, not meeting my eye. "I know what you did. To me."

The backs of my eyes burn as I register Minnie's stiff shoulders, the darkness beneath her eyes. The darkness in her voice.

She's right. What I did was inexcusable. Nothing will fix it.

"I'm sorry, Min," I whisper, bile rising in my throat. "I can't make this better, I'm so—"

"Please," she whispers. If she had tears left, I think she'd be crying again. "Please, just leave."

Biting my lip hard before I break down, I flee the room via the secret door to Lyle's apartment, with Henry hurrying to follow while I shoot Raquel a mental message.

* * *

Fifteen minutes later, I'm on the floor of Lyle's shower with Henry, sobbing into my arms under the onslaught of warm water, when I hear it.

Male voices arguing. Leaving the water running, I crawl out of the bathroom and wrap a towel around myself. Heading into the bedroom, I shove my ear up against the door and train my ears to hear what my mates are talking so heatedly about.

I hear everything.

"We don't even know the beginnings of what she's capable of," Lyle says, clearly pacing up and down the living room. "Has anyone even stopped to consider what the hell she can do?"

"Lyle, you're projecting your own insecurities onto her," Scythe's cold, emotionless voice replies.

"You were the one who told me we should be wary of her power, Scythe."

"In the wrong hands, she's a weapon," Scythe says. "Mace Naga isn't truly her father. He's a man who saw an opportunity with his offspring and wants to capitalise on it."

My stomach churns.

"You're talking about her like she's a business asset," Savage snarls. "She's a human, for the Mother's sake."

"Only part human," Lyle murmurs. "And her anima is fighting back."

"You're projecting again," Savage growls.

"And you are blinded by love!" Lyle says. Then more quietly, "As I was. I've been a fool not to see it."

My breath catches and I clutch my stomach as his words hit me. I really want to vomit now.

"It's not natural to fight your instincts like this," Savage says. "That's half your problem, Lyle."

"If I let my animus out, no one would fucking survive," Lyle sneers. "Including me."

"Well, that sounds like a grand plan to me," Xander says drolly.

I've heard enough.

Climbing to my feet, I wipe my nose on the edge of my towel and make sure my boobs are covered before I wrestle open the door and step out.

Four heads whip up as I walk out, and whatever anger I have dissipates in a whoosh of emptiness. There are bluish bags under Lyle's eyes and he's bracing his hands on the kitchen bench like he's about to lose it. Or lost it already. Savage looks sort of pale under his tan as he leans against the fireplace. His face lights up as he stalks towards me. Both Scythe and Xander sit on an armchair each, smoking that weed they like so much. Their faces are grave. Their energy is like a maelstrom in the centre of the room.

And it's all because of me.

"It's little Boneweaver," Xander says nastily. "The one who's more dangerous than we thought."

"What are you talking about?" I grit out, trying to fight my own clashing emotions.

He shrugs his broad shoulders. "Just that what you did, is the exact reason we wanted you dead. You have powers that no one, including you, knows anything about. You're an unknown. A danger. To us. To everyone."

Rage thrusts its sharp claws through my veins. "I am not! I've never hurt anyone!"

The room is dead silent, the words hanging in the air like a corpse from a tree. I still feel Minnie's dead weight in my arms.

Savage takes both my hands and kisses them, smiling down at me like I'm the best thing in the world and suddenly I can't look at him.

Lyle asks in a tight voice that makes me stare at him, "*Can you control your powers, Aurelia?*"

I see it in his eyes. He's thinking about his school. His other students. If I'm a danger to them. If he will have to protect them from *me*.

When everything I've done was to protect my friends, the unfairness of it tears at my heart. The wet wounds on my stomach burn incessantly like an echo of my mad efforts.

"What?" I step away from Savage. "Yes, Yes, I can. Of course. I've been in control this entire time."

Xander snorts. "Have you? Then what was that you did to your so-called best friend?"

My words get stuck in my throat. I'd used my mating mark shield to protect myself from the very males standing before me.

Savage steps forward "She just needs to learn—"

"She needs a fucking muzzle!" Xander cries.

"Shut the fuck up, Xander," Savage growls, stepping in front of me like he can defend me from the rest of them. "I love her the way she is. Dangerous and all."

Xander moves his head like he's rolling his eyes and leans back into the armchair.

"I didn't mean to do that to Minnie," I say firmly. "I don't care if you don't believe me, Lyle. I don't fucking care if *any* of you don't believe me."

"I believe you, regina," Savage says helpfully.

"I believe you about your intentions," Lyle sighs. "But others might not be so understanding. I've spoken to Minnie, and she wants space. She wants to get to know Yeti better and come to terms with all of this."

I swallow against the memory of Minnie's face. "I understand. She told me to leave the dorm."

Savage sighs, putting his arm around me and resting his chin on my head. "Come and stay with me, regina. I've wanted you with me forever."

"I've allocated Minnie and Yeti a room in the pack-dorms," Lyle says. "That way, she's far from Titus."

"And far from me," I complete for him.

It makes me want to curl up into a ball and hide at the way asking this question makes me feel, but I do it anyway. "Can't I stay here?"

Lyle straightens, a small crease forming between his brows, and my heart stutters. I know the answer. I've always known it.

"No." It's firm and strong and made of something stronger than steel. And then he continues in that way of his, unyielding. unbreakable. "We've done this for too long. We've had our fun. Now it's time to go back to normal."

"Our *fun?*" I repeat with disgust. "Is that what we're calling it?"

"You should not have come here and you know it. Have you forgotten that you *still* have an order out for your execution?

That at *any* moment, the council can decide to overrule the injunction?"

It's a low blow and by the way Savage growls, he thinks so too.

I blink at him, my fists clenching as I try with every ounce of willpower not to let the tears spill. "Where else would I have gone?" My voice rises to a shrill cry, "Where the fuck else would I have gone where people don't want to kill me at every *fucking* turn?"

Savage's arms tighten around me, like he can hold me together with his strength.

"Where any other student would have gone, Miss Aquinas," Lyle grits out, stepping towards me. "To Sabrina and Raquel's room, or to Stacey's room."

I stand there, staring at him, my body still, my bones rattling. This is really him kicking me out of here.

Kicking me out of his life. Forever.

It stings like a hot barb pressed into my chest. But I will not buckle before him. I refuse.

"So that's it then?" I ask, breathing heavily against the oncoming storm that's about to wrack my body.

He stares me down, hard, commanding, unmovable. "That's all it can be."

I snarl at him, baring my teeth, "You're a *lying* asshole, Lyle Pardalia."

He strides out of the apartment, leaving only a chill to rival Scythe's in his wake. Even Savage's warmth wrapping around mine can barely stave away that icy burn.

Chapter 69

Aurelia

With my arms wrapped around myself, I ascend the stairs to the hidden floor in the animus door in front of Eugene and Savage, the latter of whom holds my duffle bag.

I planned to fulfil my promise to Savage and spend weekends in his dorm, but between one thing and another, we've never had the chance. It's been delayed long enough. People have already been wondering where I went those days I had my casts on and stayed in Lyle's apartment. The last thing I want is people getting suspicious about me getting special treatment.

I made my point in that courtroom the day my bones were broken and it seems to have granted me some respect amongst the animuses. Respect or fear of my unstable mental state. One of the two.

And after *that* conversation with Lyle, I'm definitely not feeling any sort of stable, but it's time for me to bite the bullet and finally sleep in Savage's den and in the same room as Scythe and Xander.

"Everything will be okay, pup," Raquel's voice floats into my mind. *"Just rest easy. Minnie is okay. She was shy with Yeti at*

first, but I think seeing their mating marks made them happy. She cried, and he held her. It was beautiful. He's feeding her now. Mr Pardalia made sure."

"I just wish I'd been there to support her."

Raquel is silent for a moment. *"She has her mate now. We'll miss her in our dorm, but she is where she belongs... and so are you. With your mates, Lia."*

Raquel is right. Fuck, they are really right on this.

"But we just wanted to check." Raquel's mental voice turns tentative. *"You didn't accidentally put Boneweaver magic on the rest of us did you? With the mating mark thing?"*

"No." I say quickly. *"I checked as soon as I realised."*

There's silence and then, *"Sabrina says she doesn't know whether to be insulted or relieved."*

I snort. *"You're all safe from me now."*

"Take care, Lia. We'll see you soon."

We close our mental connection as I walk into the living room of my mates' hidden suite. So what Lyle kicked me out of his nest? I have a second one anyway.

I previously snooped around here when I snuck in that one time to take revenge on Savage stealing my underwear, but the space feels completely different now. A little pang of sadness hits me, and for a moment, I want to steal my panties back from Lyle's bedside table.

But I can't. My anima keens and whines and I just... can't. Taking that little piece of myself from his apartment feels so wrong and my anima vehemently agrees.

Scythe and Xander are, thankfully, not present when we enter, and Savage enthusiastically shows me and Henry around. My faithful ball of blue fluff immediately leaves me to take a detailed look at everything, and Eugene finds his usual perch on Savage's bedside table.

I try to focus on my new way of living away from my dorm. There's the main living area with couches, the dining table, and the alcohol cabinet. There are a few adjoining rooms. The first is the massive bedroom with the three beds, the second has a giant TV and PlayStation set up, and the last one is a locked room Savage does not open. My wolf leads me into the bedroom and places my duffle bag on the bed in the middle. His bed. He grins at me and shows me the wardrobes allocated to each of them, and then leads me into the bathroom.

It's huge and luxurious. All shiny black tile with ornate gold finishings and two chandeliers, all worthy of a dragon manor.

There's a massive shower with three sparkling gold heads, with all their shower products lined into a recess in the tiled wall. Opposite that are three sinks beneath a wide mirror with a gilded frame of flying dragons.

Savage explains that Xander instructed the school's magic to make adjustments for the three of them and, if he wants to, we can make a fourth set of everything. But I shake my head because I don't actually think Xander would appreciate me coming in and changing things, being the awful serpent princess I am.

But it's what's on the other side of the showers that makes me gape a little. There's a spa—no, *pool* would probably be a more appropriate word—built into the floor. Ten people could easily fit within its depths, and it's currently filled with steaming water that looks divine. There are black dragon-head faucets all around, ready to spew water from their mouths.

"I know," Savage says proudly. "Wherever we go, we have to have something like this. Scythe needs it because he always has to be around water or he's hard to deal with, and Xander needs it to blow off steam because..." Savage rubs the back of his head and gives me a grin. "Well, he also becomes hard to deal with."

I step closer to him and trace a finger over his chest, covered in a T-shirt for once. "Does that mean you're the only one who's easy to deal with?"

He chuckles and places a hand over my own. "Nope. I'm still going to hassle you the entire time you're here."

We spend the rest of the afternoon curled up on the couch in front of the TV, eating the blessed pizza delivered by Ernie, one of the big bear shifter guards on Scythe's payroll. He smiles at my offered hand when Savage introduces me and *bows* at me instead.

"Regina," Savage chides after he leaves. "None of our beasts can touch you. You belong to me."

"Oh right," I say, frowning into my barbeque chicken pizza. "I'd forgotten about that."

It's been seven and a bit years since I left my father's household, but I've forgotten some of the minor rules of etiquette when it comes to animas and reginas. It's considered impolite to touch an anima if they belong to a pack. In fact, it's an outright breach if you do. If you want to start a fight, it's the best way to do it.

There's still no sign of Scythe or Xander by the time I ask Savage to go to bed. I change into my cute lacy purple sleep shorts and tank top set and, in the darkened room, crawl into Savage's single bed. He pulls me into his arms, smelling of spearmint toothpaste and soap.

"We really need to do something about these beds," he says, wriggling himself into a comfortable position where he's spooning me. "I wonder if Scythe will let us get a pack bed."

The pack dorms have big bedrooms where there are massive communal beds for each pack to sleep in. Together.

"Unlikely," I snort as Henry zips over to where I've set up his nesting pillow on Savage's bedside table.

Eugene clucks sleepily from where he sits on Savage's headboard.

"Goodnight, Eugene. Goodnight, Hen," I say sleepily. "Is Eugene your prisoner?"

"We have a friendly agreement," Savage mumbles into my hair. "Don't worry about him." The way he says 'friendly' doesn't sound so friendly at all.

It's then that I hear noises from outside. The thud of heavy males, the quiet murmur of deep voices. I don't notice I've stiffened until Savage rubs at my arms.

"Will they mind?" I whisper.

"Of course not," Savage says, but for once, the usual arrogance doesn't pepper his tone.

The bedroom door opens and both men are shadowy giants who quietly head for the bathroom. I listen intently. Having been granted access to their personal, private area, me and my anima are keen to know how they sound as they attend to their nightly routine. How they brush their teeth, how they scrub their bodies as they shower.

"You're not breathing, regina," Savage grumbles.

I huff a little at being caught out. "Sorry."

"Just don't try and start anything."

I'm suddenly wide awake. "Pardon?"

"You know what I mean."

"No, I don't." I sit up to glare at him, and his eyes glint through the dark.

Savage sighs. "You know, don't try and sass them. Or start a fight."

I slap him on the shoulder. "How dare you! If I want to start something, I bloody well will!"

He chuckles and tugs on my arm. I hear the shower turn off, so I quickly lie back down.

"I'm going to sleep now," I announce.

"Good girl."

I smile despite myself and am happy he can't see it. But it also means that when they're finished, I have a perfect view of the bathroom as the door opens and light and steam cascades out. The smell of male soap and marijuana fills my nose.

Xander's massive form trudges to the other side of the room to his bed, white eyes glowing. And Gods, it's pretty creepy at night to see two white glowing balls floating through the air, the glowing red of the joint stuck in his mouth beneath that. I lose sight of him as he climbs onto his bed.

Scythe is a little less dramatic, but I keep my eyes closed as his near-silent movements make my heart drum up a dance. He opens the window between his and Savage's bed and it's only then that I crack open my lids to see what he's doing.

Moonlight streams through where he's opened the curtain and his towering form stands predator-still by the window. His eyes are closed, and his head upturned a little as if in prayer. As if in soaking in the moonlight on his bare face and torso. Scythe's skin is made blue-silver by the moon, and it graces every perfect muscle of his tattooed neck, chest, arms, abs and...

He could be Poseidon himself. Or a warrior-god worshipping the night in humble silence. In another time, someone would have written a song about Scythe. He's worthy of an epic ballad or a poem.

I gulp as he turns away from me to drape himself prone upon his bed, his movement liquid and sensual.

In the dark of night, while I pretend to be asleep, I have one earth-shattering revelation.

Scythe sleeps naked.

I stare. And stare. And stare.

A moonbeam cuts through the window, highlighting the supreme curve of his naked, muscular ass and thighs, letting me see that both of which are covered in sprawling ink. Not an inch of his skin is left unmarked. And it feels like this is quite purposeful.

A shudder wracks my body right down to my toes. By the Wild Goddess, how the *hell* am I going to survive spending every night in this bedroom?

Chapter 70

Scythe

urelia's heartbeat is like a doe's rapid tenor in the presence of three predators. And the fourth who is forever watching.

It's fluttery and soft. Almost featherlight. I wonder how it would feel against my cheek. I don't really sleep. Above the sea, I never really do.

But tonight, for the first time in decades, I sigh a long sigh and listen to that fluttery song as it gradually turns slower and more even. I let it lull me as gentle ocean waves lull a boat.

I know the exact moment sleep takes her and only then do I turn my head to look. At this woman who is destined for me and my brothers. She's swathed in the shadows of the room, but her mating mark glows for me, as I commanded her. I watch her breathing. I watch the glow of her soft skin through the night. I watch the way she twitches alongside Savage, who has also always twitched in his sleep since he was a baby. I watch the way my brother huddles into her and the way she relaxes into him, her body softening, almost melting into him, like she's received some silent, primitive communication of safety.

"I would never be safe with you."

Those words uttered by her mouth, torn out by anger and fear, still sit within my bones. I thought about them every night since she said it many full moons ago.

And here she is now, in a place her anima is telling her it's safe to sleep.

"*Do it,*" she'd commanded my brothers. To break her arms in my courtroom. To make a *point*. She ignored my mercy and defied my order.

The sound of her bones cracking echoes through me. The way her heart quaked in that moment.

Dangerous, she might be. But I've lived my life alongside danger. Alongside death. And I walk hand in hand with madness as if it's a lifelong friend.

I can see the beauty in her danger. In her.

It's as if fate knew the exact type of woman who could look me in my mad eyes and bring me crashing to my knees.

I stare at her long into the night.

Chapter 71

Aurelia

Scythe and Xander are gone when I wake up in the morning. And I'm thankful for it.

And so begins a week of nightmares.

In which, every day, I sit on my phone, stare at old photos of Frank Ulman and try to find a way out of my father's plans.

In which I get to watch Scythe sleep every night. In which I get to be cuddled by Savage.

In which, despite my worries, I get the best sleep of my life.

I can't stomach going to class and Savage says I don't have to. Raquel asks me to come back to attend classes like normal, but I make some pathetic excuse about feeling sick. Stacey sends me texts with memes and emojis, also demanding I come have dinner with them at the very least, but I decline her too. I have all the food I want with Savage bringing me whatever I ask for, including the fairy bread, which he makes himself. I have that multiple times because he told me it was Minnie's idea in the first place. He's getting pretty good at it too, and even cuts off the crusts in neat slices so I don't 'hurt my gums'.

Theresa isn't allowed in the animus dorms, only the male teachers are, so she can't come in here to accost me either. I don't hear from Lyle, and I suspect he's avoiding me. I get to add him to the list of people I need in my life and who don't want to be near me.

In a nutshell, it's all sunshine and roses. Well, not roses, because some days I don't even shower. I can't summon the energy.

My father is supposed to come here in one week and he expects me to present myself on a platter to him. And if I don't... my friends will certainly be put on a platter themselves.

I ask Savage if there's a way for me to bundle them up and whisk them away to somewhere safe that's beyond the reach of the Serpent Court. But the answer always comes back as *impossible*. Plus, none of my friends would agree to it. They're all at the academy under legal order.

Well, it was worth a try.

So I double down on my protections, burrowing into them like a wombat and constantly monitoring them so I never slip up. Lyle's words the day Minnie kicked me out were completely stupid. I'm not dangerous at all. I'm practically harmless. If I'm so dangerous, I would have come up with a way to deal with my father by now. If I'm *actually* a princess of the Serpent Court, I would have put some genius, malevolent plan in place to kill my father and overthrow him. It's probably what my dad himself would have done if he were in my place.

One day, after a few days of radio silence, Ghoul sends me a message.

> I can't stop thinking about that beautiful mouth, snakelet

I frown down at it before tossing my phone aside and returning to my second run of *The Twilight Saga: New Moon*. It suits my mood perfectly.

Reading the words over and over again in a sort of daze sends my memories back to the night three of my mates worshipped me, and I worshipped them right back. I tilt my head back on the couch's headrest, remembering the taste of Ghoul, power and poison all wrapped up in tattooed steel.

I hear it then. A shift in the air. Like a tiny pulse surging outward. Frowning, I sit up straight. Eugene lets out a low croon from where he's perched on the armchair adjacent to me.

Henry zips into the air, shifting this way and that like a dragonfly, as if sensing the air too.

"You guys feel that?" I whisper.

Both let out clucks of assent.

Shit.

I check my protections around the school, but they're all sound, and there's no movement outside them. Pushing my fleece blanket off my knees, I get off the couch, straining my ears, and step out of the TV room. Henry and Eugene make to follow me but I hold a hand up in a silent instruction to stay put. That primitive sense in my depths urges me to turn right. Within a few steps, I find myself standing outside a wide, black door. I've never taken too much notice of it before, but there is a pressure resonating from it, red and fiery.

There's also a lock.

And if there is a door locked with Xander's power, I would like to know exactly what's behind it. Especially since that pulse from before seems to be coming from within. Quickly fetching the set of lock picks Sabrina gifted me, I return and set to my task on the old-fashioned antique gold lock, almost exactly the same type on Lyle's office door. A style the academy seems to favour.

Perhaps for that exact reason, I can't pick the lock. Squinting at it, I tap the handle.

"Open!" I command.

When the door clicks open this time, I'm not stupid enough to traipse through it. I push it open, and immediately note the shimmery heat of a dragon-lock spanning the entire doorway.

I also immediately note the lone person chained to a metal

rack on the wall, covered in blood, her hair caked and stringy with it.

"Natalia?" I breathe in horror.

The cobra winces, before raising her head to glare at me. She looks haggard, with deep circles around her eyes and fresh wounds cutting into her cheek.

"Whore," Natalia rasps.

Xander did this. Scythe did this. Savage probably also did this. I'm stricken by the sight of her.

There's a toilet on one side of the room and a small table with a tray of leftovers and a water bottle, so I know they let her off sometimes. But... she's been here weeks now. *Weeks.*

"I'm so sorry," I whisper.

"Yeah, right," Natalia spits. "We did the same thing to you. Why the fuck do you care?"

Because I'm not the same as you. I don't say it out loud, but I know it to be true. I might have grown up in my father's court, where such things are normal. Where such things are encouraged. But the part of me that accepted this as normal died the day Theo Krait died.

"I'm getting you out."

She smiles without humour. "Yeah? I fucking dare you to try."

I stare at her and the dragon-trick door. Then out the dining-room window, where the glittering veil of the school's protections form a dome against freedom. I've never been able to find a way to get out of this place, and it's all I've wanted to do since the day I arrived.

And then it hits me.

There is only one person I know who can enter and exit the academy without being detected. I whip out my phone.

I need a favour

And what do I get in return, snakelet?

I could regina order you but I'm practising being nice

It's cute you think that would work on me

Alright, you get a favour in return

A blank cheque. Consider my interest piqued

I'm playing with poison, but somehow, I don't care. It's also turning me on that he's using fancy words. I add that to the list of things I know about Ghoul. He's educated. I text back quick instructions and the only thing I get back is:

I foresee you regretting this, snakelet

Five minutes later, an apex monster enters the academy. I don't know how he gets here so fast, no doubt a part of that monstrous power granted to him by fate. The walls quiver at the same time as my heart does. His body never manifests, but I feel his shadowy power as if he were breathing down my neck. A possessive, dominating caress tingles down my spine, before the room before me darkens.

I get to my feet from where I'm sitting cross-legged before the open door.

"Wait, what?" Natalia rasps and her eyes widen in surprise.

She stares at me in shock before the shadows wrap around her like a cloak. They both disappear and the only thing left is a whisper of a breeze and one last caress down my cheek.

With my heart pounding, I return to the TV room, where I wait for my mates to return.

Two hours later, when class ends and I feel Savage's wild, hectic energy bounce into the building, I summon the energy to assume an arms-crossed position in front of the torture room door.

All three of them file up the stairs, with Savage in the lead, jogging towards me. But when he sees where I stand, the smile falls off his face and he stalks up to me.

A shiver passes through my body as I sense the change in his energy. Like the moment the forest trembles as a predator walks through it.

"Regina," he says, stopping in front of me. His eyes flick over my head, and upon finding his prisoner missing, he meets my eye again. "What did you do?"

My eyes slide to Xander, then Scythe, both of whom stop just behind Savage. Their rage is like a living thing between us—hot, wild, and dark. But I weather it. I fucking grit my teeth and stand my ground as their combined rage dances a mad, malevolent circle around me.

To my surprise, it's Savage who speaks first, his voice trembling with restraint. "You had no right, regina," he whispers.

I turn my face towards his and meet him eye to eye. "I had the only right," I hiss. "She wronged *me*."

"Once a snake, always a snake," the dragon sneers.

Savage's mouth twists into a wry smile as he leans down into my face to whisper, "When will you understand, regina? You are *mine*. *My* regina. *My* everything. And an animus has every fucking right to destroy the beast who hurt their regina."

"Yeah, and what excuse do the others have?"

Xander scoffs. "She doesn't get it. Such a life of privilege to have never had to torture anyone."

Scythe has been staring at me this whole time, the only indication of his rage, the pure maelstrom that turns in his cold blue eyes. But in a blink, it's gone, and he turns away from me to sit down on his favourite black couch. "Come here, Aurelia."

Savage snarls softly in my face, not moving a muscle to yield me to his brother. "It was my right, regina," he whispers.

I snarl softly back. "And you did enough. Two weeks was enough. I ended it."

He angles his head as if considering this, eyes never leaving mine. Then, to my surprise, he takes my hand and kisses it. "I'm not happy, regina. But if that is your wish..."

"It is," I say firmly.

He kisses my hand again and straightens, the anger fading away and leaving only his normal, wild self behind. "Then that is all I need to hear."

Xander snorts, very much like a real dragon, and shakes his head where he's leaning against the windows, smoking a fresh hand-rolled joint. Savage steps aside, leaving me with a direct path to Scythe.

I approach the Great White with sure, confident steps as we regard each other. He sits on that couch not only like he owns the entire school, but like he owns his own emotions, too. He's the picture not of restraint—or control, like Lyle—but cold, cold death.

"It was enough, Scythe," I say slowly. "You did enough to her."

"Why do you think we did what we did, Aurelia?"

"Because that is what men like you do."

The corner of his mouth twitches. "And who are 'men like me'?"

"Men who hurt and torture and maim without thought."

Xander snorts again. "I assure you, we think quite deeply about it."

Scythe blinks slowly, like he's considering my response. Then he licks his lips. "And did you consider the consequences of your actions?"

Well, no. So I say, "I considered the consequences of my *in*action."

A minute tilting of the head tells me he's surprised by my response. "You thought we would kill her."

I wince at the memory of her condition. "I thought you would let that go on for too long. It was already too long. It's not humane."

"We have a protocol for how we extract information."

A chill passes down my spine at the directness of this conversation. At the matter-of-factness about how Scythe speaks about torture.

He continues in that cold, matter-of-fact tone, "What do you think will happen now that you've released her?"

I swallow. She's safe now. I told Ghoul to drop her somewhere close to her home. But...

Xander snaps. "She'll go straight to Mace Naga to run her fucking mouth. That's the answer you're looking for ex-serpent *princess*."

I shoot him a glare.

Scythe stands and I'm not prepared for the way his dominance washes over me as he comes to stand close, his mating mark glowing on the side of his neck. I can't help but glance at it and I know he notices. I meet him eye to eye.

"Next time," he says, his voice a terrifying, quiet rasp that I might hear in my nightmares. "If you have an issue with the way I run my business, you come to *me*."

I blink up at him, my heart hammering, my veins burning, my mind whirring in mild panic.

"Do you understand me, Aurelia?"

Dangerous. So fucking dangerous. And yet, he's right. I *should* have considered everything before I released an enemy. Natalia threatened my friends. Threatened everything.

I swallow down my instinctual panic and attempt to meet that terrifying gaze. "I understand, Scythe."

"Now go back to your TV."

In a sort of daze, I do exactly that.

It's not until I've sat down on the couch and pulled my blanket over me that I realise Scythe just *dismissed* me. He asked me to reconsider my actions, told me off, and dismissed me like one of his... men.

A weird feeling inserts itself in my stomach. One part of me is seriously turned on by this and another part of me is... strangely deflated. Like I've disappointed them. Him.

Quite suddenly, I don't know what to do.

I stare at the TV without watching it as Scythe's, Savage's, then Xander's eyes flash into my mind's eye. Then Natalia's black eyes, filled with exhaustion and agony. I did the right thing. And yet, it feels like I made a big mistake.

I start questioning every move I've ever made. If any decision I made had been the right one.

Well, it turns out that, if the universe wants you to do something, it's gonna force you to do it. It's going to cut your chain and set you free, even if it's in the most painful way possible.

For me, that's on day four, when Lyle comes calling one evening.

And everything changes.

* * *

I'm sitting on the comfortable sofa in the TV room, watching *Mean Girls* when the boss lion storms into the room like he's ready for murder. Well, this girl's heart he already butchered, so what is he wanting to achieve?

It's after classes and, uncharacteristically, he's wearing only a shirt today and slacks. He stops short in the TV room doorway and furious amber eyes take me in: The lovely, soft purple blanket I'm draped in, the multiple empty food wrappers around me, the bag of microwaveable popcorn and a wolf plushie with eyes hand painted in blue. All gifts from Savage. A little part of me wonders if Lyle is jealous my wolf has me all to himself. A little part of me wonders if he kept away as long as he could, each day tearing at him little by little until he discarded first his suit jacket, then his vest, and finally his reason.

"Really, Aurelia?" he snaps, that voice a scorching growl. "At this rate, you'll be missing most of the semester."

He's so angry he doesn't realise he's slipped up and used my name. I cheers to him with my glass of coke.

"Never liked the curriculum anyway, sir," I say with false bravado, then I take a long sip.

"Are you—" His pupils dilate before his voice descends into a whole new baritone. "You've been drinking."

"Only a teensy bit, sir. It's a Wednesday afternoon, you see. Perfectly accept— Hey!"

He snatches my glass right from my hands and sniffs it with disgust before storming out of the room with it.

"Hey!" I'm forced to extract myself from my most perfect nest of fleece and chocolate wrappers and hurry after him, pulling my tank top and shorts back into place over my bandages. My hair is in a messy bun, but I'm otherwise presentable as far as I'm concerned, sans bra. But now I'm angry my peace has been breached by this *imposter*. The imposter who rejected me and *threw* me out of his nest and shattered my fucking already broken heart.

"You have no right!" I shout at him, pointing an accusing finger at him from across the dining table. "Give that back!"

"Enough of this wallowing," Lyle says, exasperated. "You need to—"

"Don't fucking tell me what to do!" I shout back. "You have no right! Not after—" I suddenly lose my breath and pant, bracing my hands on the table. I want to cry, but I don't want to show him vulnerability either. "Get out of here!" I shout, pointing to the stairs.

He looks at me, highly unimpressed.

"I can hear you from downstairs," Xander's voice drones as he climbs up the staircase. Scythe is behind him.

Savage comes out from the bedroom fully naked, hair wet from his shower.

Suddenly embarrassed that *everyone* is now here, I shut my mouth and reassess. I huff and cross my arms because that seems like the best thing to do in this situation.

"What's wrong, regina?" Savage says, leaning on the black wood of the doorway. Even he wants to give me space right now, likely sensing I'm about to implode.

"I'm sick of this," I mutter. "I'm fucking sick of everything."

Henry clucks softly in support from where he hovers by my ear.

Lyle blows out air and runs a hand over his golden head but doesn't move from his position—the furthest position away from me the room will allow. "Look, I—"

"*What*," I say with venom, "*the fuck* do you have to say, Lyle Pardalia?"

Lyle's face darkens. "Watch the way you speak to me, Aurelia."

I glare at him and he glares back, the full force of his dominance on display. Amber eyes flicker with rage, anger... and a tinge of pain. I'm his regina and I'm perfectly attuned to see that. Suddenly, the very air in the room drags at my shoulders, my ribs, my legs, and I'm weary. So weary from months of fighting and fleeing and stressing.

I turn to look out the window, staring at the open sky. A great blue that once beckoned with freedom now suddenly demands my attention. I turn back to the room and let my eyes wander to each of their faces, one by one.

This is never going to work.

And I've fooled myself this entire time. Lulled into a false sense of... happiness. It was fuelled by lust and desire. These men can never be mine. Lyle is never going to be with me. Who am I kidding? Scythe and Xander will never yield to me as their regina. Xander said it himself. I'm an unknown. They will never relinquish power to me.

And Savage. Though he might actually feel something for me, I can never take him away from his brothers.

"I'm sorry," I say to my wolf.

Savage straightens and uncrosses his arms. "Regina?"

I'm tired, so tired that my voice is barely a whisper as I reveal my truth. "I can't do this anymore."

"What do you mean?" Savage's voice sounds hollow.

My hands are trembling, my knees are shaking as the full force of the truth wracks my very bones.

"Aurelia." Lyle is still angry, but a thread of uncertainty weaves through that gold tinted rage.

But I'm shaking my head and coming to a decision. I've had enough. I've fucking. Had. Enough. "I can't do this anymore."

Silence echoes around me and darkness opens at my centre, and that primitive void calls to me like it did a month ago. My anima rises, wings thrashing in my ears, talons scraping at my insides as if they want to shred the human in me apart.

With a sob, I let her take over. And it's like a breath of fresh air as I explode into feather and wing.

And also glass.

It's glass that shatters around me as my wedge-tailed eagle body hurls through the windows of the hidden floor and finds her freedom.

I'm greeted by cold wind and the long rays of afternoon sun, and it's a feeling of pure pleasure that pummels through me. Like I can breathe again. Like I have *space* to think. The academy is spread out beneath me, and though that powerful dome of magic shimmers with warning above, I let out a cry of open release.

Shouts resound behind me and I bank, shifting on the current to see the commotion while still flying away from it. Broken glass borders the window of the hidden floor, now visible to me above the animus dormitory. And within that, four faces stare at me, getting smaller and smaller.

One of them, golden and terrible, is honed into something purely predatory.

A shot rings out from below.

I bank again, missing that dart by inches, and have no choice but to flee from the guards shooting below.

And then Lyle Pardalia, with a hunter's fixed, predatory focus, jumps out the window.

I let out a cry of horror, high-pitched and shrill. But Lyle is not falling. Borne on the wings of some insane telekinesis, he shoots towards me like a rocket—

Something viciously injects itself into my shields, like someone has put the jaws of life through my psychic barrier and is cranking it open with brutal force.

There's only one person with the skill and power to do that.

I yelp. Pain and panic shoot through my skull and my wings stutter in mid-air. Within a breath, I'm careening towards the ground, my wings flapping feebly. A glance towards the road past the academy reveals a convoy of black vehicles advancing towards the front gate.

Holy shit.

He's not supposed to come for days yet.

Pain shoots through me again and the world becomes nothing but a blur as I fall and fall.

A dark shadow scoops me up and the roar of the wind and the scream in my head come to an abrupt halt. Despite the pain splitting my brain open, I know I'm safe in someone's arms and back on the ground.

I have no time to ponder the how of it as my senses come back online and my vision sharpens within my eagle eyes. My four mates surround me, and behind them, academy guards watch on warily.

Both Lyle's and Scythe's phones go off at the same time.

Scythe brings his phone out to look at a text while I'm jostled in Lyle's arms as he answers a call. "What?" he snaps.

We all hear the deep timbre of the voice on the other side of the line. It's Ruben.

"Mace Naga is at the front gate. Him and his contingent with a warrant."

"What does he want?"

"He's saying he's come to hold you and Animus Academy accountable for the treatment of the serpents at the school. The ones in the cages. He's saying it's against the Species Anti-discrimination Act—"

"I'll be down shortly."

The ones in the cages? But I thought Lyle sent them all home.

But that attack on my shields is not done. With a psychic wail, my shield is shredded apart by brusque, efficient force.

Malevolent pain slashes across my stomach. Dark, venomous fangs scorch hot through my already necrotic skin.

I scream, flailing in Lyle's arms, wings flapping, legs kicking out. I can't breathe. I can't think. My head is whirling, my very reality slipping.

Savage's scent envelopes me. His voice is panicked. "Aurelia, baby, what's wrong?"

Lyle's hands grip me firmly as I struggle to maintain consciousness under the assault. But the pain, the burn, the sheer blinding *shredding* of it is driving me near mad. At this rate, I won't have a stomach left.

Burn. Burn. Burn.

Shred. Shred. Shred.

I buck and thrash, trying to bring up my shields, shoving both mates away. But they hold fast. They're talking, arguing, but I can't hear what they're saying.

And then a command, sharp enough to cut through the fog invading my mind. "*Shift.*"

On instinct, I obey.

Cold air hits my skin, my stomach, and I scream in agony. I manage to set my feet on the grass, but large, firm hands stop me from crashing to the ground.

Then it stops. The assault ceases and I'm left with a malicious slicing afterburn.

I open my eyes and look up in horror.

All four of my mates surround me, staring at my stomach and the four now bleeding, gaping necrotic wounds that have torn the once smooth skin of my stomach into shreds.

Savage is holding one of my arms, his face contorted into pure animalistic outrage.

Lyle's face is white as he holds my other wrist. His nostrils flare as he stares at me.

Scythe's glacial figure seems frozen in time and space as his pupils are blown out, engulfing his irises completely.

And Xander's glowing white eyes have turned *black*.

Behind them, the guards try to crane their necks to see me.

"Aurelia." Lyle's strangled voice hits me like a fist to the gut. There's agony and torment, but I barely have time to register that before I see it happen, like a wave breaking along a beach.

One by one, I watch my mates fall into their animuses. Fall into pure animal rabidity.

Chapter 72

Lyle

It's happening again.

Chains that have been rattling in my head for the last three months finally snap like brittle twigs.

An old door, secured with a decade of bloody tendons, cartilage and sheer, disciplined will, slams open with the force of a lion's screaming roar.

And the power behind it shatters forth, a raging monster. Terrible. Uncontrollable.

I choke out my regina's name before everything turns red.

My regina has been gravely maimed so badly that she reeks of death. That she reeks of decay. Unholy black marks mar her precious, perfect skin.

She was covering it before. Weathering it, for how long?

Hiding it from me. From us all.

"*Death,*" I say to my brothers by fate. A command. An offer.

"*Death,*" they agree in unison.

A single name comes to us, sung on a black, poisoned wind.

And the beast who owns that name is on *my* territory.

Chapter 73

Aurelia

Four powers sweep around me. Around my world. As if electricity is charging the air, malevolent and dark. Calling for death. Calling for no mercy. It's icy and scorching hot at the same time.

The hairs on the back of my neck stand on end. My mating mark burns like a brand.

Within seconds, I'm standing in a circle of four towering monsters, powerful shoulders heaving, lungs breathing heavily, mating marks blazing in a hue of melted gold and silver.

In their eyes, I see nothing but unadulterated rage. The group of academy guards behind them, sensing the danger, slowly back away.

Shit. Shit, shit, shit.

"Lyle?" I pant through my pain, covering what I can of my naked body. "Savage?"

But Lyle suddenly lets out a sound that is all lion and not at all man, and I jump back from him as he explodes out of his human skin. The fabric of his clothes flies in all directions as he turns into something that is at once magnificent and terrifying.

Lyle's animus is easily the biggest lion I've ever seen.

Standing eye to eye with me, those terrible amber eyes are wide in fury. His mane is long and beautiful, fanning out from his face and trailing down his back and stomach in hues of gold and amber. And his pelt... that pelt shines in a stunning colour between bronze and gold, tight over a heavily muscled body. Lions like this haven't been seen in the wild in over a century. The photograph from his apartment comes to mind.

Lyle roars into the air.

I want to cower from that sound, just as the guards now are. I want to cover my ears and flee from the power and rage I sense from my mate.

But I don't. Instead, I take it all and feel the full force of his terrifying sound. The full force of his fury for me as it seeps into my very bones. This is Lyle's long-leashed animus. He is mine, and I am not afraid of him.

But Lyle's shifting seems to trigger Savage, because a heartbeat later, he too explodes into fur and tooth and claw. They prowl around each other, snapping and growling, the sound filling the air and making my heart pound as if they're speaking in an ancient, primitive way that talks only of the spilling of blood and the tearing of flesh.

Suddenly, they seem to come to an understanding.

As one, they both turn to me and *bow*. Leaning down on their two front paws, their heads bend low.

I only have time to suck in a shocked, reverent breath before they both whip around and storm away from me, their heavy footfalls thudding on the academy turf. The guards scatter, shocked and in awe, I think, and one of them stutters into his walkie-talkie.

Scythe snarls and there's no sign of a man in his face. His shark is visible in his eyes, those irises now a dark, malevolent navy blue, and his teeth—dear Goddess, his *teeth*—are no longer a human's, but the many-pointed rows of shark's teeth. He bares them and follows after his bond-brothers a heartbeat later.

"Wait!" I cry.

But of course he doesn't listen. They're headed to the front gates. To kill my father, the cause of my wounds. But my father will be ready for this and they'll get themselves killed in the process. Mace Naga takes guns and strong males with him everywhere. Guns loaded with things worse than plain bullets...

Struggling to calm down, and sending healing power to my shredded stomach, I turn to my remaining mate.

Xander's glowing black eyes flash gold and are trained on my naked abdomen.

"Regina." The heat hits me in a wave as he stalks towards me. His voice is like the dark, powerful places where the Earth's core glows red. "Tell me who did this and I will tear their skull apart and eat their brain, piece by piece."

"No," I say quickly, sidestepping him and heading for the side gate where my other mates were headed. I have to stop them. I have to stop Lyle from ruining his entire career. I have to stop my father from killing them all.

"Then command me." His own voice rings with command.

I pause, thinking rapidly about how best to handle this, eyeing the remaining guards unabashedly staring between us. A frantic Henry and Eugene appear from the bushes outside the animus dorm, where they must have been hiding in fear. Students are now streaming out of the dorm and the dining hall to see what the commotion is about.

"Stay here, keep the students inside," I say quickly to Xander. "Keep them safe. Tell Yeti what's happened. Shit is about to go down."

He says it through gritted teeth, but I know in my bones he will not disobey me. "Very well, regina."

"And take care of these two." My little nimpin doesn't want to leave me, but with a stern look from me, he zips over to Xander's shoulder. Eugene follows.

"Aquinas," one of the female guards barks, taking off her sunglasses to stare at me. "What the hell is going on?"

"We need to get to Lyle," I say quickly. "He's... I don't think they're in control."

"You need to get back inside," she says, rounding on me. "Right now." Her walkie-talkie goes off and Ruben's voice orders the guards to secure the students.

As we talk, I seal my new wounds. "Listen, everyone is in danger if Lyle is in his beast form."

Another guard throws an orange academy jumpsuit at me. "You're out of line, Aquinas. Get back inside with the rest of the students."

I don't have time for this.

Shifting into my eagle form, I launch into the sky. The sound of curses and guns being swung up follow me as I sweep powerful strokes to gain height. One shot is fired and I twist sideways, avoiding it entirely. By the time the next shot sounds, I'm flying over the animus dorm and headed for the main entrance.

If Lyle and Savage die on my account, I will never be able to live with myself.

One look at the front aspect of the academy shows me guards letting Lyle, Savage and Scythe through the side gate that leads up to the drive. A second look at the closed front gates reveal a convoy of many black cars, lined up as if ready and eager to enter.

Panicking, I mentally call out to Raquel as I bank.

"What's wrong, cub?"

"My dad's here. Shit's turned crazy. Savage and Lyle have shifted. And... you guys need to be careful. You might be in danger."

"Slow down. What the hell?"

"My dad's here, Raquel. Tell the others and... I don't know, keep away. Keep safe."

I can only race after my three mates, who have no idea what they're doing except seeking revenge for me.

My father's going to kill them. I just know it.

I have to do something, I just don't know what.

Cresting over the anima dorm, Christine shouts out to me from her station above the door and a sudden thought strikes me.

"Christine!" I scream mentally, hoping she can hear telepathic messages. *"Secure the school, don't let anyone out, including Lyle!"*

The stone gargoyle salutes me with her stick-like hand as I fly past.

I beat my wings to gain height, soaring above the mounting chaos as the wind stings at the fresh open wounds on my belly. Guards are streaming in from all corners, shouting and running, guns raised, following my three mates. My barely healed wounds burst open at the physical activity and I send more healing to staunch the bleeding, but it's hard to concentrate on everything at the same time.

"Shoot, shoot, shoot!" cries one of the guards.

The protective magical dome looms ahead of me along the perimeter of the concrete wall surrounding the school grounds— buzzing faintly and threatening to chargrill me into KFC on impact. I need to go to ground to stop my mates, except there's five guards standing at the head of the driveway, each with a darting rifle trained on my flying ass.

I dodge the first, but the second clips me on my shoulder. Letting out a shrill cry, I stutter in mid-air, my left wing hanging limply.

Then I'm falling. My functional right wing frantically flaps to try and slow my landing, but it does nothing. It's too much. The pain in my stomach, the weakness from the psychic shields being torn apart, from the sedative dart...

I hit the eucalyptus trees bordering the long driveway, tumbling through the branches, each impact rattling my brain and jarring my bones. Somehow, my powerful feet manage to claw into one of the branches and find a grip. I sway precariously, before righting myself and sagging against the tree trunk.

My shoulder burns like acid has been poured into it, but I'm pretty sure it's just a graze, with no sedative injected. Thanking my lucky stars, I try to hide within the sparse foliage of the young eucalypt. The guards race for me, but I lose sight of them as I huddle behind the thick, smooth trunk.

"Come out, Aquinas!" shouts a female guard. "We've got you surrounded!"

Catching my breath, I angle myself so I can see the front gates at the end of the long driveway.

The harsh light of the setting sun washes the scene in red-orange light that hurts my eyes, but it means I can see what's happening easily. There are at least six school guards gathered by the ornate cast iron gate, along with the giant figure of Ruben. He's pushing both gates wide open while the guards look back and forth in confusion.

Because before them, prowling back and forth across the width of the school driveway, like three angry, impatient predators, are my mates.

Lyle, Savage and even Scythe appear huge compared to everyone else, hair and fur glinting like dawn, dusk, and starlight under the golden, setting sun.

"*Lyle!*" I scream telepathically. "*Scythe, Savage, stop!*"

None of them falter in their pacing.

But then the school gates are fully open.

Three heavy black Jeeps sit on the other side, their engines rumbling through my eagle's ears.

They're parked sideways. Like they're blocking the exit.

I silently thank Christine. The electrified dragon-magic that surrounds the school in a dome extends right down to the ground because I can see it shimmering a pale blue between my mates and the outside world.

It's the only reason they haven't charged through yet.

The school guards look confused, shifting uncertainly. No doubt a couple of them are on Scythe's payroll. They leave their guns angled across their bodies and talk to each other, monitoring the interaction between Ruben and someone in the Jeep closest to them.

The window of the first Jeep rolls back up and I'm close enough now to see the Naga family coat of arms glinting silver on the side door.

It opens, admitting a long, black leg and booted foot.

"I can sense you." My father has a dangerous sort of smirk on his thin lips as he steps out of the Jeep. *"Not this time, Aurelia. Not this time."*

I freeze in shock and fear. The wounds across my abdomen burn in an echo of his words. A promise of what will come to pass here.

My father stands with the presence of a born king. Wiry and tall, an impenetrable wraith made of will and venom and power. His signature long black duster flaps in the breeze and he clasps his hands in front of himself as if he's not at all bothered by the line of predators with their eyes fixed on him. I share his olive complexion, his raven-black hair. But our eyes are different. His are sunken and dark, as if he can see all the bad things in the world and doesn't give a single damn.

There's a knowing smirk on his face as he stares defiantly at the three males who have now fallen still.

I'm so stricken by the sight before me that I don't even see the danger behind me.

"I knew I'd get you eventually, bitch."

Orange and black striped fur hurtles from beneath me as my body is seized and I'm swept right off my claws. I shriek in terror as damp heat encloses around both wings and sharp canines dig painfully into the tender flesh beneath my plumage. My stomach lurches as that sharp-toothed maw drags me down to the ground.

Claws scrape along the tree trunk as a human voice shouts from below.

"What the hell, Clawson?"

Even without them saying it, I would know the malefic, vile scent of the mate that rejected Minnie anywhere.

I thrash and a growl resonates from Titus' throat, vibrating through my body as he clamps down hard enough to burn and squeeze around vital organs. I have no choice but to submit.

"Leave him be," someone else commands.

Fuck. Do the Clawsons have some of the guards on their payroll, too?

My entire body is at the mercy of Titus Clawson while he holds me like a fox with a chicken, my neck dangling precariously as we land on the ground. But Titus does nothing more than hold me as everyone watches the goings on at the gate from a distance. I'm forced to remain limp and stare at the unfolding tableau.

My father jerks his head to the right, where two sleek black Mercedes are pulling up next to him. The windows roll down.

"Oh shit," the guard next to Titus mutters. "Is the *entire* council here?"

If I didn't recognise them from the *Animalia Today* news app, I'd recognise them from my own trial.

The Queen of Wolf Court, a round-faced woman in many-layered skirts, is frowning as she speaks to my father, asking him a question. Behind her sits the Queen of the Avians, a long-limbed, graceful woman called Irma Goldwing and in the other car I can make out the dark features of the King of the Feline Court, Ablo Obon.

"*Lyle!*" I project as hard as I can, despite the pain and panic. "*You need to stop!*"

But of course, Lyle does not register my voice. He registers nothing except his mark.

Instead, he *charges*.

I swallow a scream as I watch my mate rampage into the electric shield. Sparks fly, flesh sizzles, and my massive lion is thrown backwards through the air, crashing onto the concrete with a sick thud. But he's climbing back to his feet in an instant, new, angry burnt flesh bubbling across his face as he snarls angrily, seemingly unaffected by the pain.

A breeze whistles past, encasing my heart in its chill as my father talks rather calmly to the cars with the council members.

He gestures to his own three vehicles.

And one by one, doors open, and males pile out.

My father has come with his whole contingent and then some. In addition to large males who are clearly Clawson tigers, five serpent generals in their skull-painted masks and black combat gear all climb out of the SUVs. They bear semi-automatic weapons emblazoned with a silver 'V'.

These are serpent-made rifles.

Titus growls in approval and recognition, the sound filling my head with deathly promise.

My blood runs cold.

The five generals stand on the other side of the shield, armed and ready to shoot at my three mates, who are fully ready and completely open to their bullets.

Chapter 74

Xander

Apparently, I'm the only sane fucking person in this entire God-forsaken place.

This time, my dragon allows me to be conscious when he takes over by force. It takes everything I have to shove him back down, and he only does it on the condition that I follow my... *orders.*

If I was like the other degenerates here, I would have spat on the ground at the thought of it.

"Follow our regina's orders," my dragon huffs, *"or I'm taking power back."*

"Fuck you," I snarl in return.

Eugene, with Henry riding on his back because he's terrified of me, follows in my wake; my angry, rooster-nimpin hybrid shadow.

The flash of a telepathic image explodes in my mind. I can tell it's from Savage because it's got that unhinged, feral signature.

Mace Naga and his entire fucking contingent stand there with rifles drawn, flanking the council in their cars. The school guards don't even know what to do when they see the silver 'V' emblazoned on the guns.

Our worst suspicions have been confirmed.

The serpents have successfully developed venom-infused bullets. According to my research, they fragment on impact, spraying Eastern Taipan venom through the person's body. More brutal than any actual snakebite, it's a certain way of killing a beast with even the graze of a bullet.

Dirty reptile trash.

Outside the animus dorm, guards are racing around, shooting and causing a general commotion. I survey them with disdain. If these were our people, they wouldn't be reacting like this. Common idiots, the lot of them.

"Fuck it," I say, kicking off my favourite boots. I turn behind me to make sure there's no one in maiming proximity.

But there is.

"What are you doing here?" I snarl.

Chapter 75

Aurelia

Lyle roars, and it hits my eardrums with the force of a thunderclap. The guards cringe under it.

"Dart them!" one of the guards cry, raising his gun to shoot.

But my dad shakes his head, and it's directed at Ruben.

Ruben shouts, his booming voice cutting all the way down the drive. "Hold fire!"

My heart sinks in my chest. Somehow, Ruben has succumbed to the Serpent Court. Perhaps he's made a deal of some sort. That's usually how my father gets them. That or outright blackmail.

When the Serpent King speaks, his voice is unfathomable, coldness laced with venom.

"We all came to speak to the most honourable deputy head-master of this so-called academy," Mace calls for everyone to hear, to what seems like the entirety of the school guards amassed in the driveway. "Instead, I'm met with this rabid creature."

The Clawson tigers and his generals laugh behind their masks, their shoulders shaking with the dark, malevolent sounds of their humour. The council members get out of their cars, seemingly to get a better look.

To my surprise, Georgia gets out of the car after the impressive feline king. Her beautiful face is controlled, but her eyes betray her, shock and dismay leeching through as she stares at Lyle.

That bitch must've given evidence against him.

Also stepping out of a council car is the King of Dragon Court, impossibly tall and imposing, with broad shoulders, long black hair and a tailored black suit and many gold rings that glint in the remaining light. The corners of his handsome mouth are kicked up in a hint of a smile.

As if he finds this display amusing.

Lyle, Savage, and Scythe regard them all with cold, cursory glances.

"I wonder what it was that set you off?" My father's voice is mildly pensive, but his smile tells me that he knows exactly what it was. "Such a shame." He glances at the council members. "I think we can all agree he is not fit to serve in his position."

Holy shit, this is really happening.

"This is not what I expected!" exclaims the wolf queen, her many crescent moon necklaces chiming softly as she gestures towards my lion. "Very disappointing indeed, Lyle."

My father brings out a brown folder leaden with over a hundred pages of printed text. "We found all manner of interesting things from your stay at Blackwater, Lyle. Things that were hidden by your predecessor, Your Majesty." He inclines his head to the feline queen, whose pert mouth is twisted in disdain. "But it's all out in the open now. All your unusual diagnoses and issues with rabidity."

"He must be darted," the dragon king suggests without emotion. "He'll need to be assessed... not by his own team, of course. But by the council's psychiatrists."

The avian queen nods regally, her poise and bearing of a

once successful ballet dancer. "If he needs to go back to Blackwater, then so be it."

This is happening too fast. There's no discussion. This isn't fair.

Lyle is prowling back and forth, panting hard, hissing at the barrier, at the assembled group of people, not listening to or understanding what is being discussed. It's like he isn't even here. His animus is in full protection mode... combined with a mate drive. There was no way for him to defend himself against my father's claims. He's only proving them correct.

My father holds out a second set of stapled papers for the guards to see through the magic barrier. "We have here a council-approved warrant for the arrest of Lyle Pardalia, Savage Fengari and Aurelia Aquinas. Mr Fengari should never have been enrolled into this school, as he is very much a felon and should be put back into Blackwater Penitentiary. Miss Aquinas, of course, was always meant to return to Serpent Court for her execution. I will also be retrieving the serpent students who are being held against council laws. It's time things changed in this school."

The council members all nod in aristocratic agreement.

Savage is cocking his head now, apparently listening. I'm a little surprised, but out of all of my mates, my wolf has always been one and the same with his animus. They've never fought each other for dominance.

Ruben is glancing at Savage and nodding. "We've been having problems with Savage Fengari. I've known him since he was a kid and he's not changed one bit. He's not safe to be around the general population."

This screams of betrayal to me. Ruben was the one coaching Savage. Supposedly helping him this entire time.

"None of them will come willingly," Ruben warns.

The raptor queen tosses her head of thick blonde locks and says, "Lucky we came prepared. Mace?"

"Indeed, Your Majesty." He nods benevolently and gestures to something behind him. Another two vehicles park behind the rest. Armoured transport trucks, military grade, covered in steel and obsidian. Big enough to hold bears if need be.

Big enough to transport a Boneweaver, a lion, and a wolf.

"Scythe?" the wolf queen calls to the Great White standing still as a glacier next to Savage. "I don't believe he's quite with us."

"We might as well take the shark to the asylum," the dragon king says darkly. Then he casts his dark eyes around the drive. "Where is the headmistress? Why has she not greeted us at her gates?"

"Hiding, I suspect," my father says, as if he's really sad about it. "Such a shame. I wanted her to be here for the reunion. To think I'd found a long-lost friend of yours, Lyle. A great effort we went to, but we found him in the end. All for our investigation, and as a witness, of course. He's quite eager to see you. Consider it a little parting gift from me."

We all stare as the entire top of the third Jeep folds back and down. In the passenger seat, a khaki, wide-brimmed bush hat comes into view, followed by a red beard and a cunning gleam of black-eyed recognition that chills me to my core.

He's much older than when I saw him in Lyle's memories, but for what he did to my mate and his family, I would recognise Frank Ulman anywhere.

Apparently, he didn't die that fateful day Lyle was freed from his so-called sanctuary.

Ulman hefts up the rifle in his hands and says in a voice like old, dead things, "Hello, Lyle."

I scream, but of course, it comes out in a strangled squawk.

My lion goes still before letting out an earth-shattering roar that makes everyone cringe. Then he does something that surprises even me, who has seen all his memories. He prowls towards the magical barrier and puts a single paw through it. Flesh sizzles and smoke coils through the air.

I gasp in disbelief, but Lyle doesn't stop. He proceeds to walk through the barrier slowly, as if he doesn't feel the pain. As if he doesn't care that his pelt is literally melting off his muscle.

His leg is through. Then comes his head.

Smoke and the smell of burning fur and mane tunnels through the air. Lyle is hissing, growling, baring his canines, but not stopping his advance. And doesn't take his eyes off my father.

The very ground trembles.

In that moment, I hate what we are. I hate that Lyle's mating drive is forcing him to do the insane. Is forcing him to maim and torture himself for me. I throw up, retching and spitting out the contents of my stomach onto the grass beneath.

Titus takes a couple of steps forward, as if he wants to get a better look.

"Holy shit!" Ruben calls. "He's going to blow the shield! Everyone get back!"

"Pass me the obsidian!" the feline king booms. He doesn't wait for the serpent generals to pass it to him, he just zips it from their hands via telekinesis.

Everything seems to happen in slow motion.

The electrified dragon protection between the two parties stutters in one last effort to remain stable before dissipating like smoke into nothing.

But they don't know that obsidian doesn't work on Lyle.

The feline king throws the obsidian chains onto the massive lion, but they slide right off him, as he leaps not for Frank Ulman, but Mace Naga.

Shots are fired.

Right. For. My. mate.

Rage thrums inside my veins with explosive force.

That gaping maw of ancient, primitive darkness, that has always beckoned to me, opens at my centre.

And I gladly fall into it.

With vicious, savage power, I erupt.

My anima roars and I become not a human woman, but only a Boneweaver regina saving her mate. Only speed and canines and pure, bloodthirsty vengeance hellbent on a singular, lethal purpose.

My eagle's body shifts with explosive force inside Titus' mouth. Bone cracks and something falls beneath me but I don't care. Titus stumbles back and I am free.

In my fastest form, it takes only three strides to reach peak speed. The fastest land animal on earth.

I'm down the driveway in seconds.

There are screams and shouts, but I don't hear any of it. I only hear the roar of my mate. I only hear the vicious call of death.

Chapter 76

Savage

Bloodlust sings through my veins in an old, sacred song, but my mind quickly turns into confusion as shots ring out through the air.

My lion brother crashes to the ground as combined feline and dragon magic shoves his attack away. The obsidian chains and the bullets in his chest and side, of course, do nothing.

Scythe and I, protected by his psychic shields, charge after her, wanting to find our mark, wanting to rip the cobra's head off his shoulders for what he did to our queen.

The feline king moves his hands, but it has no effect on us thanks to my shark-brother.

Then a power like I've never known comes battering towards us like a herd of raging, screaming rhinoceros.

I whip around only to see the blur of golden power that is my regina, passing us at break-neck speed through the sunset.

Like some ancient, wild Boneweaver queen, *my regina* has taken her cheetah form.

"Shoot!" the serpent king roars.

Bullets spray from five automatic guns. Aimed right at my regina and the path she is making towards our enemy.

Fury tears through me, red hot like fire but desperate. *"No!"* I cry.

But dying to protect my regina is the only way for me to leave this world with my head held high.

So I launch myself into a dive between the bullets and my regina, my life, my one hope. I let myself meet death. And I meet it with my eyes open. *"I love you,"* I send into her mind. For her, anything.

I wait for the battering of bullets. I wait for the pain.

But it doesn't come.

Instead, a foreign power surges all around us like a gale force wind. I land back on all fours, and everyone screeches to a halt because something funny is happening.

Those black serpent guns are wrenched upwards with that same forceful power. And none of the bullets land.

The little black pieces of metal remain suspended in the air, moving slowly as if through water. I let out a happy, wolfy cackle. My regina turns around to see whose force is stopping the guns from firing and bullets from landing. So do I.

My dragon-brother lands heavily on the concrete driveway, blue-tinged black scales shining like living gems. But it's not him who's stopped the bullets, but the tiny, round figure sliding off his back.

Minnie. It's Minnie with her small hands outstretched, her face dark in its anger and concentration. Yeti comes to stand behind her, placing his arms around his regina as if to protect her.

Elation tears through me, until my lion-brother growls in anger and I swing back to lock in focus on our enemies.

Tyres screech because Mace Naga has jumped into his Jeep as he peels away from the school at full speed. The other serpents leap to do the same.

In my lion-brother's rush to follow the enemy, he doesn't see the human who has stepped out of the car, swinging a gun and aiming straight between his eyes.

I bark a warning

But my regina is already flying through the air on the paws of the fastest beast on Earth, heading straight for the human's throat.

But he's seen her. He's ready for her.

That human swings around his rifle and shoots.

My regina shifts—no, shrinks—so rapidly it's hard to follow. Her muzzle becomes a beak and paws that are now small wings lift her into the sky. She's a rosella. Beautiful red and blue but small. The shot misses.

Someone shouts and I think it's the feline king.

My regina smacks into Ulman's chest as she changes for a third and final time.

In a burst of power, she becomes *huge*, leathery skinned and powerful, slamming into the human male with all the colossal weight of a fully grown saltwater crocodile.

The human's gun clatters to the ground as more people scream. But he's completely helpless as Aurelia's massive, elongated jaws take his human head between them.

And *squeezes*.

The human screams. Aurelia thrashes, her bloodlust reigning supreme. I howl into the dusk with real happiness.

Then the human is silent and still, his lifeblood spilling onto the road.

My regina shifts into a human woman, scrambling off the human on her hands and knees, blood smeared across her mouth and teeth. And I realise that I've never seen a more magical sight. My regina is a wild, furious beast. A destroyer of men.

Chapter 77

Aurelia

My head is ringing, my mouth is full of the disgusting metallic taste of blood, and I've just killed a man. I retch and gag, spitting, trying to bring up the remnants of the awful truth as horror crushes me in a vise-like grip.

I'd just *shifted* in front of everyone.

I'd just shown *everyone* what I was.

Seven years of fearful hiding, lying and crying all gone in one moment of—

"I think that's quite enough," comes a deep, feminine voice.

Fire that's more than fire surrounds us all in a semi-circle, blocking any exit to the main road. Lyle jumps backwards from the heat. His skin is already starting to heal, but it's red and shiny. My father's Jeep is long gone. I actually can't believe he ran, and if the orange blur I saw was Titus' being dragged away, he's also gone. The rest of the members of his contingent are hauling ass back to Serpent Court close behind, but neither Lyle nor the council members can leave through the fiery semicircle.

They leave Ulman on the ground and I pointedly ignore the bloody mess that is left of him.

If I can't see it, I can pretend it didn't happen. I am an emu with her head in the sand.

It's bullshit and I know it. I've ruined everything I've ever worked for.

We all turn to see Lady Celeste striding down the driveway towards us, the phoenix fire lighting up her face and hair in the most ethereal way. Like a creature of myth that she is, she glows with that heavenly power and it turns her irises molten gold.

"Forgive me for the delay," she says breezily, "Some people deemed it fit to try and hold me in my office. Luckily, I am not easily deterred by a couple of vagrants."

One guess who sent them. One guess who'd orchestrated this entire operation. The only thing my father hadn't counted on was me...defying him.

The members of the Council of Beasts start talking all at once, but I can't even register what they're saying. My eyes are on my mate.

My power reaches out to Lyle, who doesn't even seem to realise he's been shot multiple times and is trying to find a way through the fire. I quickly seek out every bullet in his body and push them out, dissolving the venom that's already starting to spread into his bloodstream. Luckily, I've caught them all in time. None of it has made it to his vital organs.

"Cover the Boneweaver girl," someone says.

I go still at those condemning words. Words that mean my death. Mean my captivity.

Then I gather my shit together and turn to see that it was the raptor queen, who'd spoken, and now shaking her head at me. In wonder or dismay, who can tell? Because I sure can't. I can't fucking see or think straight right at this minute.

Savage, who is already on his way to me, curls around my body and obstructs my female parts from view. Savage, who threw himself in front of an oncoming bullet for me. My wolf whines softly and I bury my hands in his midnight fur to ground myself. To reassure myself that he's still alive. That we're all still alive. And yet.

I fucked up.

Really badly.

My heart is pounding erratically in some sort of arrhythmia that might actually kill me if anyone else doesn't want to give it a go right now. Are they going to lock me up now? Are they going to take me to the council labs to be studied? There's no way they're going to allow me to just walk free from this.

It's out now.

There's no taking this back. No covering it up. No... lying about it. I feel naked down to my marrow. I feel like a noose hovers over me, ready to circle around my neck.

Scythe comes to stand next to us, distracting me from my panic. He looks up at the phoenix fire wall in wonder, and I think that's what snapped him out of his shark-mode. His eyes are no longer glazed, his teeth now definitely human.

As Lady Celeste tries to calm down the regents of the courts, Scythe does something strange. He cups my cheek, tilting my face up to look at him. Phoenix fire reflects in his sky-blue irises, turning them into glacial fire. He runs his thumb across my bottom lip. Then proceeds to put that same thumb in his mouth.

I stare at him in rapt shock.

Lady Celeste's voice enters my head on a lick of mythic flame. *"You need to bring back Lyle, Aurelia,"* she says firmly. *"You need to bring the man back or Goddess help us all right now because they* will *take him."*

That red-orange fire cuts through the night and the sound of people talking is abruptly cut off as Lyle, Savage, Scythe and I are suddenly in our own bubble of warm, shimmering, *towering* power. The flames are terrifying as they roar upward towards the night sky in a column, the stars just beginning to blink into existence.

But then a naked human Xander strolls through a blip in the

wall of phoenix fire, his eyes that deep golden colour that tells me his dragon is in control.

I rise to face my mates.

"Shift, Savage," I command. "Lyle needs us."

Savage shifts into his human skin and straightens to standing, his eyes a little glazed as blown out hazel irises stare down at me with simmering tension and, to my surprise, arousal. His voice is deeply husky when he says, "He needs *you*, regina."

Nodding, I turn around and find Lyle still has his back to us, still looking for a way out to follow our enemy. I have a feeling that if the wall of phoenix fire wasn't stopping him, he'd be running at full pelt down the road until he found the serpent king.

"Lyle," I say.

My lion doesn't turn around, his tail swishing irritably as he sniffs and growls, pacing the length of the fire wall.

I cross the five steps it takes to get to him in slow, controlled strides. "Lyle," I repeat.

He comes to a stop, but keeps his aggressive eyes trained on the fire. Tentatively, I step up behind him and reach out my fingers to touch his rear. A tingle shoots up my arms as human skin comes into contact with that golden bronze pelt and Lyle's tail goes still. Taking a deep breath, with deep care and my senses on alert for his every movement, I trail my fingers over his rear and up along his spine, healing the awful flesh burns as I go. Burns that were made on my behalf.

His ears twitch. But he lets out a hiss, baring his canines at the fire in protest. The powerful muscles beneath my fingers vibrate with restrained force.

"Lyle," I breathe, closer to his head now. "Come back to me."

I reach his shoulders, and he's so big that I'm reaching up a little to stroke the bottom of his singed mane. I heal that too. "Such a pretty lion," I coo.

Those ears twitch again.

"Regina," Savage warns.

"He won't hurt me," I say softly. "Will you, my big lion?"

Sucking in a breath, I take in the damage to his face. His flesh is red and shiny, in some places nearly burned down to the bone. Somehow, his eyes are intact, but his fur has completely melted away.

Biting my lip against a sob, I press my cheek to his mane, in the way of cats, both big and small. I gently rub my cheek against my mate and send my power to heal the worst of his burns across his face, chest, forelegs. Muscle, skin and fur grow anew across the horrible damage, stopping the bleeding, and no doubt the pain and burning.

A low rumbling purr begins and cuts itself off.

"We will get him another day," I reassure him, stroking his mane. "Our enemy. For now, my strong, strong, animus, give my man back."

I let out a pulse of power towards him, dominating him, demanding he submit to me as his regina.

Only then does he turn that magnificent, huge head to look at me.

Untamed, ferocious amber eyes take my breath away. So different from the man and yet not. I see the defiance of Lyle in them. The power, the discipline. But his animus is infinitely wild and free. A beast that can never be successfully restrained by another based on sheer will alone.

This is not a tame lion, nor will he ever be. No, Lyle's animus is like a bush fire. Uncontrollable. Devastating.

"Regina?" comes a deep, bestial voice in my head, like rumbling mountains and sloping, rocky valleys.

"My one lion," I say softly. "My mate."

I feel my other mates at my back, towering over me. Lyle's animus marks their presence, one at a time.

"You are all mine?" he asks, baring his teeth at them in challenge.

My throat tightens at the question.

"We have lived many lifetimes with our regina," Dragon-Xander says. "We will be with her in this lifetime, too."

Lyle's eyes slide back to me, searching for confirmation.

I swallow and run my palm over the side of his newly healed face, admiring his fresh, long whiskers. "You were the sun for me down there in my cave," I whisper to him. "I heard you. I listened. You are mine."

No one expects what he says next.

"If you wish to kill me for what I have done, it would be your right. I would die gladly, having known your gentle touch. I would spend my last heartbeats worshipping you."

This is an apology he doesn't expect me to accept. My anima keens and I allow a whine to leave my throat.

He senses it and immediately steps forward, rubbing his face gently along my cheek.

"I am yours in every way that is possible," I whisper into his ear. "I have been since the moment I met you. I just didn't know it."

He purrs and I continue, tracing my finger along the lines of his glowing mating mark. "I want to kiss you. I want you to hold me and tell me it's going to be okay. I want you to tell me to put more clothes on and to wash my hair."

Lyle nuzzles my neck with his face, long whiskers brushing against me.

"I killed for you," I say into his head. *"For you alone."*

He closes his eyes and I feel something in him moving. Shifting.

"And I would do it again," I say into his head, only for him to hear. *"You, my mate, will never fight alone again. You will never be alone again."*

And then Savage, Xander and Scythe are there, crowding us in, nuzzling against Lyle's massive mane, and talking silently to him in their own private conversations.

Something in me shifts too. The backs of my eyes burn. Four scents surround me in a torrent of emotion, of desire, of... potential. There are so many things those scents could mean to me.

Lyle's animus chuffs in contentment.

And shifts.

Chapter 78

Lyle

You will never fight alone.

She acknowledged us.

She killed for us. One mortal enemy who deserved to die in the brutal way she dealt him.

She did it for *me* alone. Risked her life for *me*.

And that eternal ache in my bones, sharp as canines and heavy as a cattle prod to the sternum, finally, *finally* eases.

For the first time since he came into full power, my animus takes a slow, measured breath and sighs.

Each breath our regina, our pack, takes is the same. It's still torture to look upon her beauty, only now it's sweet and crisp, like the sensation of her nails dragging down my back.

It's not a gentle union with our regina that my animus wants. But a brutal, possessive force that will stake our claim over her forever. For all of eternity.

The desire to fuck her, to come in her, to feel her power twining around mine becomes unbearable.

My animus slips back behind the door I made so long ago with the help of the Lady Phoenix. He doesn't allow me to close it, not anymore, but I sense I don't need to. While Aurelia is here, I don't need the chains. While our regina is here, we can be free. My human side takes back our body and fur becomes skin, mane becomes hair.

We are both already naked. Perfect.

"Lyle?" she asks softly. The hope in her voice and sapphire eyes makes my cock twitch and my heart turn golden.

I can't waste any more time. I lunge for her, grabbing her around the waist and taking her to the rough ground, protecting her soft skin with my arms.

She fights me and the scramble of her delectable skin on mine ignites me further.

"I need you on your back," I growl, my animus speaking through me, with me. "Submitting to me. To my cock."

"Lyle," she moans, understanding what we need from her. Her sweet sound of assent tells me everything I need to know.

I thrust into her in one powerful stroke.

We cry out together. As we always will from now on. I know it because I will make sure of it.

My claiming is vigorous and thorough, nothing more than a beast rutting into his mate, a lion king claiming his lion queen, strong and hard, her wetness flooding us both, making her entire centre slick.

I claim her panting mouth and she moans around my tongue, my lips, my teeth. My tongue sweeps around hers, as I dominate every part of her body so completely that she shudders and cries and moans my name.

But it's not enough. It's not complete.

The skin of her neck, beautiful and perfect, beckons to me. I scrape my teeth around her skin, and without warning, I bite down.

Aurelia screams as she comes, shuddering around my cock, her warm, incredible pussy sucking me in, holding me, needing me just as much as I need her.

I come into her, emptying my heavy, aching balls in deep,

short thrusts right up against her womb as I hold her in the circle of my arms, our pack watching us in awe. As they should be.

She bites my neck in return, marking me with her tiny, beautiful, still bloody little teeth. I moan at the sensation.

"My angel," I whisper in prayer as I fuck my seed into her. "I waited for you. Mine. *Mine.*"

Our power twines together, her golden wisps against my darker chains, and together they form something new within me.

I've been born again while inside her.

Maybe that's why men seek to invade the insides of a woman with such desperation—in search of that magical thing that will put our broken parts back together in the same way all humans are put together inside a woman in the first place.

Freud would cackle in his grave to hear it.

My animus purrs with pleasure at the base of my being, never again to be truly locked away but to live as an integral part of me.

The world is suddenly different. We are suddenly stronger than before. The strongest predator stalking through the arid plain with singular focus. Through him I see that being with our regina is the only solution. It's every solution to every problem we've ever had. That the only real fear I now have is losing her.

"Yours," Aurelia sobs into my shoulder, before coming again with a cry.

And it's the sweetest sound in the universe.

Chapter 79

Aurelia

Lyle claims me with all the fervour of a beast claiming his regina. As if he no longer cares about the consequences. As if he no longer cares about anything except me. The power of his animus thrums through my stomach, through my veins, and through my body like he's a part of me. Like he is soothed by me. Lyle raises his glorious head just enough to look me in the eye.

His own eyes glimmer burnished gold with that powerful animus sitting present, like a summer sunset leading the way into the dark. My neck aches from his bite, my pussy aches from his girth, but I'm the happiest woman in the world.

"Kiss me," I whisper. My voice is heavy with a restrained sob.

His face crumples, and he swoops in, capturing my mouth with those torturous lips. I groan into him, clawing this back, as if I can inhale all of him into my body.

"Angel," he groans, kissing me deeply. Whatever he's doing to my mouth feels like heaven itself resides in us both.

Someone huffs impatiently behind me.

"This is my regina," Lyle snarls up at them, guttural and savage. "I will not let her go."

"And mine too." It's my wolf who growls back.

Both Lyle's and Savage's possessive words make something wonderful dance inside my core. I cup Lyle's jaw. "We'd better deal with…"

His eyes darken, but he pulls me up with him nonetheless, possessively holding my naked form to his side. The phoenix fire burning around us loses its height as Lady Celeste brings it down.

With slight alarm, I realise Lyle is still hard, his huge erection at full mast for all to see.

As the licking red flames fade away into nothing, I quickly step in front of him and Lyle hugs me close against him, his palm flat and light over the diagonal black slashes of the wounds across my abdomen. His touch doesn't hurt them and actually I feel better for it.

Lady Celeste's eyes widen when she sees what Lyle is trying to cover before she shrugs off her long white coat and offers it. Lyle uses his telekinesis to soar it through the air towards us and I grab it, clutching it to my chest. Savage comes to stand on my other side, holding my hand and lacing his fingers through mine.

Georgia stands next to Celeste, her face pale and drawn, her nostrils flaring in anger and shock.

"This is highly improper, Lyle," says the raptor queen, her voice dripping with distaste, even as she tries and fails not to look him up and down. I know then that they heard his claiming of me. "If you sought to hide this from us—"

"As I'm sure Lady Celeste explained," Lyle says, his deep voice still hung on his animus, "my regina chose not to disclose her order."

"And the matter of you hiding your relationship with her," the wolf queen says evenly. "A bad judgement call. We cannot let this incident go, you understand."

"There is also the matter of a human murder." The dragon king's eyes glimmer as he stares at me, and it suddenly strikes me. I risk a glance at Xander, but the dragon is nowhere to be seen. Only Scythe stands next to Savage, cutting me a look of warning.

This is Xander's father. They have the same almond-shaped eyes. The same long, silken black hair. The same air of superiority.

"He tried to kill my mate," I say, trying not to think about the fact that this dragon has seen me naked. That the entire council and my father's men have all seen my bare body. "It was purely self-defence."

"We will need to prepare a statement," Lady Celeste says, nodding. "All will be done according to the proper laws."

"Laws that do not include Boneweavers," the feline king says ruefully, eyeing me with interest before flicking his gaze respectfully up to my lion. "This changes everything, Lyle."

"Mace needs to be held accountable," Lyle says, his voice simmering with rage. "For psychic attacks on Aurelia. For luring me out with sinister intentions."

The dragon king chuckles as if this is all a cute joke. "Are you accusing the regent of Serpent Court of knowingly inciting your... mental state? Really, Lyle, I expected better of you." He waves his bejewelled hand flippantly. "But you can no longer be deputy headmaster of this institution."

I clench my fists with the sudden and furious urge to break this guy's nose. Silence hangs heavy between my pack and the council. Through the gathering dark, the school floodlights come on, white beams slicing through the air. The school's guards are gathered around, watching carefully. Listening to everything.

Ruben, I notice, is conveniently missing.

"I will write up a list of recommendations for what needs to be done," Celeste says with authority. "For now, Aurelia requires extensive healing, and Lyle needs to be assessed. The legalities will be discussed at length in the morning."

The wolf queen breaks off from the council group and approaches me with a smile. Her eyes are kind and my intuition tells me that I like her. "Apparently, you are queen of a court of one, Aurelia... Well! I suppose we call you Aurelia Boneweaver now, do we not?" She beams at me.

I flush under her gaze. "I'm not so sure about that, Your Majesty."

She nods, searching my eyes. "I never thought I'd see the day. I should like to meet with you sometime. We should talk."

I bow. "Of course, Your Majesty."

She turns to my wolf. "Savage," she says, her voice that of an amused mother. "Of course you would be tangled up in this."

To my surprise, Savage grins and sweeps a gallant bow. "Always, Your Majesty."

"Well," she says, addressing Lyle last, "I've always said that sometimes all an animus needs is a strong regina to set him straight. Wouldn't you say, Mr Pardalia?"

Lyle's lips twitch and I'm never going to let him hear the end of this. "Indeed, Your Majesty."

The wolf queen smiles sadly and steps back, nodding to someone behind us. "It's a shame we need to separate you."

Panic flares as Savage's grip is yanked out of mine. I whirl around to see Ruben and the massive feline king himself, chaining Savage with obsidian to a metal gurney. I cry out, but Lyle holds onto me and I get one last look at my handsome, wild wolf before a black bag is shoved over his head.

"No!" I cry, trying to wrest free of Lyle's grip. Something in my heart tears open as Savage is wheeled into a waiting military grade van. "Do something!" I say to Scythe, who has calmly watched the entire thing. A muscle in his jaw feathers before he looks at me.

They slam the door shut with a resounding thud.

"They have a legal warrant for his arrest, Aurelia," Scythe rasps. "There is nothing we can do."

"No," I say again, weakly holding a hand up as if I can stop what's happening.

I love you. Savage said it as he'd thrown himself in front of me. I hadn't had the time to say it back. I tunnel my mind through the air toward his. Trying to sense that unhinged, bouncing power. But of course, the obsidian blocks any telepathic communication.

Ruben gets into the driver's seat, and I suddenly want to tear that beast apart. I stifle a sob as the truck's engine roars and Savage is taken away.

"No!" I cry.

"Easy," Lyle whispers in my ear. "Easy, my angel. Savage can look after himself."

I bury my face in Lyle's chest. Savage, my one comfort in the darkness. My first.

The feline king comes up to us and I barely restrain an open, threatening growl. His midnight skin glints under the floodlights, and though his expression is serious, his eyes glimmer with interest. "I'll be in touch in the morning, Lyle. We have much to discuss. Rules to make, etcetera."

"Of course, Your Majesty," comes Lyle's stiff reply.

The remaining council members leave with wary looks towards us and the dragon king doesn't even look at us at all.

Then it's just Georgia, glancing between me and Lyle.

But he acts as if the lioness isn't even there. As if she wasn't the one who gave evidence against him. My lion sighs through his nose, tugging me towards the medical clinic and Celeste, who is watching us assessingly.

But I don't want to leave. I want to run after that van. "Where are they taking him?" I ask as Lyle tugs me up the drive.

"Blackwater," Scythe says.

"Scythe." My voice is hardly more than a sob.

The shark angles his head as he considers me through the night. "You have other things to worry about, Aurelia."

"But—"

"Angel." Lyle shakes his head as he tugs me through the academy gates. "Savage would want you to focus."

I take a deep breath of night air and turn around to face the academy. Right, because the guards lining the drive are staring at me. The expressions range from pure shock and awe to wariness and fear. I wonder how long it will take for word to spread.

Boneweaver Female. Unbred. Offers of 20M.

That unholy voice resounds in my head, but my anima brushes it away.

Savage. My anima keens for our wolf, getting further and further away from me.

"I'm sorry I couldn't get here sooner," Celeste says. "But there are currently two serpents tied up in my office."

"You should have killed them," Lyle growls.

She gives him an amused look. "You know I don't do that. But I suppose we'll all have to get used to the newly integrated you, Lyle."

I wonder about the same thing. And about how everything will be different now.

Georgia starts to say something, but Lyle dismisses her without a thought, pulling me towards the glaring lights of the medical wing.

Celeste's voice is barely a warning hiss. "Do *not* approach a newly mated male, Georgia. You know better than that."

"Yes, my lady," comes the quiet reply. Georgia leaves in a hurry, her stilettos clicking a fast pace away from us.

"I will talk to you in the morning," Celeste says. "For now, I think you need to process what's happened, Aurelia. And what it will mean for you."

I nod slowly. My stomach feels hollow, my heart twisting in agony. I've gained and lost something at the same time.

Lady Celeste takes a small glass vial out of her pocket. "No avian healing will fix those wounds, Aurelia," she says softly. "But phoenix tears will do the trick."

I stare at her and the gift she's offering me. "These are *your* tears?" I breathe. Of course, as I wanted to be a healer, I studied the effects of phoenix tears as extensively as I could. But they're mostly shrouded in mystery and hard to come by, phoenixes being rare as they are.

"They are." She smiles kindly. "And I think if anyone deserves it, it's you. Those wounds look old and vicious, Aurelia. You should have come to us."

"They were what caused all of this," I admit. And to Celeste's credit, she never says 'I told you so' for this or choosing not to share my secret.

Lyle's arm tightens around me.

"I think this little display was inevitable," Celeste says. "Mace would have found a way to achieve his goal of discrediting Lyle eventually."

And word of what happened will get out to my father. That I disobeyed an order that was seven years old.

"And, um... what of Frank Ulman?" I ask, not wanting to turn around and see them scraping his brains from the bitumen. The last thing I want is a van of my own to take me to Blackwater... although if it landed me with Savage, I might consider it.

Lady Celeste smiles at me. "You should only be thanked, Aurelia. For his crimes against Lyle's family and our kind, he was given the sentence he finally deserved. I'm sure he regretted coming out of hiding in his last moments."

I gape at her, not expecting to hear such vicious words from a refined, genteel woman. But then Lyle kisses me on the head and Celeste's eyes soften at the sight, her eyes filling with tears.

"A worthy regina," she murmurs. "Worthy indeed."

* * *

I'm lying on a medical centre table five minutes later, my wounds being carefully inspected under a spotlight by my favourite lead nurse, Hope, as Lyle watches on, his eyes dark and dangerous at the sight of my injuries. He's thankfully been given track pants, although my lion stalked into the medical clinic with his dick swinging like he didn't care. Scythe remains with us as well, though his unblinking gaze I can't read.

"Is what the guards say true?" Hope murmurs as she swabs my wound to send for testing.

Lyle lets out a rumbling growl of warning from where he sits next to me, holding my hand like he needs contact with me at all times, but I shake my head at him. The secret is out now. There's no point denying it to anyone anymore. "Yes. I'm a Boneweaver."

"But Mace Naga is definitely a serpent, so that means it comes from your mother?"

"It does."

She hums with interest. "I sensed you were something to each other when Mr Pardalia came in here that day after your kidnapping," she says, smiling faintly.

"It was always going to be difficult to hide," I say darkly. "But we tried anyway."

She's quiet as she uses a glass pipette to drop the phoenix tears onto my wounds. The magical fluid is surprisingly warm as it hits my darkened skin and starts to tingle immediately.

"It'll take a full night to work, although Celeste's tears usually work faster. You need anything else?"

"I'd really like some mouthwash," I admit. I'm pretty sure there are things between my teeth I don't want to think about. "But I'm fine otherwise."

If Savage were here, he'd make a joke about it and make me feel better. The backs of my eyes sear and I close my eyes.

"Minnie was asking for you when I checked on her," Hope says, reaching into a cupboard and setting a bottle on the table. "I heard what she did. She's a real hero."

The tears spill freely then. The fact that Minnie had enough power to stop the velocity of multiple bullets from rifles was astonishing. I had no idea she had that sort of control or strength. "She really is," I whisper.

If Savage were here, I imagine him rolling his eyes and grumbling, "I suppose I owe her now. I'll never hear the end of it."

Hope bandages my stomach to protect the wounds and leaves. As soon as she does, Xander is thrusting the drawn curtains aside and storming into the room like a fiery tornado. The room goes from mild to sweltering immediately.

"You manipulative little—"

"Xander," Lyle barks in warning.

"No, let him speak," I say evenly, sitting up to look Xander in the eyes and keeping my shoulders up and back. "What do you have to say?"

He leans down, putting a hand around my neck and hisses into my face with pure, terrifying menace only a dragon can muster, "You will *not* order me ever again. You will not so much as speak to me. I will pretend that you do not exist. *Do you understand me?*"

I stare into his glowing white eyes, currently flicking a dangerous molten red. This anger is more than anything I've seen of him before, and something tells me it's about more than just me.

So I don't mention the fact that Xander's dragon requested *me* to command *him*. Instead, my voice is even and clear when I say, "I understand, Xander."

He releases me in silence and stalks out.

"That was his dad, wasn't it?" I ask. "The king of dragon court."

Lyle nods silently. Scythe just stares at me. So I sigh and drag myself out of the bed. My lion is at my side in an instant.

"Do you need me to carry you?" he asks, almost sounding hopeful.

I smile up at him for a moment, then reach up to brush my lips against his. "I can walk."

He takes my hand, and together we walk out of the medical clinic. The staff stare at us, so do the guards.

"They'll get used to it," Scythe rasps. "It's just strange for them to see Lyle not being an asshole."

To my surprise, Lyle snorts in amusement.

"You need to keep a firm hand on them, Lia," comes a quiet familiar voice, "otherwise they'll take full advantage."

I wildly swing around. Rising from where she was waiting with Yeti, is Minnie, in a mauve maxi-dress that goes perfectly with her pink hair.

Her face crumples when she sees me bandaged up under my loaned crop top. "Oh Goddess," she says.

I launch myself at her and we meet in the middle.

"You saved my life, Min," I sob into her curls. "I'm so fucking sorry—"

"None of that," she scolds into my neck. "Not anymore. Not after everything." She pulls away from me and reaches up to take my face in her hands. Her wide, doe-like brown eyes are brimming with tears and she takes a shaky breath. "I've always believed that things happen for a reason. And I think what happened"—she swallows—"was going to happen anyway. You're my best friend. And I hope you will always be."

I glance at Yeti, eyeing me warily from behind Minnie. Before I can say anything, his face splits into a grin. "We have a Boneweaver on the team now? I'd swap that for that fucker Titus *any* day of the week."

"You don't blame me?" I gape at him, wiping my nose on my wrist as Lyle squeezes my shoulder possessively.

Yeti shrugs his broad shoulders as Minnie steps back into his body, his muscled arm coming around her as if she's always been his. "Titus is a psychopath without anyone's help. Always was."

Chapter 80

Scythe

Striding back to the academy behind Lyle and Aurelia, my blood roars in awareness and anger. From what I've seen and heard today. Even the vision of my brother being taken away cannot supersede the purely ravenous joy I felt at seeing my bloodthirsty regina slaughter Frederick Ulman. It had broken the spell of vengeance over me. Because the only thing that could break the song of revenge saturating my mind was the vision of her. Primal. Raw. Beautiful.

Aurelia killed a man. Without hesitation. Without courtesy. It was a brutal thing to watch. And she'd done it for Lyle, as his regina.

She might not realise it now, but the impact of it will hit her like a heavy wave later.

And Lyle. With his animus fully integrated, now thrums with its overtly violent power. While his aura now roils with black, red and golden power, his eyes, and even his walk, have changed. That violent power now prowls after Aurelia, a mated male, possessive and dangerous.

Things are going to be different now, and Aurelia has no

fucking idea. While Savage was bad enough with his regina, his energy was playful. Lyle's energy is not. Mine is not.

There's a storm coming, and a nasty one at that. There are preparations to be made. Calls to make.

I get out my phone, texting a quick message.

I've found a tigress who's strong enough to be a match at the academy.

The reply comes back quick as the swipe of a claw.

I'm leaving now.

Dinner is in full swing, so we head outside to bypass the dining hall. As we do, Stacey runs out from the direction of the anima dorm, pulling at her dark hair, a panicked expression twisting her face.

Lia and Minnie break into a run, heading for their friend. "Everything's okay, Stace!" Aurelia says. "Wait till—"

"No!" Stacey grabs onto Aurelia's arms. "It's Sabrina!" the lioness cries. "Sabrina is missing!"

"She's not in the animus dorm?" Minnie asks.

"No, I've checked. None of her friends there have seen her for a while, either. Oh, fuck!"

I veer towards the anima dorm, Lyle shooting Stacey questions in rapid succession, and then to Christine at the door to the building. But the gargoyle seems confused.

"Don't recall," she says, scratching her head and making an odd grating sound. "Haven't seen her come in or out."

She lets us into the dorm and I assume the lead, taking the steps two at a time. I know Sabrina's history. I know her criminal record. I know of what use she could be to the wrong sort of people. I also know of her value to Aurelia and the insane lengths my regina will go to for not only her mates, but her friends.

Suspicion is a wave that crests as I reach the third-floor corridor, scenting the air and striding down. My footfalls are heavy thumps on the old carpet. The others race behind me, Lyle with angry, dark energy pulsing around him.

I kick open the door to Sabrina and Raquel's bedroom and that wave inside of me crashes with certainty.

"Not missing." Everyone gathers behind me as I point to the wall. "Taken."

Aurelia lets out a scream.

Because over Sabrina's bed, nailed with a black knife, is the bloody, spotted, cut-off end of a leopard's tail.

* * *

Get ready for Her Psycho Beasts (Scythe's book). Order it now.

Did you know there's a competition to guess the identity and order of Lia's fifth mate? If you're the first person to guess both correctly, you'll win an entire set of special edition, sprayed edge books.

Submit your entry before book three comes out: https://forms.gle/xKEdhycm7kwPnQm78

About the Author

Ektaa P. Bali was born in Fiji and spent most of her life in Melbourne, Australia.

She published her first novel in 2020, the beginning of a middle grade fantasy series, before going on to pursue her true passion: Young & New Adult Fantasy.

Her Vicious Beasts is her fourth series set in the Chrysalis-verse and Her Rabid Beasts is the second in the series.

She currently lives in Brisbane, Australia.

facebook.com/ektaabaliauthor

instagram.com/ektaabaliauthor

youtube.com/ektaabali

Also by E.P. Bali